"Have I Told You How Beautiful You Look Today?"

A soft smile curved Julia's lips. "Funny, I was about to remark on how you look today."

"Oh?"

"Indeed. You look like a man who is about to kiss somebody."

"Is that an invitation?" he inquired.

"Merely an observation."

Morgan gathered her against him, reveling in the taste of her lips against his. In the past he had always considered a kiss a prelude to seduction. His courtships had all been meticulously prescribed: the right wine, the right flowers, the right glow of moonlight, the right trinket to be bartered to sate his lust. Now he had something entirely different, something that threw that pretty little formula completely askew.

Julia.

The right woman.

HIGH PRAISE FOR
VICTORIA LYNNE'S PREVIOUS NOVEL

What Wild Moonlight

"From the mesmerizing beginning to the surprising climax, *What Wild Moonlight* is a wild ride of an adventure-romance destined to keep you reading all night. Simmering with sexual tension and the perfect amount of suspense, Victoria Lynne secures a place on readers' bookshelves."
—*Romantic Times*

"Ms. Lynne combines adventure, suspense, and romance in a tale that will delight any reader."
—*Rendezvous*

"Readers need to provide themselves adequate time when they begin *What Wild Moonlight* in order to avoid sleep deprivation, because this is a one-sitting tale. The action-packed story line is suspense at its most intense. The characters are charming, and placing this Victorian couple in the new aristocratic playpen of Monte Carlo adds freshness to the novel."
—Harriet Klausner

Books by Victoria Lynne

Chasing Rainbows

What Wild Moonlight

With This Kiss

With This Kiss

Victoria Lynne

A Dell Book

Published by
Dell Publishing
a division of
Random House, Inc.
1540 Broadway
New York, New York 10036

ISBN: 0-440-22334-2

Printed in the United States of America

Published simultaneously in Canada

July 1999

10 9 8 7 6 5 4 3 2 1
OPM

For
David and Catherine

Prologue

1855

*L*ondon slept.

A curtain of darkness blanketed the city. The gas-lights that lined the grand boulevards had flickered off, as all respectable folk had long since abandoned their evening pursuits for the safety and comfort of their beds. Hollow silence echoed from within the shops, pubs, and alehouses. The cab drivers, costermongers, coal porters, and crossing sweepers had retired. Even the thieves and prostitutes that normally filled the narrow alleys and darkened doorways had returned to their homes, content with whatever meager profit they had gained from their night's work.

And so it was that Morgan St. James, Viscount Barlowe, made his way alone through the deserted streets. He had dismissed his driver hours earlier, sending Markum home rather than expecting him to wait while he conducted what had evolved into a series of lengthy business meetings, followed by an equally long evening at

Black's, his private club. Prowling the dark streets of London on foot was admittedly a peculiar pleasure but one Morgan had indulged in for nearly a decade. Besides, Markum's wife had only recently given birth to a baby boy—the couple's fifth child in as many years. Although his driver had taken pains to hide it, he had clearly been anxious to return to his family and had been effusively grateful when Morgan had sent him home.

The night sky was clear and cloudless. Although the moon was not full, it provided ample light. But as Morgan made his way from Regent Street onto Oxford, an early morning fog began to creep in. It was not a timid fog, the kind that curled softly around corners and seeped between passageways, but a bold, assertive fog that rolled over the city, wrapping everything it touched in a shimmering, shifting blanket of glistening silver.

As the swirling mist increasingly obstructed his vision, his other senses grew sharper. The odors that surrounded him seemed more pungent: the sharp tang of fried eel, the rank stench of manure, the sweet spice that drifted from the darkened tobacco stand. He was pleasantly aware of the cool dampness of the fog against his skin. The echo of his own boots striking pavement seemed unnaturally loud, as did the snorting protests of the tired nags that pulled the milk carts as they were hitched for duty. Even the low calls of the stevedores and sailors, furiously loading cargo in hopes of catching the morning tide, seemed to come from a point just over his shoulder rather than the distant docks.

Morgan reached Bond Street and glanced east. Sometimes, if his timing was just right, he was rewarded with a view of the early morning sun gilding the cross upon the summit of St. Paul's. But not that morning. He was too early and the fog was too thick. He walked on, his long strides carrying him swiftly to Mayfair.

His home did not sit in the fashionable West End. Unmoved by the splendor of Park Lane—an area where the real estate had become so prime the stately homes were packed shoulder to shoulder like workers on an evening trolley—he had purchased instead a five-acre tract of land east of Grosvenor Square. There he had constructed a town house that rivaled any in London, complete with private stables, manicured gardens, indoor plumbing, and a formal ballroom. Rather than razing the original estate that stood on the grounds, he had converted the modest structure into separate living quarters for his servants.

He reached his home and stopped. His gaze moved automatically toward the window of his bedchamber. A single candle flickered softly against the glass pane, as though bidding him welcome. Inside, Isabelle Cartwright lay waiting for him in his bed. A familiar scene, but one of which he doubted he would ever grow weary. He took a moment to picture her: dark hair cascading over his pillow, full lips slightly parted in sleep, lush body completely bare save for the soft linen of his sheets.

In two weeks' time she would be his wife.

Morgan stood in the predawn silence, contemplating his future. He was thirty years old and anticipating his upcoming nuptials with a sense of smug contentment that was as absurd as it was embarrassing. Theirs was not a love match; neither of them was foolish enough to expect that. Isabelle was undeniably beautiful, gracious, cultured—perhaps a bit pampered and spoiled, but the ideal wife nonetheless. He certainly had his own faults—far too many to list.

Still, they would do well together. They both enjoyed a strong sexual appetite and a prominent position in society. Moreover, they had reached that critical understanding of roles that was so essential for a contented marriage. She would handle their social calendar, the running of their home, and God willing, the care of their children. He, in turn, would provide her with his title, money, and lands.

An arrangement that was eminently satisfactory for them both.

She had spent the past months completely immersed in planning the details of the wedding: checking and rechecking the silver, the china, the linen, the candles, the flowers, the guest list; flitting to never-ending meetings with seamstresses, bakers, chefs, wine stewards; and generally turning his house upside down. To that end, she had insisted on moving in her own staff to help prepare for the wedding.

The unfortunate result was a veritable plethora of groomsmen and gardeners, housemaids and butlers, cooks and laundresses, all of whom were adjusting to the unhappy disruption in their lives. A situation undoubtedly made worse by the cramped quarters under which they were forced to dwell—in some cases, three to a room that had been designed for one. Markum, his wife, and their four children—now five, he amended silently—shared one single apartment. Morgan let out a sigh and shook his head. The joining of two households was always a messy business. There was no way around it.

At least he was taking steps to relieve the pressure. Plans had already been drawn up that would more than triple the size of the narrow four-story structure that served as the servants' lodgings. Great piles of brick and lumber were stacked haphazardly against the side wall, awaiting the tradesmen due later that morning. A small frown touched his lips as he considered that. The sleep he had envisioned would be impossible once the din of construction was under way. He shook off the thought with a shrug. The work was being done, and that was what mattered.

That resolved, his mind moved on to a more pleasant occupation. He imagined slipping into bed beside Isabelle and taking her in his arms while she was still drowsy with sleep, making slow and languorous love—

A movement near the lumber pile caught his attention, cutting off his thoughts. At first he thought it was a trick of the fog or a shadow cast by one of the aged oaks that bordered the grounds. But the shadow moved: stealthily at first, crouched low, then gaining speed as it crossed the lawn between the servants' quarters and the main house.

A thief, by God.

"You there! Stop!" Morgan cried instinctively.

The thief moved faster.

Cursing his stupidity at having lost the element of surprise, Morgan sprinted after the man, chasing him down the street and into an alley. He almost lost him as the thief disappeared into the swirling fog. Then he heard a man's sharp grunt, followed by the sound of stumbling feet scraping cobblestone. The thief was closer than expected, merely two arm's lengths away.

Morgan doubled his speed. *Got you, you son of a—*

His grim flush of triumph abruptly dissipated as a large shape suddenly loomed in the foggy mist before them. A horse. The thief had a horse waiting.

Damn it!

The man leaped for his mount. Morgan lunged after him in a flying tackle, throwing his arms forward to catch the thief before he hit the saddle. But he was too late. He felt the brush of the man's leather boots against his fingertips, the coarse hair of the horse's tail slapping him in the face, then nothing. He fell hard, sliding headlong against the damp cobblestones.

The thunder of the horse's hooves echoed into the distance. Morgan let out a dark oath, followed almost immediately by a bark of laughter. At least there was a bright side: he hadn't been hurt. The thief's mount had obligingly broken his fall by leaving behind a fresh, steaming pile of dung—into which he had fallen face first.

Groaning as he rose, he brushed the horse's droppings from his face and clothing. Old. He was getting old. Five years ago he would have caught the man handily. He

made his way slowly back to his town house, limping
slightly and shaking his head as he went. A report would
have to be made to the local constable, of course. Then it
was only a matter of time before word of the incident
spread. He could see the headline of *The Times* now:
VISCOUNT BARLOWE LOSES CHASE WITH THIEF AND LANDS IN
MANURE PILE IN PROCESS.

A wry smile curved his lips. It might have been worse
yet. Isabelle would have had a fit if the housebreaker had
managed to make off with the wedding silver. He reached
his home and studied the classical facade, looking for any
damage that might indicate the man's point of entry. As
he did so, a puzzled frown touched his brow. The thief, he
suddenly recalled, had come from the direction of the
servants' quarters, not the main house.

Odd.

Then it hit him. Faintly at first, nothing but a soft
whisper of an odor, almost undetectable. Steadily it grew
stronger. The smells of London were not pleasant, but
Morgan knew them. This one was unmistakable. Sharp,
acrid, burning.

His gaze snapped to the servants' lodgings.

A soft, curling cloud emerged from beneath the quarters' main door. A gray cloud, but not the glistening silver
of fog. A dark, sinister cloud that absorbed light and everything else around it.

Smoke.

Morgan bolted for the door and threw it open. The
heat within hit him like a blast from a blacksmith's forge.
Too late he remembered the warnings he had heard about
taking care not to cause a draft. The quarters were already
an inferno. Flames licked the walls, shrouding them in
writhing bands of crimson, gold, and orange. Smoke
burned his lungs. As he moved inside, the stench of kerosene gagged him. The fumes were so thick, he could
taste them in his throat.

His heart pounded erratically as his lungs constricted

within his chest. *There was still time. There had to be time. He could get everyone out.*

Morgan knew the servants' quarters almost as well as he knew his own home. There was the ground floor, then three flights of stairs leading to various landings, each of which branched off to pockets of separate rooms. Then there was the attic, which had been converted to a private apartment for the Markum family.

He slammed his fist against the first door he could find. "Fire! Get out! Fire!"

He raced from door to door, pounding his fists and shouting to rouse the servants.

On the landing above him appeared an elderly man dressed in a flapping nightgown, his nightcap sitting askew on his bald head. Piers, head butler. The righteous indignation that filled his expression at the predawn racket turned at once to appalled understanding.

"Wake them up!" Morgan screamed. "Get everyone out! *Now!*"

Piers nodded and turned away, his form swallowed up by the smoke and haze.

Morgan took a precious second to fasten a handkerchief over his nose and mouth, then vaulted up the steps toward the second-floor landing. As he shouted his warnings, doors began to open and people began to emerge: confused and disoriented at first, then engulfed by panic. He heard one scream, then another and another, until the voices met in an ungodly crescendo of pure terror.

Smoke and fire were everywhere. Heat cracked the floorboards. Tongues of flame licked the walls, jumping from floor to ceiling and back again. More and more people poured from their rooms, fighting blindly for the main stairwell.

"Not the stairs!" Morgan shouted. "The windows! Use the windows!"

His warnings went unheeded. A crush of bodies pressed against him, shoving and screaming as they fought their way toward the narrow stair. Horror clogged his throat. It was worse than he ever dreamed possible. Worse than he ever imagined.

Where did they all come from? How many were there? Too many, too many. Blistering remorse knifed through him. *He should have been firmer. He shouldn't have allowed it. Not this many people. Why hadn't he seen the danger?*

He wheeled around to vault the stairs to the next level when he collided into a girl of perhaps fifteen, her eyes round with terror. Morgan recognized her—the cook's daughter. She stood unmoving, her back pressed flat against the wall, her mouth hanging open in a silent scream.

He grabbed her arm and dragged her to the hallway's end. There he smashed the window with his elbow. He swung his arm around the rough pane to clear it as best he could of glass debris, then lifted the terrified girl. Ignoring her screams of protest, he dropped her from the second story to the boxwood gardens below.

He felt a body brush past him and leap from the window, followed immediately by another.

Good. Use the windows. You'll break a bone or two, but you'll live.

He fought his way against the tide of bodies until he had reached the top floor. The heat was worse. Everywhere. Fire. Smoke. Greedy, scorching flame licking and hissing, devouring everything in its path.

Grimly determined, he staggered forward. The instant he gained the upper landing, he heard a sharp crack of timber as the stair rail beneath him gave way. Screams filled the hall, followed by the dull thunder of bodies falling into the stairwell.

Morgan hesitated, ready to turn back to give aid, when an inner voice stopped him.

Move! Now! Get to the attic! The rest can get out. Please, God. The rest can get out. But Markum's children—

The door to the attic was shut. To hell with the warnings about creating a draft. He had to get them out.

He tried the knob. It blistered his palm but wouldn't give. Locked. He slammed his shoulder against the wooden door and felt it sag. One more hard shove, and it cracked open, splintering apart at the jam. He stumbled through.

More smoke. Black, billowing smoke. Heat. Burning, savage heat, surely worse than hell.

He scanned the room. Nothing. Too late. He was too late. He tried to breathe but couldn't. His lungs were charred, shrunken, useless. Sweat and ash blinded him. As he lifted his arm to wipe his eyes, a flaming motion caught his attention. His shirtsleeve was on fire. He ripped the cloak from his back to smother the flames, then realized that that garment was on fire as well.

He was on fire.

He dropped to the ground and rolled back and forth to extinguish the flames. Gasping and choking, he came to a stop in the center of the floor, struggling to catch his breath.

Then he saw it.

A tiny, whimpering figure huddled in a tight ball beneath a corner cot. A child. Alive. Dazed elation surged within him. He lunged across the room and pulled the quivering, terrified body into his arms.

Clutching the child against his chest, he crawled toward the attic window. He knocked out the glass, thrust his torso through the space, and peered below.

People. Mobs of people swarmed beneath him, their shapes lost in the fog and smoke. He heard cries of "Jump!" and thought he saw a blanket stretched out between them. Could they see what he held? He tried to call out, but his voice was nothing but a raw, hoarse whisper. He had no choice. Saying a silent prayer, he released the child and ducked back into the room.

Where were the rest of the children? Where were Markum, his wife, the babe?

His vision blurred. The world seemed to quiver and spin, then the edges went red. He knew he was losing consciousness. *Not yet. Not yet.* He took a step forward. *Not yet. He had to find them.*

He scanned the room. His gaze stopped at a bright, shimmering flame that seemed to dance in one corner, to leap and sway with a life all its own. Strangely captivated, he moved toward it. Then he heard the screaming.

High pitched. Agonized. Ceaseless.

Hideous understanding flooded through him, locking him in a paralysis of frozen horror.

The screams were coming from within the flame.

Before he could move, a thundering *crack!* filled the room. A ceiling joist broke free and swung down from the rafters. The smoking beam struck him directly in the chest, sending a sharp, searing pain radiating through him. The force of the blow lifted him off his feet and propelled him backward, knocking him through the window.

Morgan reached out to grab hold of something to arrest his descent, but he couldn't stop.

He was falling. Falling and falling. Falling forever.

Then blissful black nothingness.

Chapter I

London, 1857

The woman was putting on one hell of a show.

Morgan St. James's gaze drifted back to the redhead for perhaps the third time that hour. She stood by herself at the foot of the *trente-et-quarante* table, betting consistently on black. Her stack of chips had increased since she had started to play, but her winnings were not substantial. At least not enough to draw his attention. What caught his eye—and that of several other men in the room—was the manner in which she played.

She wanted to be noticed. Her motions were too deliberate and dramatic to be interpreted any other way. It was an altogether unnecessary performance. Her presence alone was enough to command attention. One couldn't help but notice her—for several reasons.

First and foremost was her appearance itself. Every inch of the woman was dazzling feminine perfection, from the top of her elaborately coiffed hair to the tips of her black high-heeled slippers. Her skin glowed like ivory cream, her eyes were as rich and intoxicating as warm brandy. And her body—sculpted as though every inch had been deliberately crafted to satisfy a man's most vivid fantasy. Her lush curves were wrapped in a rich, mouthwatering shade of pink satin that made Morgan think of a sugary peppermint confection.

He took a moment to study her hair. It wasn't a soft, golden-red titian or a rich, russet-tinged auburn but a bold, brazen red. Flame red.

Another thought occurred to Morgan as he watched her place her bets. The woman had money. She played with the calculated expertise of a seasoned gambler, yet she had the bold nonchalance of someone for whom winning or losing was a matter of little concern. In other words, someone whose wealth was vast indeed.

All of which begged one simple question: *Who was she?*

The fact that neither he nor any of the men with whom he was seated could answer that struck him as nearly unprecedented. The room in which they had gathered was London's notorious Devonshire House. Given the ever-increasing crowds drawn to London for the Season, something had to be done to distinguish between the high life and the rabble. Thus the establishment of an exclusive chamber to which admittance was gained solely on the basis of wealth and social status. It was the best of all worlds: an intimate club where the players could mingle freely with their peers, where only the finest champagne was served, and where fortunes that had taken twenty generations to amass were routinely won and lost on the turn of a card.

But this woman was an outsider to the rarefied atmosphere of their little club. Granted there were other women present, but their presence could easily be explained. The Boston heiresses who came to barter their wealth and virginity for an honorable British title, the dowager duchesses who sat gossiping together in one corner, the Season's Incomparables with their pretty little pouts and lowcut gowns, the French courtesans who clung to the sides of their latest paramours like pampered, well-heeled pets.

The redhead belonged to none of those cliques, yet she seemed somehow essential, as if the assembly would be seriously bereft without her. Morgan's gaze returned to the woman as if drawn there by magnetic force. She had won again, he noted, watching as the croupier pushed a thick stack of chips toward her ever-increasing pile.

His pleasure at watching her was abruptly diminished as he saw Jonathan Derrick, Earl of Bedford, cross the room and move toward her. The lust shining in his gaze was as clear and bright as a lighthouse beacon at midnight. *Pompous ass,* Morgan thought, battling a surge of possessive irritation. But to his considerable amusement, Jonathan Derrick proved no threat to the mental claim he had staked on the woman. As though aware of Derrick's amorous intent, the redhead lifted her gaze and watched him approach. Although her expression didn't change, the warmth in her brandy eyes turned to winter. She tilted her chin and turned pointedly away, giving the earl the cut direct.

Morgan applauded her silently. *Brava. Nicely done.* Derrick was the fourth man to approach her since she had arrived, the fourth man to be coolly rebuked. Very well. Let the fools rush in. All good things to those who wait.

He suddenly stopped himself, shocked at the train of his thoughts. *Idiot.* What was he thinking? He knew better. The woman was not for him. Never for him. Foolish even to entertain such an idea. He gripped the rich glass of burgundy sitting on the table before him and let out a low, steadying breath, fighting back a wave of tension. *Let it go. Let it go.*

Forcing his thoughts away from the woman, he turned his attention back to his companions and the conversation at hand.

"Did you see the *Review* today?" demanded William Conor, fifth Earl of Gravespark. He was young, excitable, and unable to handle the bourbon he drank in regrettably copious amounts. "What did I tell you? It's official now. They're engaged. Lady Isabelle Cartwright and Lord Roger Bigelow. Didn't I say it was only a matter of time before she—"

"That's enough, Gravespark," interrupted Edward Southesby curtly.

William Conor stared at Southesby with a confused frown. "What? It's right here in the paper. I don't see why . . . oh." He swung his head around, and his bloodshot eyes fastened upon Morgan. "Sorry, old man."

Morgan lifted his shoulders in an indifferent shrug. "May I?" he asked, reaching for the paper.

The *London Review* was an upstart paper, one that dared to challenge the authority and prominence of *The Times*. In all likelihood it would have failed miserably, were it not for a single column called "The Tattler," which was currently the rage among society. Mostly a gossip column, its anonymous author made occasional forays into the realm of social injustice and reform, thus giving the work a luster of moral righteousness.

He skimmed the column and felt curiously . . . flat. Nothing. As though he were reading about complete strangers, rather than a woman he had nearly married and a man he had once considered his best friend.

"She could have at least shown the decency to wait three years," asserted Conor. "I mean, really."

A sardonic smile curved Morgan's lips as he folded the paper and passed it back. "I believe that's the customary period for mourning. Contrary to popular opinion, I didn't die."

"No, of course not," Conor stammered, his face flaming. "Of course not. It's just that . . ." His gaze traveled to Morgan's hands and wrists. He studied the scars there with a look of undisguised horror. "Do you ever wonder what might have happened if—"

"No," Morgan replied, his voice steel. "Never."

An uneasy silence fell over the group. Morgan could almost hear the thoughts running through his companions' minds. Although his forays into polite society were few, he was not deaf to the rumors that circulated about him. As might be expected, the effects of the fire had necessitated a long period of recovery. In the aftermath of the tragedy, his self-imposed seclusion had led to vivid speculation among his peers. It was rumored—not entirely unjustly—that he had been grossly disfigured, a man whose hideous scars aptly reflected the true nature of his character.

The Beast.

After a long minute Edward Southesby cleared his throat, announcing in a strained voice, "I understand there's a bill before the Commons proposing to raise the tobacco tax once again."

A reply was duly offered, a contrasting opinion gamely expressed, and thus the conversation lurched awkwardly on, moving conspicuously away from the topic of Morgan's past.

Morgan leaned back in his chair and toyed absently with his glass. He shouldn't have come. After months of cajoling, he had buckled to the pressure of his few remaining friends who had insisted he take a night out, but he wouldn't do so again. It was a mistake to be here.

He swallowed his wine in one gulp, his eyes returning to the mysterious beauty he had been watching earlier. He sought nothing more than a brief, cursory check that she hadn't yet left the room.

Instead he found her gaze locked on him.

For a moment he was jolted to a stunned stop, his wineglass arrested in midair. Then instinct took over—an instinct he thought had vanished with the smoke and ash that had turned his life upside down. But old habits died hard. He set down his glass. He tipped his head in cool acknowledgment of her stare as his mouth curved into a smile of seductive greeting.

The woman didn't respond at all. Instead her expression remained curiously flat. Sitting there with a fool's grin on his face, Morgan was struck by the appalling certainty that he had completely misread her look, that he had made as big an ass of himself as Jonathan Derrick had only moments earlier.

Just as he was about to turn away, the redhead coolly returned his nod. Although her expression still didn't change, a Mona Lisa smile touched her lips; secretive and slightly superior. It was a silent yet unmistakable invitation, leaving him with the distinct impression of a she-wolf who had bestowed upon him the honor of entering her sacred lair—if he dared to accept the challenge. So be it.

"If you'll excuse me, gentlemen," he said to the table at large, "it appears I'm being summoned."

He rose and strode across the room, feeling the stunned gazes of his companions—of the entire room—upon him. It was unavoidable. The woman's presence was too dramatic not to have been noticed, particularly in a company that devoured gossip, scandal, and titillating speculation—all the more so if they could witness it for themselves. The fact that she had singled out Morgan St. James, Viscount Barlowe, for her attention, was nothing short of astonishing.

He paused beside a white-gloved waiter and removed two tall crystal flutes of sparkling wine from his tray, then presented himself at the woman's side at the *trente-et-quarante* table.

"Champagne?"

She smiled softly and took a glass from his hand. "Yes, I believe I will."

Lovely, he thought. Not so much her words, but the timbre in which she spoke. Never had he heard a voice so full of seductive promise. Low, smooth, and feminine, yet entirely confident and assured. It occurred to him that he might even enjoy this. The woman—whoever she was— was Christmas come early. He smiled as his gaze moved over her body once again. And wrapped in such a lovely package. Peppermint pink. Delicious.

She took a small sip from the delicate crystal champagne flute, then tilted her head toward the tall glass doors that overlooked the gardens. "They say the view from the balcony is lovely this time of night."

Exactly what he was about to suggest. Privacy. Evidently she was as cognizant of the curious eyes upon them as he was. He took her arm and wordlessly ushered her outside. Once they reached the sanctuary of the balcony, they stood silently against the intricate wrought-iron railing, staring out over the deep blue waters of the Thames. Moonlight bathed the gardens beneath them, casting long shadows over the neatly manicured shrubs and meandering stone pathways. The fragrance of rose, jasmine, and lavender wafted through the air. An unseen fountain gurgled nearby, setting the scene to the music of the trickling water.

Morgan took that all in with one sweeping glance, then turned his attention to the woman beside him. Incredibly, her beauty was even more astounding as one drew closer, for the details were more apparent. He noted for the first time the lushness of the lashes that framed her eyes, the delicate bridge of her nose, the sculpted curve of her cheek, the tantalizing fullness of her lips.

Disbelief tore through him at the fact that she had selected him. Then he noted that her gaze was moving over his skin, eyeing the scars that marred his neck and hands. Bitter understanding took root. In his rare social forays following the fire, he had discovered that certain women derived a queer pleasure from the sight of his scars and the notoriety of his reputation. Evidently this woman had the distinction of belonging to that select group. For a moment he hated her, hated her with an even more virulent loathing than he hated himself. Beauty in search of the Beast. So that was it. Very well. He could play that game. Lord knew he had done it before.

He watched as she drew one delicate hand absently along the balcony rail, imagining those long, slim fingers moving over his skin. Would she touch him? Was that part of her game? Or would she draw back in appalled horror once she saw—

Before he could pursue that demeaning line of speculation, a casino clerk stepped out onto the balcony to deliver her winnings. The stack of chips she had abandoned at the betting table had been dutifully exchanged for a thick wad of pound notes. With a word of gracious thanks, she peeled a five-pound note off the top and passed it to him. Then she dropped the remaining bills into her pink satin reticule.

"Do you always walk away from a lucky streak?" he asked.

"When it suits me." She gave a light shrug, then tipped her face up to his. "What about you?" she asked. "Have you been playing the tables tonight?"

"Not tonight. I'm afraid my partner failed to make an appearance."

"Oh? With whom do you prefer to play?"

"Tyche."

"I see." Adopting an expression of grave commiseration, she said, "She's deserted you this evening, has she?"

Morgan nodded, silently impressed. Whoever she was, the woman was obviously well educated, for she understood his somewhat obscure reference to Tyche, the goddess of good fortune. "Until you arrived," he replied gallantly.

A mocking smile touched her lips, as though the mundane banalities and false compliments of nascent romance were beneath them both. Clearly she neither wanted nor expected such coquettish tripe.

As her gaze moved slowly over his form, her expression changed, becoming unguardedly curious and candid. It wasn't a look he was accustomed to receiving from women—or men, for that matter. It was a look of open assessment, as though she were taking his measure and defining him against some nameless inner standard.

"Morgan St. James," she said at last. "Or do you prefer Viscount Barlowe?"

His surprise at hearing his name on her lips must have been visible, for a look of knowing amusement showed on her features. "You don't remember me at all," she said. There was no reproach in her voice. It was a simple statement of fact.

Morgan frantically searched his mind. Had he taken her to bed? Surely he would remember that. He would remember *something* about her. Her hair, her eyes, her body, her voice. But nothing came to him.

He shook his head. "I'm afraid you have me at a disadvan—"

"It doesn't matter," she said, abruptly dismissing the topic as though irritated she had brought it up. "It was long ago."

How long? Morgan wondered. A year? Five years? Ten?

His eyes moved briefly over her body, searching for some small clue that might jar his memory. But he found no blemish, no mole, no mark of any kind that would serve as a reminder of their past meeting. Nor could he distinguish her in his memory by the jewelry she wore— only by its rather startling absence. Unlike most of the patrons of the Devonshire House, who delighted in using their bodies to display their wealth, the woman was not draped in jewels. The only ornament he could discern on her person was a delicate gold chain that hung about her neck, from which was suspended a small gold medallion.

"Looking for something?" she asked. A faint hint of amusement colored her tone.

He returned his gaze to hers. "Yes."

She arched one perfectly shaped auburn brow and waited.

"An explanation."

"I'm afraid I don't—"

"When we met," he began. "Who you are and why you're here."

"Would you rather I wasn't?"

"No."

She took a small sip of champagne and regarded him steadily. "Then let it go."

"Difficult when I don't know your name."

She hesitated, then said in a tone of subtle reproof, "I've sent you three letters."

"Have you? How remiss. They must have gone astray."

A cynical smile curved her lips. "Amazing how often inconvenient mail goes astray, isn't it?" Her smile faded as she shook her head. "Actually, I received a very politely worded reply in each instance, denying me the appointment I had requested."

Morgan lifted his shoulders in a cool shrug. "My secretary handles my correspondence."

"Is it just me you refuse to see, or everyone?"

"Everyone."

"I see." She took another sip of champagne, regarding him thoughtfully. "You don't often leave your home, do you? Not since—"

"No."

Silence fell between them. Not an uncomfortable silence, but one that resonated with a remarkable degree of ease considering they had met only minutes ago—at least, to his recollection. He let the silence linger, savoring the moment. The quiet, the moonlight, the woman. So rare. It would be over soon enough, but for now it was a tiny taste of paradise.

She shifted beside him. *Restless so soon?* he thought

with a sigh. Very well. Resuming his conversational duty, he turned to her and said, "I believe you were about to tell me your name."

She parted her lips as if to speak, then hesitated as her gaze flicked past him, moving to a point just over his shoulder. Curious, Morgan turned. He followed her line of sight to a man who stood alone just inside the gaming rooms. He was elderly, beak-nosed, preposterously tall, and so long and awkward of limb that he looked as though his Maker had originally intended to fashion a stork. The painful thinness of his body was regrettably underscored by the severe lines of his black formal attire.

It wasn't so much his appearance that made him conspicuous as his general manner. An air of permanent petulance seemed to surround him, calling to mind a fussy bureaucrat or a tireless chaperone. He stood stiffly by himself in a forgotten corner of the room looking distinctly displeased, as though the world and everything in it fell far short of his lofty standards.

As Morgan watched the silent exchange between the redhead and the elderly man, the pieces clicked into place. Married. Mystery solved. That explained her unwillingness to give her name, as well as her presence at the Devonshire. Evidently her husband had grown accustomed to indulging his young, beautiful wife in her sordid little escapades and private amusements. Adventure and security. Nice if one could have both, and apparently she could. He arranged his features into a mask that he hoped would reflect both discreet understanding and solemn commiseration. An aged, impotent husband and a young, adventurous wife. A situation so common, it was almost banal.

"Do you have a timepiece?" she asked, returning her full attention to him.

He removed his sterling silver watch fob from his pocket, flipped open the engraved case, and passed it to her.

Her eyes widened, and a stark urgency filled her voice. "We must leave."

So soon? he thought to himself. A flicker of disappointment coursed through him. Pity. He enjoyed the chase—almost as much as he enjoyed the final capture. But in her case the prize was surely worth forgoing the pleasure of the hunt. There would be ample reward later.

He took a step toward her, simultaneously blocking her husband's view and closing the gap that had been between them. Gathering his courage—ridiculous how much courage it took—he looped his arm around the small of her waist and drew her gently into his embrace. "As you wish."

She pulled back—not far, but abruptly and distinctly. "Not here."

"Where?"

"Someplace . . . private." She reached into her reticule, then passed him a small linen card with an address already written on it.

A wry smile touched his lips. "How very convenient. Flattering as well. You must have known I would be here tonight."

If she was at all aware of his sarcasm, she chose to ignore it, letting her silence speak for itself. *So she isn't a wolf at all,* he thought, changing his original assessment. *Merely a married kitten playing her little kitten games.* Ignoring her sudden urgency, he idly twisted the card between his fingers as he asked, "When you dance, do you always lead? Or do you permit the man that small honor?"

Anger flared in her eyes. "I don't recall lifting you from your seat and dragging you bodily to my side."

A feisty kitten, he amended, silently pleased. That should make it interesting. "No, you didn't," he allowed.

"You'll meet me?" Again, that odd urgency in her voice.

Of course he would. He gave a brief nod and
watched the relief blossom in her expression.

"Wait fifteen minutes, then follow me there."

She lifted her skirts and moved rapidly away. He
watched as she stopped to whisper a word to her husband. The man bowed down low to hear, nodded, then
stiffened his spine and sent Morgan a disapproving
glare—a glare that Morgan returned with calm indifference. The moment quickly ended as the cuckolded husband turned and obediently followed his wife from the
room.

Well. So the evening wasn't entirely a mistake. Morgan sipped his champagne. It had been a long time. Too
long. He watched the woman leave, his gaze riveted on
the unconsciously seductive sway of her hips as she exited
the room.

Very nice.

Apparently Tyche hadn't deserted him after all.

Julia Prentisse stepped from the hackney and stared at
the ramshackle buildings before her. The address she had
given Morgan St. James led here, to a row of run-down
warehouses just off the docks. She was well acquainted
with the site and therefore accustomed to the deteriora-
tion of the buildings, but this was the first time she had
visited at night. The moonlight did little to enhance the
architectural blight.

She let out a soft sigh, telling herself it wasn't as bad
as she thought. The attempt at self-delusion was useless.
For even as she tried to bolster her confidence, the rowdy,
drunken laughter of a group of sailors spilled out from a
nearby pub. Apt, she thought, for the warehouse itself
slanted drunkenly to one side, as though the task of remaining erect were simply too formidable an undertaking
for the dilapidated structure.

Behind her, Mr. Randolph's disapproving voice

drifted out from within the confines of the hired coach. "Are you certain you wouldn't like me to stay?"

Forcing a brave smile, Julia turned toward the elderly man and shook her head. "No, really, I'm fine. You've been so kind already, and it's late—"

"Which is exactly why you shouldn't remain here alone. It's unseemly; dangerous as well."

"I won't be alone. At least, not for long."

"Hmmph. Your uncle would never—"

"My uncle isn't—" she began sharply, but let the words drift away unsaid. There was no point. She took a deep breath, then let it out slowly. "Thank you, Mr. Randolph," she said firmly. "Good night."

He let out another disapproving snort. "I don't like this. Not one bit."

Nevertheless, he pulled the coach door closed and gave the interior ceiling two sharp raps with his cane, calling his direction to the driver. As the coach began to roll away, he thrust his head through the window and sent her a stern glare. "I expect you to send word to my office first thing tomorrow morning. If I don't hear from you, I shall assume the worst."

On that dire pronouncement, he resumed his seat and the hackney rumbled away. Julia watched him leave. Feeling suddenly vulnerable, she wished she had thought to give Mr. Randolph the bills she held in her reticule. But it was too late now. She pulled her cape tightly around her shoulders, fighting back a sudden chill. No sooner had the coach faded away into the night when she heard the echo of heavy footsteps behind her. She turned sharply and scanned the wharf.

No one was there.

She took a deep breath, forcing herself to remain calm. There was a reasonable explanation. A sailor who had stepped into the pub, perhaps. Or a pursesnatch hiding in an alleyway. Or *him*. Had he been there tonight? She would swear she had felt his eyes upon her while she had been speaking with Viscount Barlowe. Had he followed her here? The thought sent a shiver racing down her spine. She retrieved her key and quickly let herself into the warehouse.

A dark, heavy stillness surrounded her. Eerie shadows leaped up the walls, weaving back and forth in the dull moonlight. Her hand moved automatically to the small desk by the door, where she felt for a box of sulfur matches. She struck one and held the flame before her, letting its meager flare guide her as she moved about the space lighting kerosene lamps.

Within seconds a gentle golden light filled the warehouse. The shadows that had seemed so menacing only moments earlier now presented themselves as nothing but tall stacks of crates and a miscellany of shipping supplies. She shrugged off her cloak and hung it from a nail, willing herself to remain calm. Morgan St. James would be here shortly. All she had to do was wait.

And wait.

Too anxious even to consider sitting, she paced back and forth between the shipping crates. The drunken laughter of the men in the nearby pub echoed through the thin walls, as did the gentle *lap, lap, lap* of the water sloshing against the pier. She strained to catch the dull clatter of a coach drawing up outside, but the street was ominously silent.

He was coming, wasn't he? Her heart skipped a beat as she considered the alternative. He *had* to come. He had to. She idly fingered the gold medallion around her neck, brushing it against her lips. Saint Rita. Patron saint of the impossible. *I wish—* She stopped abruptly. She wouldn't get greedy in her prayers. She thought for a moment, then sent a different plea heavenward. A simpler plea. *Courage. Give me the courage I need to continue.* That was small enough to ask, wasn't it?

She reached the end of the narrow aisle she had been

pacing and turned around. As she did, her stomach flipped, and she let out a startled gasp. There he was.

Morgan St. James.

He was dressed in the evening attire she had seen earlier: a black serge suit that had been immaculately cut to emphasize the breadth of his shoulders and the length of his legs, complemented by a crisp white shirt and black leather boots. Simple, yet undeniably elegant. Around his shoulders he had tossed a black cape. It billowed about his knees as he moved, giving him an almost sinister appearance.

The Beast.

She brushed the thought off impatiently. He had come. That was all that mattered.

"I didn't mean to startle you," he said.

She shook her head. "No, you didn't," she replied, relieved she didn't sound as breathless as she felt. "It's just . . . I didn't hear your coach."

"I didn't bring my coach. My mount is tied outside." He drew off his riding gloves and tucked them inside his coat pocket. "I imagine it's safe to assume that someone has stolen him by now."

A fleeting smile touched her lips. "Yes. Well . . ."

She searched for something witty to say, but her mind abandoned her. His presence was completely unnerving. He seemed larger than she remembered him and vaguely threatening somehow. Although they had stood much closer on the balcony of the Devonshire House, there had been swarms of people nearby. Now they were completely alone.

Unable to hold his gaze a moment longer, her eyes moved past him to a stack of heavy crates.

"Nervous, princess?"

Her gaze snapped back. "Hardly," she replied, drawing herself up with what she hoped was an expression of regal authority.

"I'm glad to hear it." He gestured vaguely around the warehouse. "Interesting choice."

"Yes. I thought it . . . practical."

"Rotten cabbage and sour cheese do tend to set a certain mood, but I'm not certain it's entirely appropriate to this . . ." He hesitated, as though searching for the right word. Finally he finished with "Arrangement."

"It's certainly private," she countered. "And spacious."

He arched one dark brow. "How much space do you think we'll need?"

Unthinking, she lifted her shoulders in a casual shrug. "The bigger the better."

A slow, seductive smile curved his lips. "Any other preferences I should know about?"

Julia stared at him in blank confusion, then felt her cheeks flame as understanding set in. "This isn't what you think it is."

"Oh? What do I think it is?"

She cleared her throat, tilted her chin and returned bravely, "An assignation."

"How delicately put." His gaze moved with deliberate insolence over her form, as though committing her body to memory. Then his eyes flicked back to hers. Leaning one slim hip against a makeshift trestle table, he idly swung one booted foot to and fro beneath him. "Is this part of your game, princess? This"—he paused, waving one hand in a gesture of vague boredom—"resistance? Shall I shower you with copious flattery until you succumb to the heat of my passion and fall helplessly into my embrace? Shall I praise your beauty, your soul, your wit, and swear that I will surely perish if forced to live another day without you? Is that what you're waiting for?"

Once again Julia felt the heat of embarrassment rise within her. Refusing to give him the upper hand, she greeted his words with cool silence. Then her gaze moved

over his body with the same deliberate insolence he had
shown her.

He was just as she remembered him, she thought,
then immediately corrected herself, for it wasn't true. He
still had the same aristocratic bearing, the same silky black
hair, the same lean, muscular form. But she had mis-
judged his eyes. She remembered them dark, level, rational. Not stormy gray, eyes that looked quick to passion
and quick to temper. Moreover, the man she had met
years ago had been one of London's most notorious rakes,
a man who had commanded attention and admiration
wherever he went. A man rumored to be notoriously at
ease in any situation, whether he found himself in a married woman's bedchamber or speaking before the House
of Lords.

But Morgan St. James had changed; that much was
evident even to her. It went beyond the scars that marred
his hands and the back of his neck. Years ago his gaze had
been open, warm, brazenly suggestive. Now there was a
coldness beneath his smooth charm. He seemed guarded,
inaccessible, icily distant, even as he tried to woo her to
his bed.

She brushed the thoughts away. It didn't matter. *Get
on with it.* "I suppose you're wondering why I invited you
here," she said. When he didn't reply, she continued
bravely. "I have something to show you."

Her heart pounding, she moved to a small cabinet
and unlocked the bottom drawer. She lifted a thick parchment envelope and withdrew the letter contained therein.
As she unfolded it, the words seemed to leap out at her.

> *Flame,*
> *Did you miss me? I've missed you, my love.*
> *Through circumstances beyond my control, I've*
> *had to abandon you to do our work alone. But I'm*
> *back once again.*
> *I saw you walking in Cheapside last Thursday eve,*

*and my heart leaped with joy. You were wearing a
golden gown.
How the colors of fire do become you. Crimson,
orange, gold.
So warm. So pure. So beautiful.
Lazarus*

With shaking hands, she passed the note to Morgan. He
skimmed the contents, then lifted his shoulders in an indifferent shrug. "A love letter," he replied flatly, looking
supremely bored. "If you think this charming little missive
came from me, princess, I'm afraid I must disappoint
you."

"No, not from you." Julia drew a deep breath, then
her eyes locked on his. "From the man who set your servants' quarters on fire."

Chapter 2

Julia wasn't sure what sort of response she had expected
from him. She only knew she had expected some sort of
reaction.

Something.

Instead, Morgan St. James stared at her with a look of
polite disinterest.

"Indeed," he said flatly.

"But I thought you—"

"The man's dead. Even if that letter did come from
him, I can't imagine what use it is now."

Of course. *Idiot,* Julia thought, cursing herself for her
shortsightedness. She had been so absorbed in her own
worries, she had completely forgotten that the rest of London believed the arsonist had come to a fiery end in one
of his own blazes.

Two separate fires had been deliberately set after the
one on Viscount Barlowe's property. The stables belonging to the Earl of Chilton had been set ablaze; a month

afterward the estate of Lord Webster had gone up in flames. Found among the smoldering remains of Webster's property was an unidentified man, a man presumed to be the arsonist himself. When no fires had occurred thereafter, that presumption had been considered confirmed. The city had breathed a collective sigh of relief, and life had resumed as before.

Even Julia had been lulled into a false sense of security—a security that had vanished the day she received this latest letter.

"He didn't die," she said. "I don't know who that body belonged to, but it wasn't the arsonist. He's alive, and he means to begin setting fires again. I'm certain of that."

"I see." He hadn't moved. He was posed exactly as he had been earlier: one slim hip propped upon a trestle table, one foot swinging to and fro beneath him. But his expression was entirely different. No longer coolly seductive, he regarded her with a look of naked disdain.

"Upon what evidence are you basing this rather hysterical presumption?" he asked, his voice ringing with aristocratic superiority.

"Letters," she stated succinctly, refusing to be intimidated by his tone. "Letters very like the one you now hold. All sent to me and signed by the same man—Lazarus." She turned back to the cabinet and withdrew a slim bundle of papers. "I received this the very day your servants' quarters were set ablaze." She passed him a parchment sheet and watched as he read,

Flame,
The time has come, my love. How glorious is the
wrath of the righteous. At last he shall suffer as I
have suffered. What ultimate joy. A flame shall
wither him up in his early growth, and with the
wind his blossoms shall disappear.
Lazarus

"Job, chapter fifteen, verse thirty," she said as he finished reading, referring to the last line in the letter.

"Yes. I'm familiar with the passage."

She waited for him to say more, but nothing came. The heavy silence that weighed between them was broken only by the distant echoes coming from the docks outside. He had shifted his body slightly as he read. A shadow now fell across his face, denying her any glimpse of his reaction. Nor had there been any clue in his voice as to the state of his emotions.

With little choice but to go on, she passed him the remaining letters. One she had received the day of the Earl of Chilton's fire, the other the day of Lord Webster's. Both were similar in content and style to the ones she had shown him. He skimmed them, then passed them back.

"Flame?" he asked at last.

"I believe he's alluding to the color of my hair."

"I see." He hesitated a moment, then continued coolly. "The letter referring to seeing you in Cheapside—when did you receive that?"

"Two weeks ago."

"And between Lord Webster's fire and the letter of two weeks ago . . ."

"Nothing. No word at all. Like everyone else, I assumed he had perished."

"Do you know the identity of Lazarus?"

"I'm afraid I have no idea."

"In that case, why you? Why would he send these letters to you?"

"That's rather difficult to explain," she hedged.

"Then skip the explanations. Just give me the facts."

There was a curtness to his tone that immediately rankled. She was on the verge of reminding him that she was not one of his servants to be ordered about but held her tongue. Not yet. She knew better. This had to be handled delicately if she was to have any hope of success.

"Would you care for tea?" she asked.

"Tea?" Although his face remained masked by shadow, raw incredulity was plain in his voice.

She drew her hands together, clenching them tightly against the pink satin of her gown in an effort to hide her nervousness. "The explanations—facts—are somewhat lengthy. Perhaps we would be more comfortable adjourning inside."

Silence greeted her words. Then, after what seemed an interminable pause, Morgan stood. Once again Julia was struck by how large he seemed. How overwhelmingly masculine. The awareness did little to ease her nerves.

"By all means, princess, let us adjourn for tea."

She forced a tight, polite smile, feigning a complete ignorance of his patronizing tone. Turning away, she led him through the maze of crates to an oak door. She paused to light the small lamp that stood by the entrance, then ushered him forward with a polite wave of her hand. She followed behind him, taking a moment to light a few more lamps that were scattered at various points throughout the room. Unfortunately the mellow, golden glow they provided did nothing to soften the ugliness of the space.

Julia glanced about the room, battling a surge of shame as she considered how it must appear to him. The quarters were little more than an empty corner that had been crudely partitioned off from the rest of the warehouse. The walls were bare, the floors nothing but wooden planks covered by rugs that had long since worn thin. The oversize furniture, once grand and elegant, looked ridiculously crowded and out of place, as did the damask drapery that covered the single window overlooking the docks. A thin film of grime, the result of constant exposure to a coal-burning furnace, covered everything.

To make matters even worse, each item in the room, from the smallest porcelain serving dish to the huge mahogany armoire, was conspicuously marked with a ticket from Pindler and Sons, announcing the opening bid that would be requested once the items went up for auction—

an event scheduled for next Tuesday afternoon. In her haste to meet with Morgan St. James, Julia had completely forgotten to remove the tags. Now they seemed to blaze out at her, further evidence of her family's fall from grace.

Unable to meet his eyes, she murmured an invitation for him to sit and bolted behind a bamboo screen that partitioned the kitchen from the rest of the quarters. Reveling in the temporary privacy, she hung her head and took a deep breath, battling the emotions that clogged her throat. If there had been a back door, she would have cowardly scooted out of it. Unfortunately, however, there wasn't. She had no choice but to continue with her plan. With shaking hands she lifted a poker, stirred the oven ashes to spark a fire, then went about the task of boiling water for tea.

By the time she returned to the front room a few minutes later, she felt somewhat composed. She found Morgan standing beside a curtain used to provide a modicum of privacy for the small space that served as the bedchamber. Her gowns hung in a neat row inside, all ticketed for sale. Like everything else, they were victims of a bygone era in her life. The tag that had marked the pink satin she now wore lay waiting atop the dresser, ready to be replaced as soon as she removed the gown. Five pounds, sixpence.

He turned at the sound of her setting down the tea tray. "You live here?" he asked curtly.

"No. I live with my aunt and uncle. This building belonged to my father."

"What of your husband?"

She stared at him blankly. "My what?"

"Your husband. That elderly crane who accompanied you earlier tonight."

"Oh, you mean Mr. Randolph. He is—was—my father's solicitor. Now he is in my employ. At my request, he was kind enough to escort me to the Devonshire

House tonight." She sat, then gestured at the settee across from her. "Please."

She waited until he had made himself comfortable. "Sugar?"

"Black is fine, Miss . . ."

"Prentisse," she supplied, passing him his tea. "Julia Prentisse." She waited a beat, then gathered her courage and continued. "My father was Nathaniel Prentisse."

"Ah."

"Captain of the *Mystic*."

A slight pause, then, "Yes."

Again, not the reaction she had been expecting. Cool and calm, markedly imperturbable. There was no shock, no appalled recognition. He sat with his cup and saucer balanced on one knee, the epitome of elegant, aristocratic ease. She searched his eyes but saw nothing within their gray depths but mild interest. He was merely waiting for her to continue.

Julia had prepared for this moment for over a week. But in that instant all her carefully rehearsed speeches abruptly evaporated, leaving her nothing but a collection of jumbled thoughts and worn-out phrases.

Finally she managed, "I know you're interested in the facts surrounding these letters only as they pertain to you, but there are circumstances relating to the background that can't be explained without further detail. . . ." Aware how foolish she must sound, she stopped abruptly, sending him an apologetic smile. "If you'll indulge me for just a moment?"

"By all means, Miss Prentisse, do continue."

She hesitated, searching again for the right words. "There is just one additional issue that should be addressed, Lord Barlowe. What I am about to disclose is of a rather sensitive nature. I should like your word as a gentleman that the matters discussed here tonight—whatever the outcome of our talk—will remain entirely confidential."

"Very well. I give you my word."

Satisfied, she nodded and stiffened her spine, facing him squarely. "You are aware of my father's background?"

"I am aware of what was printed in the papers."

"Good. In that case, I'll be brief. A year ago my father was convicted of smuggling. I won't defend his actions here, except to say that following my mother's death he began to drink excessively. I believe that clouded his judgment. Despite the rumors you may have heard to the contrary, he was a good man." She began to expand on that sentiment, but thought better of it and continued briskly. "We lost everything. My father was reduced to selling our home and moving here; I was sent to live with my aunt and uncle. Shortly thereafter my father died."

"My sympathies."

The words had a perfunctory edge to them that Julia did not miss. She brought up her chin and coolly met his eyes. "I relate these events not to engage your sympathies but to adequately disclose my past. I believe it only fair that you know exactly with whom you are dealing."

He bowed his head in a gesture of mild contrition. "In that case, may I say that I appreciate your excruciating honesty."

This was not going well. Not at all. But she had no choice but to continue. "As I mentioned, I am presently living with my aunt and uncle. I'm afraid my presence is rather a burden on their household. You see, they have two daughters who are also of marriageable age. The fact that I have no dowry is compounded by the scandal that has been attached to my father's name. As you might imagine, there is no legion of suitors waiting at the door to beg for my hand. It has made things rather difficult for us all."

"In what sense?"

"The shame of my family's disgrace has unfortunately tainted my cousins' reputations. Naturally, my uncle is rather anxious to see me married off so that he may attend to securing the futures of his own daughters. To that end he has managed to uncover three suitors who have asked for my hand, despite my obvious shortcomings."

"My sincerest felicitations."

"I refused them all," she returned flatly. She suppressed a shudder, pushing aside the memory of her uncle's fury. *Later.* If her plan failed tonight, she would deal with him later. "My uncle, however, has not conveyed my sentiments to the gentlemen involved. He has informed me that I must choose one, or . . ."

"Or?"

"Or there will be consequences." She hesitated, fiddling for a moment with the scalloped edge of her saucer. "I am not being fickle, nor am I ungrateful. But I fear that in his haste to see me married off, my uncle does not have my best interests at heart." Ashamed at the feelings she had expressed so freely, she glanced up at Morgan with a small, embarrassed smile. "It does me no honor to harbor thoughts like that, does it?"

He returned her smile with a look of glacial indifference. "You say you have no dowry. Yet you were gambling tonight as though you had money to squander."

"That is exactly the point I was coming to. Contrary to what my uncle may believe, I am not without funds or resources. This warehouse, for example. It belonged to my father. Now Henry and I—"

"Henry?"

"Henry Maddox. My father's former bosun. He rents the warehouse to ships in need of storage space for their cargo, and we split the profit between us. The enterprise has been quite successful."

"I see."

Julia drew a deep breath. Having dispensed with her background, it was time to address the issue at hand. "There is another matter with which I am involved," she began, "one that has indirectly come to concern you. You see, for the past three years I've written an anonymous column for the *London Review*. Perhaps you've seen it. 'The Tattler'?"

"Good God."

She set down her teacup. "I take it that's a yes."

He looked utterly appalled. Then after a moment a smile of cynical satisfaction touched his lips. "So that's you, is it?" he said. "London's foremost gossip—and thrower of stones—is hiding a dark past of her own."

"I am not a gossip. Nor do I throw stones. The purpose of that column was, and still is, to educate London's elite as to the social ills that infest this city. The workhouses, the slums, the factories where children labor from dawn to dusk, the fact that women are denied the right to vote, as well as the right to hold property in our own name, not to mention—"

"Indeed," he interrupted dryly, "how very noble."

"I would prefer not to include the gossip at all, but I found my column was neither read nor discussed without it. It has become, I'm afraid, a necessary evil."

Refusing to debate the point, he stated simply, "I believe you were eventually going to come to the subject of Lazarus?"

"Yes. Of course." She folded her hands in her lap and continued. "Shortly after I began the column, I started receiving letters from this Lazarus person. Initially they were merely praise and encouragement for my good work in exposing the evils of society. Then they began to grow darker, full of dire biblical references and vague threats of vengeance. Unfortunately I no longer have those early letters. They were so disturbing, I simply threw them away."

"How did the letters come to you?"

"The same way all my correspondence with the paper is handled: through Mr. Randolph. He delivers my column once a week and picks up any letters that may have been sent to me in the interim. I've never set foot anywhere near the *Review*'s offices myself. As far as I'm aware, no one there has any knowledge of my identity."

"Yet Lazarus was able to deduce who you are."

"Apparently." She drew her hands over her upper arms as though warding off a chill. Not only did he know who she was, but in recent weeks she had *felt* the man's presence—watching, lurking, following her every movement. She did not say as much, however. No need to get overly dramatic.

"When the fires began," she continued, "Mr. Randolph took the letters directly to Mr. Chivers, the Home Secretary at Scotland Yard. Unfortunately they proved to be of little use. And once the fires stopped . . ." Her voice trailed off as she lifted her shoulders in a helpless shrug.

"Yes. The matter was put aside." Morgan nodded thoughtfully. "Have you shown this latest letter to anyone else?"

"No, just you—and Mr. Randolph, of course."

"Can he be trusted?"

"Mr. Randolph?" she echoed with a startled laugh. "I've known him since I was a child. I would trust him with my very life."

He considered that, then nodded once again. "Very well."

"I hope you understand now why I felt it was necessary to divulge my entire background, Lord Barlowe. Ordinarily I might not have spoken so freely, but I felt it only fair that you be aware of all the surrounding circumstances . . . particularly as they pertain to the matter of marriage."

He glanced up at her with a distracted air. "Yours?"

Her heart pounding in her chest, Julia looked directly into Morgan St. James's cool gray eyes. "Ours."

Morgan's first thought was that he hadn't heard the woman correctly. But the expression on her face told him otherwise. She stared at him with a mixture of hope and dread as a small, trembling smile curved her lips.

"I beg your pardon?" he finally managed.

"Our marriage."

"You can't be serious."

"On the contrary, I've never been more serious about anything in my life." She leaned slightly forward in her seat and continued in a tone of desperate urgency. "Given my uncle's recent determination to see me married off, I have given the matter a great deal of thought. Especially the issue of a dowry. If I had something of value to bring to the marriage, my betrothal would be of considerably greater worth. It suddenly struck me that I am not as impoverished as it would appear. I do have a dowry—albeit one that is of value only to you."

"And that is?"

"Lazarus. I can help you find Lazarus."

Morgan regarded her in silence as disbelief coursed through him. Her proposal was as shocking as it was ludicrous. Marriage. The thought was too ridiculous even to entertain. A joke. Surely it was nothing but a joke—one that was made in incredibly poor taste. He straightened in his seat, intending to stand, bid her good fortune, and leave the room. But one nagging, irritating thought held him in place.

Lazarus.

Was it possible? His muscles tightened as images of that fateful morning flashed through his mind. Could this Lazarus be the same man he had chased down an alley that misty dawn morning more than two years ago? Could all of London have been mistaken as to the identity of the dead man found in the ashes? Unlikely, despite Julia Prentisse's conviction to the contrary. But as he considered the question, a flicker of uncertainty sparked somewhere deep inside him.

If it was the arsonist sending those letters . . . If the man still lived and could be found . . .

It would be worth any cost.

Realizing she was waiting for an answer, he studied her with newfound curiosity. She didn't look as though she were joking. Instead, the expression on her lovely features was one of dire earnestness. Interesting. He understood his own motivation, but what of hers? "You said your uncle has encouraged three other suitors who have asked for your hand," he said. "Why this inexplicable desire to wed me?"

A grimace of raw embarrassment crossed her features. Avoiding his eyes, she turned away with a light shrug and replied in a voice of patently false nonchalance, "They don't please me."

"Who are they?"

Her gaze snapped back to his, her sherry eyes wide with alarm. "I refused their suit. I couldn't possibly reveal—"

"Who?"

She studied his face for a long minute in stubborn silence, then a petulant frown curved her lips. "This is most—"

"Who?"

"Lord Edward Needam."

A misogynistic ass who was known to beat his mistresses when the mood struck him. "Who else?" he asked.

She let out a sigh, replying with considerable reluctance, "Sir William Bell."

A mule-faced drunk up to his ears in gaming debts. "And?"

A long pause, then, "The Honorable Peter Trevlin."

That name surprised Morgan. He had thought Trevlin's predilections ran solely toward young boys.

"That's quite a list, princess. I had no idea I had fallen into such stellar company."

"Yes. Well . . ." She hesitated for a moment, fiddling with the soft folds of her gown. "Naturally my uncle prefers that the more favored suitors turn their attentions toward his own daughters."

Naturally. Good God. What had she said? *I fear my uncle does not have my best interests at heart.* That was putting it mildly. If the man was that eager to be rid of her, he would have done his niece a greater favor in tying a stone around her neck and tossing her in the Thames.

"When one considers my alternatives," she said, "I believe it becomes understandable as to why I would take the drastic measure of pressing my own suit this evening."

"Indeed." He leaned back against the settee, a wry grin curving his lips. "Always flattering to learn that one is looked upon as a last resort."

"That's not the case at all," she protested. "The same research that led me to turning down my other suitors convinced me that you would make a tolerable husband."

"Indeed? And just what research was that?" he asked, genuinely curious.

"I spoke to your servants. You'll be happy to learn that they're a rather closemouthed bunch. Furthermore, most of them have been in your employ for years. Loyalty of that sort is generally a sign of contentment. Short of informing me that you are not romantically engaged at present and that you were undertaking a rare visit to the Devonshire House this evening, they had very little to say."

"That's good?"

"Quite. As you might imagine, the discussions I had with the servants in the employ of the other gentlemen I mentioned were rather . . . stimulating."

Morgan barely managed to suppress a smile at her prim disapproval. "Yes," he replied solemnly, "I would imagine so."

A contemplative silence fell between them. She bowed her head, her lips pursed in thought. As she moved, a strand of her incredible hair fell forward, brushing against her cheek like a silken caress. For an instant,

Morgan found himself wondering what that hair would feel like tumbling against his chest, how that fiery red would look against the linen cream of his sheets. Before he could pursue that fantasy further, she looked up and softly announced, "I believe we would do well together as husband and wife."

"And just how did you reach that astonishing conclusion?"

"I'm fluent in French," she said, evidently—perhaps deliberately—misinterpreting his sarcasm for a genuine query.

"So am I," he replied, unimpressed.

"I can cook."

"I have a cook."

"I'm very efficient in the managing of a household."

"As is my housekeeper."

"I have served as hostess at my father's parties, affairs that included as many as one hundred guests. Furthermore," she rushed on before he could comment, "I would not be a burden to you financially. As I mentioned earlier, I have a steady income from the rents on this space, and the auctioneer from Pindler and Sons has informed me that I may make as much as two hundred pounds from the sale of the furnishings. Perhaps even two hundred and fifty pounds—"

"Can you breed?"

"I beg your pardon." She studied him with an expression of queenly disdain, plainly giving him an opportunity to retract his words. When he didn't, she brought up her chin and turned away, muttering in a tone of maidenly outrage, "What a vulgar question."

He lifted his shoulders in an indifferent shrug. "Yours is a vulgar proposition. Besides, you're forgetting what a man wants most when he takes a wife."

"Love?"

He nearly choked on a mouthful of tea. "You neglected to mention a sense of humor while regaling me with your considerable attributes."

"Then I'm afraid I don't—"

"An heir."

"Oh. I hadn't considered . . . that is . . ." Her voice faltered and came to a stumbling stop. An expression of open dismay showed on her face. But she quickly rallied herself and lifted her gaze to meet his. "We would need to make some . . . arrangement for that, wouldn't we?"

"As far as I know, there is only one *arrangement* for that sort of thing. A myriad of creative possibilities when it comes to style and satisfaction, but just one basic arrangement."

He was being deliberately crude, measuring her reaction.

To his considerable amazement, she met his challenge with cool aplomb. "I am familiar with the ways of intimacy between a man and a woman," she replied succinctly, with barely a blush marring the porcelain perfection of her skin.

So she wasn't a virgin. Very well. Neither was he. He wouldn't hold that against her.

"May I speak plainly, Lord Barlowe?" she asked.

He arched his brows in an expression of mock astonishment. "Do you mean to say that you haven't been?"

A small smile curved her lips, but it was clear by her distracted manner that her thoughts had taken another direction. She stood and moved away from him, fiddling for a moment with a hodgepodge of ornamental bric-a-brac that cluttered an oversize bureau.

She turned to him and said, "We are outcasts in society, you and I. I have no dowry. I am a burden to what little family I do have. My name has been permanently besmirched—as evidenced by the quality of suitors who have asked for my hand. And as for you"—she paused, looking him directly in the eye—"I remember well what happened after the fire on your property. It wasn't long before the initial tide of sympathy turned against you, and you were vilified by all of London, condemned for awful loss of life and the callous disregard you showed in forcing your servants to live in such close confines. It was even rumored that you deserved your scars, for they mark you as the Beast you truly are."

Morgan tensed. He had heard all the rumors, of course, but never had they been so baldly tossed in his face. "Are you always this outspoken, Miss Prentisse?"

She lifted her shoulders in an elegant shrug. "I say these things not to incite your anger—nor so that we may wallow together in self-pity—but so we may examine the facts as they exist. Perhaps things might have been different once, but now we have no choice but to accept our lot and move forward. I believe we can help each other. If I didn't think so, I wouldn't be here tonight."

He regarded her in cool silence. Finally he said, "Marriage to a total stranger seems a rather desperate measure, does it not?"

"I've given the matter considerable thought, and I fear it is my only solution," she replied. "Living with my aunt and uncle is growing more intolerable every day. As I mentioned earlier, I have some income, but I would need to augment that sum in order to fully support myself. I had intended to search for a position as a governess, but it would take too long to secure a post. And short of taking another name, I'm afraid the scandal of my family's past would make finding work difficult."

Morgan contemplated that. Even if she could find a post, it would mean spending the rest of her life in dull seclusion. Furthermore, if the man were married and his wife had any sense, she would never allow a woman who looked like Julia Prentisse to live under their roof. The temptation would simply be too great.

Aloud he said only, "Very commendable. Boring work, but a respectable occupation nonetheless."

"I also thought of opening a shop. I've been told I'm rather clever with lace and feathers when it comes to decorating a hat—"

"We're full of all sorts of brash plans, aren't we, princess?"

Anger flashed across her face. "This is difficult enough as it is. If you mean to say no, I would appreciate your doing so without demeaning me further."

Morgan studied her a moment longer, as though she were an object he was about to acquire. Amazing the paths life took. He had once been known as London's most notorious rake. Now he was seriously contemplating marriage to a bluestocking reformer. But he could do worse. Much worse. His gaze moved slowly over the sculpted curves of her body beneath her shimmering gown, the flaming richness of her hair, the perfection of her delicate features. Even in the heat of anger, she was lovely.

And then there was the matter of Lazarus.

Lazarus.

If marrying Julia Prentisse meant finding the man who had set his servants' quarters ablaze, it was well worth the cost—any cost.

That decided, he rose abruptly to his feet. "Your address?"

When the question drew nothing but a blank stare, he prompted, "Your uncle's address?"

Her eyes widened with startled disbelief, then she gave him the location.

"Very good." He gave a tight nod. "You may inform him I'll be paying a call tomorrow morning."

"Does this mean . . ."

He paused at the door and turned back. "Don't sell the gowns. You can wear the pale green at our wedding ceremony."

Chapter 3

*H*er hand was trembling. Julia tried to control her reaction, but it seemed the more she focused on that quivering appendage, the more it seemed to shake. Morgan St. James had to be aware of her reaction—he was holding her hand, after all—but his expression indicated little interest or concern for the precarious state of her emotions.

"With this ring I thee wed," he said. His voice conveyed the same level of emotional intensity one might hear if reading aloud a bill of lading.

At the minister's nod he slid a thick gold band onto the fourth finger of her left hand. Centered in the band was a dazzling, square-cut sapphire wreathed by glittering diamonds.

Julia's mind reeled with disbelief. A wedding ring. It was all happening so quickly. Less than a week had passed since their initial meeting, yet in that time Morgan had operated with brisk efficiency, meeting her uncle to obtain his permission for their nuptials, securing a special license for their betrothal, locating a church in which the ceremony could be performed, and making arrangements with a minister to officiate.

Despite the discretion with which Morgan had moved, rumors had nevertheless flown throughout London that the Beast was about to take a bride. The church was packed with gossips and curiosity-seekers, all of whom had come to witness for themselves an event that was being touted as the spectacle of the year.

"With all my worldly goods I thee endow," he continued evenly. "With my body I thee worship."

His words echoed off the church walls, rebounding all around them.

Julia's hand shook even harder. Morgan St. James. Was it true what people said about him? She gazed at the long fingers that held her in his grip. The skin there was taut, deeply scarred, red and angry. Did the rest of his body look the same? A shudder tore through her at the thought. For a moment the urge to run was so overpowering, she almost succumbed to the impulse to flee the church. Morgan must have somehow divined her shameful thoughts, for in that instant his mouth tightened to a grim line, and he loosened his hold on her hand.

Startled, she lifted her eyes to his. He looked icily remote, as though the question of whether she fled—leaving him alone at the altar with more than a hundred spectators to witness his humiliation—or stayed to become his wife was one of supreme indifference to him.

Julia became dimly aware that the minister was asking her a question. She tore her attention away from Morgan to focus on the words being spoken. Would she take him for her lawfully wedded husband? Her silence lasted perhaps only a second or two, yet as she held Morgan's gaze, it seemed to stretch out between them into infinity.

She took a deep breath, then answered in a soft voice that sounded completely unlike her own, "I will."

The remainder of the ceremony passed in a blur. She repeated the minister's words by rote, as though she were a mere witness to the ceremony rather than an actual participant. Then it was over. The minister placed their hands together and declared them man and wife. Morgan signed his name on the register; she did the same.

It was customary for a new bride and groom to be received with cheers, applause, greetings of goodwill, and perhaps even a bawdy joke or two when first presented to a congregation. Julia had attended enough weddings to know that. But as she and Morgan turned and faced their audience, nothing but stony silence greeted them, punctuated occasionally by an indiscreet whisper or the flutter of fan.

It was an uncommonly warm day, and the crush of bodies only intensified the heat within the small church. But Julia found the silence even more oppressive than the temperature. It seemed to carry with it a weight of callous censure and scorn, as though she and Morgan had turned themselves into the sort of pitiful misfits normally found accompanying a traveling carnival.

Her gaze moved to her own family, who were seated in the front pews. Uncle Cyrus, dour and disapproving as ever, was dressed in a grim black suit that looked as though it should be reserved exclusively for funeral rites. Aunt Rosalind, who had made the unfortunate choice of a lavender taffeta gown that wilted in the stifling heat, looked as though she might faint at any moment. Her cousins, Theresa and Marianne, regarded her with expressions of pained endurance, as though the whole affair were nothing but one further embarrassment to be suffered through on her behalf.

With an air of total disregard for their reception, Morgan wordlessly took her arm and ushered her down the main aisle. They exited the church and stepped out into the brilliant July sunshine. His coach and driver were waiting at the bottom of the steps; a second vehicle was parked directly behind it for her family's use. Morgan handed her into his coach and immediately followed, pulling the door closed behind him.

Shortly thereafter the driver gained his seat and gave the reins a quick snap. As the team of chestnut geldings began to pull into traffic, Julia protested, "Shouldn't we wait until my aunt and uncle—"

"Your uncle is familiar with the arrangements. He'll follow us."

The words were spoken in a clipped, no-nonsense manner that left little room for argument. Julia would have pressed her point nonetheless, had the issue mattered to her. But as their destination was a wedding breakfast with the sole participants being herself, Morgan, and her family—an event she looked upon with dread rather than anticipation—she let it go.

She turned her attention to the happenings outside the coach. They made their way east, skirting the well-heeled patrons and expensive shops and restaurants that lined Regent Street, then continued north through the boisterous, bustling crowds that filled Covent Garden. As they neared Mayfair and Grosvenor Square, a dignified quiet settled over the streets.

With little left for her to see but the strikingly similar facades of the mansions they passed, Julia returned her attention to the other occupant of the coach, Morgan St. James.

Her husband.

Her plan had worked perfectly. She had avoided her uncle's odious suitors and taken a husband of her own choosing. But somehow that knowledge did little to engender an emotion of celebratory bliss. Instead, the realization that they were truly married caused a tight, fluttering vibration through her belly, filling her with equal measures of dread, disbelief, and nervous wonder.

She cast a discreet glance at the stranger she had married. Morgan was engaged in the same pastime that had previously occupied her: watching the scenery pass as they drove toward his home. Conscious of the silence that resonated between them, she decided to strike up a conversation.

"The ring is beautiful," she said. "Thank you."

For a moment it appeared he hadn't heard her, so total was his absorption in the view outside the carriage. But after a minute he slowly turned to face her. "I don't blame you."

She regarded him in blank confusion. "I beg your—"

A small, cynical smile curved his lips. "Were I in your position, I would have wanted to run as well."

She could think of no reply, nor did any seem appropriate. So she did the only thing she could think of. She turned away, directing her attention outside the carriage once again.

Seconds later the coach slowed before a large tract of land that was markedly different from the homes that surrounded it. There was no elegant facade, no neatly manicured lawn, no smoothly paved drive. Instead, all that could be seen was a tall iron gate connected by imposing brick columns that encircled the property. Thick, thorny vines had woven their way through the iron rails, obliterating any view of what was contained within.

Julia went cold at the sight. Had she escaped one hell only to make herself a prisoner in another? As most of London knew, the gate that circled the St. James estate had been erected shortly after the fire. With its appearance—and further isolation of the man within—rumors had begun to spread throughout the city as to exactly what was behind those gates.

The Beast.

Embarrassed by her own foolishness, she pushed the thought away with an irritated sigh. Ridiculous. She had researched the man carefully. Hadn't Morgan's own servants spoken well on his behalf? Furthermore, she was here of her own free will. This was entirely her choice, her decision.

Nevertheless, as the broad gates opened to admit them, her breath caught in her throat and her heart thundered at twice its normal tempo. This step—entering what was to be her home for the remainder of her days—seemed far more final than any she had taken to date, including the wedding vows they had exchanged earlier. She had once read an account written by a man who had been sentenced to life imprisonment. In his recollection, it wasn't the sentencing itself that had caused him to break down. The stark, cold realization of what was happening to him had come when the metal bars of his cell clanged shut behind him.

And so it was for her.

Perhaps because that grim analogy filled her mind, because she had prepared herself for the worst, the reality that greeted her was all the more startling. Stretching out as far as her eye could see were lush green lawns that rolled over gently sloping hills. Stone pathways traversed the grounds, leading to pockets of tall, shady trees and intimate gardens that bloomed with a riot of color. She noted a brook that meandered across the property from north to south, and a formal, bubbling fountain centered in the courtyard to the west of Morgan's estate.

The house itself was classic in design, with tall columns, an ornate oak door, and broad steps composing the facade. Constructed of brick, it had been painted a dazzling white that seemed to shimmer in the summer sunlight. Black shutters flanked the windows; matching black window boxes were bursting with bold crimson geraniums and neatly trimmed ivy.

She turned to him and smiled. "It's lovely."

A look of cynical amusement touched his features. "What did you expect?"

Refusing to be intimidated yet again, she replied honestly, "A deteriorating estate with crumbling walls, shutters hanging askew, rotted steps, and broken window-panes. I thought it would be surrounded by dying trees that cast ghostly shadows on the walls, and dismal gardens that had long since withered with neglect."

"How very dramatic. I fear I disappoint you."

"You surprise me."

For a moment she thought she saw something other than cool indifference in his gaze. But the expression, whatever it was, vanished too quickly for her to be certain. As the carriage shuddered to a stop a footman was instantly at the door, pulling it open. Morgan stepped out first, then turned and assisted Julia. They stood together in silence for a moment, contemplating the broad steps that led to the front door.

"I believe we can dispense with the customary carrying of the bride over the threshold," he announced.

The implication that she had been expecting him to do exactly that was clear. Biting back a stab of annoyance, she matched his cool tone. "I would be exceedingly grateful."

"In that case, shall we?"

Julia lifted her skirts and wordlessly preceded him up the stairs. Once she reached the entrance, the door swung open almost instantly. Waiting within the main foyer was a small army of servants, all immaculately dressed and standing in the tight, orderly formation of troops waiting to be reviewed.

She arched one brow and shot a silent, questioning glance at Morgan.

He shrugged. "I thought we might see to the introductions straightaway."

"How very efficient."

Taking her words for assent, he addressed his waiting staff. "I present your new mistress, my bride, Viscountess Barlowe. I would have you serve her as you would serve me. What she wishes is what I would wish. What she would have done is what I would have done. Please her, and you will have pleased me."

His words were brisk and concise. But to Julia, who hadn't the faintest notion of what her place would be in his household, they were deeply reassuring. At her request, his remarks were followed by personal introductions. Aside from the few faces she recognized from her earlier encounters, she knew she couldn't possibly remember the name of every housemaid, parlormaid, scullery-maid, chambermaid, and dairymaid; nor that of every footman, butler, cook, groomsman, and gardener. But she felt the attempt to offer a personal greeting to those with whom she would be living was at least a step in the right direction.

The introductions completed, the servants went back to their duties. "I expected your family would have joined us by now," he said.

"Yes." She cast an anxious glance out the front window, but there was no sign of the second coach. Facing the inevitable, she let out a sigh and sent Morgan an apologetic smile. "Given that he has temporarily retained a private coach, Uncle Cyrus may have decided to run a few errands before joining us." The obvious implication—that her uncle was too miserly to lease a coach of his own, selfish enough to take advantage of Morgan's hospitality, and rude enough to keep them waiting for their own wedding breakfast—was undeniably true. But stating it so baldly did not shed the best light on the situation. Therefore she added hastily, "With this heat it's so difficult to find a coach for hire. I'm sure you understand."

Judging by Morgan's expression, he did understand. All too well. But his only reply was "If we are to wait, perhaps we would be more comfortable doing so on the veranda."

He led her through a maze of long hallways and elegant rooms to an informal back parlor that was filled with chintz-covered sofas, enormous bookcases, and pretty floral rugs. A set of tall French doors at the far end of the room opened onto a shady veranda that overlooked the gardens below. She moved immediately to the banister, leaning out over the rail to more fully enjoy a soft breeze that chose just that moment to stir. Unfortunately the breeze died away as quickly as it had erupted, leaving nothing but the stifling warmth of the day.

Behind her, Morgan asked, "Would you care for tea or something cooler?"

She turned to see one of the parlormaids she had met earlier standing just outside the glass doors, waiting for her reply. Julia sent her a soft smile. "Something cool, thank you."

The maid gave a brief curtsy and turned to obey. As the girl left, Morgan abandoned his place near the rear of the veranda and moved closer, positioning himself to receive the shade of a potted palm. A slight frown touched Julia's lips as she considered the movement. In each instance they had been together, Morgan St. James seemed to surround himself with shadows, whether it was a matter of pulling the coach shade partially closed or taking up a position in a darkened corner of a room. The maneuver was subtle but consistent. Was it an acquired habit, she wondered, or something that he consciously thought about?

"Tell me more about your Uncle Cyrus," he said.

The topic surprised her, both in its boldness and in the rather odd subject matter. Now that they were alone, she had expected to be immediately questioned about Lazarus.

She lifted her shoulders in a casual shrug. "Are you always this inquisitive?"

"Yes. Every time I marry, I succumb to a strange desire to know my bride."

A small smile touched her lips. In admitting their situation was as bizarre to him as it was to her, his words had an unexpected calming effect. Realizing she had little to hide or defend, she replied, "My Uncle Cyrus was my father's older brother. The two were never close. As a result, our families had very little contact. Thus it was difficult for all of us when I was suddenly thrust into their midst—particularly given the circumstances."

"I would imagine so." He shifted slightly, folding his arms across his chest as he leaned against the balcony rail. "I met Cyrus Prentisse some years ago. At the time he was most interested in pressing the suit of his daughters. They were quite young then, perhaps only fourteen or fifteen, but he was already prowling about searching for husbands for them."

An image of her cousins, both of whom had inherited their mother's blond beauty, flashed before her. "They're quite lovely," she said.

"So I was informed. Repeatedly."

She smiled again. "I fear Uncle Cyrus sometimes appears overly zealous when it comes to the matter of their marriages. You see, he is determined that his daughters marry no less than a peer." She paused, then added mischievously, "Perhaps he was considering you for a candidate."

"Actually, I was under the distinct impression that was the case. I'm afraid I disappointed him." He regarded her quizzically. "Why the obsession with marrying a peer?"

Julia was surprised by the question. She had assumed that all of London had been subjected to her uncle's dreary, dismal recital of how he had been denied his rightful place in society. "I'm afraid that requires a rather laborious answer."

Morgan shot a glance toward the front gates. No sign of the coach was in sight. "It appears we have time."

She followed his gaze and let out a soft sigh. "Yes. So we have." She hesitated for a moment, collecting her thoughts. Finally she began. "The matter originated some six hundred years ago. My uncle was doing a bit of genealogical research and chanced to discover that the original Earl of Giffin did not die in the Crusades, as was assumed. Instead, he was badly wounded and languished for some years near Constantinople. There he met a Saxon woman who nursed him back to health. He took her for his wife, and they were blessed with a son. Eventually the earl recovered sufficiently to attempt the trip back to England. Unfortunately he never reached his home. The trip proved too great a strain for him, and he died in France."

"And what of his son?"

"As he was only an infant at the time, it was up to his mother to press her son's claim to the earl's title. She attempted to do so, but despite the evidence she held of her son's birthright, her claims were rejected. In time she gave up and returned to her own family."

"I take it your uncle is a descendant of that neglected child."

"A direct descendant," she affirmed. "Had the original earl survived to reach England, in all likelihood Uncle Cyrus would now hold that title, rather than a mere baronet." She paused, then continued lightly. "I suppose most men would have regarded the issue as an example of the fickle twist of fate, but to my uncle it was a matter of profound wrongdoing. He even went so far as to hire a solicitor to press his case before the High Court of Chancery."

"What happened?"

A rueful smile touched her lips. "As you might imagine, the current Earl of Giffin was not keen on the idea of relinquishing his title and all his estates. Naturally he used the sum of his power to protect what is his. The claim was dismissed as being without merit."

"Did your father participate in the suit?"

"My father?" She gave a startled laugh. "He thought it was an embarrassment and told my uncle so directly. Of course, that only deepened the rift between them." She lifted her shoulders in a light shrug. "And that leads us

back to the present day. Uncle Cyrus may have been denied his rightful place in society, but he is determined to
secure a place in the peerage for Marianne and Theresa."

"I see."

Morgan's gaze moved to the doorway, where a young
maid stood balancing a silver tray. At his nod she stepped
out onto the veranda and placed the tray on a small table,
then exited without a word. He reached down, removed a
tall, frosty glass from the tray, and passed it to Julia.

The glass was brimming with ice chips and felt won-
derfully cool and moist to the touch. Fighting back an
urge to press it against her cheeks and temples, she lifted
it to her lips instead and took a sip of the contents. Lem-
onade. An icy concoction that was at once tart and sweet,
a perfect antidote to the heat of the day.

As she drank, a fat drop of water trickled down the
side of the glass. It plummeted off the bottom of the glass
like a heavy raindrop, striking her collarbone. Before she
could catch it, the droplet cascaded down the soft swell of
her bosom, disappearing into the shadowy cleavage of her
breasts. Mortified, Julia raised her eyes to Morgan's, hoping he hadn't noticed.

His gaze was locked on the exact point where the
droplet had disappeared.

A sudden sensual tension surged between them, a
tension that was as unexpected as it was unwelcome. She
swallowed hard, searching for something to say to ease the
awkwardness of the moment. Before she could speak,
however, he lifted his gaze to hers.

"I'm glad you wore the pale green," he said. "It becomes you."

As usual, his expression was unreadable. Not certain
how to respond, she set down her glass and turned away,
directing her attention toward the fountain that bubbled
in the courtyard, a gardener engaged in pulling weeds,
two squirrels clucking over a single acorn. In short, anywhere but at the man she had married.

Unfortunately Morgan St. James wasn't ready to be so easily dismissed.

"You mentioned at the Devonshire House that we had met before, yet I don't recall doing so."

She gave a curt nod, forcing her gaze back to his. "I'm not surprised you don't remember," she replied, relieved to find that her tone was remarkably even. "It was a brief, inconsequential meeting. The occasion was Lady Catrell's annual ball, and I recall the affair was quite a crush."

As Julia spoke, the memory of that meeting surged to the front of her mind. She remembered the way Lady Catrell's giddy whisper had filled her ear: *Here he comes. Morgan St. James. Notorious rakehell. Despoiler of innocents. Beware. Beware.* Yet even as she had pressed the warning upon her, Lady Catrell's eyes had danced over Morgan's form with a hungry intensity that radiated naked longing and desire. And Julia had waited, breathless, her heart in her throat as he had approached. A beautiful, strutting peacock in a sea of plain brown hens. He had greeted Julia politely. She had murmured a cordial response in return. He had excused himself and moved on.

Morgan seemed to be searching his mind, attempting to place their meeting. Apparently failing to do so, he changed the topic. "Your father was a captain, was he not? A merchant seaman."

"Yes."

"Then we have something in common. My ancestors earned their living by the sea as well."

"Oh?"

"They were pirates. Quite successful ones at that." Her shock must have shown on her face, for a small smile curved his lips as he said, "You didn't think my family came by all this wealth honorably, did you?"

In truth, she hadn't considered his wealth at all. What surprised her was his bald admission of its source. Most

men in his position would have taken great pains to hide
that. Assuming a light, teasing tone, she said as much.

Although his smile didn't fade, an icy chill returned
to his gray eyes. "Yes. I do have my reputation to protect,
don't I?" He turned away before she could reply, fixing
his gaze on the heavy iron gates to his estate as they
groaned open. "It appears your family has decided to join
us at last. Shall we go and greet them?"

Julia watched the carriage swing up the drive. At that
moment she experienced an emotion she had never in her
life dreamed possible.

She was actually happy to see her Uncle Cyrus.

*M*oonlight drifted in through the broad windows of
Julia's bedroom, casting silvery shadows over the apple
green silk of her bedspread and curtains. Like every other
room in the house, the decor was impeccable, from the
Aubusson carpets that covered the floor to the collection
of fine porcelain vases that sat atop a corner dresser. Still,
a slight frown touched her lips as she surveyed the room,
for it was startlingly devoid of any semblance of warmth.
She had felt much the same way when the housekeeper
had shown her through the remainder of the estate earlier that afternoon. Expensive. Immaculate. Profoundly
empty.

She let out a sigh and glanced about her bedchamber,
looking for something to occupy her thoughts. A stack of
books had been thoughtfully placed on the nightstand beside her bed, but she was too restless to read. The delicate
corner desk was well stocked with exquisite linen parchment and pen and ink, but there was no one to whom she
wanted to write. She had even discovered a deck of playing cards, but she was not in the mood for that frivolous
pastime.

On the southern wall was a set of narrow doors that
opened onto a small balcony. Julia moved toward them

and stepped outside, hoping to catch a breeze. But the heat of the day had faded only slightly. A heavy, sticky warmth still clung to the air, impervious to the night. She ran her hand along the balcony rail, considering the day's events. She was married and therefore removed from her uncle's authority. The wedding breakfast had passed tolerably well. The home in which she was to live was lovely.

All things considered, she should have been quite happy. But she couldn't shake the subtle, clinging discontent that hung over her. Shortly after her family had departed, Morgan had disappeared into his study and she had not seen him since. He had not even appeared at supper, leaving her to dine alone at a table that could easily accommodate twenty.

She was, she realized, profoundly lonely. She missed her parents, she missed her home, she missed her two Yorkshire terriers, she missed . . . her life. Her fingers moved automatically to the gold medallion she wore around her neck. Saint Rita. Patron saint of the impossible. But she could not think of a single prayer or wish that would do her any good at the moment.

Suddenly disgusted with her own misery, she brought up her chin as steel resolve coursed through her. Tomorrow would be better, she vowed. Tomorrow she would—

A soft, insistent knocking at her door interrupted her thoughts. Frowning slightly at the late hour, she padded in bare feet across the room and pulled open the door.

Morgan.

A startled gasp escaped her lips before she could stop it. She had not expected to see him until tomorrow morning—if then. Her gaze moved briefly over his form. With the exception of loosening his cravat, he was dressed in the same formal attire he had worn earlier.

"May I enter?" he asked.

Her thoughts immediately turned to her own clothing. She was dressed in a simple cotton nightrail and matching robe. She had removed the pins from her hair, releasing it from the elaborate arrangement she had worn earlier, but had not yet braided it for bed. It hung in loose, careless waves that cascaded over her shoulders and down her back.

"I should dress," she said.

"For bed?" He arched one dark brow as a tight, mocking grin touched his lips. "Given that we have embarked together into the sacred state of matrimony, I believe it entirely proper and acceptable that I see you in your nightrail."

Something in his tone sent a tremor of nervous apprehension flooding through her belly. But short of refusing him entrance, there was little she could do. She forced a polite smile and stepped away from the door.

He strode into the center of her bedchamber, pausing for a moment as his gaze moved around the space. "I trust you find your room adequate?"

"It's lovely, thank you."

"I take it everything else is satisfactory as well?"

She hesitated. Rather than chastise him for having left her alone all day, she chose instead a softer approach. "I'm afraid I must have missed you at supper."

"Ah, yes," he said, as though suddenly reminded of the fact. "If you find time in the next few days, you might pass a note to Mrs. Nagle, the cook. Let her know when you prefer to dine, what you enjoy, that sort of thing."

"What about you?"

"I am accustomed to taking my supper late, and generally in the privacy of my study."

"I see." Silence fell between them. Believing their interview at an end, she pulled her robe closed and tightened the belt around her waist, saying primly, "Thank you for calling upon me to say good night. It was kind of you to do so."

The mocking smile returned to his lips. "Kind, was it?" He turned abruptly away, crossing to stand before the collection of ornamental bric-a-brac that had belonged to her parents.

Julia realized she had forgotten to thank him for purchasing the items when they had gone up for auction. She had found the pieces earlier, when the maid had shown her to her room, and the thoughtfulness of the gesture had deeply touched her. "They belonged to my parents," she said to Morgan, watching as his gaze moved over the lot. "They're of little monetary value, but have great sentimental—"

"Why did you want to sell them?"

There was an accusatory edge to his voice that she did not miss. She stiffened her spine and replied with unabashed honesty, "I needed the money. I did what was absolutely necessary."

His expression hardened as a cool, determined light filled his smoky gaze. "What a beautiful martyr you make. Resolved to make the ultimate sacrifice, aren't you? How very brave."

Before she could guess his intent, he moved to a small gas lamp that sat near the door and extinguished the flame. Then he turned to yet another lamp and did the same.

"What are you doing?" Her voice came out in a high, trembling rush.

"What does it look like I'm doing?"

"It appears as though you're turning down all the lamps."

"Remarkable. Perceptive as well as brave."

The last of the lamps extinguished, they stood together in a hushed darkness that was broken only by the silvery glow of the moon.

Morgan crossed the room and stood before her. Brandy. She could smell brandy on his breath. Her mind whirled, sending her thoughts spinning in sickening circles. He had been drinking, but how much? Would he force her? Legally he had every right to do so. The thought sent a tremor of fear and anticipation flooding through her.

Julia licked her suddenly parched lips as her heart began to race. She stared at her husband in horrified fascination, refusing to believe what was about to happen. She had known this moment would come, of course, just not so soon. Not until they knew each other better. Not until they shared some level of emotional intimacy. She had imagined a gradual period of reckoning, rather like wading slowly into a pool of icy water. Instead she found herself being flung headfirst into the deepest end. Although they had never spoken of it, she had assumed Morgan was of a like mind. Apparently not.

Unable to adequately put her shock and dismay into words, she murmured only, "I don't understand."

"Don't you?"

He moved to her side and gently brushed the weight of her hair off her shoulder. He bent and trailed a series of light kisses along the sensitive skin of her neck and collarbone. His touch served only to increase her panic. He couldn't mean to take her tonight, could he? A shiver ran down her spine as her heart doubled its tempo. Her limbs felt brittle and weak, yet at the same time she was seized by an almost uncontrollable urge to flee.

"You said you were familiar with the ways of intimacy between a man and a woman," he pointed out.

"I had no idea that such knowledge implied consent," she replied, amazed that she was capable of forming any words at all.

"Our vows implied consent."

"I was under the impression that was a wedding license we signed. Not a bill of sale."

"Such modern thinking," he said, making a *tsk*ing sound with his tongue. "I shall have to cure you of that, won't I?"

"Furthermore," she continued, "when I didn't see you at supper—"

"You assumed I would fail to make an appearance for dessert."

Julia failed to see the levity in the situation. Stoically she replied, "In a manner of speaking, yes."

Morgan shrugged. "You were wrong."

"I need time."

He paused, lifting his head. For a moment she thought she saw a flicker of compassion cross his face. But it vanished with the shadows of the night. His voice was unrelenting. "You'll only make it worse, waiting and dreading. Better for both of us if we finish this now."

His hands moved to the shoulders of her robe. A second later the garment pooled about her feet.

A shudder tore through her. "Please. Don't."

At last Morgan stopped, his eyes narrowed on her face.

Julia stood frozen in place, trembling and hating herself for trembling, unable to control it.

The moment seemed to stretch out forever.

Then she felt his touch once again. He caught her hand and lifted it to his mouth. Bending slightly, he brushed his lips against her knuckles, just above her wedding ring. She followed the movement, but all she could see were her husband's broad shoulders and silky black hair. He straightened and dropped her hand. "Very well," he said. "You have your reprieve."

He turned abruptly and strode to the door, reaching it in four long strides. He pulled it open with a sharp tug, then spun around to face her. Golden lamplight from the hallway spilled around him, casting his form in dark, menacing silhouette. "But know this," he said softly. "You've made your bed, princess. And I intend to sleep in it."

He pulled the door shut behind him and was gone.

Julia waited a beat, then her shaking knees gave out. She sank to the floor in a puddle of quivering emotions. After a span of perhaps twenty minutes, one single emotion rose to the forefront. Resolution. What had happened was as much her fault as it was Morgan's. She had assumed they had been of a like mind regarding their nuptial privileges and duties, but obviously she had been wrong. It was a simple mistake, that was all.

Nevertheless, she would not tolerate intrusions of that sort ever again. She would stick to her bargain and give her husband an heir—but when she was ready, and not a day before. First thing tomorrow morning she would tell Morgan so herself.

That decided, she was able to sufficiently compose herself to rise and cross to her bed. Unfortunately the rest she hoped to find eluded her completely. As the light of dawn broke through her windows, she finally sank into an exhausted slumber. It was a fitful sleep at best, full of tossing and turning, combating vague premonitions of dread.

Then, abruptly, she awoke.

Her heart pounding in her chest, she gazed about her bedchamber. She wasn't sure what had awakened her so suddenly. Perhaps a noise, perhaps something—

Suddenly it hit her.

Faint, acrid, burning.

Smoke.

Chapter 4

Morgan stood on the south lawn, watching the flames build. The vivid oranges, reds, and golds leaped and twisted, quivering before him in an erratic sideways dance that was oddly beautiful. As the blaze intensified, the blue-tongued flames shot higher, greedily devouring everything in their path with a hiss and a snap, like a nest of fiery vipers battling over prey. Then the fury of the flame abruptly peaked. With a final shooting spark the scorched tips spit against the sky and disappeared in a serpentine stream of dark gray smoke.

The smoldering heat of the blaze warmed Morgan's face. Although he wasn't certain what he was searching for, some insatiable urge prevented him from looking away. Some days it was the fire itself that drew his attention, the mesmeric beauty of the dancing flame. Other days it was a darker need that drew him. Like a fortune-teller guided by a crystal ball, he was grimly certain there was a message waiting for him within the flame. Something lurking within the heat and flickering light of the blaze. Something he hadn't seen before, some part of the past he hadn't acknowledged, or perhaps a glimpse into the smoky blur that was his future.

Occasionally he looked for no answers at all. He merely wanted to probe his memory of that writhing flame, to experience anew what he had seen and felt that foggy morning two years past. If he focused intently, he was there again; in the middle of the blaze, in the middle of those crumbling, burning quarters. He could hear the screams and feel the shrill terror that surrounded him. He could smell the sharp tang of kerosene as the flame licked the walls and ravaged the floorboards. At first his old wounds only tickled. Then the scars came alive, throbbing and burning as though the fire once again blistered his skin. Last came the vision. The tiny, dancing flame that reached out for him; the tiny, agonized face within the flame.

In moments like those he was gripped by an inconsolable sense of loss and incompleteness. Gripped by despair so overwhelming, the weight of it nearly forced him to his knees. He had been pulled back too soon. He wanted to return, to fling himself headlong into the searing inferno. The child was waiting for him within the flame. But this time he would make it. This time—

"Viscount Barlowe?"

Morgan turned abruptly, startled by the intrusion. His gaze fell immediately on Julia. So engrossed had he been in the fire, he hadn't heard her approach. Judging by the anxious expression on her face and the tentative sound to her voice, she had been watching him, perhaps even calling his name, for some time. She glanced nervously at the blaze, then back at him.

"I didn't mean to disturb you."

"But you have, haven't you?"

He hadn't meant to sound so curt. But she had caught him off guard and in the midst of an intensely personal reverie. Had he the time to school his reaction to her presence, he might have chosen a softer tone. But it was too late now. The words had been spoken and duly registered. He watched as the wariness she had displayed earlier abruptly dissolved. She brought up her chin and regarded him coolly, adopting an attitude of regal condescension.

"My apologies, Lord—"

"I believe we can dispense with the formalities, can we not?" he said evenly, in what he hoped was a more amicable tone. "I prefer you address me as Morgan. With your permission I shall call you by your given name as well."

She hesitated. Then, after what struck him as an inordinate amount of consideration, nodded in reluctant agreement. "As you wish." They stood together in uncomfortable silence. After a moment she shifted slightly, turning away. "I'll leave you to your thoughts."

"Wait."

"Yes?" She stopped in midstride, studying him expectantly.

Morgan had uttered the command impulsively. Now he found himself foolishly at a loss for words. He hadn't wanted her to leave, but he couldn't contrive a plausible excuse for her to stay. As he searched his mind for something to say, his gaze moved from her face to her attire. Clearly she had just been roused from bed. A lightweight cloak was tossed haphazardly about her shoulders, and from beneath it peeked her bare toes and the lace trim of her nightshirt. Her hair hung in a loose, disorderly braid that fell over her left shoulder. Its fiery richness was even more brilliant in the light of day, he noted, particularly becoming against the pale blue of her cloak.

Aware of the path of his gaze, an embarrassed grimace touched her lips. She lifted one hand in an attempt to restore order to her hair and said, "I smelled smoke. . . ."

"I see." He gave a curt nod. "I should have mentioned it. Rubbish is collected and burned every Tuesday morning." He gestured to the thick metal drum that had been constructed for the purpose of disposing of the waste. "As you can see, the flames are quite safely contained."

"So they are." A long pause, then, "I thought—"

"Lazarus had struck and the house was burning down around us?" he supplied.

Aware of his mocking tone, she coolly leveled her gaze on his. "Something in that vein, yes."

"How very dramatic. Fortunately it appears we will not begin our marriage on so spectacular a note."

Although his thoughts had not been moving in that direction, his words immediately called to mind an image of the scene they had played out together last night. Hardly an auspicious beginning. It had taken him hours to approach her, and even that small feat had necessitated gathering his courage from a bottle of brandy. Never in his life had he felt so grimly determined yet so profoundly inept. So cowardly and clumsy. And it had all been for naught. Julia—*his wife,* he reminded himself—had cast him out of her bedchamber without so much as an excuse or an apology.

In retrospect, he hadn't expected the encounter to be enjoyable, merely bearable for them both. For him the matter had been a straightforward attempt to fulfill his marital obligations. Getting her with child as quickly as possible so that they might leave one another alone had seemed the best solution to their rather unconventional union. The finer points—such as how to deal with a wife who was so openly repulsed by his scars—left him blank. Nor could he really summon the energy to try.

They had made a bargain. He was married to this woman standing before him. The fact struck him in that instant as both ludicrous and gravely regrettable. But the deed was done now, and there was nothing either of them could do but make the best of it.

Apparently her thoughts had moved in the same direction, for she surprised him by saying, "While we are on the subject of our marriage, I thought a discussion of last night might be in order."

"Indeed," he answered coolly. His gaze skimmed over her cloak and nightrail once again. "Have you breakfasted?" At the negative shake of her head, he said, "Why don't you join me in the morning room in . . ." He paused, mentally calculating the time it took a female to bathe and dress. Given that the average man could accomplish the task in five minutes, he doubled that amount, tripled the sum, then hazarded a guess. "Thirty minutes?"

A worried frown touched her brow. "Yes, I suppose if I hurry . . ."

She turned away and moved toward the house, leaving him alone with the fire once again. But the blistering blaze had died down to nothing but heat and smoldering ash. Nor was he able to pick up on the thread of his earlier thoughts. Morgan frowned in irritation. His days had a neat, orderly rhythm that his new bride was already interrupting.

The Tuesday morning fire had become a ritual of sorts. His servants collected the rubbish and began the burning, then left him undisturbed to watch the flames. An odd habit, perhaps, but one he did not intend to give up because it might strike Julia as peculiar. He brushed the thought off with a mental shrug. The household idiosyncrasies would be made clear to her soon enough.

In the meantime—what? He thrust his hands in his pockets and gazed about the grounds, unsure how to fill the intervening thirty minutes. He had already read the morning papers, and there wasn't time to retreat to his study to immerse himself in his business affairs, so he wandered to the stables. There he had a brief discussion with a groomsman as to the quality of a pair of young colts he had recently acquired, and he checked the condition of a mare who was nearly ready to foal. The discussion, although generally pointless, did serve one convenient function: by the time he adjourned to the morning room, Julia was already there.

She stood with a slight frown on her lips and an empty plate in her hands, contemplating a sideboard that groaned with a variety of rich dishes. Spread before her was a veritable banquet consisting of eggs, both scrambled and poached, potatoes, scones, muffins, biscuits, toast, porridge, cheese, sausage, bacon, kidneys, oysters, fruit, jellies, marmalades, coffee, tea, and hot chocolate.

As he entered, she glanced up at him and arched one delicate auburn brow. "You must be ravenous in the mornings."

He helped himself to a cup of tea, then took a seat in his customary chair at the head of the large oval table. "Actually I rarely eat before noon. But as I didn't know your preferences, I had Cook prepare—"

"One of everything," she supplied with a small smile.

He shrugged. "Perhaps you'll find the time later to let Cook know what you like."

"I shall," she agreed easily. "It looks wonderful, but in future she needn't bother. Tea and toast suit me just fine." That said, she dabbed a light pat of butter on her toast and moved to join him at the table.

His gaze followed her as she moved. Although she had attended her toilette and donned her clothing, the result was hardly an improvement. She wore a drab gown of coarse brown bombazine, over which hung a badly stained white linen apron. A crudely knit mobcap covered her hair; the fingers of her gloves reached her knuckles and went no further.

"If it was your intent that by dressing as a fishmonger's wife I might set a clothing allowance for you," he said, "you may consider your plan a success. Will one hundred pounds a month be adequate?"

She sipped her tea and regarded him levelly. "Quite generous, actually. But that was not my intent at all. I am perfectly satisfied with my wardrobe."

"I, however, am not."

She lifted her shoulders in an indifferent shrug. "I have no intention of going about society dressed as I am. But I happen to have a routine of my own on Tuesday mornings—one for which I am dressed entirely appropriately."

"Exactly what sort of routine?"

"If you don't mind, we'll get to that shortly. I should like to discuss last night first."

"Very well," he replied, somewhat surprised at her eagerness to engage in a conversation that would no doubt be unpleasant for them both. He settled back in his chair, folded his arms across his chest, and waited for her to begin.

She took a moment to collect her thoughts. Next she set down her teacup and squared her shoulders. Lifting her gaze to his, she regarded him with an expression of stern disapproval, reminding him of the time he was nine years old and had been caught slipping a toad into the headmaster's case. "I shall be honest with you, Lord Barlowe—"

"Morgan," he corrected.

Obviously flustered by the interruption, she looked up at him and blinked. "Yes, that's right." She sent him a brief, cursory smile, then delicately cleared her throat and began again. "I shall be honest with you . . . Morgan. I was quite taken aback at the events of last night. Quite dismayed, actually. After you left, I resolved that I would never permit that sort of incident to occur again." She paused, a reflective look on her face as she finished. "Then, after much debate, I thought better of forbidding you from entering my bedchamber."

"Wise of you."

She did not miss the threat veiled within his silky tone. "Not because I am intimidated by you," she shot back, sending him a significant glare. "But because I thought it more prudent to the future of our marriage that we make a bargain, you and I."

"It was my understanding that we had already made a bargain."

"Yes, in general. I believe we have a basic understanding—"

"I believe we have an explicit understanding," he corrected firmly.

"You want an heir."

"Yes."

"Very well. I am not disputing my obligations in that regard. I am simply asking for a little more time to get to know each other before we undertake such an . . . intimate endeavor."

"How much time?"

"I'm not certain. How long does it take a husband and wife to truly get to know one another?"

"It has been my impression that most married couples try to avoid that at all costs. Particularly those who wish their marriages to be bearable."

"I'm serious."

"So am I." Nevertheless, he considered her question and gave an indifferent shrug. "Years."

"Years," she repeated, a slight frown touching her lips. "I see."

Silence followed as she sipped her tea and mulled over his reply. Morgan wasn't certain exactly what he had expected from her; perhaps a tearful scene begging his forbearance, dramatic vows of apology and reconciliation, or even outright disdain at his attempts to press his marital rights. In some ways her reaction was infinitely more degrading. Instead of fighting him with female hysterics, she chose an entirely pragmatic approach, as though the burden of bedding her husband was one that could be overcome with a little logical thinking.

"Well," she said at last, "perhaps expecting you to wait years until we consummate our vows is asking a bit too much."

"Remarkable. I would have reached the same conclusion."

Anger flashed in her eyes at his mocking tone. "There is no need for sarcasm. I was hoping we might resolve this problem amiably. I am simply attempting to be reasonable."

"By what folly of logic did you convince yourself that I would be reasonable in regard to this problem—as you so expressively put it?"

"Because it is to both our benefit that we come to a mutually satisfactory resolution."

"A mutually satisfactory resolution. How very civilized." He lifted the butter knife from the table and absently toyed with it, brushing the dull edge against his thumb. Then he fixed his gaze on her. "But what you sound like, princess, is a woman who has made an unhappy bargain and is attempting to renege on her word."

Julia instantly bristled. "I can assure you that is not the case at all."

"Isn't it?"

Overcome by a sudden impatience with their conversation, Morgan sprang from his chair and moved to stand beside the tall bank of windows that overlooked the gardens below. He had never been embarrassed by his sexual drive before, but now he felt vaguely shamed by it—as though he were an ogre hiding in wait for a beautiful maiden upon whom he could pounce and unleash his carnal desires. The Beast. Ridiculous. And yet even as that assertion formed in his mind, he couldn't quite banish the image of Julia on their wedding night, trembling in disgust as his fingers had traced her skin. She had looked so fragile and pale in the moonlight, like a porcelain doll that might shatter at any moment. Granted he could have forced her, but he had never sunk so low in his life and had no intention of starting now.

He considered their predicament for a long moment, then turned to his wife and carefully asked, "Is the thought of our making love so horrific to you?"

A small, sad smile touched her lips. "Therein lies the crux of our problem. Why do men persist in calling it lovemaking when there is no love in it at all?" Before he could reply, she shifted her chair and leaned forward, asking with an expression of eager earnestness, "What do you feel for me? Answer honestly, if you please."

The question surprised him—all the more so because he had no ready reply. It was not a matter to which he had given any thought. She was simply a means to an end. A way to capture the man who had set his servants' quarters on fire or, failing that, a way to provide him with an heir to his estate. But what did he feel for the woman herself? Another time he might have said lust, but that didn't seem entirely appropriate in this instance. For with lust came the vague hope that one might be desired in return. Certainly he had no expectations in that regard.

He hesitated, giving the question deeper consideration. He pictured her as he had first seen her, standing at the Devonshire House, looking like a cool confection in peppermint pink as she placed her wagers. Then later at the rundown warehouse, as she faced him with the audacious proposal that they marry. All fluttery nerves while she introduced him to her aunt, uncle, and cousins. The raw panic in her eyes as they had exchanged their wedding vows. A broad variety of images, but none that gave him a clear notion of Julia herself or helped him define his feelings for her.

Finally he replied, "A base attraction to your beauty. A limited amount of curiosity."

She nodded slowly, considering his words. "But nothing deeper," she said. "Nothing that might convey any sort of warmth or caring."

She didn't seem to be searching for any false assurances, so Morgan didn't offer her any. "No," he said flatly. "Nothing."

Glowing approval showed on her face. "Very good. I appreciate your honesty, Lord, er . . . Morgan."

"I assume you wouldn't define your feelings for me as warm."

"Not at all," she replied promptly. Color suffused her cheeks as she immediately realized her gaffe. Lifting her shoulders in a light shrug, she said, "I would define my feelings for you as wary."

He frowned. "How do you mean?"

"Look at our respective positions," she said, clearly working into the heart of her argument. "You hold all the power. Granted, you have been a gracious host—last night notwithstanding, of course. But with that singular exception, I would say you've been most kind."

Morgan folded his arms across his chest and waited for her to continue.

"Nevertheless, I can't help but feel that were I to acquiesce to your base needs immediately, I would be nothing in this household but an object you had acquired, an object that has very little value once Lazarus has been uncovered. From that point forward, what would we have between us to last the rest of our marriage?"

"Much the same as any other husband and wife."

A thoughtful frown touched her lips as she rose and moved to stand across from him. "That does not satisfy me," she said. "Nor do I believe it would satisfy you. I realize the circumstances that brought us together were rather unusual, but we ought to make the best of our arrangement. It has been my observation in life that one should begin a relationship at the level where one means to continue it. In short, I would like to attempt to establish a precedent of mutual caring and respect before we"—she hesitated, a rosy blush staining her cheeks, then bravely raised her gaze to his and finished—"commence the intimate work of creating an heir."

"I see."

"That may be too lofty a goal, it may very well elude us completely, but I would like to try nevertheless."

He regarded her in silence, impressed despite himself. Had she defied him entirely, he might very well have forced the issue, seducing her that very night despite her resistance. Instead, Julia had made the astonishing argument that refusing him was for their mutual good. All in all, it was not a bad argument. He cringed as he thought of his own approach—entering her bedchamber slightly drunk, grimly determined, and profoundly inept. In retrospect he felt like a boorish oaf. He knew better. But years had passed since he had courted a woman, and the thought that there might be anything between them had simply not occurred to him. Now that she had presented her position, appealing to his sense of honor and chivalry, it would be exceedingly difficult for him to refuse her.

"Nicely done," he said. "It occurs to me that I have taken a bride who is entirely too shrewd. Remind me never to sit opposite you at a negotiating table."

A look of cautious pride showed on her face—a look he immediately eradicated by saying, "Very well, you shall have three months' reprieve. At the end of which time I expect you to have developed enough warm feelings toward me that we may—how did you put it?—commence the intimate work of creating an heir. Does that satisfy you?"

A look of prim disapproval curved her lips. "I am not under the impression that it is supposed to."

True, but that wasn't the point. "I want your word," he said sternly. "Three months and no more. At the end of which time I will expect you to uphold your end of the bargain and assume your wifely duties. Are we in agreement?"

"Yes," she said stiffly, "We are in agreement."

She turned away, focusing her gaze on the gardens below. As she did, a strand of fiery hair slipped out from beneath her ridiculous cap to curl softly against her temple. Morning sunlight streamed in around her, revealing the shadowy outline of her body through the drab brown linen. As she lifted her hand to trace one finger along the sparkling glass pane, her bosom strained against the pleated bodice of her gown. The sight, and the unexpected pleasure it brought him, made Morgan wonder if perhaps she had received the better end of their bargain. In that instant three months seemed a very long time to wait to claim his bride.

He shifted slightly, impatiently banishing the thought. Aloud he said, "Very good. Now that that issue has been dispensed with, let us move on to the matter of your absurd attire. I assume there is an explanation?"

Julia seemed as relieved as he was to drop the intimate topic and move on. "I mentioned that I am in the habit of talking to servants in order to procure the various tidbits of gossip I use in my weekly column. Naturally, if I wish to be spoken to freely, I can't appear as a lady who might carry their stories back to their employer."

"Hence the mobcap and stained apron."

"Yes. A rather dreary disguise but effective nonetheless. I've yet to be taken for anything but a common housemaid."

"So you intend to continue that ridiculous column."

She looked startled at the suggestion that he might think otherwise.

"Of course. Why wouldn't I?"

He shrugged. "You no longer need the income."

"My motivation in writing the column was never financial. It's the moral satisfaction I receive in exposing society's ills that makes me continue."

A slight frown touched Morgan's lips as he considered her words. From what he had seen of her work, it was composed of scandalous gossip and very little else. Writing "The Tattler" might amuse her, but the pastime was one he considered eminently unsuitable for his wife. Testing her reaction, he said, "And if I were to recommend that you discontinue the column, it being an inappropriate occupation given your new station as Viscountess Barlowe?"

"I would recommend you not do such a thing."

"You would disobey me?"

She smiled sweetly. "Without hesitation."

Morgan stiffened. "As your husband, it is my responsibility to determine what pastimes are fit for my wife."

"And as your wife, it is my duty to accommodate your wishes. I will attempt to do so—within reason."

"Whose determination is it if my requests are reasonable?"

"Mine, of course."

A small tremor of alarm shot through him as he perceived a dangerous trend, one he had heretofore overlooked. She had defied her uncle in finding a suitor of her own choosing. She had defied convention in earning an income of her own by leasing her father's warehouse space. Now she was openly defying him. He had relented in the matter of his nuptial rights, but he would not indulge her whim on every issue. Better she learn now who commanded the household.

He leaned one broad shoulder against the window frame, eyeing her coolly. "I'm afraid you overestimate your influence in this matter. I need only send word to the editor of the *Review,* informing him that you are my wife and that I wish for him to cease publication of your column immediately."

Heavy silence filled the room. "Yes, you have that authority," she agreed at last. "But if you do, I will resent you for it and that resentment will fester between us for the remainder of our married life."

"Perhaps that is a risk I am willing to take."

She returned his stare with one of glacial self-assurance. "While I cannot prevent you from doing so, I can assure you it would be a mistake. I ask that you consider what you will have gained, for it will accomplish nothing but my undying hostility. Furthermore, it was my understanding that the primary goal of our union was to find Lazarus. How do you expect to accomplish that if he can no longer contact me through the *Review*?"

Damn. Morgan scanned his memory but could not recall a single instance when he had blundered so thoroughly. Had he thought the matter through, rather than reacting on emotion, he would have come to the same conclusion. Instead, his response had been both idiotic and embarrassing. But rather than admit that directly, he temporized. "Has it occurred to you that we may have driven Lazarus away by uniting openly? He had perceived you as a partner; our alliance may be seen by him as the ultimate treachery."

A worried frown knit her brow. "Yes," she conceded with a sigh. "I did consider that." She paused, then continued hesitantly. "But there was something in his communications, something that gave me confidence he would not do so. I may have read too much into them, but his letters seemed to indicate that he had formed a rather profound attachment toward me—an attachment he would not easily abandon."

Morgan nodded. After viewing the man's letters, he had reached the same conclusion.

Setting that issue aside for the moment, she continued. "It has occurred to me that Lazarus may not have been working alone. I thought our first step in uncovering his identity should be to determine exactly whose body was discovered among the ashes of Lord Webster's fire. If the two men were working in conjunction, his corpse may very well lead us to the identity of Lazarus himself."

"A laudable goal, but as no one was able to identify

the man at the time, and two years have since passed, I would imagine those ashes have grown even cooler."

"Very likely, yes. Nevertheless, I suggest we begin our search by eliminating the loose ends." She retrieved a worn vellum notebook from the pocket of her skirt and flipped through the pages with a concentrated frown. "Yesterday I took a moment to review the notes I took at the time of Lord Webster's fire, and—"

"You took notes?"

"I always take notes. In writing my column, it's vital that I capture exactly what is said. A word or two repeated in error can change the entire nuance of a sentence. I was particularly careful in getting down all the details of the events described by Lord Webster's servants, especially as they pertained to the night of the fire."

"What did you discover?"

"At first glance nothing unusual," she replied, her tone brisk and businesslike. "No strangers lurking about the grounds, no sudden dismissal of any of the servants, no unexpected visitors. Lord Webster was preparing to host a large party, hence the household was somewhat hectic, but there was nothing to indicate the disaster that was to come."

Just as it had been at his own home, Morgan thought.

"It was how the servants reacted when they were questioned after the fire that caught my attention," Julia continued.

"What do you mean?"

"They were uniformly distraught, naturally, having lost all their worldly goods as well as their source of income. But there was one woman who appeared more shaken than the rest—a Miss Sarah Montgomery. She had been employed as a housemaid at the time of the fire. I recall seeing her days afterward at a pub where Lord Webster's servants frequently gathered. She was ashen and inconsolable, breaking into tears at the mere mention of the fire."

"An understandable reaction, I would think."

"Yes," Julia agreed, but it was clear in her expression that she wasn't quite convinced. Her next words confirmed it. "Something in her manner disturbed me," she said. "Miss Montgomery wasn't simply upset. She was nervous and frightened, as though she had a secret she was terrified might be found out. I had made a note to myself to question her later, but she left London before I had a chance. Apparently her sister had found her employment in Sussex."

"What of Mr. Chivers at the Yard? Did he find her behavior suspicious?"

"Not at all. Aside from being so distraught, she was very cooperative. Like everyone else, she reported seeing nothing unusual the day of the fire, nor did she claim to know the identity of the man found among the ashes. Furthermore, she received a letter of high commendation from Lord Webster himself."

Morgan shrugged. "I would think that would settle the matter."

"Perhaps it might have, had Lazarus remained buried in the ashes of that fire. But as he has resurrected himself, I thought I ought to begin my search where I left off two years ago. Short of waiting for Lazarus to come to me—or worse, waiting until he sets another fire—it seemed the most prudent course of action."

Logical enough, he supposed. Yet still . . . "You intend to travel to Sussex to question her?"

"Fortunately, there's no need for that. Evidently Sussex was not to Miss Montgomery's liking. She returned to the city after an absence of only seven months. She is presently working as a kitchenmaid in Lady Escher's employ. I've done a bit of research into her habits and discovered a tea shop she frequents once her morning marketing is finished."

He nodded, impressed. "You believe she'll discuss the fire with you?"

"I have no idea." She tucked her notebook inside her pocket, facing him with an air of breezy determination. "I won't know until I try, will I?"

"You mean, until we try."

She looked startled, then dismayed. "That's very kind, but there's no need for you to accompany me, I assure you. I've been making these forays to the East End for years and—"

"In search of a few choice morsels of gossip to sprinkle through your column," he pointed out. "Not following the trail of a deadly arsonist who has apparently singled you out for his attention. Need I remind you that there is a difference?"

"Nevertheless, I would rather—"

"I insist."

Their eyes met and held for a long moment. "I don't suppose there's anything I can say that might dissuade you?" she said at last.

"No."

"I thought not." She let out a soft sigh. "Very well." She paused, eyeing him critically. "Do you have anything disreputable to wear?"

He arched one dark brow. "I thought my reputation was disreputable enough. I wasn't aware my clothing needed to reinforce it."

"For our purposes it does. There is a ragman who operates a cart not far from here. Perhaps you have a footman who might run an errand for me, were I to tell him what I want?"

Now it was his turn to look appalled. "You're not suggesting—"

"A chimney sweep," she announced definitively. "If your scars show, they will not be questioned. In fact, they should serve to add a bit of authenticity to your costume. Perhaps then no one will notice your face."

"My face?" Morgan had not been aware there was a problem with his face. In fact, just the opposite was true.

Through some absurd twist of fate, his face was one of the few areas on his person that hadn't been scarred by the fire.

"You look"—she hesitated, as though searching for just the right word—"imperious. Aristocratic. As though you were used to giving orders rather than receiving them. If you speak, that will be even more evident. It might be best if you accompany me as a mute chimney sweep."

Before he could reply to that preposterous statement, she turned her attention from him and removed her notebook from her pocket. She scribbled furiously for a moment, then tore off the page and passed it to him. "I believe that should suffice. Do ask your footman to hurry, however. And for heaven's sake don't dally in dressing. I should like to be under way within the hour."

With that imperious announcement, she swept from the room, her drab brown skirts trailing in her wake. Morgan watched her leave, battling alternating surges of admiration and irritation. In the space of a single morning, she had thoroughly disrupted his routine, put him in the ridiculous position of bartering over his nuptial rights, directly challenged his domestic authority, and openly, *casually,* referred to his scars, something no one—no one—ever did. Now she expected him to trail after her in the ridiculous guise of a mute chimney sweep.

Again, an inauspicious beginning. When Julia Prentisse had come to him with the extraordinary proposition that they wed, capturing Lazarus had been paramount in his mind. But as usual, hindsight provided the better view of events. As he stood alone in the breakfast parlor, the list of ragged clothing dangling from his fingertips, it occurred to Morgan that he ought to have spent more time getting to know his new bride.

Chapter 5

Julia stood in the main foyer, tapping her fingernails impatiently along the smooth oak balustrade as she waited for Morgan to make his appearance downstairs. She glanced at the set of matching settees that had been upholstered in a rich midnight blue brocade, but was too restless to sit. The footman had returned some minutes ago with the bundle of charred rags she had requested. After considerable reluctance on his part, Morgan had at last relented to what he termed her ridiculous whim and retreated to his chamber to don the apparel.

At the sound of a footfall above her, she turned her attention to her husband as he descended the stairs. He wore a pair of threadbare pants, torn and sloppily patched at the knees, and a collarless jacket that was badly stained with soot. His wrinkled shirt, perhaps white originally, was now a dull mushroom gray. A dirty houndstooth cap crowned his head. His shoes didn't quite reach the point where his pants abruptly stopped. He wore no stockings on his feet, resulting in the prominent display of his bare ankles.

Julia eyed him critically as he approached, looking for glaring imperfections that might give his costume away. Finding nothing amiss, she nodded slowly. "Yes, I think so," she said. "It suits you."

"No need to be insulting."

She didn't know whether to laugh or say something encouraging. Deciding that the latter was a more prudent course, she sent him a small, fleeting smile. "I realize the clothing is somewhat bizarre, but I find it's the only way." When that prompted no reply, she continued. "You're being quite cooperative."

A sardonic smile curved his lips. "Exactly what I've always aspired to be known as: cooperative."

He leaned against the balustrade and folded his arms against his chest, regarding her with a look she couldn't begin to interpret. That absence of understanding made her feel intensely awkward, for her mind instantly conjured a thousand possibilities of what he might be thinking—none of which was particularly flattering to her. Something about his gaze was unlike that of other men. She felt as though he could see right through her, unveiling her innermost thoughts and desires. The sensation was not a comfortable one.

Abruptly abandoning the subject of his clothing, she turned and gestured to the oil portraits that filled the hall, latching almost desperately onto the fresh topic. "I've been admiring your collection of portraits," she lied, having given the oils nothing but a cursory glance. "Your ancestors, I assume."

"Indeed." He gave a brief nod, then studied her with a look of mild curiosity. "Which do you like best?"

Surprised by the question, Julia returned her attention to the majestic paintings that towered above her. Judging by the style of dress and the way the subjects had been posed, the portraits went back in time at least ten generations. Although they were all fine works of art, only one painting truly caught and held her attention. Imperiously peering down at her was a dark-haired man dressed in sixteenth-century finery, an elaborate lace collar, and cuffs peeking out from beneath what appeared to be a velvet jacket.

Something in the man's expression reminded her sharply of Morgan. His posture of stiff formality was softened by the subtle grin that curved his lips, as though he were aware of a secret no one else knew. He exuded an air of mastery, self-reliance, and self-control—coupled with just a hint of self-mockery, as though he was sharply aware of the humor in his posing for such a flamboyant portrait. Seated in a thronelike chair before him was a lovely woman with chestnut hair and warm green eyes. Unlike the other women depicted in the various oils, she exuded an air of genuine happiness. In a gesture of intimacy not found in the other portraits, she held her husband's hand in hers. Through a broad open window behind the pair could be seen a vista of the sea. A tall three-masted schooner floated in the calm azure waters.

"This one," she said, not certain whether it was the subject's resemblance to Morgan or the intimacy conveyed between the man and the woman that drew her to it. She knew only that the painting intrigued her far more than any of the others.

"Interesting choice." He turned to the painting she had indicated and cocked one dark eyebrow. "My namesake, the original Morgan St. James. He was hanged for piracy six months after that portrait was finished."

Julia studied the painting with renewed interest. "What happened to his wife?"

"I'm told she lived into old age in relative comfort. Her husband's wealth might have been of rather dubious origin, but it was nevertheless quite securely invested. During the course of their marriage, she bore six children, only one of whom lived into adulthood."

"How awful," she murmured. "First to lose her husband, then to suffer the heartbreak of watching her children die."

Morgan shrugged. "The St. James family is marked by a distinct propensity to die young. On the whole it's rather a nuisance, but I suppose it rids us of the ghastly spectacle of squabbling among cousins over the rights of inheritance."

She smiled. "I suppose so."

"I might add that it also explains my urge to create an heir. I would hate for the entire line of noble scoundrels to come to an end at my door. I've beaten death once; I doubt I'll be given a second chance."

Julia's smile abruptly faded. She wondered fleetingly if he was deliberately being perverse and attempting to make her feel guilty for temporarily denying him his conjugal rights. But somehow that didn't seem like Morgan's style. Even if it were the case, she decided, they had made a bargain and firmly settled the matter. There was no point in revisiting the issue.

That decided, she directed her reply to the subject of the artwork. Beyond the mere images of the men and women who were Morgan's ancestors, several paintings featured a unique item that appeared significant to the couple portrayed. In one case it was a pair of dueling pistols, in another a magnificent piece of jewelry, in another an ancient map. "I notice that some of the paintings seem more like illustrations to a story than portraits," she remarked.

He nodded. "A bit of insurance that the family legends will be passed on from generation to generation, I suppose. I'll relate them to you another time if you like. Our own portrait will have to be done as well. I thought of engaging Thomas Fike for the position, unless you have someone else you might recommend."

His words brought a frown to her lips. Although Thomas Fike was an artist of great renown, Julia couldn't quite imagine herself and Morgan standing side by side, peering down at succeeding generations like ancient exemplars of matrimonial happiness and duty.

Misinterpreting her expression, Morgan said, "If his work doesn't suit you, there are any number of artists who—"

"No, I have no objection to Mr. Fike at all," she assured him. "It's just that . . ." She hesitated, searching for the right words. "That seems so . . . permanent, doesn't it?"

"Marriages generally are. Perhaps someone should have warned you about that before you entered into this arrangement."

This time there was no mistaking his deliberate baiting. Refusing to display any reaction to his words, she eyed him coolly, then turned her attention to what appeared to be the most recent of the portraits.

"Your parents?" she guessed.

"Yes."

She scanned the portrait but found no hint as to the nature or temperament of the couple portrayed. Although the work had been commissioned when the man and woman were young, there was no sign of youthful gaiety on their faces. Instead they stared at the viewer with expressions of stodgy pomposity. They were posed in a library, sitting in stiffly backed chairs, distinctly apart from one another. No further clues were offered as to their temperament or their lives.

"What were they like?" she asked.

"Imperious and aristocratic."

Julia's first thought was that he was teasing her again, throwing back her own observation about him in her face. A fleeting smile touched her lips, but it disappeared at his stony expression. As usual, his gray eyes were cool and unfathomable. A dark and foreboding image of the future suddenly loomed before her. She couldn't imagine herself ever growing closer to the man she had taken for her husband. They would forever be strangers, sharing a relationship that was polite but empty.

In that instant she experienced a sudden urgency to be under way, desperate for any action that might divert her stark thoughts. Forcing a tone of cheerful purpose, she said, "I believe the groomsman brought the coach around some minutes ago."

Morgan didn't move. "Did he?"

"Yes. And the horses too."

"How very thorough of the man."

"I believe they're waiting. Just for us." When the statement still provoked no action on his part, she urged, "We should go."

Finally he straightened. "By all means, princess. Heaven forbid we keep the horses waiting."

The Blue Kettle was located on Chanhurst Lane, a narrow, unlovely street shadowed by tall tenement buildings with pockmarked brick facades. A chaotic mix of women running errands, children playing, dogs barking, babies shrieking, and men selling everything from fish and milk to bones and rags jammed the lane. The stench of rotting refuse hung in the air. Wet laundry, hampered by the lack of sunlight and fresh air, dripped soured suds from clotheslines that had been stretched between buildings. A miscellany of carts and wagons choked the street. As was the case with most sections of London's East End, life was bare and exposed.

Julia and Morgan had sent their driver away some blocks ago, having decided to continue their journey on foot. That decision had been reached partly out of concern for appearances—it would not do for a scullerymaid and a chimney sweep to descend from a coach as regal as that of Morgan's—and partly out of pure logistics: the vehicle was simply too broad to navigate the narrow streets.

Julia deftly lifted her skirts to dodge a particularly offensive pile of refuse. Having spent the past several years visiting the haunts of the servants who worked for London's elite, she had grown somewhat accustomed to the squalor that surrounded them. But she doubted Morgan St. James had ever been exposed to London's crueler side. Men of his class rarely ventured beyond their manicured gardens and private clubs and thus were perfectly comfortable blaming the poor for the abysmal conditions in which they lived. Curious to see if Morgan fit that same mold, she cast a surreptitious glance at his face as they walked. She searched for signs of repulsion or contempt but found nothing in his gaze but remote indifference.

At last they came to the shop she had been seeking. No distinct sign welcomed them, just a tin teakettle that had been thickly coated with chipped blue paint. The door was propped open. The sounds of raised voices and laughter, the scuffing of chairs, and the clatter of dishes drifted out from within the shop. Julia nodded to Morgan, then stepped inside. After taking a moment to adjust her eyes to the dimness of the interior, she scanned the room for Sarah Montgomery.

Their arrival was poorly timed. It being noon, the small tea shop swarmed with men and women taking a brief break from their labors, making it difficult to see through the crowds. Nevertheless they had arrived, and there was nothing to be done now but proceed as best as they could. With that in mind she gave Morgan a brief nod and moved through the stuffy room. The long plank tables were crowded with workers hunched over their food; there wasn't a chair to be had. Standing room was available in a far corner, however, and it was there that they stationed themselves. A stout woman with a floppy mobcap and no-nonsense manner approached them and recited the special of the day in a flat monotone: baked cod and fried potatoes. Julia asked for tea and a biscuit, Morgan requested ale. The woman nodded, removed dirty dishes from a shelf that protruded from the wall, and moved off.

Julia scanned the room, convinced that they had missed Miss Montgomery completely. Then a movement near the front door caught her eye.

"That's her," she whispered to Morgan, indicating a pretty young woman with light brown hair.

Sarah Montgomery's attire was simple but neat—a pale blue muslin gown trimmed with a touch of lace. She carried two cloth bags packed with what appeared to be a variety of produce, bread, and goods from the butcher. She moved through the crowds with a breezy familiarity, then disappeared through an open door that led to the kitchens. Julia assumed that the woman had simply ducked inside to deposit her parcels before taking a seat for her midday meal, but when Miss Montgomery didn't reappear after a few minutes, she turned to Morgan with a puzzled frown.

"Perhaps she does the marketing for this establishment as well," he said.

"Yes, perhaps."

A reasonable explanation, but one that didn't quite feel right. Nor did it make sense that Miss Montgomery would spend her hard-earned wages on a meal. One of the distinct advantages of working as a kitchenmaid was the rather liberal opportunity one had to sample any number of leftovers, from soups and breads to the finest quality meats. Julia had learned to trust her instincts, and those instincts told her that something else was at play here.

Before she could speculate further as to Miss Montgomery's doings, the serving woman reappeared and set down their tea and ale. With a word of thanks, Morgan pulled a billfold from his coat, extracted a pound note, and passed it to her. The woman took the note with some surprise, eyeing the rich leather billfold from which it had come. Then her gaze moved appraisingly over Morgan, as though to reconcile the money with the man from whom it had come. She seemed to brush the matter off with a mental shrug, for she dug deep into her apron pocket for the proper change, passed Morgan the coins, and moved off without a word.

"That was foolish," Julia reproved softly.

"Paying for our beverages?"

"The manner in which you paid," she corrected. "You never know who might be watching. It isn't wise to flash one's money about so carelessly."

An amused smile curved his lips. "I didn't flash my money about. I merely removed my billfold and paid for our drinks."

"Nevertheless, it's hardly in keeping with your attire."

He lifted his shoulders in a bored shrug, dismissing the topic.

Frustrated at his indifference, she glanced around to see if anyone else had noticed his gaffe. She was almost disappointed when she saw that his movement brought them no undue attention. Why wasn't it glaringly obvious to everyone in the room that he didn't belong? The fact was evident in more ways than the carelessness with which he displayed his billfold. It showed in the way Morgan moved, in his carriage, his mannerisms, his way of looking around the room and coolly sizing up the occupants. Nothing about him suggested a lifetime of meek servitude—regardless of his ragged attire.

Fortunately, she didn't have long to dwell on the matter, for Miss Montgomery chose that moment to reappear through the kitchen doors. Her hands were once again occupied, but not with the cumbersome cloth bags she had carried earlier. Now she held a young child against her hip. She sat down at a small table positioned in the hallway between the kitchens and the main dining area, a contented smile on her lips as she proceeded to bounce the little girl on her knee.

"Her daughter?" Morgan asked after a moment.

"It would appear so."

"How old, do you suppose?"

Obviously he was performing the same arithmetic that was running through her mind. She sized the little girl up and replied, "Perhaps a year and a half, give or take a month or so."

"Yes. That was my estimate as well."

Which would have made Miss Montgomery approximately three months with child when the fire occurred. So there it was. They stood together in deflated silence, mulling over this newest bit of information. That explained the distraught, frightened stage Julia had found the woman in two years ago. She had taken a lover and had been carrying his child. Her nerves had been excitable because of her own private condition—a condition that had nothing whatsoever to do with Lazarus or Lord Webster's fire.

Again, Morgan's thoughts were clearly running along the same lines, for he said, "Very good. We came all this way to discover that a young parlormaid left London to hide an illegitimate child. Shocking. I do hope you'll make room for this unprecedented bit of news in your next column."

His tone of dry amusement immediately served to set Julia's nerves on edge.

She took a sip of her tea, then set the cup down with deliberate care. "I must go and speak with her."

Startled surprise showed on Morgan's face. "What do you intend to say?" he demanded. " 'Pardon me, but is your daughter a bastard? Furthermore, is that the reason you left London two years ago, or was it due to some nefarious connection to the fire that occurred on your employer's property?' "

Julia gave a cool shrug. "All we have at this point are conjectures and assumptions. Miss Montgomery is the only person who can tell us whether those assumptions are correct."

She turned away before he could offer an argument

and headed in the direction of the kitchens. But as she moved through the crowded room, she wondered what on earth she would say to the woman. Direct confrontation had never been her style. Nearly every word that went into her column had been obtained through friendly gossip or casual eavesdropping. But Morgan's words had goaded her into action. Perhaps her instincts about Miss Montgomery had been entirely misguided, perhaps not. She wasn't leaving until she knew for certain.

All too soon she found herself standing before Sarah Montgomery's table. The woman was younger than Julia remembered, perhaps as young as eighteen or nineteen. Two pair of wide blue eyes stared up at her with open curiosity as she paused before them. The resemblance between mother and daughter was even more striking up close.

"Can I help you?" Sarah asked with a puzzled smile.

"I hope so, Miss Montgomery." She hesitated a moment, still searching for words, then continued in a voice she hoped sounded softly reassuring. "I'd like to speak to you about Lord Webster's fire."

Sarah Montgomery's smile abruptly faded. "I see." For a long moment the young woman didn't speak, nor did she move. Then she bent her head and kissed her daughter softly on the cheek. "You'll be a good little girl for Mrs. Lowry until Mama can come and get you, won't you?"

The little girl bobbed her head up and down.

"Run along then, sweetums. Mama'll be back soon." The little girl threw her chubby arms around her mother's neck and gave her a quick hug, then climbed off her lap and tottered away toward the kitchen.

"You have a beautiful daughter," Julia said.

Sarah nodded flatly, making it clear her mind was no longer on her daughter. Instead her gaze moved over Julia in open appraisal, taking in her face and attire. Apparently somewhat comfortable with what she saw, she gestured to a chair across from her. "Please."

"Thank you." Julia sat.

The younger woman studied her curiously. "I don't think I know you."

"My name is Miss Prentisse," Julia replied, automatically using her maiden name. "You and I met once before, very briefly, after the fire."

"I don't remember."

"I didn't think you would. That was a very difficult time."

"Yes."

Heavy silence fell between them. Forcing a deliberately cheerful tone, Julia said, "This is rather awkward, isn't it?"

"Yes." Sarah matched her fleeting smile with one of her own. She fiddled with her hands for a long moment, then looked up and said, "I always knew that someday someone would want to talk to me about that fire. I didn't think it would be someone like you. I was afraid it would be someone coming to arrest me for . . . some of the things I said about that night."

Resisting the urge to immediately pounce on the young woman's words, Julia replied instead, "I'm not here to arrest you."

Sarah's gaze moved once again over Julia's drab clothing. "No, I didn't think so."

"The truth is, Miss Montgomery, I wouldn't be here if I was simply prying into your affairs. But there were so many people hurt in the fires, and I don't mean to see it happen again. The problem is, I'm afraid it's already started."

"You don't mean—has there been another fire?" Sarah looked aghast.

"No, not yet," Julia rushed to reassure her. "But whoever started them may be active again soon."

The younger woman studied her curiously. "How do you know that?"

Julia hesitated, choosing her words carefully. "My work occasionally brings me into contact with Mr. Chivers, Home Secretary of Scotland Yard." Honest, she thought, yet sufficiently vague that the other woman might think she did his wash or scrubbed his floors. Bending the truth a bit, she continued, "Sometimes when you're working in a great house, you hear things that you're not meant to hear. Do you know what I mean?"

As eavesdropping and gossiping were pastimes as common among servants as drinking tea and pitching horseshoes, Sarah didn't bother to deny it. She did, however, have the grace to blush slightly as she nodded her head.

Julia continued. "Last week I heard Mr. Chivers speaking with another gentleman. He said that letters have recently been circulated that appear to be coming from the man who set the original fires. Of course, it's quite confounding. Everyone assumed that man died in Lord Webster's fire."

"I see." The color abruptly drained from the younger woman's face. Her gaze moved past Julia to the spot just inside the kitchens where her daughter sat playing with a wooden toy.

As Julia studied the small child, a thought suddenly occurred to her, one she hadn't explored until just that moment. Where was the baby's father? Leaning across the table, she said softly, "I'm going to be blunt, Miss Montgomery, because I can think of no other way to say what needs to be said. I hope you'll forgive me."

"This is about Jack, isn't it?"

Julia carefully controlled her reaction. "Jack?"

Tears welled in Sarah's eyes as an expression of stubborn denial showed on her face. "Jack never set that fire," she declared fiercely. "He never hurt anybody. He was as kind as they come, and brave too. He went back into the

flames to save old Mr. Potter, that's what happened. But
. . . he never came out."

"Was Jack the man they found in the ashes? The man
everyone had assumed had set the fires?"

Sarah took a deep breath, then nodded tightly.

"I'm sorry."

Heavy silence fell between them once again as Sarah
fidgeted with her fingers. At last she took a deep breath
and said, "Jack and I were going to get married right
away, but when we found out about the baby, we decided
to wait a bit so I could keep working." She sent Julia a
faltering smile and continued. "You know how it is. Make
a little extra money so we'd get off to a better start." She
paused again, then let out a shuddering sigh. "He was
visiting me the night of the fire."

"I see."

"I didn't mean to lie about it, but I was so scared. If I
had let on that I was in a family way and that Jack had
been in my room that night, Lord Webster would have
turned me out without a reference. Then what would I
have done? What would have happened to my little Margaret? How would I have taken care of her?" She shook
her head, studying the tabletop. "It seemed like the best
thing for me to do was just leave things alone. My sister in
Sussex helped me out for a while, but I had to find work
again. There wasn't anything else I could do."

"If I were in your position, I might have done the
same thing."

Sarah lifted her gaze to Julia's once again. An expression of pensive weariness shadowed her eyes, making her
appear much older than her years. "Sometimes I wonder
about it," she said softly. "Jack's out there lying in a pau-
per's grave without so much as a stone to mark his name.
And I keep waiting for another fire. Sometimes I wake up
trembling in the dead of night, afraid I hear those fire
bells ringing. I'm afraid that whoever really started those
fires might just decide that he wants to start them again.

Maybe if somebody knew that Jack wasn't their man, they might have kept looking. They might have found who killed him."

Julia let out a soft sigh. "We can't change what's past, Miss Montgomery. But there is something you can do now."

Sarah studied her warily. "What?"

"Will you allow me to tell Mr. Chivers what you've just told me?"

"Tell Mr.—" Sarah looked appalled. "I can't do that. If Lady Escher finds out, she'll dismiss me for certain."

"Mr. Chivers is a very discreet man; very kind as well. He won't spread word of any of this to your employer, I can assure you of that."

The younger woman looked away, her expression troubled. Minutes passed. Then her gaze fixed on her daughter once again. Very softly she said, "I heard that in that first fire four children were burned to death. One of them a little girl not much older than my Margaret. Another just a newborn babe."

The fire that had occurred on Morgan's property. "Yes," Julia said.

"What if it happens again? What if more babies burn to death and I don't do anything to help stop it?"

Knowing when to keep silent is as important a skill as knowing when to speak—in some cases far more so. As there was no reply that could possibly answer the depth of those questions, Julia held her tongue, waiting for Sarah to come to her own conclusions. Soon an expression of firm resolve slowly showed on the young woman's face. She turned and quietly said, "Tell him. Tell Mr. Chivers what I said. His name was Jack Wilcox. He worked as a smith at a forge down near Thorne's Alley. Tell Mr. Chivers I'm sorry for not talking about it earlier. If he needs to find me, I come here every day at this time to see my Margaret."

Julia nodded. "Thank you, Miss Montgomery. I'll let him know."

Sarah smiled the first genuine smile Julia had seen since she sat down. "I'm glad," she said. "I'm glad it's finally out. Jack was a good man. He never set those fires. He deserves a proper stone."

Julia thanked her again, then stood and left, making her way through the crowded room to the front entrance. As she stepped outside, she found herself temporarily blinded by the sudden glare of brilliant sunlight. The heat of the day was even more intense than it had been earlier. Too troubled by the conversation she had just finished with Sarah Montgomery to stand idly by and wait for Morgan, she strode purposefully down Chanhurst Lane, retracing the path they had taken earlier that morning. Three blocks later he fell in step beside her.

"Any luck?" he asked.

"Some. You were right about her reason for leaving London; it was because of the child she carried."

"So her nervousness at the time had nothing to do with Lord Webster's fire."

"Not entirely. Her lover was with her that night. It was his body that was found among the ashes. Miss Montgomery was too frightened to admit it at the time. Given the precariousness of her position, I don't entirely blame her."

He studied her in surprise. "She told you that much?"

Julia shrugged. "Apparently the lie has been weighing heavily upon her. She seemed almost relieved to be able to finally unburden herself. She's been living in fear for two years now, afraid the arsonist would strike again unless she did something to stop him."

Morgan nodded, an expression of dark contemplation on his face. "He's alive, then."

"Yes. I believe that should finally lay to rest the question of whether the letters I've been receiving are genuine. Lazarus is out there somewhere."

They walked together a few more blocks in silence, both occupied with their own thoughts. After a few minutes Julia felt Morgan's gaze on her. A quick glance in his direction confirmed that he was indeed watching her, studying her face with a look of somber curiosity.

"Yes?" she said, somewhat irritated at his scrutiny.

"You look upset. I would have thought you would be thrilled to be proven correct about Miss Montgomery's deceit."

"On the contrary," she corrected, "I found her circumstances most distressing. I can't imagine what it must have been like to be in her place—a young woman barely past childhood with a baby of her own on the way; her fiancé dead and her employment ended. She was terrified she would bring further ruin on herself if she spoke out and identified the the man found in the ashes, terrified of what might happen if she didn't." Julia let out a sigh and shook her head. "She didn't deserve to be put in that predicament."

"No, she didn't. But I don't know that that justifies her silence. Two years were wasted—time that could have been spent hunting Lazarus."

"No harm was done, was it? Lazarus himself was kind enough to announce his resurrection; Miss Montgomery merely confirms it."

He made no direct reply, just a thoughtful murmur that might have been interpreted to mean anything.

They came to a busy corner and paused as a farmer's dray rumbled by. Julia, who had been walking mechanically without taking any particular note of their direction, glanced around to gain her bearings. Down an alleyway to her left were Duck the Stairs and the Three O'Clock Inn, both popular taverns for local servants. Nicely timed.

"Well," she said, sending Morgan a businesslike smile, "I believe that concludes our venture. If you continue north, you'll run into Stafford Street. You should be able to hire a hackney there without too much difficulty."

Morgan arched one dark brow and regarded her coolly. "Exactly where will you be while I'm running into Stafford Street?"

"As I explained earlier, I'm here to research my column. That will take me at least an hour, perhaps more. There's no need for you to wait, however. In fact, I would prefer that you didn't."

"Nevertheless, I insist."

"You'll only be bored."

"I'll live."

"Maybe you will," said a gruff male voice from just over Julia's left shoulder, "but I'm not so sure about the lady."

She felt a strong arm lock around her waist before she could react—before she could even consider what the appropriate reaction might be. Then the tip of a blade bit into her ribs.

Three men seemed to materialize out of nowhere, crowding in tightly around her. Although she couldn't see the man who held her, she could feel his brute strength as he pressed himself against her. Judging from the stench emanating from his body, bathing was not a ritual to which he had accustomed himself. His breath reeked of stale gin. The profuse sweat dripping from his skin served to plaster his thin clothing against hers, enabling her to feel every detail of his thickly muscled anatomy.

Swallowing her disgust, she quickly surveyed his partners. They were lean, hardened men dressed in rough, tattered clothing. Nothing about them distinguished them from any other man found in London's East End—except perhaps their eyes. They had the cruel, hollow-eyed look of dogs that had been bred to kill for sport.

"I'll take that purse you're carrying, sweep," said the man to her right. "Hand it over nice and slow."

Her immediate reaction was not fear but outright disbelief. Preposterous. A robbery? On a busy street corner in the middle of the day? She had heard of such outlandish things happening, of course, but always to other people. Never had she dreamed that it might happen to her.

The man behind her shifted, inching the blade slightly deeper against her ribs. She let out an instinctive gasp as her pulse began to race. The fact that she had been correct in warning Morgan to be less conspicuous with his money was of little consolation now.

Her eyes darted to her surroundings. Nothing. The thieves had timed their action well. Granted, it wasn't as crowded as it had been earlier, but there were still people milling in the streets and going about the business of their day. Unfortunately, the passersby continued to glide past them, evidently oblivious to what was occurring in their midst.

Her gaze fastened on an elderly man pushing a rickety cart that was piled with kindling. If she screamed, would he come to their aid? Although he might not provide much actual help, perhaps his presence would discourage the thieves from pursuing their audacious act. She had to try, she thought, opening her mouth to call out for help. Before she did so, however, her gaze caught Morgan's. As though reading her thoughts, he gave a slight shake of his head.

She instinctively obeyed his silent command. Taking a deep breath, she scanned his face for some sign of what she should do. But as usual her husband's expression was completely composed. He looked neither alarmed nor frightened. Merely mildly alert, as though he were watching an event unfold that temporarily held his interest.

"Easy, gentlemen," he said. "The money is yours." He reached into his coat pocket and withdrew his leather billfold, holding it before him. "But first," he said with a small smile, "please be so kind as to unhand the lady."

The man who had spoken earlier gave a deep guffaw. " 'Unhand the lady,' " he mimicked. Then his expression hardened. "We're giving the orders here, sweep. You don't want to see your lady friend sliced in two, you'll hand it over. Now."

"Very well." Morgan extended his billfold. Before it reached the thief, the leather case slipped from his fingers, landing on the ground between them. "My apologies," he said.

The thief let out a curse and began to reach for it. Apparently thinking better of it, however, he suddenly straightened, eyeing Morgan warily. "You pick it up," he ordered.

Morgan shrugged. "Certainly."

Calmly obeying the command, he bent low. His fingers brushed the pavement as he reached for his billfold. As he completed the motion, his gaze connected with Julia's for a fraction of a second. But in that instant she read both tension and readiness in the smoky gray depths of his eyes.

Then he nodded slightly.

That was all the warning she had.

Chapter 6

Morgan lunged forward, slamming his full weight against the shoulder of the giant who held the knife against Julia's ribs. The impact of the collision sent them all reeling off balance. Julia didn't miss the opportunity to gain her freedom. As they stumbled backward, she twisted away, moving out of her assailant's reach. Grim satisfaction surged through Morgan. She was relatively safe—at least for the moment. If the woman had any sense at all, she'd run like hell in the opposite direction.

Unfortunately his wife's reaction—or lack thereof—was not something he could control. Not when the giant wielding the knife recovered his footing and slashed his broad-bladed weapon through the air, barely missing Morgan's midsection. The near miss gave Morgan two immediate goals: disarm the man and get him out of the fight. The first was relatively easily accomplished. Morgan feigned a stumble to his left, knowing the man wouldn't waste an opportunity to strike at him again. It worked. As the giant thrust his knife forward, Morgan caught the man by the wrist and twisted down hard, causing the thief to emit a sharp grunt of pain as his fingers reflexively shot open. The knife clattered to the pavement.

The second goal, getting him out of the fight, wasn't so easily accomplished. The giant wasn't about to give up. He swung about, leading with a beefy left fist that caught Morgan dead center in the stomach, nearly doubling him over.

Then he heard Julia's scream.

He spun around just in time to see his wife, her forearm caught by one of the thieves, stumble backward in an attempt to escape his grasp. The jerky movement knocked them both against a cart of kindling, toppling the rickety vehicle. Cries of outrage from the elderly vendor added to the melee as the cart crashed to the pavement, spewing the loosely bundled sticks in all directions.

Morgan moved to help Julia but was stopped as the giant he had been fighting took advantage of his momentary distraction. The man's thick fist connected with his jaw. Morgan fell hard against the brick wall of the alleyway as the giant's partner shot forward, the fallen knife in his grasp.

The thief swung the blade in a vicious arc at his chest. Morgan caught the man's fist in his left hand, temporarily stilling the motion of the knife. He drove his right fist into the thief's belly, then slammed an uppercut into his jaw.

The giant lumbered forward with a roar of raw fury, obviously intent on finishing the brawl. At the same instant Morgan caught a glimpse of drab brown skirts. Julia—apparently lacking the sense to run for her life— stepped into the fray. Her hands wrapped around a thick piece of kindling, she swung at the thief's head.

While her intention might have been admirable, her aim definitely needed improvement. The stick flew by Morgan, missing his cheek by a fraction of an inch. Although far off its mark, the blow did provide a welcome distraction. The knife-wielding thief paused for an instant, blinking in confusion. That was all the opening Morgan needed. He drove his fist into the thief's chin, knocking him flat. The man hit the ground hard.

Julia swung again, this time aiming for the giant. Morgan barely managed to dodge the blow. The giant, however, wasn't so lucky. The broadest part of the heavy stick hit him dead center in the groin. The giant's features reflected a split second of shocked agony, then his skin went ashen. His knees abruptly buckled as he hit the pavement with the force of a fallen oak.

After the raucous noise of the fight, the heavy silence that followed seemed eerily oppressive. Morgan gripped his knees and hung his head down low, struggling to catch his breath. After a long moment he raised his gaze to his wife. Julia stood looking at the giant in shocked wonder. Then she shifted her attention to the stick she held. In that instant both Morgan and the elderly kindling vendor shared identical, instinctive reactions: they winced, then turned their lower bodies slightly sideways, as though to protect themselves from a similar blow. Clearly embarrassed, Julia dropped the stick.

Morgan's eyes moved assessingly over her body. Her gown was torn and dirty, her apron drooped half-untied across her bodice, her hair tumbled around her shoulders in fiery disarray. "Are you injured?"

"No, I'm quite well, thank you very much." Amazingly, her voice sounded remarkably composed. She brushed back her hair and smoothed her skirts, as though this sort of bothersome event happened regularly.

"Where's the third man?" he asked.

"He ran away after the cart fell."

The shrill peal of a police whistle echoed in the distance.

"Would you like to file a complaint with the local magistrate?"

Julia's gaze moved to the two remaining assailants,

both of whom lay groaning in the street. She considered the question, then slowly shook her head. "No, I think not. It might be rather awkward should this incident make the daily papers."

His thoughts exactly. The whistle drew closer. "In that case," said Morgan, "I suggest we remove ourselves from this scene." He bent to retrieve his billfold from the spot where it had fallen, opened it, and passed a twenty-pound note to the elderly vendor. "I trust this will cover the damage to your vehicle, sir."

The vendor's eyes widened. The money was more than triple the value of his cart and all the kindling it carried. "Yes. Yes, I believe it will," he agreed, hastily tucking the bill away.

Moving with brisk efficiency, Morgan took Julia by the arm and waved at a passing hackney. The driver pulled to a stop, then gave a sigh of deep annoyance as he took in their state of battered dishevelment. "What the hell do you think—"

Morgan wiped the blood from his chin and slapped a five-pound note on the seat beside the driver. "Grosvenor Square." He pulled open the hackney door and thrust Julia inside. He followed after her, slammed the door shut, and banged his fist against the ceiling. "Now," he commanded.

The driver flicked the reins, and the hackney pulled off. Glancing outside the window, Morgan saw two of the local police arrive behind them. As he had hoped, the twenty-pound note was enough to buy the kindling vendor's silence. In reply to their questions, the old man lifted his shoulders in a convincing shrug, pointing to his upset cart.

Satisfied, Morgan leaned back in his seat and directed his attention toward Julia. Although she seemed unharmed, the trauma of such an experience often took time to manifest itself. With that in mind he carefully scrutinized her face, searching for signs of shock or hysteria.

But instead of being near tears, Julia met his concerned gaze with a victorious smile. She clasped her hands together and leaned forward, her sherry eyes sparkling. "We did it, didn't we?" she said, almost giddy. "We bested those hooligans. That was marvelous. Truly marvelous."

Disbelief tore through him, followed immediately by a surge of anger. "I'm delighted to hear that at least one of us enjoyed that debacle."

Confusion showed on her delicate, dirt-streaked features. She cocked her head and studied him across the dimly lit confines of the coach, as though stunned by the suggestion that he might not relish a midday brawl with three knife-wielding thieves.

"You can't be angry," she said.

"Can't I?" Morgan brushed a clump of dirt from his sleeve, grimacing in disgust as the torn garment ripped even further.

She watched him in silence, then primly straightened her shoulders and folded her hands in her lap. "For the record," she said, "I didn't enjoy it. As a matter of fact, I was quite terrified. I was merely expressing my appreciation for the fact that our assailants are lying in the street right now, rather than you and me."

"It was foolish in the extreme to travel to this section of London. I shouldn't have allowed it in the first place."

"I have journeyed here hundreds of times in the course of researching my column. Never have I been assaulted."

"You've been lucky."

"I've been alone," she corrected, coolly meeting his gaze. "Fortunately, I am not in the habit of flashing my money about as though I were using the bills to swat away flies."

A sardonic smile touched his lips. "A bit of an exaggeration, don't you think?"

"Hardly." She turned pointedly away, directing her

attention out the window and to the heavily populated borough in which they traveled.

Just as well, Morgan thought. He was in no mood to be civil. Judging from the brooding expression on Julia's face, neither was she. Simmering resentment hung between them, and the air felt thick with unspoken words. He shifted impatiently, attempting to divert his attention by watching the passersby, but was regrettably unable to do so. It might have been possible had they been in his coach, where he could have disappeared into the plush luxury of the rich leather squabs. But the hackney's seats were cracked and torn, the brittle leather bit into his legs. The sour stench of the interior was intensified by the heat. The springs were so badly worn as to be nonexistent. He and Julia were continually bumping knees, no matter how deliberately rigid his wife held herself in her blatant attempt to avoid contact.

The driver plodded doggedly forward, jostling for position among the phaetons, hansoms, hackneys, tillburies, growlers, dogcarts, gigs, broughams, and landaus that choked the narrow streets. Half-naked children romped in the alleyways, searching for relief from the heat by splashing in oozing brown puddles. Ragged and despairing mothers sat on front stoops, holding wailing babes in their arms. Drunks staggered through fetid piles of household refuse. The blind and crippled begged for alms. Glancing to his left, Morgan caught sight of a battered wooden sign that hung suspended from the corner of a crumbling brick tenement building: Paradise Place.

"Incredible," he muttered. "They would do well to raze this entire section of London."

Julia turned to him and arched one delicate auburn brow. "What a caring and compassionate sentiment. Where would you propose these people live?"

"Anywhere would be better than this."

"That's not an answer, is it?"

Morgan released a sigh of disgust and folded his arms

across his chest. "Let me see if I can divine where this conversation is heading. Because I was born to a life of wealth and privilege, I must be inherently evil, morally responsible for the plight you see around you."

"Your standing in society does not make you evil," she returned coolly. "Your indifference does. Apparently you belong to the legions of men and women who have yet to understand that human beings ought to dwell differently from cattle."

"Forgive me," he said, nodding his head in a grave bow. "I had forgotten I was speaking with such an enlightened reformer. The exalted Tattler herself. Naturally you have a solution to all the city's most abhorrent plights."

"Not at all. But at least I attempt to incite change."

He smiled. "I take it you are referring to your column."

Grim defiance glittered in her eyes. "I am."

Although Morgan knew better than to engage in a fruitless and antagonistic discussion of what Julia obviously considered her life's great work, her tone of haughty moral superiority rankled too much for him to simply let the matter drop.

"As it appears we are to be stuck in this rotting hell for at least another few minutes," he remarked, "this would seem an ideal opportunity for you to share your benevolent wisdom. Let us see if you can cast light into the darkened corners of my soul, shall we?"

"I don't understand."

"Your column. What do you have in mind for next week's column?"

"You want to hear it now?"

"Yes."

"Why?"

"Indulge me."

She eyed him warily for a long moment, then reached into her pocket and felt for her notebook. Miraculously, it hadn't fallen out during their tussle with the thieves. She flipped open the slim volume and scanned the contents. "I have a few items left from last week's research that I didn't have room to mention earlier. Not my best work, but it will suffice."

"Oh?"

She lifted her shoulders in a bored shrug, tapping her finger against the slim volume as she recited, "Lady Bartholomew served her guests chicken liver at her latest soirée, rather than the pâté de foie gras indicated on the menu. Lord Lionel Winfrey has been seen riding unchaperoned with a certain attractive lady who is young enough to be his granddaughter. Although they have been acquainted only a fortnight, they have already formed a rather intimate romantic attachment—an attachment that remarkably coincides with the recent death of Winfrey's elder brother and the passing of the family title and estates to Lord Lionel. And finally the beautiful Audrey Winter, mistress of Sir Augustus Campbell, is reputedly carrying his child."

"Shocking," he said. "I can see why you would receive a certain elevated satisfaction in printing that. Such profound revelations must be told." As the hackney turned onto Regent Street, Morgan leaned out the window and gave the driver direction to his estate.

Julia waited until he had finished and resumed his seat. Then she said, "Those items are mere filler to the central subject of this week's column. As you are undoubtedly aware, my work is not read unless it is couched between such frivolous bits of gossip."

"What would that central subject be?"

"It concerns Messieurs Matthews and Hornsby, makers of the pretty little cakes of soap I've seen in your household."

Morgan arched a dark brow. "When did the making of soap become a threat to English society?"

"It is not the making of soap to which I object, but

the manner in which it is made." She paused, a look of pained reflection etched on her face. "Matthews and Hornsby operate a vast factory in Cheshire that employs predominantly women and children. In return for mere pennies a day, they are expected to toil from dawn to dusk over boiling vats of tallow and lye."

"Mere pennies, granted, but does it occur to you that those meager sums might be the only thing keeping those children and their mothers from starving to death?"

"Nevertheless, the chemicals with which they work are frightfully caustic, and the vats are far too heavy to be lifted by such tiny arms. Two weeks ago a vat of boiling tallow spilled, severely injuring four children. One of them, a little boy only six years of age, was blinded. The physician who attended him reports that the child's sight has been permanently damaged."

Morgan frowned. "Unfortunately that sort of incident is not unusual in the factories."

"The frequency of its occurrence does not make it any less shameful."

"Did you have a remedy in mind, or are you merely calling this tragedy to light?"

"Ideally, I would like to see the issue of child labor addressed by the House of Lords," she replied, naming the institution of which he was naturally a member. "But as I recall, that august body was too busy determining which artist should be awarded the employ of designing the statues for Regent's Park to properly focus on the plight of England's impoverished children." She gave a light shrug. "I suppose it's all a matter of priorities, isn't it?"

Refusing to be baited, Morgan gave a curt nod for her to continue. "Do go on."

"If Matthews and Hornsby cannot be legislated into doing the right thing, perhaps they can be driven to it economically. Currently it is quite fashionable to buy their soap—as evidenced by the fact that it is purchased for homes such as your own. I propose to make it even more fashionable *not* to buy it. At least, not until the children are removed from working in the vat rooms. I have no objection to them wrapping the soaps in pretty tissue or packing the crates in which it is shipped."

"I'm sure Messieurs Matthews and Hornsby will be delighted to hear that."

"I do not seek their friendship. Merely their cooperation in removing children from the hazards they currently face."

"You believe you exert enough influence to effect that sort of change?"

"I am merely one voice, but I am not afraid to speak."

"Evidently not."

She eyed him coolly for a long moment. "Do I detect a note of disapproval in your voice?"

"The poor have existed for centuries, they will continue to exist for centuries to come. You would do well to thank providence for your station in life and leave alone matters that do not concern you."

"Remarkable. Does blind arrogance come naturally to the peerage, or is it a skill one must cultivate, like fencing or fisticuffs?"

"If you wanted a lesser man, princess, you should have married one."

The hackney came to an abrupt stop before the tall, ivy-covered gates to Morgan's estate. Recognizing his master within the confines of the cramped coach, the gatekeeper ceremoniously opened the gates and ushered them inside. The hackney gave an abrupt jolt, then creaked forward once again, carrying them up the broad drive that led to Morgan's door.

Julia observed the practiced ease with which his servants shepherded them forward, then turned to face him once again. A small, disapproving frown touched her lips. "Life—with all its unpleasantries—must occasionally be faced, Lord Barlowe. Not everyone can afford to build gates to hide behind."

Heavy silence rang between them. At length he said, "It appears you've developed a fondness for testing my limits, haven't you?"

"Is speaking my mind testing your limits?"

"A word of advice. Don't push too hard. You might not like the results. Three months is a very short time."

A deep flush suffused her cheeks at his blatant reference to their future intimacy. It was, he had come to discover, a weapon he held over her, and he had no qualms about brandishing it now. The sooner she respected his authority, the sooner life would become bearable for them both.

"Furthermore," he continued coolly, "I believe I've given you permission to call me by my given name. You may thank me for that courtesy by addressing me as such in the future."

A footman appeared, silently let down the stair, and pulled open the carriage door. Morgan exited the decrepit hackney, then turned to assist his wife. Refusing his hand, Julia tilted her chin and lifted her drab brown skirts, no doubt intending to sweep grandly past him in a regal fit of feminine pique. But she took only two steps before she came to an abrupt stop, an expression of crestfallen dismay on her face.

Morgan turned and followed her gaze. As his focus had been on his wife, he had not noticed the other vehicle, a hired coach, that was blocking his drive. Gathered around his front stoop were Cyrus Prentisse, his wife Rosalind, their two daughters, the coach driver, and Morgan's head butler. From the looks of it, a rather heated discussion was under way. Biting back a sigh of impatience at his uninvited guests, he took Julia's arm and ushered her forward into the fray.

By way of greeting, Cyrus Prentisse turned to Morgan with an air of pinched displeasure and stated, "The driver has the temerity to inform me that he does not carry the proper change for a fifty-pound note."

The cab fare. Of course, Morgan thought, stifling a sigh. Although he doubted Cyrus Prentisse had ever so much as seen a fifty-pound note, let alone presently carry one on him, at least that explained the general air of domestic calamity.

The coach driver took in Morgan's ragged attire with an air of total bewilderment. After casting a glance at the butler to make certain he was in fact speaking with the lord of the manor, he doffed his hat and gave a quick bow, looking embarrassed but determined. "Beggin' your pardon, sir," he said, "but I can't carry that kind of blunt. Not with crime being what it is."

Morgan directed a meaningful stare at Julia. "Yes," he said dryly, "you have my full sympathies."

"Right," the driver muttered, shifting uncomfortably. "Well . . . the fare's one shilling, sixpence."

Morgan gave his butler a brisk nod. "See to it."

Cyrus cleared his throat. "I presume the cost will be the same on our return."

"Indeed. What remarkable foresight," Morgan replied dryly.

Cyrus gave a pompous sniff. "One cannot advance in life without it."

"How very true."

The driver looked from Morgan to Cyrus with a worried frown, twisting his cap in his hands. "I don't know that I can wait too long. I'm missing fares as it is."

"I can assure you it won't be long," Morgan replied with a tight smile. "See to his fare, Piers. Make it worth the man's while."

That business handled, Morgan ushered his guests into the west parlor but did not offer them the courtesy of a beverage. Neither, he noted, did his wife. Instead Julia regarded her relatives with an expression of pained forbearance as they settled themselves on the plush chintz-covered sofas. Morgan elected to remain standing. He propped one elbow upon the marble mantel as his gaze moved over Cyrus and Rosalind Prentisse. He had initially made their acquaintance when Cyrus had begun his quest for a match for his daughters. He hadn't liked them then; he liked them even less now.

Rosalind was plump and florid, given to indulging in minor dramatics. Cyrus was tall and stern and wore an expression of constant displeasure. Between them they had produced two pale and insipid daughters who appeared to have inherited their parents' voracious appetite for money and status. Even now their eyes moved around the room as though judging the value of each object contained therein.

"This heat," moaned Rosalind as she waved a silk fan before her, her features arranged in an expression of exaggerated misery. "I simply cannot abide it much longer. Something must be done about it."

"What would you suggest, Aunt?" Julia asked.

Rosalind blinked, then snapped her fan in a gesture of peevish irritation. "Really, Julia," she muttered. "I haven't the faintest." As her gaze moved over her niece, her eyes widened in appalled horror, as though truly seeing her for the first time since their arrival. "Julia, what in heaven's name are you wearing?" she demanded.

"I'm afraid you caught us rather unawares," she replied unapologetically, making no attempt to correct her state of scandalous dishevelment. "I visited an acquaintance in the East End this morning and—"

"The East End?" Rosalind interrupted, her brows shooting skyward. "Surely you don't personally associate with anyone in the East End."

"On occasion, yes."

"You permit this, Lord Barlowe?" Rosalind demanded, her gaze moving over Morgan in horrified bewilderment.

"As you might divine from his attire," Julia replied coolly, "Morgan was kind enough to accompany me."

"Good heavens." Rosalind's fan flew back and forth before her in a flurry of shocked outrage.

Cyrus stiffened in displeasure, studying his niece with an accusatory air.

"What possible business could you have in the East End? The area is rife with nothing but thieves and derelicts."

"Private business, Uncle Cyrus. Nothing that need concern you."

Her uncle's eyes narrowed intently. "You are forgetting that we are family. Naturally I am concerned. This wouldn't have anything to do with the men your father disgraced himself with in that awful smuggling episode, would it?"

"Oh, dear," Rosalind gasped as her fan fell to rest on her pudgy chest. "Not another scandal. I simply cannot abide another scandal. Think of your poor cousins. How will we ever succeed in finding them suitable husbands if you persist in ruining the family name? Have you not brought enough shame—"

Morgan had had enough. "Julia has caused you no scandal or shame," he interrupted, his tone one of icy authority. "This morning's adventure was a mere lark. She is guilty of nothing but choosing a husband who too freely indulges his young bride's whims."

As uneasy silence descended over the room, Morgan returned his gaze to Julia. She looked surprised that he had come to her defense.

"I would suggest you not do so again in the future," Cyrus said. "The girl is too high-spirited as it is. Her parents indulged her unmercifully, and that has done her no service at all. What Julia needs is a husband who can offer her firm guidance. You would do well to remember the scripture," he continued solemnly. "There is scarce any evil like that in a woman. Keep a strict watch over an unruly wife. A bad wife is a chafing yoke; he who marries her seizes a scorpion."

"Thank you," Morgan returned dryly. "I'm sure I'll find that helpful in the days to come."

Cyrus gave a pompous nod. "I trust you will."

The conversation lurched awkwardly forward. They touched for a moment on the latest gossip, then finally rested on what Morgan was certain was the true purpose of their visit: a lucrative business venture that Cyrus Prentisse was certain would interest his newest family member. It required a small investment of twenty thousand pounds, surely a mere pittance to a man such as Viscount Barlowe. . . .

Morgan withstood the oral assault for as long as he could. Finally, after relaying a cool promise that his secretary would look into the matter, he invited his guests to take their leave. Once their departure was complete, he moved to a sideboard and poured a generous splash of bourbon into a crystal tumbler. He lifted the glass to Julia, offering her the same refreshment. At the shake of her head, he gave an indifferent shrug and drank deeply, as though driving away a bad taste that had been left in his mouth.

Julia watched him for a moment, then quietly stood. "If you'll excuse me," she said stiffly.

He stopped her at the door. "Julia."

She turned, an expression of wary reluctance on her face. "Yes?"

"How long did you live with them?"

"Six months."

"No wonder you were so anxious to escape."

"I—" she began, then stopped abruptly. Her fingers moved to the small gold medallion she wore about her neck as she gave a tight nod. "It was a difficult time for us all."

"I imagine so."

"Yes."

"Cook generally serves supper in the Blue Room at seven," he informed her before she could turn away. "It's not a formal affair, particularly as it will only be you and me tonight."

A slight pause, then, "Actually, I'm not terribly hungry. I had thought to take a small meal in my room if that's possible."

"Of course. I hope you're not unwell."

Her lips curved in a tight, fleeting smile as she shook her head. "I'm sure it's just the heat."

"Yes."

She stood before him for an awkward moment, neither one quite able to breach the silence that followed.

"Well," she said at last, "if you'll excuse me."

Morgan gave a small, polite bow. This time he didn't attempt to stop her. He turned to the window and looked out at the gardens below, sipping his bourbon as he contemplated the day's events. Their idiotic adventure into London's East End had left them both unharmed, but that was pure caprice. It could have been worse. Much worse. It was all larks and escapades until someone was hurt—until Julia's tender flesh was torn by a knife, her body ravaged by a common thief.

What his wife suffered from, he decided, was not immaturity but a lack of experience. She was too idealistic. She didn't understand the depth of horror to which life was capable of subjecting one. In many ways she reminded him of himself, before the fire: moving from day to day with the cocky certainty that life was a glorious feast to be devoured, a game meant to be enjoyed.

Morgan had failed even in that. Looking into his past, he saw no joy there, only unmitigated foolishness. Reckless, selfish arrogance. Drunken races through St. James Park. Lurid affairs conducted in married women's bedchambers. Forcing his servants to live four to a room that had been designed for one.

He clenched his glass in his fist, studying the sharp

contrast between the purity of the crystal and the morbid scarring of his skin. The adage that time healed all wounds had been invented by a fool who had never been hurt. There was no divine moment of healing. Time passed, that was all. One didn't rise above grief. Grief had a life and a force of its own. One simply learned how to move around it.

He watched as the tall iron gates to his estate were swung shut and secured for the night, experiencing an undeniable sense of relief. He had held all manner of potential disaster at bay for one more day. Although he was loath to admit it, in many ways Cyrus Prentisse was right. Control, that was the key. That was the only way to get through life.

He had spent the past two years unburdened by emotions. Julia disturbed that comfort. She demanded things of him that he couldn't possibly give. Although she hadn't said as much directly, he could see it in her eyes. His bride had once had dreams of her own. She held no wealth or title, but her beauty was remarkable—even when dressed in drab brown rags. Under different circumstances she would have attracted a man who would love and cherish her. Instead she had been forced to wed him. Life had betrayed her. He understood that all too well.

Morgan gave a soft sigh. It was regrettable, but there was nothing he could do to change it. He was not cruel enough to hold out any false promises. Julia was smart enough to accept her circumstances and make the best of them. She would bend, but she wouldn't break. She would learn. Given time she would adjust. And so would he.

Even more importantly, together they would find Lazarus.

In the end that was all that mattered.

Chapter 7

Julia hesitated before Morgan's door. In the two days that had passed since their ill-fated excursion into London's East End, she had done her best to avoid direct contact with her husband. A petty game, perhaps, but wars were often won and lost based on the outcomes of small skirmishes. And there was no denying the fact that she needed the time to accustom herself to Morgan's presence. Although she considered herself fairly level-headed—and judged Morgan to be the same—an inexplicable volatility seemed to erupt between them whenever they were together, throwing her completely off balance.

Unfortunately, she could no longer avoid his presence. She took a deep breath to gather her courage, then lifted her hand and rapped sharply on his door. At his call to enter, she turned the heavy brass knob and stepped inside.

Julia had never visited Morgan's bedchamber before. That had not stopped her from forming an opinion as to

what she might find inside, however. She expected to see
a masculine version of her own opulent chamber, replete
with satin drapery, lush carpets, magnificent oil paintings,
and an exquisite suite of expensive furniture. Instead she
stepped into a large room that was almost medicinal in its
starkness. A bank of tall windows flooded the space with
light. In the center of the chamber stood a tall four-poster
that had been dressed in crisp linen sheets and plump
feather pillows. A simple chest of drawers occupied one
corner. There were no rugs, but the oak floors had been
polished to a high sheen. Glancing around, she saw no
personal belongings whatever. The only soft touch was the
sheer muslin curtains that hung limply in the midday heat.

Morgan stood with his back to her, peering into a
small mirror as he dragged a razor blade across his chin.
The shallow puddles that surrounded a large tin tub told
her that he had just emerged from his bath. His dark hair
clung in sleek, wet waves to his scalp. His feet were bare,
as was his back. Judging from the way his pants hung
loosely about his hips, they were still unfastened.

"I hope you didn't trouble yourself boiling hot water
this morning," he called over his shoulder. "I certainly
didn't need it in this heat."

Julia hesitated, then replied softly, "No, I wouldn't
think so."

The long, steady strokes of Morgan's razor halted in
midair. After a moment he set the blade upon a nearby
washstand. Moving his hands to the front of his trousers,
he made a motion that could only be interpreted as but-
toning his fly. Then he turned to face her. His cool gray
eyes offered neither welcome nor warmth. "I was expecting my valet."

Heat suffused her cheeks. "So I gathered." Her gaze
skimmed briefly over his chest, focusing on a thin, reddened scar that looked relatively new. A knife wound, she
realized, immediately attributing it to their recent alterca-
tion. "I didn't realize you had been hurt," she said.

"It's nothing," he replied. "Another beauty mark. Imagine how the women would be swooning over me if I wasn't already taken."

Although there was no doubt he meant the remark sarcastically, Julia couldn't help but wonder if there wasn't some truth to it. Morgan's body had been deeply scarred; there was no denying that. His back and shoulders, hands and arms, had been brutally ravaged, profoundly damaged by the flames. Yet the dark bronze beauty of his chest remained undisturbed. The incongruity was strangely compelling. Darkness and light. What he was now and what he had been. The rake and the Beast.

Moreover, Morgan St. James radiated a wealth of virility and strength. His muscles were lean and long, giving an athletic grace to his movements. Generations of nobility were bred into his chiseled features. His gaze smoldered with heat and purpose. Despite the havoc the fire had wreaked upon his body, the man exuded a raw masculine beauty that was utterly captivating.

Abruptly realizing that her husband had been politely enduring her penetrating inspection, Julia quickly returned her gaze to his. Lost in the awkwardness of the moment, but determined to say something optimistic, she observed, "They say life leaves its mark on us all."

He folded his arms across his chest and regarded her levelly. "Yes. In my case, however, I had hoped it might leave a less indelible impression."

"You're still a very attractive man."

A tight smile twisted his lips. "Love is blind." That said, he lifted his razor and resumed his task of shaving.

Julia noticed a streak of soapy film on his left shoulder blade. She moved to the washstand, removed a clean cloth, and immersed it in a basin of tepid water. Without thinking the matter through, she pressed the cloth against Morgan's shoulder, gently removing the soapy residue from his skin. His muscles instantly tensed beneath her touch.

He set down his razor and turned to face her once again. "May I ask what you're doing?"

Embarrassed by her action, she lifted her shoulders in what she hoped would be interpreted as a shrug of cool nonchalance. "It will itch unmercifully if you don't remove the soap properly."

"Fascinating. If only I had known. All this time I thought it itched because the flesh had been burned from my bones."

"My apologies. I was simply trying to help."

"If I find myself in need of a nursemaid, I shall hire one. I have other uses in mind for my wife."

"Indeed," she concurred briskly. "Whom would you heap your abuse upon if I were not here?"

"My servants have become quite adept at that task."

"I imagine so. Years of practice, no doubt."

A ghost of a smile flashed across his face. "No doubt." His smile slowly faded as a look of somber intensity entered his eyes. "As there obviously appears to be some confusion on the matter, I wonder if I should further define the uses I have in mind for my wife."

Julia felt a flush of heat that had nothing to do with the weather. "I can assure you that's entirely unnecessary. You've made your wishes abundantly clear in that area."

"I'm delighted to hear it."

There was a firmness to his tone that was unmistakable, a hard edge running just beneath the surface. Her gaze moved to his body once again. A shudder of nervous apprehension tore through her as she studied his sinewy strength and unyielding masculinity. She swallowed hard, willing herself not to show her fear. But Morgan's body was so totally foreign to her own—so much larger and more powerful in every way. Even if she willingly complied with his demands, how could their encounter not be one of sheer dominance on his part? The thought was not a pleasant one. She returned her gaze to his face just in time to see a muscle leap to life along his jawline.

"I sincerely regret it," he said tightly, "but this is the best I can do."

She blinked at him in confusion. "What do you mean?"

"I've tried all the cures, princess. Packs of mud, herb balms, holy water, vinegar solutions. One esteemed physician—whom I shall have the grace to allow to remain nameless—swore that bathing in a foul concoction of milk and cat urine would restore the youthful luster to my skin. As you can see, none of it worked."

Her eyes moved over his ravaged skin. Gathering her courage, she quietly asked, "What was it like?"

"Bearable."

She regarded him in silence for a long moment. "That sounds very polite, and very untrue."

"It pacifies most people who ask."

"Does it?"

"Yes."

She turned her attention to the washcloth she held in her hands, absently twisting it between her fingers. "I don't want to pry."

"But you will anyway."

"I would like for us to be able to speak frankly to one another, without fear of reprimands or reprisals. If that is too much to ask, however—"

He gave a beleaguered sigh and replied flatly, "Apparently the smoke didn't weaken my lungs."

"I don't understand."

"I'm told my screams could be heard all the way to Newcastle." He leaned one broad shoulder against the window casing, regarding her with a look of cool detachment. "Is that what you wanted to hear?"

Julia hesitated. She knew she was asking too much, wanting him to share a memory that was so intensely personal. But the fire was part of him—a central part. Her

need to know what he had gone through went beyond
mere prying. That understanding seemed central to their
relationship, critical to building their future together. She
was also aware, however, that to him her rationale would
sound undeniably selfish, nothing but a convenient excuse
to satisfy her curiosity. So in the end all she did was nod.
"Yes."

"Very well." He shifted slightly, folding his arms
across his chest. "You were right. It wasn't bearable at all.
It was unending, unendurable. The worst of it was the
isolation. Weeks on end, lying alone in my bed, wracked
by pain so intense, there were days I thought I might lose
my mind. Yet it was worse when someone entered the
room. The faintest disturbance of air seemed to whip my
skin raw. Perhaps it was just the suspense that made it feel
that way. For I knew if someone was in the room, they
would want to touch. To change my bandages or apply
a salve. That was an agony all its own."

His tone was flat and dry, as though the memories he
shared belonged to someone else.

"I remember experiencing an unendurable longing to
ride, to leap on my mount and race through the cool, dark
streets of London, shrouded in a soothing mist of early
morning fog. That longing was particularly strong later in
my recovery, when my physician allowed me visitors. I
suspect my friends meant well, but they were never quite
able to hide their pity and horror when they looked at me.
After one of their well-meaning visits, I would wallow for
days in shame and rage. In the end it was easier to bar
everyone entirely."

Julia struggled to find her voice. "What pulled you
through it?"

"Prayer," he replied succinctly. At her nod of understanding, a wry grin curved his lips. "Not the kind of
prayer you're thinking of, I'm afraid. As I was convinced
God had turned his back on me, I turned my back on
Him. I tried to strike a deal with the devil instead. My

eternal soul in return for his turning time back just twenty-four hours before the fire. That's all I wanted. A mere twenty-four hours to have that day and live it all over again."

She lowered her gaze, appalled at the casual blasphemy.

"I thought it a very blackened, depraved soul. A fit bargain in every way. But the devil must have reckoned me beneath his notice, for he never showed his heathen face. In the end I despaired of ever being heard at all." He hesitated for a long moment, then said, "Yet I was. Someone was listening to my lurid ranting—although I can't imagine why."

She frowned. "What do you mean?"

"A traveling minister came to my room at my lowest moment. I could feel my strength draining away and remember being vaguely relieved. I knew I could simply let go and it would all be over. I wouldn't have to fight any longer. I was falling in and out of a troubled sleep, contemplating death. That was when he appeared at the foot of my bed. My servants must have announced him, but when I questioned them later, none remembered doing so. I have no idea of his name, merely the memory of a fair-haired man wearing the collar of a cleric. We talked, and he brought me a strange sense of peace. When he left, I was committed to live. I felt there was still purpose in my life. You may question my sanity, but he was there. He was real."

Julia felt a shiver run down her spine. "I sometimes think angels come into our lives just when we need them most."

Morgan must have felt he had revealed too much, for he took a step back, moving away from her physically as well as emotionally. They had enjoyed a momentary truce of sorts, but apparently it was over. "I thought that was your role, princess," he said.

"I'm no angel."

"No? Society's ultimate redeemer," he intoned dramatically, "out to save all of London. The whores, the thieves, the orphans, the poor and downtrodden. So pure you should have wings. In fact, I find myself constantly searching for a trail of downy feathers in your wake." He paused, a sardonic smile curving his lips. "But I never do. Neatness must be one of your virtues as well."

"Must you make a joke of everything?" she asked tightly.

He shrugged. "After the fire I was furious with the world, beside myself with rage. When that subsided, I wallowed in self-pity. That was even more disgusting. Morbid humor is infinitely preferable, don't you think?"

Julia said nothing, watching as he lifted a shirt of finely woven white lawn and shrugged it on. Next he slipped on his socks, then stepped into a pair of beautifully crafted leather riding boots. As he went through the motions of dressing, he seemed to withdraw even further from her. It was almost as though he used his clothing as a weapon of defense, or perhaps simply as a barrier between them. Standing scarred and half naked before her Morgan had emanated a vague air of male vulnerability, reminding her of Samson with his shorn locks, or a medieval warrior who had lost his sword. But that momentary weakness—if it had existed at all—was gone now. He appeared coolly aloof once again, projecting an air of almost icy indifference.

Nevertheless, she was not yet ready to abandon their discussion. "You must take some comfort in the way your wounds were acquired," she said. "You were a hero to go in after those children."

"I was an idiot," he corrected curtly. "If I had to do it all over again, I wouldn't."

"I don't believe you."

"Suit yourself."

"There was a little girl you saved," she pressed. "I

remember reading about her in the paper. She was taken in by her aunt and uncle after the fire. Emily, wasn't it?"

Morgan stilled for a moment, then slowly turned his attention to a drawer of neckties. After much contemplation, he lifted a piece of pale gray silk and wrapped it around his throat. "Yes," he said at last. "Emily."

"I understand you regularly send her a sizable amount of money."

He shrugged. "It's nothing. A bit of pin money to help assuage my guilt."

"Pin money? The sum of one thousand pounds per annum? That's quite generous."

"Is it?" he retorted. "Tell me then, how do you compensate a five-year-old girl for watching her family burn to death before her eyes? One hundred pounds per annum? Five hundred? So sorry about the fire, my dear, but here's a few quid for your trouble. Run along and buy yourself a pretty new doll, and you'll forget all about it." A look of naked disgust showed on his face. "The generous lord of the manor."

"It wasn't your fault. You couldn't have predicted—"

"No, but I could have prevented it."

"It was the Lord's will."

"Really?" he parried dryly. "I thought it was the will of some madman named Lazarus. Isn't that what brought us to these heights of marital bliss?"

A knock sounded on the door before she could reply. At Morgan's call to enter, the valet he had been expecting earlier entered with a freshly pressed navy linen suit jacket. He draped the garment over a wooden clothes-horse and said, "Andrew has asked me to relay that your coach is waiting."

"Very good."

"Will there be anything else, sir?"

"No, thank you, Robert."

He gave a polite nod to his employer, a similarly respectful bow to Julia, then quietly exited the room.

The valet's interruption gave Julia time to reflect upon their conversation. Morgan's reticence to talk confirmed something she had suspected but hadn't been certain of. He had spoken with relative ease about his physical wounds; obviously he had come to some sort of healing. But his emotional wounds were still too raw. Deciding to let the matter drop for the moment, she watched as he shrugged on the navy jacket. "It appears as though you have plans for the day," she remarked.

"The usual."

An answer that told her nothing. "I see," she replied.

He turned and briefly surveyed her attire. She wore a lightweight Swiss muslin dress with a crisp emerald overskirt and a heart-shaped neckline. It was a simple gown, but one she had always felt pretty in. In a nod to the heat, she had styled her hair in a sleek twist. A broad-brimmed straw hat, adorned with a small cluster of pink field flowers and a green and white ribbon, provided protection from the sun.

"You have a distinct air of purpose about you as well," he said. "May I inquire as to what glorious deeds you have planned for the day? Leading a bread riot? Storming Windsor Castle? Feeding chocolate pudding to the mudlarks along the Thames?"

"Actually, nothing quite so noble or dramatic," she replied, matching his light tone. "I thought I might visit Henry and Annie Maddox instead." She hesitated, then plunged into the matter that had brought her to his room, blurting before she could change her mind, "In fact, I thought you might like to join me."

A look of surprise showed on Morgan's features. "To what do I owe the honor of this unexpected invitation?"

"Actually," Julia replied with a small smile, "you might consider it a summons rather than an invitation."

"Oh?"

"As you may recall, Henry Maddox was my father's bosun mate. They sailed together for years and were quite close. In many ways Henry and his wife are like family: I'm much closer to them than I am to my Uncle Cyrus. After my father's death Henry felt responsible for my welfare. That's why he assisted me in managing the leasing of my father's warehouse, and why he has daily been sending me letters demanding to meet you."

"They didn't attend our wedding?"

She shook her head. "I invited them, of course, but Henry refused. He said he didn't want to shame me by showing up, a seafaring tar and his innkeeper wife at a gentry wedding. But that has not dimmed their desire to make certain of my happiness and to bestow their blessing upon us. In fact, they expect to receive us both today at noon." When that elicited no response from Morgan, she continued. "Normally I wouldn't intrude upon your time, but this is rather important to me. We may not be related by blood, but they're the only real family I have left."

"I see."

His words constituted neither a refusal nor an acceptance. Just a perfunctory reply that was open to a thousand different interpretations. Refusing to lower herself to pleading for his acquiescence, she said stiffly, "I am aware I've given you no notice. If you've other plans, I shall simply convey your apologies—"

"That won't be necessary," he said. "I believe I can accommodate you in my schedule."

"How very kind," she returned, matching his tone of regal aloofness. Putting her irritation with his manner aside for the moment, her gaze moved once again to his elegantly tailored attire. "You needn't dress so formally for the visit. They're quite simple people."

"I take it they would probably feel more at home with my guise as a chimney sweep."

She smiled. "Actually, they probably would."

"I, however, would not."

"Very well."

Evidently he didn't miss the terse disapproval in her

tone. "I believe we've enjoyed enough costumed buffoon-
ery for one week, don't you?" he said.

"Must you always speak like that?"

"Like what?"

"So . . . pompous."

"I speak like a viscount who was educated at Eton
and Oxford." He paused, critically eyeing his tie in the
looking glass before him. Apparently satisfied, he turned
to her and asked, "How else could I earn my colleagues'
respect and attention while debating the merits of the various artists' conceptions for the statues in Regent's Park?
You know what a crucial issue that is for the future of
England."

"How indeed?" she retorted lightly, biting back the
sharp retort that sprang to her lips. This was not the time
to allow their conversation to degenerate into its usual
petty bickering. Particularly as there remained one nagging little issue to discuss. Stalling for time, she folded the
washcloth she held into quarters and set it on the basin as
she considered the best way to approach the sensitive issue.

"There is one more thing you should be aware of,"
she said at last. "Henry and Annie don't know about our
arrangement."

"I shudder to think what that means."

"Well, they are aware of our marriage, of course. But
they are ignorant as to the circumstances."

He arched one dark brow and regarded her with a
look of piercing scrutiny. "Meaning?"

Deciding to adhere to a policy of strict honesty—at
least insofar as this specific matter was concerned—she
continued. "They think we're madly in love with one another. That ours was an impetuous union based on the
fact that we simply couldn't wait to be together."

"Ah." He flicked a speck of lint from his sleeve. In a
tone of utter boredom, he inquired, "Exactly what
brought them to that idiotic conclusion?"

"I suppose I did. I couldn't very well tell them the truth, could I?"

A small smile curved his lips. "Heaven forbid."

Refusing to be baited, she continued. "They happen to take the sanctity of marriage very seriously. They would not understand the caprice with which we entered into our union. To them, marital vows are a pledge meant to be taken for eternity and nothing less." She paused, shaking her head. "Quite frankly, I can't even begin to contemplate eternity, can you?"

"I've spent a few evenings in the company of the royals. That should qualify, shouldn't it?"

Julia studied her husband's face for a long moment. "You seem to regard this marriage of ours as nothing but a mildly diverting hindrance to what might otherwise be occupying your time."

"That depends on my mood. On other occasions it seems a contrivance, pathetic, spurious, laughable, ill-conceived, brash, and completely inane. I fluctuate."

"Thank you so much for that edifying bit of information."

"If I were to fall down upon one knee and swear my undying devotion to you, would you believe it?"

"Certainly not."

"Then let us spare ourselves that embarrassing bit of nonsense, shall we, princess? I have made it clear that I desire you physically—you shall have to content yourself with that."

That might suit him, but it would not suit her. Julia knew herself well enough to know that. The circumstances that brought them together might have been unusual, but that did not mean that all hope was lost. She would not settle for a marriage of mere convenience, punctuated by occasional episodes of compassionless lust. And despite his mocking bravado, she was not yet willing to believe that Morgan would content himself with such a dismally shallow relationship either.

With that flash of insight came a peculiar sense of strength and purpose. Until that point she had had only vague notions of what she wanted from Morgan. Now she was able to compact her hopes and desires into a single word: *more.* More depth, more emotion, more warmth. Surely that was not asking too much. Granted there were untold barriers between them, but in time they could be breached. And if she failed? Julia brushed the thought off with a shrug. She had yet to back away from a struggle or a cause because the odds of success were against her.

Before she could speak Morgan turned and strode toward the door, dissolving the temporary intimacy that had existed between them. "Come," he said. "It's late. I know how you hate to keep the horses waiting."

The Tern's Rest was like any of the hundreds of other dockside taverns that crowded the Thames's southeastern shore. The structure itself was tall and narrow, built of the same crude lumber that had been used to construct the dock it sat upon. The main floor served as a pub; a flight of crooked stairs led to second-story lodgings. Raucous laughter, calls for more ale, and the tinny sound of a badly played pianoforte spilled out from unshuttered windows.

Inside, however, the atmosphere was markedly better than Morgan had expected. The floors were clean and dry, and the long trestle tables were free of the sticky residue of spilled ale and bitters. A huge beveled mirror sat behind the bar, reflecting the day's bright sunlight across the room. Squat casks of beer sat in a neat row against the back wall. Pretty young barmaids moved through the crowded room, serving tall pints of beer and generous plates of food that looked surprisingly edible. The clientele, although boisterous, generated an air of warmth and friendliness.

"I hope you'll excuse the china, your grace," said Annie Maddox, setting a slightly chipped cup and saucer before him. "As you can see, we're not set up for entertaining royalty."

Morgan, of course, was neither a duke—as Annie had addressed him—nor royalty. Nevertheless he sent the woman a benign smile, neglecting to correct her. "Not at all," he said smoothly, hoping to put her at ease. "I thank you for your kind hospitality."

The woman had clearly gone to some trouble on his behalf, and Morgan found himself reluctantly touched by her efforts. The small, rickety table at which they sat had been positioned in a corner of the room, offering them a modicum of privacy from the rest of the tavern guests. A lace tablecloth, a pair of sterling silver candlesticks—with candles blazing despite the hour and the heat of the day— and a glass vase brimming with fresh summer daisies served to distinguish the space even further. In addition to freshly brewed tea, the fare consisted of dainty sandwiches of cucumber and watercress, wafer-thin almond biscuits, and fresh orange slices. The menu was based, no doubt, on the ill-conceived but surprisingly popular notion that the gentry were given to weak constitutions and preferred to eat like rabbits.

"I can't recall the last time I was served such a delightful luncheon," he remarked.

Annie beamed with pride. She was short and plump, her blond hair generously streaked with gray. Her face was as round as a cherub's, pleasant and kind, if somewhat flushed from working in an overheated kitchen. Although she had no apron over her modest cotton gown, clearly she was accustomed to wearing one. Her hands moved repeatedly to the fabric of her dress, as though seeking the nonexistent apron upon which she could wipe them.

"That's Annie's business," put in the man Julia had introduced as Henry Maddox. "Hospitality. What with me being off at sea as much as I was, it was up to her to run this place. She's made a fine job of it. A real fine job of it." A small, private smile passed between them, expressive of the obvious affection that had not waned in the two decades they had been wed.

So perfectly did Henry Maddox fit the description of a sailor, he was almost a caricature. He was short in stature, barrel-chested, and given to a distinctive swaying walk that identified him at once as being more accustomed to the pitch of a rolling deck beneath his feet than solid ground. His skin was weathered from constant exposure to wind and sea, and his hair and beard were cropped into short gray bristles. But his most striking feature was his intensely pale blue eyes—eyes that looked at a man as though taking his measure and rating him against some unwavering inner standard. To Morgan's surprise and irritation, he was not yet sure he had gained Henry Maddox's approval.

"We didn't want to shame Julia by coming to the wedding, not with all the fancy guests you'd have," said Annie. "But we couldn't wait much longer to meet her new husband. We just wanted to make sure she was as happy as she said she was. It looks like she made a fine match, doesn't it, Henry?"

Henry Maddox gave a noncommittal grunt. "A title don't make you a good man. Money don't make you a good man."

"Try going without it for a fortnight," teased Annie lightly. To Morgan she said, "Don't mind him. We were never blessed with a child, but we've watched Julia grow since she was a tiny baby swaddled in pink blankets and covered in ribbons and lace. I guess that makes it hard to see her grow up and start a family of her own."

From there the conversation lapsed into a series of warm reminiscences, recalling better times when Julia's parents were still alive. Morgan leaned back and listened, alternately amused and entertained, depending upon the nature of the story. The conversation might have drifted on for hours were it not for a nearby ship releasing its hands for a brief respite from the exhausting chore of loading the hold. Within minutes the tavern was swarmed with sailors demanding to have their hunger and thirst quenched.

Henry immediately stood and assumed a position behind the bar, while Annie excused herself and hurried off to the kitchens. Even Julia abandoned their table. Murmuring a word of apology, she accepted an apron passed to her by one of the barmaids and began circulating among the tables with breezy familiarity, running back and forth with cool drinks and plates of hot food.

Morgan watched her work, battling a vague sense of unease. There was, he decided with a frown, a decidedly chameleonlike quality to his bride that he wasn't entirely certain he approved of. She had seemed so regal and aloof the night they had met at the Devonshire House—an unearthly goddess sculpted in peppermint pink. Yet here she was, the Viscountess Barlowe, serving beer and ale to a group of rowdy sailors. Incomprehensible. Worse still, Julia was smiling as she worked, exchanging good-natured banter with the men who crowded around her.

It soon became evident that it would be some time until the sailors were properly served and fed. Left to his own amusement, Morgan allowed himself to be drawn into a game of pitch-and-toss. After a lapse of perhaps an hour, the tavern cleared somewhat, and Julia—looking tired but content—plopped onto a nearby bench and watched him play. Morgan took a few more shots, then left to sit beside her.

"Any luck?" she asked with a soft smile.

His game, as she well knew from what little she had witnessed, had been less than stellar. He gave a light shrug and replied, "I shall sleep easier knowing I have done my part to keep the local population in generous supply of coin for at least the next month or so."

"It was good of you to play."

"You're commending me on my ability to blend with the common rabble?"

Her smile instantly faded. "I should commend you on your ability to nonchalantly refer to my friends as common rabble without the least bit of embarrassment on your part. I consider that an even more extraordinary skill."

"If I didn't know better, princess, I'd swear you were calling me a snob."

"There is nothing common about either Henry or Annie."

"I don't recall saying that there was."

"Perhaps not directly, but—"

"One more game," called one of the sailors with whom Morgan had been playing, his voice carrying across the room. "But this time let's sweeten the pot. Rather than mere coin, the winner is rewarded with an even greater victory: a kiss from the bride—our own fair Julia."

The suggestion was greeted with a round of good-natured cheers and friendly laughter. The game was played just as before, but with one minor variation. The winner received a chaste kiss on the cheek instead of coins. The money from that round of play went to the bride and groom, accompanied by wishes of prosperity and good fortune. It was, Morgan knew, a harmless bit of innocent fun and well-meaning tradition.

Despite that knowledge, he was struck by an impulsive sense of possessiveness. The appreciative looks Julia had received as she had moved among the tavern's patrons had not escaped his notice. Nor did the bawdy jokes that circulated among the men at the prospect of winning her kiss, even under such innocuous circumstances. Thus when she—after a questioning glance directed at Morgan—offered her reluctant assent, he immediately countered, "Under one condition. I am allowed to play as well."

"But you already claim her," objected the sailor who had proposed the game.

"My point exactly," replied Morgan. Catching Julia's wrist, he lifted it and pressed a dramatic kiss against the back of her hand. Smiling as he raised his head, he asked the crowd, "What man could blame me for not wanting to share such a prize?"

Fortunately he succeeded in setting the right tone. His question was received with more cheers and laughter as the men crowded around, eager to participate. The game began almost at once. Pitch-and-toss was perhaps one of the simplest pub contests. A large glass stein was set on the floor some distance from the players. Each man tossed a coin at the glass, the object being to strike the glass and bounce off, the player whose coin landed closest to the stein—and in the heads-up position—being declared the winner.

When Morgan had played earlier, he had not given the game much thought, for he had been too distracted watching Julia move about the room. But now as his turn arrived, he gave the glass stein careful measure. Then he drew a twopence from his pocket and tossed it in the air. The coin struck the glass with a satisfying *clink,* then dropped flat, heads up, one smooth edge still touching the stein.

A round of groans immediately filled the room. A few more men lined up and gave their best throws, but the game was effectively over. Despite the reception his toss received, Morgan experienced a ridiculous sense of victory. He was well aware that he had ruined the spirit of the game by participating, but he had not been able to resist. Never having been given to fits of jealousy, he was loath to put that label to his emotions. But the prospect of Julia pressing her lips against another man, no matter how innocent the gesture, struck him as simply intolerable. For better or worse, she belonged to him.

With the eyes of the room upon them, he turned to his wife to receive his prize. She hesitated for a moment, seemingly lost as to how to proceed. A roar of bawdy recommendations immediately filled the room. "Let's see how the better half lives!" called one slightly inebriated sailor. "Show us how you kiss your husband!" This, one of the mildest of suggestions, seemed to finally prompt her into action. As a delicate peach blush spread across her cheeks Julia leaned forward, pursed her lips in an exaggerated pucker, and pressed a fleeting peck against Morgan's cheek.

Morgan caught her as she pulled away. Tucking his arm around the small of her back, he pulled her tightly to him and pressed her body against his own until he could feel her every soft curve, her every gentle breath. The heat of her skin seeped through the thin fabric of her gown, wrapping him in a bewitching cloud of her soft scent and gentle warmth. Julia immediately stiffened in resistance and attempted to escape his grasp. Ignoring her tacit protest, he bent his head and crushed her lips beneath his own.

It was not a lover's kiss. There was no finesse, no softness in his touch, no subtle seduction. As much as Morgan would have liked to please her, he was far too aware of his own needs. He had wanted this from the moment he had seen her, and he was not about to let the opportunity pass him by. In a desire born part of possessiveness and part of urgent need, he used the pressure of his jaw to force her lips apart. That accomplished, he thrust his tongue inside her mouth. He was rewarded with a taste of infinite sweetness, accompanied by an overwhelming longing for more than just that kiss. But the Tern's Rest was not the place for it. As that bitter understanding slowly seeped into his consciousness, he reluctantly released her.

Julia staggered backward, her breath coming in hard,

deep gulps. She stared at him with a mixture of shock and dismay as a roar of merry cheers sounded behind them.

Morgan merely lifted his shoulders in an indifferent shrug. "That, princess, is how you kiss a husband."

Chapter 8

M organ moved through a sinister world of twisting
gray phantoms. The smoke intensified as he moved forward.
It billowed about him and curled into his lungs, constricting
his breath. He could feel the strength draining from his
body. He had forgotten what he was seeking, he knew only
that he had to look. Time was running out. Not yet, he
pleaded silently. Not yet. He had to find them. Who? He
focused intently, straining to maintain a cohesive line of
thought. Then he remembered. The children. Markum's
children. He had to find them, he had to get them out.

Smoke turned to flame. Everywhere. Burning, blistering, hissing flame. Choking, Morgan shoved open a door
and staggered blindly into a room. The floorboards cracked
beneath his feet. Fire licked the walls. The ceiling peeled
away, raining down upon him in sheets of smoking ash and
plaster. His gaze shifted to a small, quivering form huddled
beneath a cot.

Emily.

A surge of elation temporarily replaced the anguished despair that had gripped him. He lunged for the child and gathered her into his arms, carrying her with him to the window. Left with no other choice, he blindly dropped her into the crowd gathered below.

Swaying slightly, he turned back and scanned the room, searching for the rest of the children. His gaze stopped at a bright, shimmering flame that seemed to dance in one corner. Strangely captivated, he moved toward it. Then he heard the screaming.

High-pitched. Terrified. Ceaseless.

The screams were coming from within the flame.

Hideous understanding flooded through him, locking him in a paralysis of frozen horror. The knowledge of what he was seeing seized him in an absolute grip, obliterating all pain, all weakness, all other thoughts. Nothing mattered but the flame.

And the child trapped inside the flame.

Markum's-four-year-old daughter Patricia. Patty. Morgan instinctively knew. Recognition was automatic and absolute. For a fraction of a second, he saw her as she had been yesterday, a giggling sprite playing peek-a-boo in his gardens, squealing in delight as she hid behind a mulberry bush. Everything came back to him in vivid detail: the way the sunlight had danced in her mop of light brown curls, how her dress had been stained with grass and mud. The sight, just a distracted glance from his study window, had meant nothing to him at the time. Now it loomed before him in painstaking detail. Patty's eyes wide with innocence and wonder, clapping her chubby hands as she sang patty-cake, patty-cake . . . her gleeful screams as her brother thrust a frog in her face.

Now just the screaming remained.

Agonized, piercing screaming.

And flame.

Before he could move, a thundering crack! filled the room as a ceiling joist broke free and swung down from the *rafters. Morgan was aware of a sharp, radiating pain as the smoking beam hit him directly in the chest, propelling him backward and knocking him through the window.*

He reached out to grab hold of something to stop his descent, but he was too late.

He was falling. Falling and falling. Falling forever.

Then blissful black nothingness.

Morgan opened his eyes.

For a long moment he lay motionless in his bed, studying the shadows that flickered across the ceiling of his room. He almost expected to see a message there, some divine sign that might offer direction or meaning to his life. But the shapes and shadows amounted to nothing—just moonlight sifting through the branches of an old oak in the gardens outside his room. He had left his windows and curtains open in the hope of catching a breeze. A vain hope, apparently, for the air that filled his bedchamber was as hot and stifling now as it had been hours earlier when he had retired.

With nowhere for his thoughts to turn, he let his mind drift back to the nightmare that had awakened him. It was a familiar one. In sleep he relived that dark moment again and again; never able, even in his imagination, to alter the outcome. But in its recurrence the dream had lost its original power. He felt oddly removed from it, able to dissect the images with an almost dispassionate interest, as though the thoughts and feelings they generated belonged to someone else. Perhaps that wasn't unusual. Two years had passed since the fire had occurred.

Now his emotions, like his scars, were deadened by time. He felt only . . . what? he wondered. Regret? But surely that was too shallow and trifling a word for the enormity of the weight pressing down on him. Finality, perhaps. A sense of irreparable damage, of having made a mistake so immense, there was no way to ever correct it.

But even that didn't quite satisfy the scale or the scope of his emotions.

Irritated at his ineptitude in failing to find the right words—at his own foolishness for even trying—Morgan threw back the pale linen sheet that covered his body and stood. He prowled naked about his room, consumed with restless energy. Needing an escape but not sure where to go, he drew on a lightweight cotton robe and stepped out onto the balcony that overlooked the gardens. He drummed his fingers restlessly over the wrought-iron rail, then gripped the cool metal in his fists. He glanced up at the sky. Judging by the path of the stars, there remained at least an hour before dawn.

As he moved to return inside, the soft flicker of lamplight coming from a window to his left caught his eye. Julia's room. Thoughts of his beautiful bride instantly filled his mind. Unfortunately, they weren't the lofty, inspired sort of thoughts of which Julia might approve. Instead his reflections were decidedly carnal in nature. As he recalled the brief kiss they had shared earlier that afternoon, raw need blossomed within him, accompanied by an ache he could feel deep within his bones. He would not seek comfort in her arms, merely a blind, meaningless release from the tension that held him in its grip. Surely that was not too much to ask.

Had the noise of him moving about disturbed her sleep, or was it the heat that kept her from slumber? In either case the discovery that she was awake offered him the perfect opportunity to enter her room in the guise of checking on her. A rather transparent excuse, he recognized, but it would suffice.

He exited his chamber, moving down the hall toward Julia's room. He reached her door and rapped softly on the heavy oak. Silence greeted him. He knocked again, louder this time. When she still failed to reply, he turned the knob and slowly opened the door. Like him, she had kept her windows and drapes open when she retired. The soft, silvery glow of moonlight filled the room. He scanned the space, his gaze stopping abruptly when he found her.

She was lying on her back in bed, sound asleep. Naked. Beautifully, blissfully, naked. Apparently she had been reading when she had fallen asleep. An open book lay beside her pillow. An oil lamp—the light he had seen from his room—flickered softly on the nightstand beside her. The soft glow warmed her skin, providing a dramatic contrast to the cool moonlight that otherwise filled the space.

Her sheets were pooled about her hips, draped in a pose of such artful perfection, one might suspect she had arranged to serve as inspiration for a Renaissance painter. An apt analogy, Morgan thought, for it would take a master like Botticelli to truly capture her. Venus in the flesh.

His gaze moved slowly over Julia's body. Her rich copper hair tumbled over her shoulders in a luxuriant mass, spilling across the soft white sheets. Her face was relaxed, her lips slightly parted as she slept. The pale shadow of her dark russet lashes fell against her cheek. Her rib cage rose and fell in time to her breathing, creating a serene in-and-out pulse that was entirely mesmerizing. Her breasts were slightly flattened due to her position, but they looked full and incredibly soft. The deep rose of her nipples made his mouth water in anticipation of their taste. Her waist was tight and narrow, the lush curve of her hips suggested beneath the thin weight of her sheet.

She was his wife. His by all means legal, religious, and moral. He could take her any time he wanted her. He gave their ridiculous bargain cursory thought, then abruptly dismissed it. He had promised her three months, but the fact that he had given his word did little to tame the desire that pulsed through him. Hunger overrode honor. Therein lay the trouble. Opportunity only knocks. Temptation breaks down doors.

He could even convince himself it was for her own good. He wouldn't take her against her will, naturally, but he was skilled enough in the art of seduction that she would quickly enough become a willing partner. That decided, Morgan loosened the belt to his robe and shrugged the garment off.

He moved to slip in bed beside her when a flicker of light from the oil lamp reflected in a mirror across the room. Distracted, he glanced up, then froze as he caught a glimpse of the tableau they made. Julia, the porcelain perfection of her skin glowing in the warmth of the lamp. A goddess come to life. Then his gaze shifted to his own body. The fire hadn't marred his skin everywhere. But there were hideous patches where it had licked his skin raw, leaving it puckered and grotesque, reddened and angry, stretched taut over his muscles. His back. His hands and forearms. The nape of his neck. His left hip.

After the fire he had made it a point to avoid mirrors when he bathed, waiting until he was fully clothed to check his appearance. Now he couldn't help but stare.

The Beast.

Fragments of his dream rushed back to him. The smoke, the heat, the flame.

Patty-cake, patty-cake.

His fault. All of it his fault.

His desire, the pounding pulse that had driven him to seek out his wife, instantly shriveled and vanished. He reached for his robe and shrugged it on. Extinguishing the oil lamp, he retraced his steps and left the room, quietly pulling the door shut behind him.

"*I* beg your pardon?" Lionel Oakes, Morgan's private secretary, studied his employer with an expression of blatant disbelief. "Did you say—"

"Accept it," Morgan affirmed. "And the rest."

"All of them?"

Morgan turned from his position at the window of his study. He crossed the room to the small desk where Mr. Oakes sat. Impatiently he held out his hand. "Here, let me see them."

He rifled through the minuscule stack of engraved linen cards, privately amazed that invitations still arrived at all. Particularly since he hadn't accepted an invitation to a ball or dinner in over two years, as evidenced by his secretary's shock at his abrupt turnabout.

"Yes," he said, passing the invitations back. "Accept them all, and mark my calendar accordingly."

"Including tomorrow night's gala at Lord and Lady Winterbourne's?"

"Send a note this afternoon," Morgan replied. " 'Viscount Barlowe exceedingly regrets his late reply, but is honored to accept the kind invitation,' et cetera, et cetera.' " He waved his hand dismissively in his secretary's direction. "You know what to say."

"Yes," Lionel Oakes stuttered. He was a young man with a round face, round glasses, and meticulously neat attire. Despite his youth he projected a decidedly stodgy air. Given to an innate dislike of the unexpected, he carried an umbrella with him everywhere he went. Morgan's response had obviously taken him by surprise, but he was quickly recovering. "Yes, of course," he replied.

"Mention that my wife, Viscountess Barlowe, will be accompanying me as well."

His secretary bowed his head and made a note. "To tomorrow night's engagement or all of them?"

"All of them. Have you met her?"

"I beg your pardon?" Lionel Oakes looked decidedly confused by the question. Their discussions had always pertained exclusively to Morgan's business affairs. Never once had they shared anything that might be considered a personal conversation.

Nevertheless, Morgan doggedly continued. "My wife. Have you met her?"

"Oh. Ah . . . yes. Indeed. I have had that honor."

"What was your impression of her?"

"My impression?" Lionel Oakes fiddled uncomfortably with his glasses for a moment, giving the matter what seemed to Morgan undue thought. He looked distinctly put out, as though asking for his personal opinion were clearly outside the purview of his duties. At last, apparently resigning himself to the fact that he would not be granted a reprieve from answering, he reluctantly replied, "My impression is that she is quite lovely, Lord Barlowe. Quite . . . genteel."

"Genteel," Morgan echoed, a wry smile curving his lips. "Were you aware that we were assaulted at knifepoint last week?"

"Good God."

"There were three assailants. When one of the men came at me with a knife, my genteel wife lifted a heavy stick of kindling and swung at the man's groin with all her might. As you might imagine, the blow was quite effective." He paused, shaking his head. "I don't think I've ever seen a man turn that particular shade of green before."

Oakes looked horrified. "I'm afraid I don't know what to say."

"Nor did he."

Morgan moved away from his secretary's desk and returned to his former station near the window. He leaned one shoulder against the windowpane, listening as the sounds from the street drifted toward him. He heard a heavy cart rumbling by, a barking dog, the steady *clip-clop* of a horse and carriage, the sound of a young boy—a newspaper vendor, perhaps?—shouting out the price of his wares. They were mere guesses as to what he was hearing, however. Just as the tall gates that surrounded his estate prevented anyone from seeing inside, he was equally prevented from seeing what was occurring outside. He had a view of the city in the distance, but the tall gates rendered him blind to his immediate surroundings. A fact that had never elicited much interest or concern on his part. But now he couldn't help but wonder what he might be missing.

"Viscountess Barlow informed me last week that I have been using the walls of this estate to hide behind," he announced. "Would you concur with that opinion, Mr. Oakes?"

"I would say that you were recuperating from your injuries," his secretary returned loyally.

"Really. Is that what I've been doing?"

Morgan's gaze drifted out over the gardens. Despite the sweltering heat he had seen Julia head in the direction of the rose arbor some thirty minutes ago. A broad straw hat had covered her head, and a large basket had been tucked under her arm. A glance in that direction confirmed that she was still there. From his vantage point he could not see her face, just her shapely rear and the soles of her shoes. Apparently she was on her hands and knees, mucking about in the dirt. Such odd habits.

Returning his attention to his study, he noted how dark and dim the room was, compared with the shimmering brilliance of the day. How stuffy. In a nod to the heat Morgan was attired in a loose white linen shirt and lightweight buff-colored pants. His secretary, however, was apparently immune to the weather. Lionel Oakes was dressed in a somber brown suit, starched shirt, necktie, and sturdy walking boots. His ever-present umbrella was at his side.

"I have examined their portfolio at length," Oakes droned on, his nose buried in a thick folder. "The return on investment is quite high, as might be expected for such a risky venture, but there remains the problem of negative capital expenditure. Not an insurmountable problem, granted, but one that should be examined more closely before—"

"What brand of soap do you use, Mr. Oakes?"

Lionel Oakes's head snapped up. He studied Morgan blankly, then blinked twice behind his gold-rimmed glasses. "I beg your pardon?"

"Matthews and Hornsby. Do you ever purchase it?"

"No, I do not."

Morgan frowned. "I see."

Oakes hesitated a moment, then added helpfully, "Perhaps it will interest you to know that my mother did. She mentioned just yesterday, however, that she will not continue to do so in the future. I don't recall exactly why; something to do with spilled tallow, I believe."

"Remarkable."

A small smile touched Morgan's lips, but he offered nothing further. Clearly trying to make sense of the question, his secretary asked, "Were you considering buying an interest in that firm?"

"No, not particularly," he replied with a shrug. "Just indulging a bit of curiosity, I suppose."

Lionel Oakes shifted uncomfortably. "Ah."

Taking pity on the man, as well as resigning himself to the fact that he was not going to get any work done, Morgan turned abruptly from his station near the window and crossed the room, pausing at the door to his study. "You'll excuse me, Mr. Oakes. I believe we're quite finished for the day."

His secretary's mouth fell agape at the unprecedented midday dismissal. "But what about . . ." he began, gesturing to the thick pile of untouched papers beside him. Then, abruptly recalling himself, he stood and executed a tight bow. "Of course. Very good, Lord Barlowe."

Morgan turned from the study and left the house. As he stepped outside, the heat of the day greeted him like a blast from a coal furnace. *Damned unseasonably warm,* he thought in irritation. The weather had been fairly tolerable when he had gone riding earlier that morning. Now it was sweltering. Shimmering bands of heat pulsated in blistering waves in the distance. The sky was cloudless, and so pale a blue, it was almost white, as though overbaked by the sun. The gardeners and groomsmen, normally at the peak of their labors, moved listlessly about in the shade.

He strode across the grounds in the direction of the rose arbor. There he found Julia in the same position he had seen her from his study window: kneeling down on all fours near the base of a rosebush. She held a pair of pruning shears in one hand; the basket beside her brimmed with freshly cut flowers.

Morgan stopped behind her, waiting for her to take note of his presence. When she failed to do so, he made himself known with a soft "Ahem."

Visibly startled at the intrusion, Julia spun about and squinted up at him. "Oh. It's you."

Hardly the warmest of welcomes, but he supposed it would do. "If you have a moment, I should like to speak with you."

"Actually, I've been most anxious to see you," she replied, adopting a brisk, businesslike demeanor. She rose and withdrew a parchment envelope from her pocket, passing it to him. "Mr. Randolph delivered this earlier this morning."

Morgan took the note and read,

Flame,
How greatly you disappoint me, my love. We could have accomplished great things together. Instead you choose to lay with filth. Now you leave me no choice.
You must pay for your treachery.
When I have assembled you, I will blast you with the heat of my anger and smelt you with it.
Lazarus

His fingers tightened on the letter as a surge of grim victory swelled in his chest. "Lazarus. So he hasn't abandoned us after all."

"I wanted to show you the note the moment it arrived, but you were in conference with your secretary. I didn't wish to disturb you."

"In the future, you may feel free to do so immediately."

"Very well."

Despite the threatening nature of the missive, Morgan noted that Julia didn't appear the least bit intimidated or frightened by it. Or even surprised, for that matter. "You were expecting this, weren't you?" he remarked, studying her intently.

"Let us say that I was not shocked when it arrived."

"Why?"

She hesitated, then lifted her shoulders in a small shrug. "Yesterday I bought a lace shawl at a small shop near Coventry Market. While I was there, I *felt* him watching me. I know it must sound foolish, given that I have no idea who the man is, but I knew he was there nonetheless. In the middle of that crowded street . . . lurking, waiting, and watching. Just as I felt him watching me at the Devonshire House the night you and I met."

"He was at the Devonshire House?"

"I can't say for certain, but—"

"But you felt his presence."

"Yes."

"Very good," he murmured, thinking aloud. He would not discount or belittle intuition. In his experience it was just as valid as any other sense, consisting primarily of information that the mind had collected but hadn't yet processed logically. "That would be in agreement with my own speculations."

"Oh?"

"I believe the man we seek is a member of the peerage. If you recall, the thinking at the time of the fires was that the arsonist was probably a disgruntled servant, someone who wanted to take some measure of revenge against his betters."

Julia nodded. "Yes, I remember."

"I was never convinced of the right of that reasoning. The morning of the fire on my property, it was densely foggy, too foggy for me to get a close look at the man. At the time I thought I was chasing a common thief. But later, when I examined my memory at greater length, it was evident that that was not the case."

She regarded him curiously. "Why?"

"His boots. When I leaped to tackle the man, I missed. My hands came in contact with his boots instead. I distinctly remember that the leather was remarkably sleek and supple, and that the soles were barely worn. Granted, he could have stolen them, but there were other things about him that marked him as an individual of some means. The fact that he had a horse waiting—a fine piece of horseflesh, not a tired old nag. Would a common thief be able to afford the boarding and upkeep of such an animal here in London?"

She nodded thoughtfully. "That could all be explained, of course," she said after a moment.

"True. I'm merely stating my impression of the man, combined with my own instincts, if you will."

"Yes." She considered that for a moment, then remarked, "I took the liberty of writing Mr. Chivers of Scotland Yard and informing him of these latest developments. I expect he shall pay us a call soon."

"He'll likely tell us we are a pair of fools."

She shrugged. "Perhaps."

Uncomfortably aware of the thick heat pulsing down upon them, Morgan nodded toward his estate. "May I accompany you inside?"

Julia hesitated, then gestured with her pruning shears to the bush she was working on. "It will just take me a minute or two to finish, if you don't mind. . . ."

"Not at all."

He nodded politely and stepped past her, seating himself upon a stone bench as he watched her at her task. The pile of deep yellow roses in the basket beside her steadily grew. Shifting his attention slightly, Morgan's gaze moved to the simple cotton gown she wore. In what was likely a concession to the weather, she wore minimal undergarments beneath it. The lightweight fabric clung to her body as she moved, pulling at her hips and thighs. She had unbuttoned the top of her bodice as she worked; a faint sheen of perspiration glistened in the shadowy cleft between her breasts.

Although he had never before found the sight of a woman clipping roses the least bit erotic, her movements struck him as dazzlingly sensual. A memory of Julia as she had appeared last night, naked and tranquil in repose, blurred with the sight of her as she was now: damp, warm, and gracefully lithe as she moved among the rosebushes. It did not require a great leap of imagination to combine the two images and envision what she might be like in his bed. In a reaction of pure adolescent idiocy, Morgan felt himself stiffen in response to the lecherous conjecture; his manhood grew thick and hard against his thigh. Annoyed by his inability to control his response to his own wife, he shifted slightly to make his dilemma less obvious.

Julia glanced up at him and frowned. Clearly misinterpreting his impatience with himself with a desire for her to finish her task, she tucked her pruning shears into her basket and briskly announced, "I believe that should do."

He stood and extended a hand, helping her to her feet. Either his dilemma was not as apparent as he feared, or she was simply too intent on brushing the dirt from her gown to notice. In either case she looked up at him and said, "I suppose I should have asked permission before clipping so many of your roses."

"Not at all. But you needn't bother with the chore. I'll direct the servants to see to the flowers."

"I wish you wouldn't. I don't mind at all. In fact, I quite enjoy it." She hesitated, then looked around her with a small frown. "The lawns are magnificent, but it appears the groundskeepers haven't quite put their hearts into the flowers."

"What do you mean?"

"Your peonies are choking. They're hopelessly tangled in this holly bush." An expression of bossy exasperation showed on her face as she pointed to a clump of weak green stems. "And I can't imagine when your rhododendron was last pruned. Furthermore, all of your bulbs need thinning if you expect the poor things to bloom next year."

He folded his arms across his chest, regarding her with undisguised amusement. "You're determined to save everything you come into contact with, aren't you, princess? Even the flowers."

"Almost," she replied, studying him with an expression of cool intractability. "Not everything is redeemable."

The implication that she was referring to him was unmistakable. Instead of taking affront, his smile only widened. "Wise of you to come to that understanding so quickly."

Without commenting further, he took the basket from her arm and carried it for her. Rather than returning directly to the house, he escorted her on a more circuitous route through the gardens in order that they might enjoy a bit more privacy. "It occurs to me that we may have made a fundamental error in our strategy regarding Lazarus," he said after a moment. "Receipt of his letter is quite encouraging, but it is not enough. If we intend to prod him into making his presence known, we must dangle a bit of bait. Unfortunately, that bait is you."

"Yes."

"To that end I have directed my secretary to accept every invitation we receive. We must flaunt the fact that you, Lazarus's true desire, have taken refuge in my arms. You rejected him for me. With any luck that will serve to further flame his fury."

"That seems logical."

"If we hope to be successful, it will require that we appear disgustingly happy and in love. Positively enraptured with one another."

"Yes," she agreed, her expression giving nothing away.

"I thought we might begin this charade tomorrow night, at Lord and Lady Winterbourne's affair."

"Very well."

She was taking it so matter-of-factly that Morgan doubted she fully understood what he was driving at. As they approached his home, he paused beneath the shade of a tall cypress to finish their conversation. Intent on making himself as clear as possible, he lifted his hand and lightly stroked it against her cheek. "I take it you can list persuasive acting skills among your considerable accomplishments?"

While she didn't flinch, neither did she give any indication that his touch was welcome. "We made a bargain," she said. "I understand what needs to be done."

He felt himself go cold. "How very commendable," he said with a tight smile. "A woman of her word, willing to make the ultimate sacrifice."

"You know how fond I am of lost causes."

"Indeed." Deciding it would be pointless to pursue the matter further, he let the subject drop and guided her up the front steps. "By the way," he remarked as they stepped into the foyer, "my congratulations on the formidable wrath of your pen. I conducted an informal survey this morning and discovered that my secretary's mother has ceased purchasing Matthews and Hornsby soap."

"Has she? That's wonderful."

"Apparently there is a method to your madness after all."

An unmistakable glint of victory entered her soft sherry eyes. "Wise of you to come to that understanding so quickly."

$\mathcal{J}$ulia leaned back against the plush leather squabs of
Morgan's coach, listening to the rhythmic drumming of
the horses' hooves as they journeyed to Lord and Lady
Winterbourne's. The crowded streets made their movement slow, negating any chance they might have had for
stirring a breeze through the open windows. Although she
had taken a cool bath less than an hour earlier and thoroughly dusted herself with a sweet-scented talc, the effects
of her ministrations were already beginning to lessen. She
felt warm and damp, her nerves as strained and excitable
as those of her Aunt Rosalind.

In an effort to distract her thoughts from the coming
evening, she turned her attention to her gown, running
her fingers over the intricate pleats to prevent their wrin-
kling. She had selected a deep apricot silk with cap
sleeves, a square bodice, and a full bustle that gave an
elegant sway to her movements. Her elbow-length brown
kid gloves, made to match her shoes and reticule, rested in

her lap. She wore her hair piled high, with just a strand or two left to curl softly against the nape of her neck. The gown was too tight to be comfortable, and as a result she found herself constantly fidgeting with the fabric, gently tugging at it in a vain attempt to gain a bit more room.

"You needn't fuss with your gown," Morgan said after a moment. "You look lovely."

Julia instantly stilled her hands, unaware he had been watching her.

"An interesting color," he continued. "I wouldn't have selected it, but it suits you well."

She felt a gentle bump. Their movement, sluggish as it had been, abruptly halted. "We've arrived?" she asked breathlessly.

He glanced out the window. "No," he replied. "There's a queue. Blocks long, by the looks of it." He released an impatient sigh. "One of the reasons I've taken to hiding behind my gates, as you so eloquently put it. Rarely does the effort required to attend an event equal the enjoyment one receives once arrived."

She made a noncommittal noise and shifted her gaze to the long line of coaches. "Do you think he'll be here tonight?"

He didn't pretend to misunderstand who she meant. "Lazarus?" he said, lifting his shoulders in an indifferent shrug. "Possibly." Returning his full attention to her, he observed, "You're nervous."

The note of condescending amusement in his voice was unmistakable. "Hardly," she replied.

"Then it must be the prospect of being introduced to all of London as my bride that has you aflutter."

She stiffened her spine, arranging her posture into one of prim disapproval. "Contrary to what you obviously believe, not everything that occurs in life directly revolves around you."

Smiling broadly, he leaned back in his seat and

crossed his right leg over his opposite knee. "Is that what I believe, princess?"

Something in his voice caused her to raise her eyes to his. Unable to stop herself, her gaze moved assessingly over her husband. His scars notwithstanding, he was still a strikingly beautiful man. He wore a black formal suit of lightweight wool. Having removed his jacket before entering the coach, he sat opposite her in a shirt of starched ivory linen, his cravat tied in an intricate knot that managed to simultaneously suggest a careless yet fashionable air. It wasn't simply the elegance of his attire that made him appear so compellingly regal, however. He seemed to project an air of aloof, aristocratic authority, as though he were watching and judging from afar—a Greek god surveying the petty mortals from his seat upon Olympus.

"You're amused by this," she said.

"What?" he asked, arching one dark brow. "The Season? Society?" He waved his hand in a coolly dismissive motion. "The lords and ladies of the peerage taking turns making a spectacle of themselves fawning over one another, parading about like the naked emperor of legend, each convinced his robes are the richest in the land. Perhaps Lazarus is right to set us all aflame."

His words seemed vaguely prescient. The darkness of that intuitive recognition caused a chill to run down her spine, doing little to ease her nerves. Deliberately choosing to steer their conversation to a somewhat brighter tone, she said, "It's all fairly new to me. I've never had a Season."

"Not even a coming out?"

"No."

He frowned. "Why?"

She managed a light shrug. "My parents wanted me to have a Season, of course. That's what this gown was intended for, as well as the others you've seen. They were all ordered for my eighteenth birthday, in anticipation of my grand debut in society." She paused, sending him a self-deprecating smile. "I don't know if you've noticed, but the gowns are all a bit tight now. Apparently I don't enjoy the same lithesome, girlish figure I did when I was eighteen. Particularly—" She lifted her hand to indicate her bosom, then stopped abruptly, horrified at her gaffe.

But she was too late. Following the path of her gesture, his gaze had come to rest directly on the creamy expanse of skin revealed above her bodice. Molding her body to the hourglass shape dictated by the gown had necessitated the use of an almost painfully tight corset. As her lungs were already tightly constricted, the unavoidable chore of breathing could only be accomplished by lifting her breasts and pushing them out and upward. Although the gown remained well within the bounds of fashion and modesty, Julia felt dreadfully exposed. Particularly now, when she could feel the heat of Morgan's smoky gaze on her skin as clearly as if he were touching her. The breathless tension she had experienced when he had shocked her with his kiss at the Tern's Rest ran through her again now.

"Yes," he said, his voice like dark silk, "so it would appear."

She cast about for something to say to relieve the awkwardness of the moment, but her mind refused to cooperate. "My mother abruptly fell ill," she said, doggedly continuing her story, "and my Season was cut short after just one night."

"What about the following year? You could have made your coming out at nineteen."

"Perhaps. But my heart just wasn't in it. It seemed like such a frivolous waste. And my father . . ." She hesitated for a moment, searching for the right words. "He was never quite the same after my mother passed away. He had always been so competent, so strong. But he began drinking heavily, and his business affairs fell apart. Then there was that awful scandal, the smuggling and the trial that followed. . . ." She paused, toying for a moment with a beaded fringe that hung from her reticule. "We lost everything: our money, our reputation, our home."

"Did you hate him for it?"

Her shocked gaze flew to Morgan. "My father?"

"Most women would. He owed you more than that."

"No," she replied softly. "No, I didn't hate him."

He searched her face for a moment, as though judging the truth of that statement. Apparently satisfied, or perhaps merely indifferent to the true state of her emotions, he shifted his posture, extending one long arm along the seat back. "So you had just the one night," he said. "One brief night to glory in the wonder of London's exalted society. Tell me about it."

"It was crowded."

"Come now, you can do better than that."

"I don't underst—"

"I've yet to meet a woman—any woman—who hasn't experienced an impassioned epiphany on the eve of her first Season. I believe it's practically a requisite. Surely some dashing Lothario managed to sweep you off your feet and fill your head with dreams of romantic nonsense." Although Julia didn't reply, the blush that heated her cheeks must have been evident, for a triumphant smile curved Morgan's lips. "I thought so."

She looked pointedly away. "It's a silly story."

"Did you fall madly in love?"

Julia considered her reply. Harboring the vague hope that if she opened up a bit to him, he might be coaxed into doing the same thing, she answered honestly, "Yes. Or at least I imagined myself so. For an entire week."

He smiled. "As long as that?"

"An eternity when one is eighteen."

"True. So who was your mysterious Lothario?"

She shook her head. "His name doesn't matter. He was dashing, wealthy, self-assured; a rake and a bounder as well. He moved through the room with an air of utter domination, as though the gala were being held solely for his amusement. At the same time he was utterly captivating. One couldn't help but watch him. You know the kind."

"Pompous, self-indulgent asses, the lot of them."

She smiled. "That was my father's opinion as well. But I thought he was wonderful."

"What happened? Did your eyes meet across the room? Did he shower you with praise for your delicate beauty, claim your every dance, steal you away to a secluded corner for your first real kiss?"

Julia hesitated, debating the depths of her honesty. But as Morgan apparently had no idea they were discussing him, she felt safe in replying, "Not exactly. Our hostess introduced us, but evidently I made little impression upon him. He barely noticed me."

"Foolish man."

"Yes," she replied, regarding him levelly. "Foolish man."

"So that was all it took," he said, his expression registering his disgust. "One brief, meaningless introduction, and you were thoroughly smitten with this strutting ass."

"As was every other woman in the room."

"I believe there's a moral to this tale, isn't there? Something about casting pearls before swine."

"Perhaps."

"You don't sound convinced."

"I'm not." A soft smile curved her lips. "For all his swaggering, there was something magnificent about him, more than just his appearance or his wealth. He seemed to project a kind of inner beauty . . . a nobility that separated him from other men."

"Nobility," he echoed. "I imagine your Lothario would be astonished to find himself thus labeled."

"I imagine he would be."

An unexpected pang of sadness washed over her. Perhaps Morgan had been right in calling it an epiphany of sorts, for on that night everything had seemed possible. She remembered the warmth that had filled the air, her first intoxicating taste of champagne, the gentle flirtations of the men with whom she danced, and the way the soft swishing of the ladies' ball gowns seemed to create a music of their own. She recalled laughing with her parents, and her unwavering conviction that life would go on that way forever. On that magic night the future had held nothing but bright promise.

Lost in her reminiscence, she continued softly. "I saw him in the gardens later that same evening. I stepped outside for a breath of fresh air and found myself meandering down a stone path. I was alone and occupied with my own thoughts—so much so that I paid little attention to my direction. I wandered past a tall hedge and nearly stumbled into him. He was with a beautiful woman. They had no idea that their privacy had been violated. Perhaps it was the wine I had been drinking that rendered me motionless, for I found myself transfixed.

"There was so much beauty and intimacy between them. I remember their soft laughter, their murmured whispers, the way he lightly brushed his body against hers. I watched her defenses melt away as he swept her up in a torrid embrace. It was just as I had always imagined it should be between a man and a woman. I turned away, of course, but the image stayed with me. That night and every night that followed for a week, I found myself lying in bed, wishing that he would come to me. That he would lock me in that same embrace, touch me as he had been touching her, that he would kiss me with all the passion and fervor that he had been kissing her."

Morgan said nothing, but his expression had changed. He regarded her with a look of raw intensity, a light she couldn't define smoldering within the depths of his gray eyes.

Abruptly recalling herself, she shrugged, sending him

a small, embarrassed smile. "I warned you it was a silly story."

"That's the ending?"

"Yes," she said definitively. "That's the ending."

An odd, intimate silence hung between them. Julia once again experienced the discomforting sensation of being too exposed, almost naked to his sight. With nowhere else to look, she directed her attention to the beaded fringe that hung from her reticule. Looking anywhere was better than meeting her husband's eyes at the moment.

At last, unable to bear the silence or the memories any longer, she announced with forced brightness, "Very well, I've confessed. Now it's your turn. Time to plumb your emotional depths. Shallow waters, granted, but let us attempt it nonetheless."

He leaned back into his seat. "This should be entertaining."

"Have you ever been in love?"

His cool, slightly superior smile returned. "I take it you mean with someone other than myself."

"You were once engaged," she pressed, ignoring his sarcasm.

"The lovely Isabelle." His tone was completely flat, devoid of any semblance of emotion.

"She's to be married soon—to Lord Roger Bigelow."

"Indeed. I seem to recall reading that enlightening bit of information in your column. Tucked in between various rantings against the cruelty of the poorhouses."

Refusing to have her temper baited or to be otherwise thrown off track, she persisted. "I imagine they'll be in attendance tonight."

"I imagine so."

In a sudden burst of comprehension, Julia came to a bittersweet understanding. His flat responses weren't mere sarcasm on his part, but a desire to keep his true emotions hidden. Feeling a sudden burst of sympathy, she asked gently, "Will it be very awkward for you to see them?"

His gaze moved over her features for a moment, then he released a short, harsh laugh. "Lord, you are a romantic, aren't you?"

"What do you mean?"

"What are you looking for, princess, heartbroken dejection? Shall I rail against the cruel twist of fate that tore my love from my side? Rue the treachery of my best friend? Will that satisfy you?"

"You misunderstand. I was merely—"

"Prying."

Julia opened her mouth to protest, then abruptly closed it at the dark amusement dancing in Morgan's eyes. So much for her attempt to grow closer to the man she had married. It had been foolish on her part to even think it possible. From all indications it would be easier to scale the gates that circled his estates than to breach the walls of his heart.

Yet even as that cynical thought took root, she couldn't help but feel that her initial instincts about him had been right. There was more to Morgan than what he let on, a depth of emotion that lurked just beneath the surface. Given time, she just might be able to draw that out. Or—more likely—fail miserably in her attempt to do so. The hope that he might one day come to care for her was undoubtedly ridiculous. Despite that knowledge, however, she knew she had no choice but to try. She released a small sigh at her own stubbornness. There was no greater fool than a woman who looked at a man and saw what he might be rather than what he actually was. But nothing died harder than a bad idea.

Their coach, having plodded forward in a series of jolting stops and starts, rumbled to an unmistakable rest. The driver leaped down from his perch above them, let down the stairs, and pulled open the door.

"Perfect," Morgan announced with a smile. "We've arrived."

He stepped down, then turned and held out his hand to assist her in alighting from the coach. Julia took a moment, deliberately keeping him waiting while she went through the elaborate motion of drawing on her gloves, arranging the soft brown kid precisely to her satisfaction. Then she gathered her skirts in one hand and extended her opposite arm, allowing him to assist in her descent. Mingling into the crowds, they moved up the broad stone steps that led to the main entrance.

"Maybe you'll get your wish after all," Morgan said, linking her arm through his. "Perhaps fortune will favor you, and your true love will be here tonight."

"Actually," she replied coolly, "I'm beginning to suspect that's a far better dream than reality."

They entered the estate and moved down a broad hallway toward the grand salon where the gala was being hosted. Candlelight flickered all around them; the sounds of the orchestra drifted out over the hushed footsteps of the guests. Julia discovered that the hall led to a plushly carpeted marble stair that descended gracefully into the ballroom. As they reached that landing, the reason for the long queue they had endured quickly became apparent. Apparently Lord and Lady Winterbourne belonged to the old school and were formally announcing each guest to the assembly, then welcoming their guests in a traditional receiving line at the base of the stair.

As the names Viscount and Viscountess Barlowe rang out, a heavy stillness descended over the room, followed immediately by a shocked murmur of scandalous delight. Julia found herself staring into a sea of upturned faces. The combination of her jittery nerves and overly tight corset had caused her to feel slightly breathless before—now she was positively dizzy. Shooting a glance Morgan's way, she discovered that he was not the least bit rattled by their reception. Instead, just the opposite appeared to be true.

He gazed out over the crowd with an expression of cool superiority, as though he were not only immune to their stares but slightly amused by them as well.

"Look at them," he murmured softly in her ear. "Like sharks in murky water. Circling about in search of a tasty morsel of gossip to sink their teeth into. Shall we oblige them, princess?"

Without waiting for her reply, he slipped his arm through hers and led her down the stairs to greet their hosts. Fortunately her manners did not fail her. Despite her state of anxiety, Julia managed a wooden smile and a graceful curtsy. They moved on, intent on losing themselves in the swirling crowds.

Unfortunately fate, as was lately its habit, chose to amuse itself at their expense. They moved directly into the path of Lord Roger Bigelow and Isabelle Cartwright. The near collision was as unavoidable as it was mutually distressing. The other couple made no attempt to hide their discomfort at the awkward meeting. Their faces mirrored the tension Julia felt when yet another embarrassing silence fell over the crowd, as those nearby strained to catch every word of their exchange.

Morgan was the first to speak. "Isabelle," he said coolly, giving his former fiancée a brief bow. Turning next to the man who had once been his best friend, he greeted him with a curt "Roger." Then he shifted his hand from Julia's arm to the small of her back, gently pressing her near. "I don't believe you've had the pleasure of meeting my wife," he said, graciously performing the introductions.

Roger and Isabelle's gazes immediately fell upon her with looks of undisguised curiosity. Julia experienced a surge of primitive satisfaction in having chosen to wear her best gown. Affecting a serene smile, she moved slightly closer to Morgan in a tacit gesture of both unity and intimacy. Although it was a subtle movement, it didn't go unnoticed. Roger's expression reflected baffled

disbelief, while Isabelle's was one of possessive disapproval.

"You look well, Morgan," said Isabelle, breaking the
stilted silence that had followed the introductions.

"So do you, my dear."

And she did, Julia thought dismally. Lady Isabelle
Cartwright had earned a reputation as a singular beauty,
and it was immediately apparent upon meeting her that
that reputation was not undeserved. Her lush figure was
draped in a gown of midnight blue satin, a shade that
served as a perfect complement to her dark hair and eyes
while bringing out the creamy ivory glow of her complexion. Julia's first thought was to wonder at her husband's
reaction—was he experiencing a flood of nostalgic lust
and longing at the sight of his former lover? As that dis-
heartening thought crossed her mind, she watched in appalled dismay as Isabelle's dark eyes scanned Morgan's
face and neck, undoubtedly searching for scars.

"Looking for something, Isabelle?" Morgan asked
coolly.

An expression of embarrassment crossed Isabelle's
lovely features at having been caught, but she recovered
quickly and gave a throaty laugh. "Morgan. How you do
like to tease."

"Yes. Don't I." Morgan turned to Roger Bigelow.
"My congratulations on your engagement," he said.

Roger nodded. He was a tall, handsome man with
dark blond hair and hazel eyes that emitted no warmth
whatsoever. Looking coolly superior, he pulled Isabelle's
arm through his.

A sardonic smile touched Morgan's lips as he arched
one dark brow. As the swell of the orchestra sounded
behind them, he gave a gracious bow of parting and lifted
Julia's hand. "If you'll pardon us, I promised my bride a
waltz."

He turned and led her away, guiding her directly onto
the dance floor. He pulled her into his arms as the open-

ing strains of a waltz filled the room. They moved silently through the beginning of the dance, each occupied with his or her own thoughts.

After a moment Morgan asked, "Can you feel him here?"

Instantly understanding that he was referring to Lazarus, she lifted her shoulders in a small shrug. "I can't say."

He frowned. "You mentioned yesterday that you could feel his presence."

"That was merely an impression, not a feat of clairvoyance that can be repeated on demand. Besides, it's rather difficult to discern his presence when the entire room is staring at us."

"Ignore them. Look at me."

Exactly what she had been attempting not to do. It was difficult enough to maintain a sense of distance and decorum when Morgan was by her side. But doing that while he held her in his arms was simply impossible. Nevertheless she obeyed his command and lifted her gaze to his. Although he appeared perfectly cool and at ease, that was not the case for her at all. As his eyes locked on hers, a spiral of hot tension coiled through her belly. Her pulse skipped a beat and her heart leaped into her throat. Everything about him overwhelmed her senses. The smell of his skin, the feel of his body swaying against hers, the smoldering intensity of his eyes. It was all too much, she realized, wishing she had left herself some route of escape.

Searching almost desperately for a topic that might relieve some of the sensual tension she felt, she blurted, "So that was Roger Bigelow."

"Yes."

"What is he like?"

"Roger?" Morgan thought for a moment, then replied, "Brash, arrogant, wealthy, self-obsessed, cocky, tasteless, and immature. In short, a pompous ass."

"If your opinion of him is so low, how is it that the two of you were such good friends?"

"I imagine that should be fairly obvious," he returned. "We had so very much in common."

A fleeting smile touched her lips at his reply, but her thoughts were elsewhere. "And what of Isabelle?" she couldn't resist asking. "What is she like?"

Morgan made a *tsk*ing sound with his tongue. "Why should I mourn the loss of Isabelle when I have my lovely bride, the enchanting Julia, to warm my bed at night and heal my deepest sorrows?"

As he already held her hand in his as they danced, it was a simple matter for him to draw it forward and brush his lips against the back of her glove. An innocuous gesture perhaps, but one that was profoundly intimate nonetheless. Julia stiffened and pulled back, instinctively jerking her hand from his grasp.

A light of mocking disdain filled his eyes. "How remiss of me to forget. My bride has made it abundantly clear that she prefers phantom lovers to the embrace of her own husband."

"Very commendable," she replied coolly. "You waited an entire ten minutes before using my confession against me. How trying that must have been for you." Her scorn at his teasing abruptly turned into alarm as Morgan's hand brushed gently over her hip, then proceeded to lightly travel up the small of her back. "What are you doing?" she demanded shrilly.

"Touching you."

"Why?"

"Do I need a reason?" When she didn't reply, he lifted his shoulders in a detached shrug. "I thought the entire point of this exercise was to demonstrate how madly impassioned we are with each other. Difficult to make that impression without engaging in a small, scandalous display of affection, don't you think?"

"Perhaps if we—"

"Do you like that?" he asked, discreetly pressing his legs against hers as they moved in time to the music.

Julia wasn't sure whether she liked it or not. She only knew that the feel of his long, masculine thighs pressed so intimately against her skirts caused her head to spin and her pulse to double its tempo. "What would you have me say?" she stalled.

"The truth, if you please."

She swallowed hard and admitted softly, "I suppose it's not intolerable."

He grinned and bent slightly forward. "Careful," he said, his breath falling in a warm whisper against her neck. "You'll ruin me for certain with such lavish praise."

Julia took a deep breath to gather her wits, then lifted her gaze to meet his. "Why do I suspect this has nothing whatsoever to do with Lazarus?"

"I'm afraid I don't know—"

"Is this a ploy to lure me into your bed?" she boldly asked.

"That depends."

"On what?"

"Whether it's working."

A reluctant smile touched her lips. "Are you always this horrible?"

"Habit, I suppose."

His jesting reply touched off a deep insecurity that Julia hadn't been aware of until that moment. Seducing women was indeed an ingrained habit as far as her husband was concerned. And yet he had acquiesced so easily to her request that they put off their lovemaking until they knew one another better. It suddenly struck her that his consent might have been obtained not out of a wish to please her, but simply because he didn't find her desirable.

Apparently sensing her shift of mood, he asked, "What is it?"

She searched his gaze, then hesitantly replied, "I know why I asked you for three months' time," she said. "But I don't know why you allowed me it."

Morgan studied her in silence for a long moment. Finally he said, "Is it so impossible to believe I'd like to be desired in return, princess? I want an heir, but I also want you to come to me willingly."

On that astonishing note the last strains of the waltz died away. He abruptly released her and stepped backward, concluding the dance with a small, polite bow. As they moved off the dance floor, an acquaintance of Morgan's joined them. After the greetings and introductions were exchanged, the man requested Julia's hand for the next dance. With little choice but to graciously accept his invitation, she left Morgan's side and stepped onto the dance floor with Edward Southesby.

She quickly discovered that her new partner was not only handsome, charming, and intelligent but a perfect gentleman as well. Yet despite her cheery smiles at the harmless bits of gossip they exchanged as they danced, Julia felt distinctly bereft. Something was missing. Edward Southesby, she finally realized, had one distinct, unalterable flaw.

He wasn't Morgan St. James.

Lazarus swallowed hard, barely able to contain his joy. A bead of sweat trickled down his collar as giddy excitement seized him. She was here. Flame. His Flame. She had come. More important, she had touched him. In a gesture of undeniable significance, her arm had brushed against his as they passed each other in the hall. Contact. What exquisite torture.

He had been angry earlier, but now he understood. Of course she had slipped away. She had been waiting for him to come to her once again, to show her his power, his compassion, his faith. But he had let her down, driving her into the arms of another. He had abandoned her for two years so she had sacrificed herself, taking Morgan St. James. The Beast. The man Lazarus had personally punished for his sins. The man Lazarus had forever marked with fire. Surely that was no coincidence.

It all made sense now. It was a game. A sweet, fickle, feminine game. Flame was testing him. She had sacrificed herself in order to get to him. He watched her move through the crowd, a beacon of purity and light within the decadent interior of the grand salon. She paused in mid-step and scanned the room. As her gaze met his, a small, polite smile curved her lips. Then she turned away and continued to survey the room as though she were looking for someone else.

But he knew better. Her look had been deliberate. She was letting him know that she recognized him. He had seen it in her eyes. It was a sign. She was letting him know that she knew what he was thinking. She understood. Together they shared a holy mission to cure London of all its evils. They alone saw the sin that gripped the city. The filth and hopelessness and despair. Tomorrow she would write about it in her column. She would write about this very room: the sanctimonious, fleshy crowd that ate fine food and smoked rich tobacco while the rest of London begged for scraps. She would describe the gluttony, the vanity, the debauchery.

She would write about his cleansing touch.

Lazarus experienced a blazing flash of insight. That was what she wanted. That was the reason she had sought him out. To offer him encouragement. To silently praise his judgment. To let him know that she had not abandoned him after all.

Joy. It swelled up within him, nearly bringing him to his knees. He swayed against the wall in an ecstasy of pure bliss. He felt omnipotent. Soaring. His emotions erupted within him like a wave of pure sexual tension. His nerves tingled, and his heart tripled its rhythm. Breathless desire seized him.

Yes.

It would be his triumph. No one would know but the two of them.

He thought he would explode. Now. It had to be now. Flame was right. A cleansing. The room needed a cleansing. He had to honor her trust. This was not the way he liked to do it. He liked privacy. Hours of meticulous planning. But he had no choice. She was waiting. He scanned the room, looking for just the right place. It had to be beautiful. Worthy of her.

Then he saw it. Near the arched entryway that led from the grand salon into the dining room. A large round table covered with a damask cloth. An artfully arranged bouquet of summer flowers and a pair of sterling silver candlesticks sat atop it. Behind it hung a pair of magnificent floor-to-ceiling drapes, framing a mirror of massive scale in which the dancers were reflected. The candles' blaze was reflected within the mirror. The tiny flames shimmered and danced, leaping and fluttering with incandescent brilliance.

A shiver of delight ran through him. Perfect. So perfect. The room was hot, crowded, engulfed in noisy confusion. It would be worse in a moment. There would be chaos. Pandemonium. Smoke. He crossed the salon, nodding politely to his acquaintances as he moved. Their blank smiles added to his sense of private exhilaration. Amazing that no one knew . . . no one would ever suspect.

At last he reached the table. He casually brushed against it, giving it a deliberate bump with his hip. That was all it took.

The candles wavered. The left stick wobbled and tipped over. It rolled across the surface and plummeted down between the table and the wall, disappearing into the heavy folds of the drapery. Lazarus held his breath, waiting in a state of delicious tension. Had the flame flickered out? Had it betrayed him?

A tiny crimson spark erupted within the rich cloth. A small puff of smoke immediately followed.

Glorious.

Deep satisfaction curled within him as he turned and stepped briskly away.

All for you, my love. All for you.

Chapter 10

Morgan was not by nature a possessive man. Nor was he in the habit of acting like an ass. Tonight, however, he seemed to be making an exception on both counts.

Raw frustration and edginess welled within him. Focus, he thought. What mattered was capturing Lazarus. But his thoughts kept tangling, moving in a grimly repetitive circle of anxiety and unease. He wanted Julia by his side, where he could keep her safe and protected. Unfortunately that defeated their purpose entirely. In the end there was nothing he could do but leave her to mingle about the room in hopes of drawing Lazarus out.

That did not mean that he enjoyed watching her dance with other men. Or watching those men make fools of themselves in an attempt to win her favor. Thus far, however, that summed up the entire dismal course of the evening. Julia talking and laughing, a swirling, shimmering vision in apricot silk. Morgan watching and brooding, waiting for Lazarus to leap out from behind a potted palm like some evil villain in a farcical melodrama.

Dutifully playing his role, he scanned the room and found his bride almost at once. She was deep in conversation with an elderly couple he didn't recognize. She caught his gaze and smiled slightly, then tilted her head, an expression of serene patience on her face as she strove to hear the elderly couple over the din of the crowds and the orchestra.

Momentarily turning his gaze away from her, he pulled a timepiece from his pocket and gave it a cursory glance. Half past midnight. The bell for supper would be rung shortly. They would eat and drink, then the evening would drag on to its merciful conclusion. Had he forgotten how tedious these galas were? Or was this event worse than the others? Impossible to imagine that he had once enjoyed this sort of thing.

The room was stifling. The uncharacteristic heat of the evening was made worse by the crush of bodies and the lack of fresh air. Winterbourne's guests had been arriving in a steady stream all evening. The salon had likely been designed to comfortably accommodate one hundred people, perhaps one hundred and fifty. Morgan glanced around the room and estimated the current capacity to be at least twice that number.

All in all, the party would doubtless be deemed a smashing success. The orchestra was excellent, the room was stunning, the guests included the best names in all of London society, and the wine and spirits were generously dispensed in an effort to compensate for the heat. To that end Morgan noted that quite a few of the company seemed to be overindulging in the libations, turning the already overheated crowd somewhat rowdy and edgy. But that hardly presented a hazard at present. There would be ample time to pay for their overindulgence tomorrow morning, when they awoke clutching their heads in misery.

He returned his attention to Julia. She had left the elderly couple and stood surrounded by her aunt, uncle, and cousins. Other than her obvious discomfort at being cornered by her relatives, she was fine. As a change of pace, Morgan decided to do something gallant and rescue her from her predicament.

Before doing so, however, he scanned the crowd one last time. His gaze fell on a little girl of perhaps six, trying and failing to stifle a yawn as she moved through the crowd carrying a tray of canapés. She wore a ridiculously formal emerald green gown; her curly blond hair—elaborately swept up earlier—now fell about her shoulders in weary disarray. The child was part of a passing fad, but one that was currently all the rage. Beautiful, impoverished children dressed in rich clothing who assisted the servants, almost as though they were part of the decor. There were a dozen boys and girls like her in the room, all wilting with the heat and noise and lateness of the hour.

While Morgan watched, a glob of hot wax dripped down from the candelabra above her and fell on her sleeve. The little girl issued a cry of alarm and jumped to the side. If the candle itself had fallen, catching the long train of her gown . . .

As that grim thought took root in his mind, a flash of flame appeared just over the child's head.

Morgan froze, unable to move. The moment seemed to stretch out forever. He knew with stark, gut-wrenching certainty it was all happening again. The little girl. The flame.

So quickly. It happened so quickly.

His pulse leaped to his throat as his muscles tensed in readiness. A split second before he lunged forward to grab the child a second movement caught his eye. The motion of a man's dark sleeve reflected within a glass pane just above the little girl's head. A man was standing on the terrace outside the grand salon. He had struck a match and lifted it to the tip of his cigar. What Morgan had witnessed was a reflection of the flame within the glass. That was all. Nothing more. Nothing dramatic. Merely an illusion. A trick of the eye.

Morgan swallowed hard, clenching his fist around the glass he held. Lifting the brandy to his lips, he took a deep swallow. Unfortunately the drink did little to steady his nerves. The fleeting image of the little girl and the flame had left him shaking, drenched in a cold sweat. As he turned away, the man he had seen lighting the cigar waved to catch his eye. Morgan recognized Joseph Perryman. Seizing the excuse for a temporary respite, he managed a tight smile in return and left the room, stepping outside to join his friend.

Julia scanned the room once again for Morgan. She wasn't desperately in need of her husband's presence as much as she was desperate to be extricated from her present situation: keeping company with Marianne and Theresa. It wasn't that she disliked her cousins. She simply had nothing in common with them. They were both completely feminine—in a manner she found completely annoying. At the moment they were engaged in a pastime they clearly found to be of the utmost enjoyment—issuing scathing critiques of the other guests' ball gowns.

"Did you *see* Lady Vackerby?" Marianne inquired in a hushed whisper, leaning forward in conspiratorial delight as she cast a sly glance at the woman whose gown had so deeply offended her sensibilities. "I mean, really. *Purple* lace? And she hasn't even the dignity to—"

A shrill scream pierced the echoing din of laughter and conversation that filled the grand salon.

Marianne paused abruptly.

A second scream followed the first.

A shocked, quizzical hush fell over the salon at the unprecedented disturbance. The orchestra paused, as did the guests who filled the crowded dance floor. Heads turned. An eerie, unnatural silence hung over the assembly. Then an audible gasp echoed through the chamber as horrified understanding set in.

Julia's gaze shot to a twisting, hissing wall of flame that licked up the damask draperies near the room's main entry. Within seconds the cloth covering the adjacent table simmered and writhed, catching flame as well.

For what seemed an infinitely long moment—although it was probably no more than a fraction of a second—a frozen stillness seemed to hold everyone in place.

Then pandemonium broke out. Cries of *fire!* mixed with shrill screams of terror. A few lone guests called for buckets of water as they bravely raced toward the flame, swatting at it with whatever was near to hand. The vast majority, however, surged toward the doors that led to the terrace, the salon's only other exit. A panicked tumult of pushing and shoving instantly engulfed the room.

With a great roar and a hiss, the tall swath of flaming drapery abruptly tore away from the rod on which it hung and fell to the floor, collapsing on top of the men and women who had attempted to flee through the main entrance.

What had been an anxious crowd disintegrated into a outbreak of mob hysteria. Screams flooded the room. One moment Marianne and Theresa were standing before her, the next they were gone, whisked away in the tumult. Julia stood frozen, unsure what to do. She desperately scanned the salon for Morgan, somehow confident that he could bring order to the melee. No sooner had that thought seized her when she was struck by another. Should she look for Lazarus? If he was behind this, surely he remained nearby. Unfortunately the moment of indecision cost her. She felt a hard blow knock her from behind, nearly driving her to her knees.

She quickly regained her balance, and in the next moment she was moving—but not of her own free will. She found herself carried away by the same desperate tide that had seized her cousins. Her feet were swept out from under her as she was dragged forward by the violent current of bodies streaming through the room. Julia fought to break free from the mob, but she had no control over the direction in which she was moving. It was all she could do to stay abreast of the chaos.

The woman beside her gave a shriek of terror, then fell and disappeared beneath the teeming throng. Horror clogged Julia's throat as she tried to reach for her, but her arms were pinned against her sides. There was nothing she could do. She was trapped, totally engulfed by the mob. Panic began to seize her. The crowd was rushing toward a series of four narrow glass doors that led to the terrace—narrow doors that couldn't possibly accommodate the thick swell of bodies.

Heat and smoke filled the room. The sound of shattering glass rose above the cries and wails of the mob. She watched as the terrace doors rushed toward her. Then the momentum of the crowd abruptly shifted. Terror seized Julia as she realized that she was about to be, not unceremoniously flung through a door, but crushed against a section of wall that separated the wooden door frames instead.

She tried to move, but her body, held captive by the stampeding masses, refused to obey. It was all she could do to turn her head, taking the blow to her temple rather than her face. For a moment she feared her knees were going to buckle beneath her. But somehow she managed to remain upright. She felt the crowd weaken behind her, then surge forward even more forcefully, as though attempting to use her as a battering ram to break through the wall itself.

The mob pressed against her, squeezing the breath from her lungs. No matter how desperately she tried, she couldn't gulp in enough air. Hysteria wrapped around her throat, further constricting her breath. Her heart raced, her pulse drummed in her ears. Smoke billowed through the room.

Then the crowd surged forward once again.

She slammed against the wall. Weakness seeped through her limbs. There was no more fight left in her. She felt bruised and broken, dizzy from the effort required to remain conscious.

Hysteria faded to acceptance. Her limbs relaxed as a state of mild euphoria seized her. From lack of oxygen? she wondered. It didn't matter, she realized, letting the thought go. She was floating now, and she felt wonderful.

As her eyes fluttered shut, she caught a glimpse of a dark-haired man who looked remarkably like Morgan. He was fighting his way through the crowd, an intense expression on his face. Coming to rescue her, she thought. A nice fantasy, but one she knew wasn't real. Just an image her mind was conjuring up. Nevertheless, her dark rescuer did possess a fierce kind of beauty. There was something magnificent about him . . . something noble. . . .

The thought brought a soft smile to her face.

The mob shoved against her once again. Julia hit the wall hard. Her legs buckled as her body at last gave way, slipping beneath the crowd.

$\mathcal{M}$organ stood at the window of Julia's bedchamber. It would be another blistering day, he thought. Although just midmorning, heat already filled the air, casting a thick, yellow haze over the city. If he looked intently enough, he imagined he could see remnants of smoke from last night's conflagration. Was it dull shadows he saw in the distance, or soft flakes of gray ash clinging to the rooftops and tree limbs?

The sound of gentle rustling of bedsheets prevented him from pursuing the question further. He turned immediately, his gaze moving toward his wife's bed. She studied the room in cloudy confusion, as though attempting to get her bearings. As her gaze locked on his, understanding seemed to set in, for her expression instantly sobered.

Releasing a soft sigh, she said flatly, "You're frowning at me."

Was he? Evidently the relief he felt at seeing her awake was not as apparent as he assumed. Lifting his shoulders in a light shrug, he replied simply, "My apologies. I'm not accustomed to seeing bruises on your face."

She raised a hand and gently probed her swollen left temple. "I must look a sight."

He ignored that. "How do you feel?"

She shifted experimentally and grimaced. "As though my body were used as a battering ram to break through a wall."

"So you do remember what happened." Morgan crossed the room and lifted a small vial of amber liquid from the nightstand near her bed. "If the pain is very bad, I have a sedative—"

"No," she said, waving it away. As she glanced down at herself and saw that she was attired in her nightgown, a subtle blush crept over her cheeks. She focused on sitting up. Morgan leaned forward to assist her, seizing a plump pillow and propping it against the headboard to make her more comfortable.

"Dr. Hammill was here to see you last night," he said. "Fortunately, you don't have any permanent injuries. Apparently the bone stays in your corset offered some protection; your ribs are bruised but not broken." He paused, shaking his head. "How do women breathe in those contraptions? It boggles the mind."

"The male mind, perhaps, not the female one. When it comes to the latest fashion, breathing is secondary to looking shapely."

"You don't need it."

She shrugged. "I'm not entirely vain, merely practical. My gowns won't fit without one."

"Then we'll order you new gowns."

Julia went silent. A deep frown marred her brow as she toyed with the lace edge of her sheet. She took a deep breath, as though bracing herself for the worst. Then she looked up at him. Studying his face intently, she asked, "How many?"

He knew instantly that she was referring not to the number of gowns she could expect but to the number of people who had been injured in last night's fire. He let out a sigh and reached for a chair. The piece was delicate and fragile, made to match the suite of feminine furniture that filled the room. He turned the chair around and straddled it, resting one arm across the embroidered back as he met her eyes.

"Seven injured, including you," he replied directly. "One fairly badly—a Mrs. Edgar Addison. Like most everyone, her injuries were a direct result, not of the fire, but of the pandemonium that ensued. Apparently she fell and was trampled beneath the crowd. She suffered several broken ribs and a broken collarbone, as well as numerous bumps and bruises."

Julia nodded. "I think I saw her. The train of her gown was caught, and she was pulled under. I tried to reach her, but I couldn't move. My arms were pinned against my sides." She stopped abruptly, giving a slight shudder. "What about the children who were in the room?"

"One little boy suffered a broken wrist. The rest were unharmed," he assured her quickly. "Some were lifted bodily and carried from the room by whoever was near, the rest managed to dart out through a side door. The servants' exits to the kitchens were overlooked completely. Everyone attempted to herd through the narrow doors that led to the terrace."

"There was no way to avoid it. There was so much smoke and confusion, so much panic and shoving. It was like being caught in the most sinister of currents. If only people had remained calm. Then there might have been time—"

"I don't know how you could have avoided panic," he interrupted. "From what I heard, the fire was both abrupt and terrifying."

She frowned. "You didn't see it?"

"Not at first. I was on the terrace speaking with a friend when the flames erupted."

"But you went back inside."

For a moment he wondered if she remembered seeing him fight his way through the mob for her. But before he could suggest as much, her gaze moved slowly over his clothing. A mirror hung on the wall opposite her bed. Glancing into it, Morgan experienced a shock. He knew he hadn't yet bothered to bathe, but he had not been aware just how dreadful his appearance really was. Flakes of filmy ash clung to his skin and hair. His white linen shirt was coated with streaks of grimy black soot. A long, narrow slash split the side of his trousers nearly in two.

"You look as though you tried to extinguish the flames single-handedly," she remarked.

He grinned. "Or like a chimney sweep."

A whisper of a smile crossed Julia's face at his jest, but it vanished as quickly as it had come. "Lazarus?" she asked.

He released a dark sigh. "Possibly. I don't know. The servants remember placing two candlesticks on the table where the fire began. An accidental bump could have knocked one over and started the fire." He paused, shrugging. "It was hot and crowded in the room, and many of the guests had been drinking excessively. A careless stagger would have been enough to start the inferno."

Although she nodded in agreement, she didn't appear any more convinced than he was. "It just seems . . ."

"A bit too coincidental?" he supplied.

"Yes. Particularly in light of the fact that you and I were both in attendance."

"Overstating our importance a bit, is it not?"

"Then there's the matter of Lazarus's letter," she continued stubbornly. "What were his exact words?"

" 'When I have assembled you, I will blast you with the heat of my anger and smelt you with it,' " he supplied, having already reread the letter numerous times since their return from the Winterbournes' gala.

Her eyes shone with victory. "There. You see? *When I have assembled you.* Clearly he's referring to a grand ball or a large assembly."

"Or when he has assembled you and me," Morgan countered. "Difficult to remember that we are dealing with someone who isn't at all sane. We can't apply our own standards of rationality to his dealings. There is also the fact that the fire was not begun in his usual manner. His earlier acts were always performed in secrecy, usually in the early morning hours, when the chances of his being discovered were practically nonexistent."

Julia let out a sigh. The victory he had seen in her eyes a moment before turned to an expression of utter frustration. "So what have we learned after the events of last night? Either the fire was coincidental or it wasn't. Either Lazarus was there or he wasn't. Furthermore, if he was there, he may or may not have had a hand in setting the fire. This entire disastrous episode could have been accidental."

"I'm afraid so."

Their conversation came to a lull. Unable to stop himself, his gaze moved slowly over Julia as though drawn there by some irresistible force. Sitting with her linens gathered about her waist in messy disarray, her fiery hair cascading down her shoulders, and her prim nightgown buttoned up to her throat, she looked unbearably fragile and delicate, lost in the enormity of her bed.

Morgan had always viewed women in a sexual way. But the impulse he experienced at that moment was decidedly asexual in nature. He wanted to climb into bed with Julia and do something positively ridiculous: gather her into his arms and cuddle her against him until they both fell asleep. It must be his own exhaustion that was twisting his thoughts, he rationalized. Whatever its cause, the urge was as unwelcome as it was unexpected, for it set off a silent alarm in his mind. A warning of sorts, but of a different kind of danger. His control was slipping away.

Forcing his thoughts back to the events of last night, he said, "When the fire first broke out, I saw you standing alone amidst the pandemonium, almost as though frozen."

"True," she admitted with a rueful smile. "But not by fear."

"Oh?"

She lifted her shoulders in a light shrug. "I didn't know whether to look for you or to begin immediately hunting for Lazarus. It seemed as though I should have been doing *something*, I just didn't know what that something was."

"I see," he replied. "In that case, might I offer a suggestion in the event that you ever find yourself again in a room that is engulfed by flame?"

"Yes?"

"Get out."

A soft smile curved her lips. "We keep coming back to this, don't we? You keep attempting to order me about."

"Consider it my husbandly duty."

"Indeed? Remarkable that I've survived at all without your divine guidance and inspiration. You forget that I've managed perfectly well without you all these years."

"It is exactly that sort of brash defiance that landed you here."

"Thus far it has worked out tolerably well."

He arched one dark brow. "Tolerably well, is it? Being assaulted at knifepoint, victimized by fire, crushed beneath a frenzied crowd. Then there is your lecherous

groom to contend with . . ." He threw the last out before he could stop himself, and immediately regretted his
words. Yet something within him couldn't resist testing
the waters, foolishly attempting to glean an idea of what
his wife thought of him.

"Yes," she said, "there is that, isn't there?" Her gaze
moved over his face, then her lips curved in a small, unfathomable smile. Reaching out, she lightly brushed her
fingers across his cheek. "The Beast."

Her soft touch sent a shiver racing down his spine,
throwing his emotions into a tumult of confusion. Initially
nothing had mattered to him but finding Lazarus. But last
night had changed everything. The panic he had felt at
witnessing Julia nearly trampled to death beneath the
thundering hordes was with him still. What if he hadn't
reached her in time? The thought was unbearable.

"We don't have to continue," he said.

"No, we don't." Reading his thoughts with amazing
accuracy, she continued. "It seems to me that in any venture one reaches a point of reckoning. It is so simple in
the beginning to say that we will use everything at our
disposal, whatever the cost, to go after Lazarus. It is something altogether different once we experience the fruits of
that intent. Then we must weigh the risks and decide if it
is worthwhile to continue."

"There is no shame in choosing a different path."

She hesitated for a moment, then said, "There are
times when I'm writing my column when I wonder if my
words have any effect at all. When I wonder if I shouldn't
just abandon my work completely. But there is one fundamental truth that makes me continue, that gives me a
sense of solace and certainty."

"And that is?"

"Good will triumph over evil. Right will overcome
wrong."

Not in the world Morgan knew. In fact, the utter
naïveté of her words brought a smile of disbelief to his

lips. He didn't consider himself a cynic, just a realist. Life held no place for purity or justice. One fought through a series of petty vengeances, harsh sufferings, and bitter animosities, and then one died. That was all. There was far more darkness than light, and pretending otherwise didn't change that fact.

Fortunately the sound of a minor commotion downstairs spared him the necessity of a reply.

Julia frowned at him. "Were you expecting company?"

Morgan stood. "No, I wasn't," he began, when a soft knock on the door interrupted him. "Enter," he called.

A young housemaid inched open the door and stepped inside. "A Mr. Chivers of Scotland Yard requests an audience, my lord. With both you and Lady Barlowe, if she is well enough to see him."

"You may inform him that she is indisposed at present—"

"No," Julia said, cutting him off. "I'd rather you wouldn't."

Morgan hesitated, studying her with grave misgivings. "Are you well enough to be up and about?"

"Quite," she returned decisively. "I suspect I'm suffering more from the effects of the laudanum than from any injuries. In fact, I'm certain I shall feel much better if I bathe and dress, rather than lie about in bed all day."

"Very well." Deciding not to challenge that, he turned instead to the housemaid and said, "Show Mr. Chivers into the west parlor. Lady Barlowe and I will be down shortly. And inform Mary . . ." He paused, turning to Julia. "Mary is your lady's maid, is she not?" At her nod he continued. "Inform Mary that her mistress is in need of her services."

"Yes, my lord." The maid gave a quick curtsy and left.

He turned back to find Julia watching him with an air of distinct amusement.

"You're very good at that," she said.

He arched one dark brow, picking up on her light-ened mood. "At what?"

"Giving orders."

He crossed to the door, pausing at the threshold. "Remarkably enough, they're generally obeyed. By every-one but my wife, that is."

On that note he softly closed the door behind him and went to his own chamber to bathe and dress. A few minutes later he made his way downstairs. Morgan had met the Home Secretary before, but that was two years earlier, shortly after the fire that had occurred on his property. But evidently that laudanum-sated, pain-wracked state had blurred both his perception and his memory. He had a vague recollection of an elderly man with a large build and long-suffering temperament. In-stead he found a man not much older than himself. Mr. Chivers was short and dark, small in stature, and dressed in a fastidious manner that reminded Morgan of his secre-tary, Lionel Oakes. He sat with a cup of steaming tea balanced on his thighs, his dark eyes moving about the parlor as though absorbing every detail.

Upon hearing Morgan's arrival, Chivers set aside his tea and came to his feet. "Lord Barlowe. Good of you to see me," he said briskly. "I received Lady Barlowe's note and thought it best if I reply in person. If my timing is poor, however—"

"Not at all," Morgan replied. He moved to the side-board and poured himself a cup of tea, then assumed a seat across from Chivers.

Dispensing quickly with the requisite pleasantries, they moved immediately into a discussion of the events that had occurred prior to last night's fire. Although the Home Secretary took no notes, he interrupted from time to time with piercing questions that served to demonstrate his keen intellect and nimble grasp of the situation.

"So there have been no other—" Chivers began, then

halted abruptly at the sound of softly rustling skirts coming from the doorway. Both men rose as Julia stepped forward.

"Lady Barlowe." Chivers gave a formal bow. "I heard you were indisposed, but the grave nature of events prompted me to come at once. I hope you can forgive my intrusion."

"As you can see, I'm perfectly well," Julia assured him. Much to Morgan's relief, she did look markedly better than she had earlier. She was dressed in a gown of pale cream muslin, her hair pulled back in a thick braid. Despite the simplicity of her attire, there was an artless freshness about her that immediately brightened the room.

"In your absence," Morgan said once she was seated, "I've taken the liberty of showing Mr. Chivers the letter you received and apprising him of the events to date."

Julia grimaced. "After Lord Webster's fire," she said to Chivers, "I had hoped that we had heard the last of Lazarus."

"As had I. But from what your husband tells me, that does not appear to be the case." He thought for a minute, then asked, "At last night's gala, did you receive any sign, any indication at all that you might have been dealing with Lazarus? Did anyone seem angry or overly attentive? Did anything occur that struck you as odd?"

"No," she replied after a moment's reflection. "Nothing seemed amiss until the fire itself."

"Very well." Chivers gave a brisk nod. "In that case let us examine what we do know of the man. Perhaps there is something we've overlooked."

"Lazarus," she said. "Surely the name itself has some special significance."

"Obviously he sees himself as someone who has risen from the dead," Morgan said. "I doubt he means it physically, for the man I chased was in solid form. But that could be significant of his standing in society. Perhaps he has been ostracized by his peers, and this is his way of extracting revenge."

"I would say there's even more to it than that," remarked Chivers. "Lazarus seems determined to purify society of what he perceives to be its sins—and to punish the sinners as well. Hence his fascination with Lady Barlowe and her column. He perceives himself as an instrument of justice."

"That was my thinking as well," Julia concurred. "He feels wronged, angry—" She paused abruptly, looking at Morgan. "By the way, do you see any connection between yourself and Lazarus's other victims?"

"No. I have a nodding acquaintance with the Earl of Chilton and Lord Webster, but that's all. We've never been involved in the same business venture, nor have we enjoyed a particular friendship. We differ in age, marital status, wealth, and political views. Other than the fact that we are all members of the peerage, I can find nothing—sinful or otherwise—that connects us directly."

Mr. Chivers delicately cleared his throat. "I believe I may be of some assistance there."

Morgan regarded the man curiously. "Oh?"

"The Earl of Chilton was a notorious gambler. I'm told he was particularly fond of betting on his own horses. Hence the fact that it was his stables that Lazarus chose to set aflame."

"What of Lord Webster?" Julia asked. "Why would Lazarus want to destroy his library? Surely there is no sin in collecting books."

At the expression of obvious discomfort on Chivers's face, a flash of understanding struck Morgan. "Of course," he said, astounded he had not considered it himself until that moment. Sparing the Home Secretary the embarrassment of answering, he said to Julia, "Lord Webster was not entirely satisfied with his collection of classic literature, plays, and philosophy. He was also known to possess one of the finest libraries of rare erotica in all of London."

"I see," Julia replied, a soft blush coloring her cheeks.

Returning his attention to Chivers, Morgan said, "And what was my great sin? Too many servants?"

"Not precisely, Lord Barlowe." Chivers hesitated, studying his tea with a diplomatic and practiced pause. Finally, he lifted his head and coolly met his gaze. "Women. You were known as quite the rake, as I recall. It is my opinion that Lazarus timed the fire so that you would personally discover it, counting on you to act exactly as you did—rushing headlong into the blaze to warn others of the danger. In disfiguring you, Lazarus tried to take away your ability to find another woman."

"As I recall, I was engaged at the time."

"Apparently he felt your attachment was of a rather superficial and fleeting nature."

"How very perceptive of him," Morgan returned dryly. "Lazarus may not be lucid, but let us give the man due credit for his discernment."

"So where does this leave us now?" Julia asked.

"I see no reason to alter the strategy you and Lord Barlowe have employed to date," said Chivers. "When does your next column appear?"

"Friday. I've already sent it to Mr. Randolph for submission to the *Review*."

"Do you have time to make revisions?"

She frowned. "I suppose so, unless the presses have been set. What did you have in mind?"

"Lazarus has formed the habit of using your column as a means to communicate with you. Would you be adverse to using your column to reply to him?"

Julia considered the question. "Yes," she replied thoughtfully, "I see what you mean." She exchanged a questioning glance with Morgan, then rose and moved to a corner desk where she retrieved a pen, ink, and sheet of

parchment. She penned a few lines, then passed the sheet
to Morgan. He lifted it and read,

> Disaster was narrowly averted at the densely
> crowded gala of Lord and Lady Winterbourne
> when an overturned candle sparked an inferno in
> the grand salon. The Tattler sends his sincerest
> wishes for a speedy recovery to those injured in the
> blaze.

A space, followed by brief editorial instructions, then:

> Lazarus,
> Was that you?
> Flame

Nothing more. Just a simple question. One that would
likely mean nothing to anyone but Lazarus himself. In
addition it was cunningly open to interpretation. Lazarus
could read fear into the question if he so desired, or admiration, or breathless appreciation, or any number of other
emotions. But most importantly, it reinforced the intimacy
between them, issuing an open invitation for the man to
establish contact with Julia once again.

Morgan gave a curt nod and passed the note to
Chivers. The strategy was contrary to every instinct he
possessed—using his wife as bait in the attempt to lure a
madman. But short of passively waiting for the next fire
and hoping to catch Lazarus in the act, it was their only
logical move. Silently acknowledging that grim but unalterable fact, he held his tongue, watching as the Home
Secretary read the missive and beamed at Julia in delight.

"Very good," Chivers said. "Very good, indeed. It just
may work. If you'll give me direction to your man, Mr.
Randolph, I'll see to it that this is personally delivered."

Once Julia had done so, the interview came to a brisk
conclusion. Morgan rose and walked Chivers to the door.

As they stepped outside, Morgan found himself surprised by the man once again. He had expected to see a hired hackney waiting. Instead the Home Secretary had chosen to ride. A high-spirited stallion paced to and fro in the shade of the towering oak to which he was tethered. The odd contrast of a small man on such a large horse was forgotten once Chivers assumed the saddle and gathered the reins in his hands, controlling his mount with considerable mastery.

"A beautiful animal," Morgan remarked, absently stroking the stallion's neck.

Chivers smiled. "You look as though you have more on your mind than the quality of my mount, Lord Barlowe."

Morgan smiled as well. "Very perceptive of you."

Yet still he hesitated before speaking. In reviewing the events of last night, his mind kept returning to one man in particular. Although there had been nothing specific in his behavior at the Winterbournes' gala to arouse suspicion, he had appeared distinctly disapproving and out of place, almost pained by the gaiety surrounding him. While that could be attributed to nothing more than his naturally sullen character, Morgan found him deeply disturbing nonetheless. Furthermore, he fit every criterion they had employed to describe Lazarus—from his proximity to Julia to his resentment of society and its perceived sins.

"I didn't want to speak of this in front of my wife," he said. "But I believe Lazarus may be closer to us than we suspect."

"I see." Chivers regarded him intently, then gave a curt nod. "If you like, I'll have my men undertake an investigation immediately."

"I think that may be wise."

"His name?"

"Sir Cyrus Prentisse."

Chapter 11

Julia lifted a copy of the *London Review* from the sterling silver tray on which it had been placed for Morgan's perusal. She noted as she did that the paper was still warm. A faint smile touched her lips as she marveled at the efficiency of Morgan's staff. The floors sparkled, the tabletops were immaculately free of dust, and the windows gleamed in streakless perfection. The feather pillows on the sofas were plumped into neat squares, the bed linens laundered daily.

It wasn't merely the impeccable housekeeping that impressed her, but the smaller niceties as well. Every whim was totally catered to. The day's papers were crisply pressed each morning to prevent the smearing of ink on one's hands. Her shoes and boots were polished after each wearing. A garment with a loose button was instantly mended and returned to her wardrobe before she could ask for a needle and thread. Crystal vases brimming with fresh flowers filled every room. Glancing at the sideboard in the morning room, she found a pot of steaming tea, warm scones, and fresh butter and jam waiting for her enjoyment—all presented, of course, on delicate bone china.

Julia let out a sigh and sank into a small settee that had been richly upholstered in pale pink, watching the sun stream through the room's leaded-glass windowpanes. Now that she had fully recovered from the injuries she had sustained at the Winterbourne gala, she felt decadently pampered and utterly useless. Exactly what, she wondered in frustration, did a lady of leisure do with herself all day? She had already prepared her column for next week, and she had no chores or marketing to keep her busy. She momentarily contemplated pouring herself a cup of tea and working on a needlepoint sampler she had begun over a year ago, but she had never managed to generate more than a tepid interest in the project. It held even less appeal at the moment.

Bored and restless, she decided to seek out Morgan's company. From the window of her bedchamber, she had seen him return from his morning ride, but he had not yet made his appearance for breakfast. As he seemed to spend the majority of his free time locked away in his study, she began her search there. Tucking the fresh copy of the *Review* under her arm, she moved down the hall and rapped softly on his paneled oak door. At the silence that greeted her from within, she edged open the door and peeked inside.

The room was empty. Curious, she stepped inside. The study was appointed with heavy masculine furnishings and dark mahogany tables and chairs. Floor-to-ceiling bookcases lined one entire wall. Exquisite oil seascapes filled another. Burgundy, navy, and hunter green rugs covered the floors. Rich tapestry drapery flanked the windows.

But what caught Julia's attention even more than the decor was the absolute orderliness of the space. The book spines were alphabetically arranged by author. Assorted busts of various ancient Greek philosophers all faced due north. Moving to Morgan's desk, she placed her hands on his leather chair and was immediately rewarded with the scent of his skin. His presence was everywhere. The slim piles of papers on his desk were arranged just so, with the corners at neat ninety-degree angles. His pen and inkwell were perfectly aligned, his drawers shut and locked. A small smile touched her lips. While she considered herself tidy, her habits clearly paled in comparison.

Leaving his study undisturbed, she wandered down the plushly carpeted halls, moving from empty room to empty room. She smiled politely at the servants she encountered but refrained from asking if they knew of Morgan's whereabouts. Although it was probably nothing but her own insecurities fueling her reservations, there seemed something vaguely pathetic about a bored and lonely wife searching for her husband.

She passed a long hallway that led to a massive salon. She had been inside only once, but she remembered the interior well. Designed for grand receptions, the room boasted ornate plaster ceilings, intricate moldings, gilded mirrors, glittering chandeliers, gleaming mahogany floors, and a podium large enough to accommodate a full orchestra. Certain she would find it empty, Julia began to move past the salon when the discordant sound of metal striking metal echoed out to her.

Swordplay? Impossible, she thought with a frown, moving cautiously toward the room. The sound grew louder, even more intense. Her curiosity piqued, Julia drew open the doors and quietly slipped inside. She found two fencers, their concentration locked on the duel in which they were engaged. Each man wore the gloves, mask, padded jacket, and white breeches the sport required. They were nearly identical in height and build. Nevertheless she had no trouble identifying her husband.

Each duelist was clearly a master at the sport. She

watched them advance and retreat across the grand ballroom in a riveting spectacle of swordsmanship. She had heard that it was impossible to hide one's temperament and personality when fencing. That once behind a weapon, a fencer will reveal his character, his mental capacities, his very essence. As she witnessed the sharp clash between the two men, she recognized the truth in that.

The man she didn't recognize fought with a technical expertise that was stunning to watch. His every movement was carried out with orchestrated precision: a thrust and lunge, a deft feint, then a straight attack. Powerful, impressive moves, executed with grace and finesse. But Morgan's swordplay was even more breathtaking. In a style that was highly erratic, he moved before his opponent like a caged animal, coolly deflecting the other man's blows. He toyed with his partner with an almost teasing playfulness, then lunged forward in an attack of disturbing ferocity.

Back and forth the two men swayed, locked in an intricate dance of clashing steel. At last the mesmerizing play came to an end. Morgan executed a flawless counterriposte, resulting in a lightning-quick flash of sword and a satisfying *tick-tack* of metal. Not about to lose the momentum of his attack, he lunged forward and lightly stuck his opponent just above his heart, scoring what was evidently the last point of the match.

Breathing hard, both men drew back and pulled off their masks. Morgan shared a few words with his fencing partner. Although she couldn't hear what was said, a burst of good-natured laughter immediately followed. Julia was shocked to realize that that was the first time she had seen Morgan truly laugh. She had become accustomed to his sardonic grin, his blatantly seductive smile, and even the look of cynical amusement he sometimes wore when they were together. But this was a smile of pure enjoyment, a flash of brilliant white teeth against the rugged bronze of his skin. An expression that instantly seared itself into her mind and her heart. For a moment Morgan St. James hadn't changed at all. He was the same dashing, carefree rogue she had seen in a moonlit garden years ago.

But the smile vanished as soon as he turned and saw her. He stiffened slightly as a look of guarded surprise fell over his features. His partner murmured something— likely a word or two of parting, for he immediately moved away, giving Julia a polite nod as he exited past her.

Feeling like a henpecking wife, she said to Morgan as he approached, "I didn't mean to disturb you."

He shook his head. "We were just finishing."

"For a man who is rumored to be so reclusive, you're rarely here."

"I'm here, merely occupied."

"So I see," she replied softly, wondering if that was meant to be a subtle admonition for her not to bother him. Was there a curtness in his voice, or had her own guilt at intruding caused her to imagine it? As usual where he was concerned, her emotions were far too near the surface for her to trust her perceptions.

Putting the matter aside for the moment, she watched as he stepped toward a small table with two chairs—the only furniture in the massive room—and tossed his fencing mask upon it. His glove, padded jacket, and sword quickly followed. Once he had stripped himself of his gear, he reached for a tall silver tumbler and took a long draught. Julia heard the ice clinking within the glass and saw the frosty droplets drip down the side. He drank in deep, thirsty gulps, his head tilted back, managing to convey a masculine elegance in even that simple motion. But then she seemed to find something smoothly attractive in everything he did, no matter how commonplace the gesture.

"Your life is so very scheduled," she said lightly, determined to force her thoughts in a different direction. "A daily ride. Monday morning business affairs with your secretary. Tuesday morning burning of refuse. Wednesday morning fencing lessons. What do you schedule for Thursday mornings?"

He lowered his tumbler and studied her with an unfathomable smoky gaze. His face was slightly flushed from the exertion of fencing, his body was damp with perspiration. The fabric of his fencing garments clung to his skin. Unable to draw her eyes away, her gaze moved slowly over his form. His broad chest and flat stomach were boldly defined, as was the raw strength in the bulging biceps of his arms. His waist and hips were sleek and narrow. His legs were long, his thighs rock solid.

"What would you suggest?" he asked.

Make love to your wife. The thought popped into her mind before she could stop it. She immediately pushed it away, feeling as flushed and warm as if she had spoken aloud. It was all Morgan's doing, she decided. Something about his gaze caused shamefully wanton thoughts to leap into her mind. Something about his presence caused a room as vast as the one in which they stood to feel shockingly intimate. Then there was the scent of his skin—

Enough, she thought firmly. She turned away, almost desperate for something—anything—to engage her attention. Spying his sword lying atop the table, she lifted it in her palm, idly testing its weight. Turning toward an imaginary opponent, she stabbed and slashed the air.

He watched as she executed a clumsy parry. "You enjoy fencing?" he asked.

"My father was fond of the sport," she said. "We attended the exhibitions at Vauxhall Gardens every year." She attempted the parry again, amazed at how foreign and awkward the motion felt. It had looked ridiculously simple when Morgan had performed the identical maneuver.

After a moment he reached for the sword and gently removed it from her grasp. "A bit redundant, don't you think, princess? You're dangerous enough without a weapon in your hands."

A small, fluttery smile touched her lips. She searched

for a witty retort, but she was too conscious of the feel of his fingers brushing hers as he removed the sword from her hand for her mind to properly function. Although she considered herself logical and rational, her thoughts seemed to tumble in flustered disorder whenever he was near.

"Anything wrong?" he inquired.

"No. I'm merely bored."

"In that case why don't you do what all other women do when they find themselves at loose ends."

"What's that?"

"Spend their husbands' money. I understand a French seamstress recently opened a shop on Bond Street. Apparently she's all the rage."

Julia frowned. "Expensive as well."

"I can afford it."

"Evidently."

He arched one dark brow and said with a smile, "Do I detect a note of dissatisfaction in your reply?"

She shrugged. "I'm unaccustomed to all this."

"All what?"

"Luxury. Wealth. Time. Having my every whim so thoroughly catered to. It feels decadent. I've done nothing to deserve it."

"Not yet," he observed coolly. "But the clock is ticking, isn't it? Where are we now? Two months, ten days to go, I believe. Would it flatter you if I told you I've been counting the hours? I haven't, but I could assign that duty to my secretary. He's very efficient in that sort of thing."

"Very amusing."

"But in the meantime . . ." He paused, giving a light shrug. "You'll suffer through somehow. Within a month I wager you'll be complaining about the decor in your bed-chamber, the color of the draperies in the front hall, the wretched state of your shoes and clothing. Your jewelry will simply no longer do. Then you'll need a coach of your own, and a driver, and so on and so forth."

"Is that so?"

Evidently he didn't miss the affront in her voice. "Ah, that's right," he said with a smile. "I married a woman who prefers dressing in rags and hobnobbing with servants, didn't I? A woman with character."

"That sounds remarkably like a regret."

"Merely an observation."

He took another long swig from the silver tumbler, then set it down. Bringing one knee up, he rested it upon a chair, leaning forward in a posture of casual indolence. He regarded her in silence, clearly waiting for her to speak.

Abruptly recalling her purpose, Julia gestured to the copy of the *London Review* she had set on the table while watching the swordplay. "I came to show you this," she said. "My column appears today."

Morgan glanced at the paper but didn't pick it up. "Our message to Lazarus?"

"Printed exactly as requested."

His expression darkened for an instant, then he gave a tight nod. Lifting his sword, he began polishing the blade with a thick cotton cloth. "Tell me about your column," he said. "What glorious causes have found favor with you this week?"

"The conditions in the workhouses on Garner Row are deplorable."

"The workhouses," he repeated. "Not exactly original material, but admirable nonetheless."

She tilted her chin. "Will ignoring the plight of the poor make them go away?"

He gave an indifferent shrug. "Apparently not. That's what the better half of London has been attempting to do for centuries, but the poor keep proliferating, don't they? Their numbers grow larger and larger by the decade. The ever-rising soufflé of poverty."

"Why does it feel as though you're constantly mocking me?"

He released a sigh and slid his sword into an embossed leather case. "Because I mock everything and everybody, princess. Myself included. You should know better by now than to take offense."

"That doesn't mean I have to like it."

"No, it doesn't."

His tone was flat and curt, devoid of any emotion. Obviously preparing to leave, he gathered his possessions without another word. But Julia wasn't quite ready to be dismissed. As she searched for a way to fill the awkward silence that followed, her gaze moved about the room. At one time the cavernous chamber had undoubtedly held such glorious promise. Now it reflected only barren expectations: unilluminated chandeliers, empty mirrors, hollow echoes, sparkling floors that had never been trodden upon. Yet the chamber appealed to her nonetheless. There was a romantic futility to the room that seemed sadly appropriate to their circumstances.

She looked back to find him watching her.

"Why did you come here?" he asked.

Gathering her courage, she ventured hesitantly, "If you're not too busy, I thought we might do something today. Together. As man and wife."

He released a bored sigh. "What did you have in mind, a waltz? Ordinarily I'd indulge your whim, but as you can see, the orchestra has temporarily abandoned its post."

"I've missed you."

The statement hung in the air between them. Morgan studied her face for a long moment, then said, "There is a term in fencing for toying with one's opponent."

"Are we opponents?"

"Are you toying?"

"I'm not sure what I'm doing."

"Forgive me if I find that difficult to believe. I've never met a more purposeful woman in my life."

A small smile touched her lips. "Is that good or bad?"

"What do you want, Julia?"

She couldn't remember him ever using her name before. The sound of it rolling off his tongue sent an unexpected rush of pleasure racing through her. Idly wondering if his reaction would be the same if she spoke his name, she said, "I thought it might be nice if we spent a little time together, Morgan."

She saw something flash in his eyes, but the emotion, whatever it was, vanished too quickly for her to properly define. "Ah. So that's it." A small, cynical smile curved his lips. His gaze moved over her body with scorching intensity, as though he were able to see right through to her drawers. He straightened and glanced around the empty room, then back at her. "Interesting timing."

Heat flooded her cheeks. "I didn't mean—"

"Didn't you."

"Certainly not. Must you always be so base?"

"You're the one who came to me."

"With the simple proposition that we attend Lord Attmark's boating party this afternoon," she said, seizing upon the sudden inspiration. "That's all I had in mind."

"Lord Attmark's boating party?"

"I thought it would be quite diverting."

"Floating along a river that smells like rancid sewage in this sweltering heat. That's what you came to see me about."

"Yes."

A knowing smile curved his lips. "Liar."

"I don't know what—"

"Liar," he repeated softly.

The word brushed against her hair, as warm and silky as the lightest of caresses. Advancing with every retreating step she took, he moved closer and closer until she felt the wall against her back. Panic tumbled with excitement as his body loomed mere inches away from hers. Although

210   Victoria Lyane

she hadn't consciously acknowledged it until that very moment, she had wanted more from him than mere companionship. Was he truly so experienced that he could read her thoughts with such amazing accuracy, or was she embarrassingly naïve and inexperienced? An interesting question, but one she would have to ponder at length some other time. At the moment it didn't matter. She relaxed back against the wall, closed her eyes, and arranged her lips in what she hoped was a seductive pout. She tilted up her chin and waited, ready to receive his kiss. When she felt no response, she opened her eyes in bewildered disappointment.

His smoky gaze searched hers. "Why the sudden change of heart, princess?"

"Does it matter?"

"It shouldn't. But I have an analytical streak in me that is difficult to quiet." When she didn't reply, he continued coolly. "Let me see if I can guess. You were lying alone in your bed, dreaming of your phantom lover again. Alas, fate has torn him away from you. Now that that's nothing but a hopeless dream, you've decided to content yourself with me."

"Jealous?" she returned, looking for some indication that he might have come to care for her, however petty and possessive that indication might be.

"You do like to invent your little dramas, don't you?"

"Is it so hard to believe that I might want you?"

He gave a small, humorless laugh. "Yes, beauty, it is. But don't worry. I won't let that stop me."

Wrapping his arm around the small of her back, Morgan pulled her to him. His touch was light at first, a mere whisper of a caress that made her breath catch in her throat. He skimmed his fingers up her thighs, over the smooth curve of her hips and the tight band of her waist. Then he drew his hand over her ribs and gently cupped her breast in his palm. Julia drew in a sharp breath, astonished at the feelings that ricocheted through her at his intimate touch. His embrace was entirely shocking, and yet somehow appropriate. A mere prelude, she suspected, to what was yet to come.

No sooner had she recognized that when Morgan shifted slightly. He slipped his thigh between her legs, gently pulling her body forward so that she was straddling his knee. She grasped his shoulders for support as he moved his leg up and down between hers, softly rocking her against him. The steady, rolling motion between her legs set off a chain of reactions within her. Heat radiated through her belly as her breath came in short gasps and a series of small tremors shot down her spine.

His hands moved over her body once again, but no longer with the light, gentle caress she had experienced earlier. Instead he touched her with a fierce possessiveness, as though he were a master sculptor and she were made of clay. He boldly massaged her breasts, her hips, her waist. He ran his hands down her spine, cupping her buttocks and pulling her ever closer to him, until she could feel the shocking length of his erection against her thigh.

She had barely accustomed herself to that sensation when he leaned forward, pressing his lips against the satiny skin exposed by the bodice of her gown. He kissed her breasts, her collarbone, and the nape of her neck, using his mouth to explore the very places his hands had caressed only moments earlier. Julia tossed back her head to allow him greater access, running her fingers through his dark, silky hair as he nuzzled his cheek against her skin.

Lifting himself slightly, he murmured into her ear, "With the right lover a woman can realize her passion over and over again, one time after another. Have you ever experienced that?"

"No," she managed breathlessly.

"Then we have a goal, don't we, princess?"

Giddy arousal collided with nervous anticipation at his words. He tightened his grip on her body, as though intent on melding them into one. Her dress was made of lightweight cotton, a fabric so thin, she could feel the heat of his skin through her gown. The barrier it provided between them was almost nonexistent. In fact, it quickly proved to offer no protection at all. Morgan slipped his hand beneath her skirts, running it up her leg until he reached the smooth expanse of thigh exposed between her stocking and her drawers. Letting out a low murmur of appreciation, he began to rhythmically stroke the velvety band of flesh.

She stiffened instinctively at his bold touch, but Morgan didn't retreat. Instead he lowered his head, slanting his lips over hers. Applying the slight pressure of his jaw, he coaxed her lips apart and slipped his tongue inside her mouth. Rocking her against him once again, he established a swelling pulse to their kiss, one that mimicked the soft sway of their bodies. Then he returned his hand to her breast, gently kneading it beneath his palm.

Within the dim recesses of Julia's mind came an awareness that something was wrong. She pulled back slightly, distancing herself from the heady rush of sensation that had engulfed her only moments earlier. It was all happening too quickly. Morgan had moved from coaxing to taking. There was no roughness in his touch—her husband was too experienced a rake to make that mistake. But neither did she feel a lover's tenderness. Instead he exercised a seductive mastery over her. Moreover there was a harshness in his kiss, as though she were an enemy that had to be conquered rather than a lover to be wooed.

What she had wanted most was missing. In her mind, she realized, she had imagined this moment before. She had imagined taking the place of the other woman in the garden. She had imagined Morgan's touch, soft and gentle and coaxing. In surrendering herself, she had longed to fill the emptiness that had existed between them. She had ached for abandonment, losing herself in his touch. Instead she was acutely aware of his every movement. They shared mutual lust but nothing deeper.

She stiffened slightly, resisting the very touch she had craved only moments earlier. It was as much her fault as it was his, she realized. She had come to him wanting something, needing something, and now she would turn him away because it wasn't quite right. Knowing that if she did so, the cycle of estrangement and frustration that existed between them would only deepen and worsen. Or she could suffer through it and not come to him again. Neither was a very palatable option.

She had simply expected too much from him. Or had she? The thought suddenly struck her that that wasn't the case at all. Occasionally she had seen glimpses of a different man. A man who wasn't harsh and cynical. A man who touched her with tenderness, who spoke to his servants with respect, and who laughed with his friends. Surely there was some part of him she could still reach. Some remnant of his former self that hadn't been completely destroyed by the fire.

To that end she decided to throw caution to the wind and show him what she wanted. After all, she had rehearsed her response so many times in her dreams. What harm could it do to ignore the reality of what he was offering and touch him as she wanted him to touch her? With that in mind she drew back slightly, turning away from his kiss. She ran her hands over the breadth of his chest, experiencing a heady thrill of sensual power as she felt his muscles stiffen beneath her fingers. She stroked his body with a soft, healing touch, intent on learning the rugged beauty of his frame.

Continuing her bold exploration, she leaned forward and touched her mouth to his neck. A light film of salt brushed her lips, a taste that was both highly erotic and evocative of the swordplay she had witnessed. Thrust, parry. Advance, retreat. A game with a rhythm so like their own. Moving ever forward, she kissed the red, puckered scars that marred the skin at the base of his neck. She felt him stiffen beneath her and try to pull away, as though experiencing an unwelcome jolt of surprise.

But Julia refused to retreat. She kissed his neck, his cheek, his chin, then pressed her lips against his. Exercising the same mastery he had shown, she gained entrance to the warmth of his mouth. Their kiss deepened and grew, moving from lustful conquest to searing intimacy. She felt Morgan respond, giving a low moan of approval as his hands moved caressingly down her spine and over her buttocks.

Julia abandoned her original purpose of deliberately gentling her husband's touch. She was no longer leading, nor was he following. Instead they had come together to establish a scorching rhythm all their own. One sensation melted into another. Desire built within her, engulfing her in a wave of selfish pleasure. The more he gave, the more she wanted. She was aware of nothing but his hand on her thigh, the feel of her breasts pressed against his chest, and the heady intensity of their kiss.

It was as though Morgan had tapped into some rich vein of feeling she had never known existed. She wanted nothing more than to lose herself in the carnal bliss that surged through her. The masculine scent of his skin, the strength of his arms, and the rock-hard solidity of his thighs—everything about him enticed her completely. She felt overwhelmed, yet had no desire to stop. She could almost feel herself sliding down a steep slope into a mysterious morass of pure feeling and sensation.

Then, like a strident noise interrupting a blissful dream, a steady knocking encroached upon their embrace. Julia willed herself to ignore it, but the annoying sound wouldn't go away. Morgan must have been aware of it as well, for after a moment he drew back, ending their kiss. He gently set her off his thigh, holding her for a moment while she regained her balance. She swayed slightly, stunned and disoriented at her own wanton abandonment. Yet she also experienced a certain amount of satisfaction, for she had felt Morgan respond to her—if only on a physical level. She might not have succeeded in destroying the barriers that existed between them, but at least they had been fractured a bit.

The knocking continued. Polite, but persistent.

Morgan turned toward the door. "Enter."

Julia hastily smoothed down her gown as Maxwell, the head footman, stepped inside. Staring straight ahead, he regally intoned, "A Mr. Thomas Fike to see you, my lord."

"You may inform him that we shall be along directly."

"Very good, my lord." Maxwell nodded and retreated.

As the door closed softly behind him, Morgan said to Julia, "I believe we discussed this earlier. I've engaged the man's services to execute our wedding portrait for the main hall."

She nodded. "Yes, I remember." She hesitated, not sure what else to say. Surely some remark on their new-found intimacy was in order. But his tone had been cool and perfunctory, so totally unlike the heated embrace they had just shared that it left her speechless.

Morgan bent to gather his sword and glove. "I do hope the man's artistic ability surpasses his sense of timing."

"Is that all you have to say to me?" she demanded at last, indignant that he would attempt to trivialize what had passed between them with such mocking indifference.

He studied her in surprise, then arched one dark brow. "Thank you?"

"Thank you?"

"Apparently your charity knows no bounds, princess. Granting me a taste of the forbidden fruit—how very generous."

Swallowing her anger, she brought up her chin, regarding him with a look of icy disdain. "My generosity has limits," she replied tartly, "as does my patience."

"Indeed? In that event I shall do my best not to excessively tax either one." He gave a low bow, then extended his arm. "Shall we?"

Refusing his arm, Julia swept by Morgan. Despite the inner turmoil that gripped her, she schooled her expression into one she hoped would reflect perfect domestic tranquillity. The household servants could be relied upon for their discretion. But she knew all too well that a stranger might not be. The last thing she needed were rumors floating about touting marital discord between her and Morgan.

Thomas Fike stood waiting for them in the main foyer. He was younger than she had expected—and far more attractive. The artist was tall and muscular, with dark blond hair that had been secured at the nape of his neck by a slim leather thong. His gloriously chiseled features looked as though they had been copied from a Roman coin, his chocolate brown eyes were deep and soulful. He wore a white ruffled shirt, with a crimson scarf knotted about his throat to provide a dashing touch. On any other man the clothing might have appeared effeminate. On him it was merely dramatically flamboyant.

According to the rumors Julia had heard about the man, he had been gifted with talent, beauty, and intelligence. In sum, everything but wealth and a title. She wondered vaguely if the other rumors that swirled about him were true—that he had seduced the majority of women whose husbands had paid him to paint their portraits. Regardless of the veracity of the gossip, it was enough to cause her to speculate as to why Morgan had hired him. It was either a bold demonstration of his trust in her, a blatant show of his lack of concern for her affairs, or more likely a simple acknowledgment that Thomas Fike was the most coveted artist of the day and therefore no one else would suffice.

At the sound of their approach, Fike greeted them with a low bow, then returned his attention to the ancient portraits that lined the hall, studying them intently. "Marvelous," he said. "Simply marvelous. Each tells a story."

"Indeed," remarked Morgan. "I hope you will be able to provide us with a work of similar distinction."

Fike's gaze moved immediately to Julia. "With a subject of such natural radiance, I would be ashamed to deliver anything less," he said, favoring her with a bold smile.

The look was entirely improper under any circumstances, but even more so given that Morgan was standing a mere two feet away. Julia shot a questioning glance at her husband, surprised to find him looking coolly unperturbed. Apparently he had deduced, as she had, that Fike's smile amounted to nothing more than sheer habit on his part. He was probably so accustomed to seducing the bored wives of the nobility that it didn't even occur to him that he was doing it.

Nevertheless, she kept her reply distinctly business-like. "My husband and I are fortunate to have engaged your services so quickly."

Fike gave a small shrug. "Lord Barlowe's secretary offered me four times my normal rate to drop my other commitments." He paused, favoring her with another seductive glance. "Had I known how beautiful my subject was, I would have offered my services gratuitously."

"And given the term *starving artist* a new life, no doubt," Morgan remarked dryly. That said, he gave a brusque nod and turned in the direction of his study. "If you'll excuse me, I'll leave you two to get better acquainted."

"Should we not discuss the manner in which you and your wife would like to pose?" Fike asked.

Morgan shook his head. "On considering the matter,

I have decided not to sit. As you have so gallantly pointed out, my wife generates enough beauty and radiance to fill the canvas on her own."

"But that's never been done before," Julia protested. Morgan shrugged. "Does that signify?"

"Of course it does. Everyone who sees the portrait shall think that I am vain."

"They shall think," Morgan corrected solemnly, his eyes meeting hers, "that you are exquisite." On that note he turned and strode away, pausing only long enough to toss over his shoulder, "Don't be too long, princess. We should leave within the hour. You were so anxious to attend Lord Attmark's boating party. It would be a shame to miss it."

"I daresay . . ." Thomas Fike began, watching with an expression of utter confusion as Morgan left the room, "I had heard . . . why, he's not a beast at all."

Julia took a deep breath, then let it out slowly. In a rebuttal so soft it could not be heard, she replied, "Looks can be deceiving."

$\mathcal{M}$organ's driver had stationed the coach beneath a row of tall cypress trees, on the circular drive that fronted his home. It was there that Morgan paced as he waited for his wife to make an appearance. Although the shade of the cypress provided a modicum of relief from the heat, it was a sweltering day nonetheless. He had removed his jacket, but the heavy humidity caused the light linen of his shirt to cling to his chest and back.

It seemed as though everything he encountered of late was nothing but a huge conspiracy against him. The weather. Lazarus. The impudent young pup of a painter who had shown the audacity to flirt with his wife while he stood a mere three feet away. And then there was Julia's kiss: a fleeting, coquettish sample of what he was missing night after night. If it had all been a trick of fate to test his patience and disposition, he had failed miserably. His mood, he recognized grimly, could only be termed as foul.

The problem, he thought, was control—the cornerstone of every intelligent action and logical decision. The path to righteousness, reason, and lucidity. Control. Something he lacked completely at the moment. He could no more control the weather than he could control Lazarus's next move or the way his body responded to his wife. The realization was galling.

He remembered the agonizing days following the fire. His skin peeling off his back, engulfed by pain so intense, no drug could free him of it. Pain that made him feel as if he were bordering on the edge of madness. Every touch, every breath, every movement had been an agony. And when it wasn't the pain that had threatened to destroy him, it was the memories themselves. The knowledge of what had happened, of what he had been directly responsible for. But somehow, through sheer will and rigid control, he had not died. He had kept himself sane and alive. He needed that same instinct for self-preservation now.

Morgan paced a bit more, battling his emotions. He had always prided himself on his rationality. But at the moment his nerves were too close to the surface. After the blaze that had destroyed his servants' quarters, he felt everything more intensely. Literally. Heat burned his skin. Cold rubbed it raw. Did the damage that had been done to his body cause those heightened sensations, or had coming so close to dying given him a new awareness of life?

He twisted his copy of the *London Review* in his hand, tapping it against his thigh as he walked. Julia's column was right there. A dare. A direct challenge for Lazarus to show himself once again. The man would. Of that Morgan was absolutely, instinctively certain. With that knowledge came the intuitive recognition that the danger they faced was internal, not external. If he was strong enough, he could protect Julia and protect himself. He could avoid any recurring disaster.

If he was strong enough. But he had failed once before, and the memory of that failure haunted him still.

Perhaps if he were a wiser man, a braver man . . . but he wasn't. As always, that realization struck him as a particularly difficult truth to come to terms with. His gaze drifted toward the boxwood gardens. Visions of children laughing and playing instantly filled his mind's eye. Patty-cake, patty-cake.

The sound of a heavy door closing drew his attention to the wide wooden porch that spanned the front of his estate. He looked up to see Julia, dressed in a gown of softly billowing blue muslin. Her hair was swept up and tucked beneath a broad straw hat from which trailed a cluster of peach and blue ribbons. She paused and scanned the grounds, one hand resting on the intricately carved balustrade. Spotting the coach, she caught her skirts and moved gracefully across the lawn toward him. With her broad straw hat trailing ribbons and her skirts floating around her, she looked the picture of graceful summer beauty.

The expression on her face, however, belied the impression of serene warmth and tranquillity she made at a distance. At his words of greeting, she favored him with a cool nod, silently refusing his assistance in entering the coach. They settled themselves opposite one another. At Morgan's command the driver gave the reins a sharp tug, and the team pulled out, moving with a sprightly step toward the sprawling estate Brynmoore, home of Lord Attmark, Duke of Connelly, host of that afternoon's gala.

Although Morgan's coach was not immodest, neither could it be considered overly grand. There was an inescapable intimacy within the confines. He had somewhat accustomed himself to the gentle jostling of the vehicle, despite the fact that the steady, rocking rhythm struck him as profoundly sexual in nature. He had could even feign a certain indifference to the teasing sensation of Julia's knees rubbing against his as they rode. But he could not ignore his wife altogether.

The scent of her skin drifted around him. She wore a

soft floral perfume, coupled with a light touch of powdery talc. Casting a surreptitious glance her way, he noted that a stray lock of her hair had escaped the tight confines in which it had been pinned. The fiery tendril curled about the nape of her neck. The bodice of her gown was modest, revealing but a glimpse of the shadowy cleft between her breasts. He perceived a faint outline of her hips and thighs through the lightweight muslin of her gown. Her arms were bare; her skin looked pale as porcelain and unimaginably silky.

Morgan had grown to enjoy his wife's company—her quick wit, her glowing smiles, her obscenely optimistic view of life. But at the moment her presence amounted to little more than pure sensual torture. Unfortunately his passion did not appear to be reciprocated. In fact, just the opposite was true. She was doing everything she could to withdraw into her seat so that contact between them would be minimal.

Breaking the silence that hung between them, he finally offered as a small gesture of atonement, "It's warm today."

His wife, however, was having none of it. "Quite," Julia agreed, her tone clipped and curt, her gaze firmly fixed out the window.

It did not require a great deal of analysis to deduce that she was waiting for an apology for his boorish behavior following their embrace. Moreover, he could readily admit that one was in order. But he couldn't determine how to offer one without an admission that her touch had affected him far more profoundly than he was willing to let on. And acknowledging that weakness was simply too damned sloppy and sentimental to be endured. Hell, it was embarrassing to even consider. Therefore he stubbornly decided to let the issue drop, relying on her generous nature to put the matter aside.

Thus they made their journey in silence, leaving the crowded, sweltering streets of London behind as they moved in a southwesterly direction, following the Thames toward Windsor. As the miles passed, Morgan felt his foul mood slowly dissipating. To his surprise he wasn't entirely dreading the event. In fact, he was actually looking forward to it, if only because it offered a welcome reprieve from the constant worry of Lazarus.

At last the coach drew up to a sprawling estate more than triple the size of his own. A centuries-old castle, looking ridiculously like something one might find in a child's storybook, sat high atop a verdant hill that rewarded its occupants and guests alike with magnificent views of lush countryside. A liveryman directed their driver away from the main entrance of the keep and around to the back of the estate. There they found vast, rolling lawns, gurgling fountains, and formal gardens deluged with massive summer blossoms. Brilliant tents dotted the gently sloping hillside. The sounds of laughter, blaring trumpets, and strolling musicians drifted out to greet them.

Julia stepped down from the carriage and gazed about the grounds with an expression of undisguised wonder.

Spying Lord Attmark, Morgan took her arm and led her in that direction. "Allow me to introduce you to our host."

He presented her to an enormous man in his late sixties, who despite the weather had costumed himself in a guise that resembled King Henry VIII. The introductions completed, they turned away from the throngs who encircled the man and moved toward a grassy knoll where a group of fine quilts were on display.

"Lord Attmark has always suffered from a rather dramatic, provincial flair," Morgan said as they walked. "He's never been interested in formal balls or midnight suppers. Instead he holds this event once a year and invites everyone to come, rank and privilege aside. It's rather like a county fair, the kind held generations ago.

You'll see families of local landowners and tenant farmers mingling elbow to elbow with London's elite. There are livestock exhibitions, dancers, magic shows, puppeteers, archery competitions, wrestling—all manner of sport and spectacle. You'll likely hear a great deal of criticism for his allowing the rabble to mix with their betters. But everyone comes, and everyone puts up with it."

"Why?"

"Because Attmark is not only rich as Croesus, he also happens to hold title to one of the oldest dukedoms in all of England."

"I gather he's rather eccentric."

"That depends on whether you consider annually beheading your wife in public as eccentric."

"You're not serious."

Morgan shrugged. "I've always found it even more extraordinary that his wife is willing to subject herself to the spectacle year after year." Determined to inject a lighter note in what had thus far been a rather somber journey, he continued. "I hope you brought your notepad and pencil."

"Actually, I didn't even consider it. Why?"

"Because we happen to be on remarkably fertile ground, should you need more material for your column. The foibles of the gentry, that sort of thing."

A small, suspicious smile curved her lips as she searched his gaze. "Such as?" she asked, a hint of a challenge in her voice.

Morgan scanned the crowd, then pointed to a beautiful blond woman with two immaculately coiffed Pekingese on long velvet leashes. The dogs' leashes and hairbows were the exact lavender shade of the woman's gown. "That," he said, "is Lady Veronica Winters, mistress of Sir Charles Kentworthy. Her dogs not only dine beside her at her table, they are also rumored to sleep in her bed—regardless of whether Sir Kentworthy chooses to join her or not."

Sensing that she was not overly impressed with that particular *on dit,* he looked for his next subject. "Do you see the man standing near the cattle pens?"

"Do you mean the rather small man with the bushy mustache?"

"Yes, Viscount Duncan. He may be small in stature, but he is certainly not lacking in vanity. He will not abide any member of his household staff having a height greater than his own. The same is true for anyone to whom he pays monthly bills, including his solicitor and his tailor. He claims one loses one's authority if one has to tilt one's head back in order to give a command."

"How very preposterous."

"True nonetheless. I've been to his home. A rather remarkable experience, as you might imagine. I felt like a goliath who had been stuffed inside a child's dollhouse."

As they walked the grounds, he regaled her with stories of who was bedding whom, who wasn't speaking to whom, who had stolen whose chef, and all manner of trivial nonsense that made up the diverse fabric of London's better class.

"I assume none of this is meant for publication in my column," Julia said.

"Actually, they would probably all be delighted to find themselves mentioned," he replied. "Though it escapes me completely why it should be, I've noted that one gains a definite stature and celebrity in finding one's name in your column. Almost as though it were an honor of sorts to be singled out for your attention."

She gave a slight shrug. "People crave being noticed, even if it's for something as silly as the type of dog they own or the manner in which they style their hair."

Their conversation drifted from point to point, not focusing long on any particular topic. They strolled through the various exhibits, more intent on each other than on what they were seeing or the crowds that swirled around them. As a result Morgan nearly breezed directly past the Earl of Reardon without so much as acknowledging the man—or his wife and newborn son. Fortunately, he caught sight of his friend in time to avoid committing that faux pas.

They greeted each other warmly, then Morgan presented Julia, feeling a ridiculous surge of pride as he did so. He heard the same pride in the earl's voice as he introduced society's newest peer, Michael Alexander Bennett Barthrowe III, a mewling infant wrapped in a lightweight blue blanket. As they parted, they exchanged felicitations on the events that had occurred since they had last seen each other, along with invitations to dine together in the near future.

"That sounded remarkably genuine," Julia remarked.

"It was."

She regarded him curiously, clearly waiting for him to say more. When he didn't, she said, "You've no stories to tell me about the Earl of Reardon?"

"I'm afraid Michael would make very poor fodder for your column."

"No eccentricities?"

"Just one. A rather unique eccentricity, as far as the peerage is concerned. Michael has always possessed a singular ability to separate the gold from the glitter."

"I take it he's a friend of yours."

Morgan thought for a long moment, then shook his head. "Not originally, no. We attended Oxford together but never developed true friendship. In many ways Michael was considered a bit of a laughingstock. He applied himself to his studies, displaying a particular interest in farming techniques, botany, and livestock breeding. He was intent on salvaging his family's crumbling estate, the value of which had been declining steadily for generations. All of that despicable earnestness could have been forgiven had he drank, gambled, and caroused. But that never interested him. As you might imagine, the rest of us found him unbearably stodgy and stuffy." He paused, shaking his head. "I have no idea what his opinion was of me. Given my behavior at the time, I have no reason to believe it might have been good."

"So you parted ways?"

"In a manner of speaking. There are, of course, the obligatory social events of the Season that even an earl cannot escape, so we saw one another from time to time." He could have ended his story there. Instead he surprised himself by continuing. "But when I think of Michael, I think of him after the fire."

"What do you mean?"

"Of all the people I knew and was close to, Michael was not among my closest friends. But we served on a few committees together in the House. During my convalescence he made it a point to drop by weekly under the pretense of needing my input on committee business." He paused, sending her a small smile. "I behaved like a complete ass. I was short-tempered, brutish, and in a great deal of pain—certainly no pleasure to be around. Nevertheless he refused to allow me to push him away. At first I hated his visits. But he was never pitying, never scornful; nor was he horrified at my scars or disgusted by my occasional displays of pain. In fact, we never discussed the accident or the events leading to it at all. He was just the same, solid Michael, Earl of Reardon.

"In time I began to look forward to seeing him. I never let on, of course, that I needed him or enjoyed his company, but I began making excuses for him to visit more often. I discovered that he's every bit as stubborn and opinionated as I am, only far more liberal, so naturally we spent a good deal of time locked in fierce political debates. It didn't matter. He offered stability, connection, and a glimpse of the world outside myself. I sometimes wonder how I would have made it through that period without him."

He stopped abruptly, embarrassed by his stark admission of weakness and need. He hadn't intended to speak on the past at all, but somehow it had seemed appropriate. Now he wondered if he had revealed too much. He cast a glance at Julia, only to find her regarding him with a soft smile of approval.

"I'm glad you told me," she said. "Now I know why I liked the earl from the moment I met him."

He smiled. "Did you?"

"Absolutely," she swore, an expression of fierce loyalty shining in her sherry eyes.

Before he could reply to that remarkable sentiment, one of Lord Attmark's servants approached, requesting Julia's aid. Apparently there were not enough ladies taking part in the mock jousting tournament. Would she be willing to lend a hand in the festivities and champion a knight? Julia graciously acquiesced, allowing herself to be led off to the games. Glancing ahead to the tournament grounds, Morgan noted that it would be a few minutes before the actual jousting began. With that in mind, he decided to stroll the grounds a bit on his own.

His attention was soon caught by the sharp clamor of steel swords clashing in battle. He stopped beneath the shade of a graceful weeping willow to watch the duelists. Fair players, he thought after a few minutes' observation, but none was truly gifted. A shame that Julia had already drifted off, however. She would have enjoyed the exhibition.

"Hello, Morgan."

He stilled, recognizing the soft voice instantly. Then he turned. "Hello, Isabelle."

She looked as lovely as ever in a gown of deep emerald green, a matching parasol twirling above her head. Exquisitely feminine and stunningly beautiful. But then, that was Isabelle.

He scanned the grounds, then regarded her with an expression of mild curiosity. "Don't tell me that Roger has left you to explore Lord Attmark's party on your own."

"I'm afraid so," She lifted her shoulders in a light

shrug. "He's already proven his skill at the archery exhibition. First prize was a five-pound hunk of ghastly-smelling cheese, but he was determined to win it. You know how he is, so dreadfully competitive."

"Yes, I remember."

"I believe he's intent on proving his prowess at fencing now."

Morgan arched one dark brow. "Five pounds isn't enough cheese?"

She smiled softly and shook her head. "The prize for this event is a mulberry pie. One of your favorites, as I recall."

"I haven't tasted it in years." It had been the speciality of his cook, a woman who had perished in the flames.

"You've changed, Morgan."

"Because I no longer care for mulberry pie?"

She ignored his poor attempt at levity and moved closer toward him, tilting her head back to search his gaze. An expression of wistful regret shadowed her features as she continued softly. "So much has changed. If we met today, I don't know that the three of us would be friends."

The three of them. It had always been the three of them, he reflected absently. Roger and Morgan, cutting a rakish swath through the fabric of London society. Yet despite their friendship there had always been a dark undercurrent between them. A competitive edge of which they had both been acutely aware, even if neither of them spoke of it directly. Who was the better swordsman, the better rider, the better gambler?

Into that simmering brew of shameless masculine rivalry had walked Isabelle, the beautiful woman who had served as the ultimate challenge. Who would win her hand? She had toyed with them both for nearly a year before finally accepting Morgan's offer of marriage. Victory. Sweet and unquestioned. In light of the intense contest that had preceded it, the aftermath had been rather mundane.

Morgan was not normally one to dwell in the past, but as it seemed to be a day of reminiscence and reflection, he indulged himself in a brief flash of bittersweet memories. He remembered coming home to find Isabelle waiting for him in his bed. Soft, naked, and endlessly desirable, every inch of her the sophisticated seductress. But he had never really known her. Aside from petty gossip, their discussions had been limited to the china patterns, the servants, and whether they ought to replace the carpets in the hall.

Amazingly enough, that had sufficed. They had both been so arrogant, so contemptuously certain that they were somehow blessed beyond other mortals, that they would never be touched by the cruel vagaries of fate. Morgan had firmly adhered to the belief that there was order and sanity in the world. One could map out one's future and expect with relative certainty that life would bend to one's will.

But the fire had changed all that.

"I didn't think you would ever recover," she said, her thoughts apparently having moved in the same direction as his.

A small smile touched his lips. "Neither did I."

"It was awful of me to leave."

She toyed with her parasol, then cast a glance at the crowd that had gathered to cheer on the fencers. Spying the Earl of Reardon sitting with his wife and newborn son, she said, "Just think, Morgan, that would have been us."

Morgan considered that for a moment. She was right. In all likelihood that would have been them. Sitting together with a child of their own: a tiny, red-faced babe wrapped in a lightweight blanket. Had the fire not occurred, there was no reason to suspect their lives would have dramatically veered from that path. He would have been satisfied, perhaps even content.

He watched as Isabelle's gaze moved past the child to admire the jewelry draped around Lady Reardon's throat. It was an inconsequential glance, probably pure habit on Isabelle's part. Yet to Morgan it seemed to ring with dire import, as though that single glance contained an answer he hadn't even been aware he was seeking.

His hand rested on the trunk of the willow where they stood. He gave it a brief glance. For so long the condition of his skin—scarred, raw, and angry—had served as a reflection of his inner state. Now, studying it anew, he saw it merely as damaged skin, the result of a horrendous accident. He would not trivialize the brutal nature of the event by characterizing his awakening as seeing the silver lining behind a cloud. But for the first time he looked at his situation, not in view of what had been taken away, but for what he had been given.

His gaze drifted past Isabelle, automatically moving in the direction he had last seen Julia. Losing Isabelle had temporarily wounded his pride. But losing Julia . . . now that would be something altogether different.

"There is something you should know, Isabelle," he said after a moment.

She looked up at him, her dark eyes shining with self-assured expectation. "Yes, Morgan?"

"I wish you and Roger every happiness."

That was clearly not what she had been expecting to hear. A look of stunned disbelief showed on her delicate features for a fraction of a second, but she quickly schooled her expression into one of regal aloofness. "Thank you."

"Now then," he said, gesturing toward the stand on which the fencers battled, "shall we watch your fiancé win his pie?"

"By all means," she replied coolly, turning away from him.

Roger disposed of challenger after challenger. There was no finesse in his swordsmanship, but he made up for it with a show of brutal force, lashing out intensely at anyone who dared to face him. As Morgan watched the play, a sensation of acute discomfort swept over him. While he was on the path of facing truths, there seemed to be one more that needed facing: Could Roger Bigelow have wanted to win Isabelle so badly, he had set the fire that had nearly destroyed Morgan's life?

He tried to brush the thought off. Unfortunately that dark speculation, once raised, loomed all too plausible a possibility.

Julia strolled across the broad expanse of lawn, grateful for the broad straw hat she wore. Aside from adding a much-needed touch of elegance to her rather simple gown, it provided some shelter from the sun's intense rays. The jousting had ended some minutes ago but still she saw no sign of Morgan. She looked for him as she walked, paying slight attention to the exhibits she passed.

Now midafternoon, the heat had apparently reached its zenith. Lord Attmark's guests drifted through the grounds, weary and uncomfortable, put out by the unseasonable warmth. There seemed to be a general rumbling consensus that someone ought to do something about the dreadful weather, but no antidote was suggested. As Morgan had predicted, there was no great enthusiasm for launching their host's boat on its maiden voyage up the foul-smelling Thames. It sat docked and forgotten, a forlorn presence listing against its moorings.

She saw her Uncle Cyrus, Aunt Rosalind, and cousins Marianne and Theresa milling about, but she wasn't quite ready to make the drastic overture of joining their party. Nor did she have any particular interest in greeting Thomas Fike, the young painter she had met earlier that morning. He appeared distinctly preoccupied in any case, flirting with a baroness who looked to be at least twice his age. Julia wondered absently if he was looking for a commission or a liaison of a more private nature. A small smile curved her lips as she contemplated the question. From what little she knew of the man, he was probably after both.

She wandered a bit more, beginning to feel as ignored and adrift as Lord Attmark's yacht. Just as she had abandoned hope of finding her husband among the teeming crowds, she caught a glimpse of a man and woman standing beneath the shade of a massive willow. Something about the man's form—or perhaps just the intimacy of the scene—struck a familiar chord. Looking again, she recognized Morgan and the woman with him: Isabelle Cartwright. Julia was not accustomed to dealing with fits of insecurity, but the sight caused a tight knot of nervous dread to curl within her belly. They looked so undeniably intimate, so very blind to anyone but themselves. It was almost as if—

"Lady Barlowe?"

Julia spun around, feeling as though she had been caught peeking through a bedroom window. She looked up to see Jonathan Derrick, the Earl of Bedford, standing a mere two feet away.

He sent her a small, apologetic smile. "Forgive me. I didn't mean to startle you."

"Not at all," she assured him. "I was just . . . enjoying the exhibits." Her words sounded stumbling and forced even to her own ears. Attempting to cover her flustered gaffe with an overly bright smile, she repeated, "You didn't startle me at all."

The earl looked past her, following her former line of sight to the spot where Morgan and Isabelle stood. He quickly looked away, his embarrassment obvious. "Yes, well . . . it is quite a spectacle, isn't it? The exhibits, I mean."

"Yes."

"Indeed."

Although he had obviously approached her with

some objective in mind, that purpose evidently escaped him. Jonathan Derrick rocked back and forth on his heels, staring about the grounds as though her presence were forgotten entirely. Unfortunately, that was in keeping with Julia's initial impression of the man. Large and somewhat bumbling in manner, he exuded an air of a perpetual distraction. His bushy blond hair and mustache were slightly damp with perspiration, his normally florid complexion was even redder due to the heat.

Abruptly recalling himself, he said at last, "I was about to take some refreshment. I wonder if you would care to join me?"

She managed a gracious smile. "That would be lovely, Lord Bedford." Anything was better than standing beneath the sweltering sun watching her husband flirt with his former mistress.

Jonathan Derrick looked momentarily surprised, then a beaming smile curved his lips as he offered her his arm. "It is my honor, Lady Barlowe."

They moved across the lush lawn toward the colorful tents under which the guests mingled. On another day the setting might have been lovely, but the heat seemed to affect everything. The floral arrangements wilted and drooped. Lord Attmark's servants rushed between the kitchens and the tents, their faces flushed and damp with perspiration.

Trays of exquisitely prepared dishes had been set out for the guests. Although the menu might be considered the height of culinary fashion, evidently the chef had not considered the weather or the nature of the gathering. The fare was mired in rich overabundance. Everything was fried or stuffed, drenched in a heavy sauce or coated with a thin film of grease. The desserts were creamy and gooey. Even the wines were dark and heavy. If the heat alone didn't suffice to make one's temples throb, the food surely would.

The Earl of Bedford chose a secluded table away

from the other diners. "I hope you don't mind," he said as he seated Julia. "But there is something I would like to discuss with you—something of a rather personal nature."

"Of course," she returned politely. As a servant set a plate before her, she listlessly lifted her fork, wondering which of the steaming dishes might be least offensive.

Like her, Jonathan Derrick studied his plate with a thoughtful frown. "Interesting," he murmured after a moment.

"Yes?"

He poked a sodden lump in the center of his plate. "A chef once instructed me as to the proper way to boil a frog. Apparently if one throws it directly into a pot of boiling water, it will quite naturally leap out. If, however, one puts a frog in a pail of cold water and slowly raises the temperature, it will sit complacently until it is boiled to death."

Julia hastily set down her fork. "Really?" she managed.

"I found it quite enlightening—illustrative of mankind as well, wouldn't you say?"

"You said there was something of a personal nature you wanted to discuss with me?"

"Oh, yes." He hesitated, then said with a small, apologetic smile, "Forgive me. I'm not very good at this sort of thing."

"What sort of thing?"

"Marriage," he replied. "I should have taken care of the chore years ago, but I simply kept putting it off. Now I find myself somewhat at a loss, particularly given my age and the fact that I have never married."

Neither of which posed an insurmountable problem in Julia's estimation. She guessed the earl to be in his early to midforties. While not young, neither was he too old to take a bride. "There are several beautiful young women making their debut this Season," she pointed out. "I imagine any of them would be flattered by your attentions."

A hint of a smile showed beneath his shaggy mustache. "May I speak bluntly?"

"Of course."

"I am not unaware that my wealth and title might serve to make up for some of my personal shortcomings. It might even serve to make me attractive to a budding young beauty of eighteen. But the thought of taking a precocious child-bride strikes me as a rather trying prospect. I am rather settled in my ways and would much prefer a woman of some maturity and experience—yet one who is still young enough to beget an heir. Furthermore, I seek a woman who has been properly reared and who would not disturb the peace and quiet of my household. That's why I thought you might be of assistance."

"I'm afraid I don't understand."

"Miss Theresa Prentisse and Miss Marianne Prentisse are your cousins, are they not?"

Of course, she thought. Her cousins. Both of whom were now in their midtwenties. Both of whom had been raised by their father to be the picture of dutiful, obedient wives.

"It was my understanding that your uncle is currently considering suitors for their hands," Jonathan Derrick pressed.

"I regret that Uncle Cyrus is making that fact painfully obvious, is he not?"

"Surely one should not hold that against your cousins."

"That's very generous of you."

"I have given the matter a considerable deal of thought," he replied with a light shrug. "If it is not too much to ask, would you consider presenting me to your family? I realize that our acquaintance has been of a rather brief nature, but I believe your husband would be willing to vouch for my good character."

"I'm sure that won't be necessary," she assured him. "Your uncle might consider me?"

An earl? Julia thought. Her uncle would do handstands. "If you like, I'll arrange an introduction this afternoon."

Jonathan Derrick beamed. "I'm forever in your debt, Lady Barlowe." He picked up his fork and dug lustily into his boiled frog.

Lazarus, Was that you? Flame.

Yes, my love, it was me. But you knew it, didn't you? You tease. You vixen. Whore.

He rolled the paper into a tight wand and employed it to swat away a bothersome gnat, then he tapped it absently against his thigh. He had been so pleased earlier in the day to see her private message to him. Now that exquisite thrill was ruined entirely.

Lord Attmark's gala was winding down at last. Shielding his eyes against the setting sun, he watched as the guests flooded the lawn and headed toward the culmination of the day's events, that idiotic beheading. Even Flame—*his* Flame—was intent on witnessing that foolish spectacle. He watched her moving across the fields with her arm locked through that of Morgan St. James.

Lazarus regarded her with acute displeasure. Although he had given her several opportunities to acknowledge him, she had not sent him one single sign that his presence pleased her. Even the gown she wore was wrong. Pale, insipid blue. Adequate on another woman, perhaps, but not her. Flame should always wear the colors of fire. Hadn't he told her so on more than one occasion?

The gown had been Morgan St. James's idea, no doubt. He was controlling her, ruining her. In time she would be nothing—just an empty receptacle for St. James's lust. Had he bedded her already? Possibly. Lazarus imagined that scarred skin touching her pristine flesh,

climbing atop her, and emptying his seed into her body.
The thought sickened his stomach. For a moment he
thought he might be physically ill.

No, not her. It couldn't be. Not his Flame. She
wouldn't allow it. Surely he was confusing her with that
other woman. The woman who moaned and slithered beneath the crimson satin sheets like a rutting sow. The
woman who writhed in the flames, screaming for mercy.
Mercy that had never come.

He clenched his fist tightly around the paper he held,
trying to shut the image out. But he was too late. His
father's enraged voice filled his mind. The woman had
been taught a lesson. Now it was his turn. Spare the rod,
spoil the child. As the lash of his whip had stung his back,
Lazarus had cowered in terror, so overcome by fear and
pain he had soiled his pants. Shame coursed through him
at the memory. His father had been right to punish him.
He had been a foul, dirty boy. Undeserving of everything
he had been given.

He could feel the ugliness taking over him. Festering.
Seething anger and rage spreading through his body,
shooting up his veins like a disease. Desperately he tried
to block it. A passage from Ezekiel drifted through his
mind. Just as silver, bronze, iron, lead, and tin are gathered into a furnace and smelted in the roaring flames, so I
will gather you together in my furious wrath, put you in,
and smelt you.

There. That was the answer. Such magnificent words.
It was up to him to carry out the Lord's work. That was
why he needed the fires. To cleanse the filth. To establish
purity and order once again. Just as his father had done. It
was his duty to find the guilty and expose them to the
world.

He knew exactly where.

Exactly who should be punished next.

He could already smell the sulfur and kerosene. He
could already see the flames licking and crawling and blis-

tering. Such raw beauty and perfection. Relaxing his grip, he ran his fingers over Flame's column once again. The Tattler. She herself had told him where to strike. This time she would know it had been him. This time there would be no doubt.

All for you, my love. All for you.

Chapter 13

The sound of sharply clanging bells woke Julia from a deep sleep. Assuming they were church bells ringing to gather parishioners together for a dawn mass, she rolled over in sleepy irritation and tried to shut them out. But the sound only intensified. The bells rang louder and louder, tolling with ugly urgency.

Succumbing at last to their call, she sat up in bed and opened her eyes. No rosy dawn glow greeted her. Nor did silver beams of moonlight illuminate her chamber. It was the dead of night. She was surrounded by nothing but varying depths of darkness and shadow, filling her room with inky purples, indigo, and ebony.

And the bells, ringing and ringing, clamoring for attention.

She frowned in cloudy confusion, turning her head in the direction of the sound. At last grim understanding dawned. She threw back her linens and left her bed, moving across the room to her balcony. Seeking confirmation of her worst fears, she stepped outside, only to be rewarded with a vista of the neighborhood estates. The bells echoed from behind her, away from Mayfair and Grosvenor Square.

Morgan's windows, she knew, faced east, affording a view of nearly the entire city. Although the house was silent, surely the bells would have awakened him as well. With that in mind she drew on a robe and padded softly down the hallway to his chamber. She rapped softly on his door. "Morgan?"

No sound greeted her from within. She boldly turned the handle and poked her head inside. It was too dim to see much. Gazing about the space, she was able to perceive only shadows and looming shapes of furniture. Her focus centered on the large four-poster. Empty. The white linen sheets cast an eerie glow in the moonlight. Searching the room, Julia finally recognized a lone figure silhouetted on the balcony, his back to her.

"Morgan?" she called again.

When he didn't reply, she stepped inside and moved across the room. She reached his balcony and joined him outside in the warm night air. Although she knew he was aware of her presence, he didn't acknowledge her. He stood silent and motionless, his hands tucked into the pockets of his dressing robe, his eyes fastened on a distant spot on the horizon. She shifted her gaze to the same place.

A ball of brilliant fiery red smoldered against the dark skyline of the city, as though a piece of the sun had tumbled down to scorch the earth. Directly above it thick charcoal clouds billowed against the ebony sky. When Julia had been a child and had accompanied her father on long voyages, he had often drawn her aside and told her that if she listened hard enough, she could hear the sun hissing and spitting flame as it struck the horizon. And so it was now. She could almost hear those flames licking and cracking, greedily devouring everything in their path.

"Charing Cross?" she said after a moment.

"Yes."

Morgan offered no more, nor did he turn to look at her. His eyes were dark and grim, watching and yet unseeing, as though he were locked in memories of his own. He wore the same chilling expression she had seen weeks ago, when she had found him watching the rubbish burn. Although she longed to breach the silence between them with a consoling word, she knew that nothing she might say would possibly be adequate. Yet retreating to her own chamber was not an option either.

The sound of a soft cough pierced the stillness of the night. She suddenly recognized that she and Morgan were not alone. The entire household was awake. The servants had gathered on the balconies that fronted the east wing, locked together in brutal camaraderie as they watched the conflagration. Most of them had been in Morgan's employ at the time of his fire. The chambermaid who had lost her daughter. The groomsman whose face still bore the damage of the flame. The butler who walked with a pained limp, the result of his leap from a third-floor window. They stood together in solemn acknowledgment, watching the blaze in the distance.

The bells rang on and on. Julia hugged herself tightly, drawing her hands up and down her arms as though to banish a chill. With nowhere else to go, she stood in silence beside her husband and watched the flames burn.

Unfortunately the blaze was not a singular occurrence. Three nights later Julia was once again roused from her bed by the shrill ringing of fire bells. The first fire destroyed the property of Lord Alfred Deerce. Four died in the blaze, including Deerce's invalid wife. The second fire ravaged the home of Sir Richard Wibberly. That conflagration resulted in one death and scores of injuries. Both fires had been deliberately set.

Julia glanced at the headlines of the papers that sat in the morning room: ARSONIST TERRORIZES LONDON. FIRES RAGE THROUGH CITY. WHO WILL BE NEXT? The entire city was abuzz with apprehension. It was happening all over again. Lazarus was back, and he was winning. London was held in a grip of terror.

By midafternoon of the fourth day, she could well feel the toll of the past week. She was edgy and exhausted, terrified of what the coming evening would bring. Those same emotions were reflected on the faces of the small group gathered around her. Morgan stood with one shoulder propped against the window frame, restlessly sifting the coins in his trouser pockets. Mr. Chivers and Mr. Goodington, a dour-looking man from Scotland Yard who had accompanied the Home Secretary, toyed with their cups of tea. Mr. Randolph, who had just delivered the latest batch of letters that had been sent to The Tattler via the *London Review,* sat utterly still, his expression appropriate to one who was witnessing a funeral procession.

The room was hot and stuffy despite the open windows. A somber heaviness filled the air, although all present made their best appearance of casual nonchalance. Determined not to belabor the moment any longer, Julia lifted the slim stack of envelopes from the sterling silver tray on which they rested. She opened the first note and scanned the page.

A small, fluttering smile crossed her lips as she looked up at the room at large and said, "Lady Georgina Chatham writes to inform me that her husband has been forcing his attentions on their chambermaid. She hopes that I might make his activities known in my column, in order that he might see what a fool he is making of himself and stop his ridiculous behavior. Apparently she has grown quite weary of replacing the never-ending parade of servants his behavior has necessitated."

Polite, empty smiles greeted her words. She set the letter aside and moved on to the next. She scanned the

contents and let out a sigh. Briefly she summarized that
Lord Daniel Franklin found the report of his liaison with
a certain French chanteuse to be both libelous in nature
and grossly erring in fact. Apparently the woman in question was an actress, not a singer, and the evenings he spent
in her company—while his heiress wife was away visiting
relatives in Dover—were purely platonic in nature. A re-
traction was demanded immediately. The letter had been
signed by both Lord and Lady Franklin.

The next note was a personal missive that had evidently been jumbled in with those addressed to The Tattler. She skimmed the contents and quietly set it aside.
Following that was an anonymous letter from a woman
who identified herself only as a matron at one of London's
largest foundling homes. She wrote to express her gratitude for Julia's scathing exposé on the plight of the children housed there. Since the column had appeared, the
quality of the children's food and care had improved dramatically.

Julia shifted impatiently and set the note aside. Normally a letter of that sort would have filled her with a
sense of purpose and accomplishment. At the moment,
however, she barely gave it any attention. Her heart in her
throat, she reached for the fifth and final letter. As she
scanned it, a rush of relief swelled within her. "Yes!" she
exclaimed breathlessly, scooting to the edge of her chair.
"It's from Lazarus."

Returning her gaze to the letter she held, she read
aloud,

> *Flame,*
> *Crusading angel. Beacon of light and righteous-*
> *ness. I have followed your words and done as you*
> *directed. Through fire we will purify this wretched*
> *city. The Lord has brought us together so that His*
> *work might be done. The guilty shall be punished.*
> *The evil that pervades our society shall at last be*

*cleansed. Fear shall grow in the hearts of those
who sin.*

*In return for my toil, I ask but a simple sign of
your trust and fidelity. It pains me to see you in
gowns of insipid blue—the mark of St. James, no
doubt. Wear the colors of fire for me, my love.
Crimson. Gold. Orange.*

So pure. So brilliant. So beautiful.

Lazarus

Home Secretary Chivers crossed the room and stood before Julia. "May I?" he asked, holding out his hand for
the letter. She obediently passed it to him. Chivers
scanned the note. "The blue gown he's referring to," he
said. "Do you know which he means?"

"Blue?" Julia knit her brows in thought. "It's not a
color I generally wear."

"You wore blue to Lord Attmark's boating party,"
Morgan said.

"Yes, you're right," she replied, sending him an appreciative smile. "I remember now. The gown is not one
of my best, but it is quite comfortable and perfectly adequate for an afternoon party. As I think on it, the day was
dreadfully warm, and—"

"Do you recall wearing blue at any other time in recent weeks?" interrupted Chivers.

She shook her head. "No. Just to Lord Attmark's."

Chivers shot a glance at Morgan for confirmation. At
his nod the Home Secretary smiled. "Very good. It may
not be much, but at least it gives us a place to begin. Now
then, who attended Lord Attmark's party?"

"Half of London," Morgan replied flatly.

Undaunted, Chivers turned to Mr. Goodington and
said, "Pay Lord Attmark a visit and see if he would be
kind enough to provide you with a list of everyone who
was in attendance—not only the guests, but the servants
as well. Then pay a call on Lord Winterbourne and see if

you can secure the same information from him. We shall compare the lists and narrow our suspects down to those who attended both events."

"Your suspect list may well be in the hundreds," Morgan pointed out.

"Perhaps," Chivers replied with a shrug. "Hundreds in a city of a hundred thousand. At least we are narrowing it down, are we not?"

That said, he gave his man a nod, silently dismissing him. Mr. Goodington bade them good day and stepped from the room. Mr. Randolph, after promising his assistance anytime they should need him, left as well. As the sound of the front door closing echoed back to them, Morgan asked tersely, "Is that all you intend to do? Compare party lists?"

"Not precisely. There is another peculiarity contained within that letter; one that is even more striking than his reference to the viscountess's blue gown."

" 'I have followed your words and done as you directed,' " quoted Julia, beating him to it. "What does he mean?"

"In the past Lazarus has always selected his own victims. This time he let you do it for him, Lady Barlowe."

"Me?" she echoed, appalled.

"As you are aware, two fires were deliberately set in the days following the publication of your column. The first occurred on Lord Alfred Deerce's estate, the second on Sir Richard Wibberly's property."

"What has that to do with my wife?"

"In addition to planting the message for Lazarus and the society news that surrounded it," responded Chivers, "the central theme of Lady Barlowe's column was the abysmal conditions found in the workhouses. Specifically, Robert's Home—the workhouse located just off Garner Row. It did not take a great deal of investigating on my part to discover that both Lord Deerce and Sir Wibberly serve on the board of guardians for Robert's Home."

Julia sank back into her chair, struck by a weight of guilt so heavy, she nearly felt ill. Five dead. The direct result of a column she had written. "I never expected that he might—"

"There was no way for any of us to predict it," Chivers reassured her immediately. "Nevertheless, it is a most interesting development, however, is it not?" He stood and began to pace the room. Despite the dismal circumstances, he looked challenged and almost delighted.

"In the past," he continued, "his letters to you have always contained a note of passion and adoration, but it was clear that he regarded you as a compatriot of sorts. A woman whose zealotry for reform neatly dovetailed with his own ideals and religious fervor. Judging by this last letter, that has changed. Now he is relinquishing the lead to you. He is doing your work and looking for a sign of acknowledgment and praise from you in return."

Julia shifted uncomfortably in her seat. "It was never my intention to inspire this sort of . . . zealotry, as you put it, Mr. Chivers."

"But the fact remains that you have, Lady Barlowe. To my way of thinking, it is quite wonderful that you have. It is incumbent upon us to seize this opportunity and capitalize upon it."

"What do you mean?" Morgan asked.

"Until this moment we have been in the frustrating position of waiting for him to strike, then searching among the embers for clues to his identity. In sum, he has controlled our actions. Now for the first time we may be able to control his. If this is any indication of Lazarus's current state of mind, Lady Barlowe is in a unique position to not only inspire the man's next move but to actually direct it."

"I see," Julia said, shooting a glance at Morgan. Judging by the grim expression on his face, Chivers's meaning was undoubtedly as clear to him as it was to her. She turned to the Home Secretary and asked briskly, "What did you have in mind, Mr. Chivers?"

"To put it in plain terms, a trap. If Lazarus is in fact taking direction from your column, we should waste no time in taking advantage of that. After discovering the connection between Sir Wibberly and Lord Deerce, I have been so bold as to presume that you would consent with my plan, Lady Barlowe. To that end I have selected a target for Lazarus."

"And that is?"

"I would ask that you write about a certain house of ill repute. If I may be so crass—a brothel. The site I have in mind strikes me as ideally suited to our purposes. The Cat's Paw. It's a rather isolated structure at the end of Canal Street. It houses less than half a dozen souls, all of whom could easily be cleared from the building in case of fire. Furthermore there are several abandoned buildings nearby in which my men could station themselves to watch for Lazarus."

She gave a tight nod.

"I have taken the liberty of assuming you would agree with this plan and written down the particulars for you," he continued, removing a sheet of paper from his coat pocket and setting it on the table before her. "If that information does not suffice, you may of course contact me."

Julia lifted the sheet and scanned the contents. As she did, a shiver of dark foreboding raced down her spine. "And if this fails?"

"To my way of thinking, we will have lost nothing," Chivers returned with a shrug. "But I believe it behooves us to take that chance, don't you? When does your column run next?"

"Not for another three days."

A flash of disappointment showed on Chivers's face. "A shame. I had hoped it might be sooner."

"I could contact my editor and see if he might place the column in tomorrow's paper—"

"No," interrupted Morgan. "To do so may very well arouse suspicion."

"I quite agree with Lord Barlowe," concurred Chivers. "Better that we take no irregular action, or do anything that might arouse Lazarus's suspicion. In the meantime, may I suggest that the two of you continue in the same vein that you have been? Attend as many social events as you are able, see and be seen. Perhaps luck will favor us, and Lazarus will say or do something to reveal himself sooner than we expect."

His business apparently finished, he flashed a quick, preoccupied smile, reached for his hat, and stepped toward the door. "Let us dangle the bait and see if he bites, shall we?"

Morgan moved to follow him. "I'll see you out."

"Not at all," Chivers returned, waving him off. "I shall put my powers of memory and deductive reasoning to work and find my own way. Good day to you both."

At the sound of the front door closing, an air of somber heaviness seemed to settle over the room.

Too restless to sit any longer, Julia rose and moved to the bay of tall windows that overlooked the gardens, standing a mere arm's length away from Morgan. "Events are escalating so rapidly, are they not?"

"You sound as though you regret that."

Until that moment her gaze had been focused on the gardens. Now she turned to face her husband. "We're forcing Lazarus's hand. I can't help but feel a sense of foreboding in doing so."

"Perhaps we're bringing things to an end."

"Perhaps."

He regarded her in silence, then said flatly, "We can call it off."

She let out a sigh. "And live like Sarah Montgomery? Spend every day waiting and wondering what might have

happened had we done something? No. We should proceed as Mr. Chivers suggests."

He nodded in agreement and turned away, glancing
about the room as though looking for an excuse to change
the topic. "You had a letter that wasn't related to your
column," he said, nodding toward the stack of parchment
envelopes that rested on the sterling silver tray. "May I be
so bold as to inquire who it was from?"

Julia regarded the tray in confusion, then abruptly
recalled the letter she had set aside. "Oh, yes. Henry. He
asked if I would pay him a call this afternoon."

"Henry?"

"Henry Maddox. My father's former bosun. You remember. He runs the warehouse down by the docks."

"I'll go with you."

A soft smile curved her lips. "If you're thinking that I
need protection, you're mistaken. Henry could not possibly be Lazarus."

"Nevertheless, I would like to accompany you."

For a moment she allowed herself to believe that he
might actually want nothing more than to enjoy an hour
or two in her company, away from the constant strain of
contemplating Lazarus's next move. But his next words
quickly disabused her of that fanciful notion.

"Henry Maddox may not be a suspect, but you've
said before that you felt Lazarus watching you when you
ventured out in public. I should like to be present should
that happen again."

"You can't follow me everywhere I go."

He gave a light shrug. "Let us just be cautious, shall
we? At least for the next week or so."

The next week or so, indeed. Her smile faded slightly
as she imagined a period of years stretching out ahead of
them, years spent constantly looking over their shoulders
for suspicious faces and ominous shadows. Years in which
she and Morgan remained nothing but aloof, polite
strangers. Refusing to consider that dismal scenario a mo-

ment longer, she sent him a brisk nod. "Very well. Give me a moment to freshen up, will you? I'll join you shortly."

As she left the room, she came to a rather unexpected and altogether unwelcome realization. Of the formidable goals she had set for herself upon entering into her marriage—capturing Lazarus and capturing her husband's heart—apprehending Lazarus might well be the simpler of the two.

*M*organ surveyed the room in which he sat. On his initial visit to the Tern's Rest, they had confined their stay to the tavern's busy front room. Had he given any thought to what he might find in the private rooms in the back of the establishment, he would have pictured exactly what he now saw. The wooden tables and chairs were old but well maintained and free of dust. The upholstered pieces were covered in neatly stitched cotton slipcovers, over which had been tossed a variety of embroidered pillows. An eclectic collection of paintings and seamen's treasures cluttered the shelves and mantel. Sheer lace curtains hung at the windows, and fresh flowers filled the vases. All in all, it was a welcoming, warm space; a room that seemed to perfectly suit Henry and Annie Maddox.

Although Morgan had tried not to intrude, he had of course been privy to their conversation. In short, Henry had invited Julia to tea in order to make her an offer for her father's warehouse. As his opinion had not been solicited, Morgan watched in silence as Julia studied the paper that outlined the terms of the sale.

"'Course, if you don't think that's enough . . ." Henry began.

"No, it's quite generous," Julia replied. "I'm merely surprised. It's all so unexpected."

"It's fairly unexpected for Henry and me too," said Annie with a smile. "But two of my regular customers came into some money and offered to buy the Tern's Rest. At first we turned them down flat, but then Henry and I got to talking." She paused and reached for her husband's hand, giving it a brief squeeze. "After all the years we missed together, what with him sailing who knows where and me running this inn, we figured it might be nice to spend our final years anchored down together. Maybe buy one of those little cottages they're building up on Drake's Hill and fix ourselves a real home."

Julia forced a small smile. "That sounds lovely."

"If you were still living with that uncle of yours," Henry said, "we wouldn't think of offering. But now that you're married to his lordship and all . . ." He made a vague gesture in Morgan's direction as his words trailed away. "Well, it didn't seem like the place mattered to you anymore, that's all."

"You haven't been by the docks in ages," Annie went on, shifting uncomfortably. "So Henry and I just figured . . . Well, we thought it just might work out for everybody."

"Yes, you're quite right," said Julia with a decisive nod. "In fact, we should have discussed this sooner. Mr. Randolph is holding the deed for me. I'll sign it over to you at first opportunity."

Henry cleared his throat. "I reckon your husband ought to sign it as well."

If Morgan didn't know Julia so well, he might have missed the subtle tension that crossed her features at the reminder that the warehouse was no longer hers to sign away. By law everything she owned had become Morgan's at their marriage. "Of course," she said, turning toward him with an artificial smile. "Morgan?"

"Certainly."

After another few minutes of rambling conversation, he and Julia made their exit. Rather than take the coach directly back to his estate, she hesitated, suggesting they walk a bit first. As it was clear that something was on her mind, Morgan acquiesced, letting her enjoy her silence as they moved along the wharf. It was not the sort of place he would have ordinarily chosen for a stroll. But at the moment a quiet, steady hum hung over the normally bustling docks. Apparently the blasted heat had rendered even the thieves, stevedores, and prostitutes too lethargic to be out of doors.

Julia seemed oblivious to their surroundings in any case. It was not until they reached the warehouse that had belonged to her father that she stopped. As Morgan eyed the dilapidated structure, he privately considered that its sale ought to be cause for celebration. But the expression on Julia's face was almost forlorn.

"Why did you sell?" he asked after a moment. "Clearly you didn't want to."

She lifted her shoulders in a light shrug. "Had Henry served in the Royal Navy all those years, rather than for my father, he would be entitled to some kind of pension. Instead, he received nothing. He and Annie deserve better than that."

"Yet it bothers you nonetheless to let it go," he observed.

"Silly, isn't it?" she said. "Of all the memories I have of my parents, my father being reduced to ending his days living here is certainly among the most painful. Yet it's also one of my last memories of him, and thus one of the hardest to let go." She shook her head, letting out a small, wistful sigh. "Why is it so hard to let go of the past?"

A good question—and one that Morgan was certainly not qualified to answer. Not after having spent the past two years reliving one single, fateful dawn. Left with a silence he could not fill, his gaze moved over his wife. She wore a gown of pale peach muslin that rustled gently as she walked, giving her a soft, distinctly feminine air. Sunlight gleamed off the burnished copper of her hair, weaving strands of pure gold through the fiery masses. Her shoulders looked unbearably slim, far too fragile to be burdened by the weight of recent events.

He lifted his hand to comfort her, then abruptly froze, lost in his own awkwardness. Despite his former reputation as a rake, that simple gesture of compassion and understanding seemed somehow beyond his capabilities, or at the very least outside his realm of experience. His mother had been a beautiful, capricious figure who had appeared in his life with great irregularity. He had been raised by a series of nannies who had always ended up displeasing one or both of his parents, and thus he had learned never to get close to them. He had no sisters. All in all, the sum of his experiences with women were purely sexual in nature—a fact that left him with a ridiculous ineptitude for comforting his own wife.

As Julia turned, he immediately lowered his hand, feeling like a common thief who had been caught delving into another man's pocket. As a glint of sunlight bounced off the medallion she habitually wore about her throat, he reached for the thin piece of gold as though that had been his intent all along.

Frowning, he rubbed the medallion between his fingers and said, "Forgive my oversight. I ought to have seen to your jewelry weeks ago."

"What do you mean?"

"A viscountess should have something of quality to wear, even for an occasion as mundane as a midday stroll along the docks." He paused, considering the matter. "There is a jeweler on Bond Street who carries an adequate stock of goods on hand. Naturally the better pieces will have to be specifically designed for you, but I believe we may be able to find a few trinkets in the interim."

"Thank you, but I prefer this."

Somewhat surprised by her refusal, Morgan glanced at the figure depicted on the medallion. "Mary?" he guessed.

"Saint Rita. Patron saint of the impossible." She

leaned against a battered warehouse wall, regarding him with a small smile. "Consistently appropriate, wouldn't you say? Always asking for too much, and yet I'm rarely disappointed."

He released the medallion. "Most women find diamonds consistently appropriate."

Her smile faltered for a fraction of an instant. "You would have been better off with a more sophisticated woman."

"Would I?"

Her sherry gaze searched his face. "Why did you marry me?"

"To find Lazarus. And because I found you breathtaking." Sensing she was looking for a reply a little less shallow, he continued with an honesty that surprised even himself. "And because you possessed an inordinate amount of spirit and courage. That much was clear from the very beginning. You did not simply bemoan your fate or berate your uncle for the predicament he put you in, although you certainly had every reason to do so. Instead you fought back."

She slowly nodded her head, as though surprised and pleased by the depth of his observation. "Aren't you going to ask me why I married you?"

"You made it abundantly clear that night," he said with a shrug. "You had no other choice."

"One always has choices."

Morgan hesitated. Feeling like a man who is about to lose his wallet to a consummate swindler in a shell-and-walnut game, he said, "Very well. I'll ask. Why did you marry me?"

"Because you were my phantom lover in the garden that night."

He froze, stunned by the admission. The jealousy he had experienced earlier at hearing of the man she had lain in bed dreaming about was replaced by a surge of overpowering sadness. "I'm afraid that man no longer exists, princess."

"Doesn't he?"

"No."

"I'm sorry to hear it."

Morgan regarded her in silence. In that instant he was vividly aware of everything around him. The barefoot children dressed in rags, the odors of gin and rotting fish brought in by the tide, the drunks snoring in alleyways.

Yet despite their desolate surroundings, the air seemed to crackle with possibility. Not beauty, but abundance. Life. There was a richness here that he had never experienced, despite his ample wealth. The recognition brought him a sense of heightened perception. He noted the way the sun brought a glow to Julia's skin and a sparkle to her eyes. Unable to stop himself, he lifted his hand and drew it gently across her cheek, fighting a sudden and ridiculous urge to pull her into his arms and renew the kiss they had shared a few days ago.

"Have I told you how beautiful you look today?"

A soft smile curved her lips. "Funny, I was about to remark on how you look today."

"Oh?"

"Indeed. You look like a man who is about to kiss somebody."

"Is that an invitation?"

"Merely an observation."

He gathered her against him, reveling in the taste of her lips against his. In the past Morgan had always considered a kiss a prelude to seduction. He wouldn't have considered sharing such an intimate moment in so public and unseemly a place. His courtships had all been meticulously prescribed: the right wine, the right flowers, the right glow of moonlight, the right trinket to be bartered to sate his lust. Now he had something entirely different, something that threw that petty little formula completely askew.

Julia.

The right woman.

As Morgan slanted his mouth over hers, he felt something open deep within him, as though a hint of lightness had managed to work its way into the darkness of his soul. A sense of wonder he hadn't known since he was a child swept over him. In complete disregard for propriety, he crushed her lips beneath his, ravaging and plundering her mouth, desperate to assuage a hunger he had barely known existed. Her touch opened a great, vast gully of need that rose up within him, choking off all other thoughts and emotions.

She locked her arms around his neck and returned his kiss with a sweet fervency that nearly made him groan aloud. He pressed her tightly against him, clutching her thighs and buttocks, kneading her flesh, as though attempting to absorb her strength, her goodness, her generosity of spirit. A slight trembling erupted between them, but he couldn't tell if its source was him or her. It didn't matter.

In that instant his lust was transcended by something else, something he vaguely recognized as more powerful and rare than anything he had experienced. His scars were forgotten, his past was forgotten. He was lost in the sweet healing redemption of her embrace.

He supported her in his arms, taking all her weight. She felt so incredibly light and fragile, and yet he had experienced firsthand the iron strength of her will. He brushed his fingers along the tops of her breasts, then, unable to stop himself, lowered his mouth to explore that lush swell of erotic flesh. Her skin felt softer than rose petals against his lips and carried the intoxicatingly feminine scent of powdered talc and lavender soap. Gently moving his hands along her spine, he felt her shudder and lean into him, as though surrendering entirely to the mastery of his touch.

His desire to take her right there and then rose to

almost unmanageable proportions. But the echoing shouts of the children playing nearby brought him to his senses. With a feeling of intense regret—coupled with a determination to continue where they had left off at the earliest opportunity—he broke their embrace, gently setting her away from him.

Julia took a moment to gain her bearings, then gazed up at him. Her face was flushed, her eyes were slightly cloudy, her lips were swollen from their kiss. In a word, she looked more beautiful than he had ever seen her.

"You have the oddest look on your face," she observed softly. "What are you thinking?"

He took a step backward, establishing a safe distance between them. "I was thinking that if we don't return soon we'll be late. Mr. Chivers recommended that we continue to make an appearance at various social events. There is a ball this evening at Viscount Trycore's that we should attend."

His wife was not good at schooling her emotions. An expression of bewildered disappointment shadowed her features at his abrupt change of mood, then brave acceptance swiftly followed.

"What should I wear?" she asked.

An easy question. Simple. One he could handle.

"The color of fire, my love."

Chapter 14

*B*rilliant red.

Not dark ruby, not purple-tinted garnet, not warm cherry. Rich, fiery crimson. Shocking scarlet. Yards of the shimmering red silk swirled around Julia as she moved.

Although she had worn the gown for Lazarus, it had seemed to cast a spell over her and Morgan as well. Rather than feeling like a pawn in a madman's game, she had experienced a strange sense of power and direction. For a while it had been a night of magic. Viscount Trycore's gala had been not merely a chore to endure but an actual pleasure.

She recalled the way Morgan's hands had slid over her body with a lover's touch as he had guided her through dance after dance. The way his eyes had smoldered with smoky intensity as his gaze had locked on hers. The way he had held her tightly and whispered in her ear. At the viscount's midnight supper, he had even selected the choicest morsels for her to eat.

As a result Julia had glided through the evening in a state of blissful sensual suspense. She had been intoxicated by her husband's touch, by the candlelight, the dancing, the champagne. Secure in the knowledge that they were taking steps to conquer Lazarus, she had relegated the arsonist to the back of her mind. Her focus had been centered entirely on Morgan. There was something in his touch, some thrilling combination of possessiveness and pride that she had never felt before. She had felt it in the kiss they had shared earlier that afternoon as well— the longing and quiet desperation, the sensation that he wanted her as badly as she wanted him.

There had been a radiant, dreamlike quality to the evening that she thought wouldn't end. Thus when their coach had drawn up in front of Morgan's estate and he had handed her down, she had been so certain he would renew the kiss they had shared earlier on the docks that she had almost pursed her lips in anticipation. Instead he had merely escorted her to her bedchamber door and politely bidden her good night.

Even then Julia had not believed that he truly meant to part from her. In time, however, her expectation that he would return dissolved into pure frustration, her light champagne intoxication soured into a dull headache, and her confidence shattered. She relived his every touch, his every smoldering look, his every word, but to no end. Inevitably she had to face the truth. Morgan was not coming to her room.

She emitted a soft sigh and cast a glance at her bed, but that promised nothing but endless hours of tossing and turning. Even if she weren't plagued by feelings of sheer unrequited frustration, the night was far too warm to expect a restful sleep. Furthermore, the thought of languishing alone in her bedchamber with nothing but her own thoughts to occupy her held absolutely no appeal.

Acknowledging the fact that she seemed destined to gain little sleep that night, she looked about her room for something else to occupy the hours until dawn. Spying a book that sat on a corner table, she went and lifted the small leather volume. A scientific survey. She wrinkled her nose in distaste. Deciding to return the volume to Morgan's library and search for something more to her liking, she left her room and quietly padded down the broad stairway that led to the main floor.

Silence greeted her as she stepped into the room. Beams of silvery moonlight filtered in through the parted drapery, but they didn't provide enough light to adequately read the titles of the volumes that filled the massive floor-to-ceiling shelves. She lit a small lamp and turned the wick down low, then moved to the bookshelves.

"Decided to join me, princess?"

Julia released a startled gasp and spun around, searching the shadows for Morgan. At last she found him. He sat in a tall wing chair that had been positioned in a far corner. On the table beside him rested a silver tray, a crystal decanter, and a set of squat crystal glasses. Like her, he had yet to change from his formal attire, though he had relaxed somewhat. His jacket was draped over the back of his chair, his cravat was loosened, and the top buttons of his shirt were undone, allowing her a glimpse the dark bronze skin of his chest.

Conscious of having intruded on his privacy, she sent him a small smile and said, "I couldn't sleep."

"That makes two of us."

His tone was neither welcoming nor curt. He studied her face with a watchful gaze, as though attempting to divine her thoughts. She shifted awkwardly, uncertain what to say next. It wasn't that she necessarily felt nervous, just strangely disconcerted. She had no idea how to interpret his mood—a mood that was so very different from the warmth and intimacy they had shared at Viscount Trycore's. Remembering the book she held, she crossed the room and set it on the table beside him. "I believe this was mistakenly left in my room. I hope you weren't looking for it."

Reluctantly removing his gaze from her, he gave the slim leather volume an indifferent glance. "Birds," he said flatly.

"I beg your pardon?"

"The book."

Her eyes returned to the volume. *Staemon's Complete Ornithological Survey.* "Oh. Yes." She clasped her hands together and sent him what felt like a patently false, overly bright smile. "Does the subject interest you?"

"Not particularly." He raised the crystal tumbler he held and abruptly drained it of its contents.

A shiver of apprehension ran through her as she watched him. "Are you drunk?"

"I have had a drink. I am about to have another. But no, I am not drunk." He splashed a generous amount of amber liquid into the glass he held, then tilted it toward her. "Can I pour you one?"

"No. Yes. Thank you." She sent him a faltering smile, then crossed her arms over her chest and rubbed her hands briskly over her forearms, as though warding off a chill. She took the glass he offered her and drank deeply, then grimaced and shuddered, staring in horror at the contents. "That's ghastly. What is it?"

"Hundred-year-old scotch."

"No wonder it tastes so vile. Do you have anything more recently brewed?"

A small smile touched his lips. "I'm afraid not."

"Oh." She frowned at the glass, unaccountably disappointed. Yet even as she did so, a relaxing warmth filled her belly, softening the edge of her nervousness. She took another small sip.

Returning her gaze to Morgan, she watched as his eyes moved over her body with smoky intensity, as though committing her every line and curve to memory. "Stunning," he said.

She ran her hand over the brilliant red of her gown. "It's French."

"I'm referring to what's underneath."

Having no idea how to reply to that, Julia didn't attempt it. At a loss for any other suitable topic, she abruptly decided to abandon all attempts at pretense and move directly to the heart of what was on her mind. Summoning her courage, she said in a rush, "I've been thinking about our bargain."

"Oh?"

"It seems rather foolish now, doesn't it?"

"As I recall, you wanted a three-month reprieve." He lifted his shoulders in a cool shrug, then took a sip of his drink. "Although little else good might be said about me, I am generally reputed to be a man of my word."

"Indeed. You've been very patient. Very honorable, as well."

A small, cynical smile curved his lips. "Not exactly the words I would have chosen."

"No?"

" 'Cuckolded fool' comes to mind."

Seizing his statement as an admission that the wait might have become as difficult for him as it was for her, she said, "In that case, if you have no objection, I thought we might commence our marital duties."

He regarded her in silence for what felt like an eternity. "May I ask what brought about this remarkable change of heart?"

Julia's courage began to crumble. She had anticipated a reaction of gratitude on his part at being released from their bargain, but she realized in that instant how exceedingly vain an expectation that had been. She hesitated, lost in her uncertainty, feeling both embarrassed and profoundly unprepared for the question.

Perhaps she would have been better served to stick to her original decision and give them a full three months to develop a more natural intimacy. Unfortunately it was too late to change her course now. It was all too easy to imagine the shame of fleeing from the room now that she had come this far. But she was determined to spare herself further embarrassment. Therefore, rather than admit the longing that kept her up at night—a longing that evidently went unshared—she searched for a reasonable excuse to abandon the terms of their bargain.

Suddenly remembering the newborn babe they had seen earlier that week at Lord Attmark's party, she said, "You made it quite clear that you wanted an heir. I hadn't given the matter much thought until I saw the Earl of Reardon's child. Now it occurs to me that you're quite right. There's no sense in waiting any longer, is there?"

Although the excuse sounded coolly plausible to her own ears, she was surprised to see Morgan's features darken as an expression that looked almost like disappointment flashed across his face.

"Ah, so that's it."

"Don't you want a child of your own?"

He finished his drink and set it aside, then stood and moved toward her. "Gilding the lily, aren't we, princess?"

"I beg your pardon?"

"You needn't dangle a carrot in front of me. You are ample lure by yourself."

Unable to meet his eyes, she fumbled with her glass, surprised to find it empty. Although she didn't remember drinking the last of it, she suddenly wished for more. Morgan now stood less than an arm's length away, but still he made no move to touch her. She swallowed hard and released a nervous, tremulous laugh. "It's funny," she said.

"What is?"

"I didn't imagine it would be like this."

"Like what?"

"This," she said, indicating the distance between them. "This formal, this stilted. I thought one was supposed to be swept away by passion, as though lost in a tumultuous sea. Not dragged there as though one's coat were caught beneath the wheels of a railcar."

Morgan released a shocked bark of laughter. Her words, and her obvious distress, knocked him out of the stupor that had befallen him. He forced himself to set aside his disappointment that it wasn't him she wanted as much as a child of her own. She had come to him, and that was all that mattered. If the fire had taught him nothing else, it was to appreciate life on its own terms. Every miracle counted, no matter how small.

For just an instant logistics filled his mind. The room was too warm, too harshly lit. While there was nothing he could do about the heat, he had no desire to dampen what little ardor she had managed to kindle for him by subjecting her to the sight of the odious scars that marked his body. He could at least spare her that. Yet while cognizant of his wife's delicate sensibilities, he did not want to rob himself of the pleasure of seeing Julia naked. In the end he settled upon a compromise position. He crossed the room and lowered the wick of the lamp, leaving nothing but a warm amber glow to fill the room.

Turning back to Julia, he hesitated once again. Like a skittish deer that had picked up the scent of the hunter, she stood poised to flee at the slightest provocation. He could take her upstairs to his room, but he didn't want to risk having her change her mind before they arrived. The chair in which he had been sitting was out of the question. The rug was undeniably plush but struck him as slightly primitive for their first encounter. At last his gaze lit upon a burgundy velvet chaise that occupied one corner. Although he had never considered the piece with a decidedly carnal purpose in mind, he realized at once that it would serve nicely.

Their ultimate destination decided, he moved to stand before her. He pried the empty glass from her hand and set it on a nearby table. Then he ran his hands along her upper arms, attempting to soothe the tense rigidity he felt in her limbs. She stubbornly avoided his gaze, but Morgan was in no hurry. He waited until she tilted her face up to his, then gently asked, "How do you know that I'm not madly overcome with lust at this very moment?"

She gave a shaky laugh and jerked her head away, but not before he had seen how perilously close to the surface her emotions were. In a choked voice she pleaded, "Please don't make this worse than it already is."

"I didn't mean to." He pulled her into his embrace, running his hands gently down her spine. As he spoke, her hair brushed his lips, as soft and feathery fine as down. "I'm not normally so clumsy. You took me by surprise, that's all."

"I should leave."

He tightened his hold. "No."

She hesitated for a long moment, then slowly lifted her eyes to meet his.

"I want you to stay," he said. "I want you, Julia. I've wanted you from the moment I saw you."

Searching her gaze, he saw a reflection of his own inner emotions. Angst, uncertainty, desire, and determination were all mirrored in her eyes. But as she had bravely taken the first step in coming to him, it was now up to him to take the second.

He bent and lifted her into his arms. Even that small act brought him pleasure. The weight of her against his body, her slight gasp of surprise as he lifted her, her small embarrassed smile, and the way she locked her arms around his neck and nuzzled her head against his chest. He moved across the room and sat down on the chaise, holding her in his lap. With his hand he traced the soft swell of her breasts, then down to her narrow waist.

Tension filled Julia's face as she jolted at his touch. Clearly embarrassed by her reaction, she sent him a taut, brave smile. She was bracing herself for his embrace, he recognized, regarding him as though he were a physician who had just shown her the torturous path his scalpel would be taking, rather than a lover who had bestowed a light caress.

A previous conversation they had shared had led Morgan to form the opinion that his wife was no longer a virgin. But her extreme nervous trepidation now gave him cause to question that assumption. Either that, or she viewed her surrender to him as a fate far worse than he had presumed. Beauty succumbing to the Beast. Although the thought sickened him, he understood it.

Deciding not to assume the worst, he schooled his expression to one of polite interest and asked, "Do I frighten you?"

"No. It's just that I've never . . ." Color stained her cheeks as her words trailed to a halting stop. She looked away, then took a deep breath and bravely returned her gaze to his. "I don't have a great deal of experience in these matters."

Morgan studied her for a long moment, then lifted his hand and softly stroked her hair. "You do me great honor."

Despite his pleasure at her admission, he found himself somewhat at a loss as to how to proceed. While he knew scores of men who preferred to bed virgins, he had always gravitated toward women whose sexual experience matched his own. He strove to find words to lessen the fear and anxiety he read in her eyes, but nothing seemed adequate.

In the end he realized that delaying the moment further would serve only to prolong her sense of anxiety. That resolved, he drew her more tightly against him. Their bodies met and molded, her soft curves yielding to the greater firmness of his lean muscles. He lowered his head, pressing his lips against hers. He waited until she had accepted the feel of his mouth, then delved deeper, using the subtle pressure of his jaw to coax her lips apart. He swept his tongue inside her mouth, savoring the sweetness of her lips and the faint flavor of scotch on her tongue.

They established a rhythm that was slow and steady, moving in a pace of sweet exploration. After a moment Julia shifted slightly and locked her arms around his neck. Her hips rocked against his in time to their embrace. Morgan felt his manhood, already wakened by their kiss, now leap to life, straining against the fabric of his trousers.

Their kiss, initially a subtle, orderly thing, grew sloppy and urgent. Julia's hands mimicked the pattern of his own, moving with an almost frantic urgency over his back, his shoulders, his hair, and his thighs, as though driven by the same raw hunger, the same aching need. Their bodies rocked together as though leaving a mere fraction of an inch between them simply could not be borne.

Without warning a sense of burning dissatisfaction took root within Morgan. The taste of Julia's lips and tongue—as profoundly sweet as they were—were no longer enough to gratify him. He wanted more.

He was suddenly overcome with a reckless eagerness to see his bride. He attacked the tiny buttons and stays of her gown, seized by a carnal yearning he couldn't contain. Frustrated by the clumsiness of his hands, he battled an adolescent urge to simply rip the garment off her back. To his surprise and pleasure, Julia once again mimicked his touch, tugging at his clothing. Together they moved with wanton, random urgency, fumbling with eagerness and giddy, almost drunk with desire.

As though playing an erotic game, they matched each other's motions one by one. Her hairpins clattered to the ground. His onyx shirt studs followed. He pulled the bodice of her gown past her shoulders. She unfastened his pants. He removed her voluminous underskirts. She tugged his cravat free and tossed it to the floor.

Morgan had the distinct pleasure of finishing his task first. Having removed the last of her clothing—from the brilliant ruby silk of her gown to the soft white cotton of her dainty underthings—he eased her off his lap and onto her back so his eyes could feast more fully on her flesh. She was neither a large woman nor exceptionally waiflike. To his delight Morgan realized instead that she fell somewhere in between.

Julia was graced with womanly curves that would have suited a Roman goddess. As the amber light flickered over her skin, he drank in every stunning detail of her form. Her hair fell in shimmering, autumn richness against the burgundy velvet of the chaise. Her breasts were round, twin globes of soft ivory peaked by the deep rosy coral of her nipples. Her waist was so tiny, he guessed he could span it with his hands. Her hips were full and lush, her legs long and shapely.

Lovely. So very lovely.

He must have spoken aloud, for Julia's expression shifted from worry and nervous uncertainty into a smile of embarrassed pleasure. "Lovely," he said, tracing his hand from her breasts to her ribs and belly. "So very lovely," he repeated, marveling at the softness of her skin, the smooth feminine perfection of her form.

Perhaps emboldened by his words, or merely succumbing to her own curiosity, Julia reached up and parted his shirt, attempting to draw the garment off his back. Instinctively he tensed, clasping her hand to stop the motion. "I'll leave it on. I don't mind."

She studied him with a small, confused frown, then understanding showed in her gaze. She lifted her hand and ran it lightly over his cheek. "I mind."

She reached for his shirt again. This time he didn't stop her as she drew it off. He held himself rigidly still and watched her face as she scanned his scarred flesh. But rather than react with disgust, revulsion, or pity, Julia simply leaned toward him, gracing him with a lover's kiss. A kiss of reverence and beauty, pressed against such ugly and undeserving flesh that Morgan almost groaned aloud. Her sweet, guileless touch was nearly his undoing. Overwhelmed by a driving need to feel his skin against hers, he drew off his boots and socks, his pants and underclothes, letting the garments tumble to the floor in a careless pile.

As her gaze moved over his body, her attention was diverted not by his scars but by the sight of his engorged manhood. Color flamed in her cheeks, and she quickly averted her eyes, as though embarrassed by her overt display of wanton curiosity.

Morgan captured her hand in his. "Touch me, princess." He placed her palm on his chest, encouraging her to explore his flesh, giving her the time to accustom herself to the sight and feel of a naked man. After a moment he guided her hand toward his penis, intent on dispelling any fear she might harbor at the very foreignness of that member.

At first her grasp was light and tentative, merely the silkiest of touches. Then she moved her fingers up and down his shaft in an experimental motion that nearly drove him to his knees. A groan of hoarse pleasure tore from his lips as he shifted reluctantly out of her grasp, lest their lovemaking end too quickly.

He braced himself on his forearms above her and explored her every lush curve and mysterious hollow. No detail was too petty to go unadmired; a freckle on the bridge of her nose deserved the same devotion as the shadowy cleft between her breasts. His caresses were no longer smooth and sophisticated but raw and necessary. His hands greedily skimmed her hips, her thighs, her belly. He pulled his mouth away from hers and traced a path of fiery kisses from the nape of her neck to her collarbone, then across her ribs, her belly, and the slender arc of her hip.

He was dimly conscious of the need to go slowly, but he couldn't force himself to do it. He was almost frantic in his desire. Morgan had made love to other women since the fire. But those had been empty, furtive episodes, lustful skirmishes that took place in darkened rooms beneath heavy sheets.

This was different.

This was Julia.

He cupped her breasts in his hands, awed at the lush weight of the soft globes and the firm, erect feel of her nipples against his palms. He heard her startled gasp as he rubbed her nipples lightly with his fingertips, gently teasing them into even stiffer peaks. When he brushed his lips over her breasts and drew one stiff peak into his mouth, caressing and teasing her nipple with his tongue, she let out a low moan and arched her back, pressing herself into him.

After devoting the same lavish attention upon her opposite breast, his hands followed the path his lips had taken, heating and caressing her flesh. He felt her shudder at his touch, heard her breathless sighs, and felt her hands clutch and release his skin. Emboldened by her responses, he shifted his body lower still, brushing his lips along her upper thighs, eager to taste the very essence of his wife. But she must have realized his goal. Until that moment she had been relaxed, almost melting in his hands, purring at his touch. But now he felt her stiffen in silent, shocked protest. Acquiescing to her unspoken wishes, he moved on, reserving that intimate pleasure for another time.

He captured her mouth with his own, restoring the mindless rhythm of passion they had enjoyed only moments earlier. As he caressed her breast with one hand, he lowered the other to the tangle of coppery curls at the juncture of her thighs. He cupped her lightly in his palm, letting her adjust to the feel of his hand, then he used his finger to gently part her innermost lips.

Julia instantly stiffened in shock and clamped her knees together.

"Shhh," he said. "I'm not going to hurt you."

He regretted the words the instant he uttered them. He would hurt her. There was no way to avoid it. Nor could he qualify his statement without causing her further distress. Therefore he simply moved on, continuing his loving, lustful ministrations. Finding the tight pearl of flesh at the entrance to her sex, he teased it with his fingertips until she was writhing beneath him, her breath coming in hot, shallow pants. Her initial reticence was transformed into glorious eagerness as she dug her fingers into his shoulders and arched her hips to allow him greater access.

At last judging her ready, he withdrew his hand and adjusted his position, bracing himself on his elbows above her. Primitive understanding showed on her features as she watched him with an expression of wariness and need.

Morgan let out a low groan as he slowly guided himself into her. She clutched him unbelievably tightly, sheathing him in her wet, silky warmth. He could have found his release that instant, but he gritted his teeth and willed himself to hold back. He pulled out slightly and eased himself more deeply inside her, only to find his passage blocked. He could go no further. Although instinctively loath to hurt her, he had no choice. Rather than belabor the moment further, he drew his hips away, then gave a sharp, quick thrust forward, tearing through the fragile barrier that had held him back.

Julia's cry of shock and betrayal was captured against Morgan's mouth.

"Shhh, let it go. The pain will ease. It will ease."

His words were nothing but foolish nonsense, based only on hearsay. Nevertheless Morgan desperately hoped that they would prove true. He moved his hands up and down her body in long, comforting strokes, doing what little he could to take away her pain.

After a moment he felt her relax beneath him. "Yes," she murmured against his cheek. "Yes. It's all right now. It's all right."

Breathing a sigh of relief, he slowly eased himself forward once again, watching her face for any sign of pain. He felt her inner walls stretch to accommodate him, tightly clutching his manhood. Soon she began to thrust her hips upward to meet his strokes, urging him on. Her breath fell against his neck, hot and shallow. He met her fervent pace, driving deep and hard into his wife. Suddenly Julia stiffened beneath him. She let out a cry of release as a shudder ran through her body.

Morgan froze, allowing himself the pleasure of watching his wife as she found her satisfaction. Her sherry eyes were glazed with wonder. A flush spread across her chest; her nipples were drawn tight and hard. A fine, silky sheen of perspiration glistened on her skin, coating her body with a fine mist that sparkled like fairy dust in the amber light.

Pressure swelled within him, a pressure so intense it was almost pain. Unable to hold back any longer, Morgan thrust forward once again. Two hard, sharp thrusts were all he needed to reach his own satisfaction. He poured into her with an explosion that rocked him to his very toes. His strength depleted, he collapsed on top of her, breathing hard.

After a moment he rolled off her and onto his side, cradling her body against his while they both fought to regain control. He traced his hand over the lush curve of her hip, her belly, and her breasts in a relaxed, unthinking motion. Like breaking free of a raging fever, he slowly regained his senses. His breathing became almost level. He was once again aware of the heat of the night, an owl hooting outside his window, a carriage passing in the street.

Julia shifted against him and released a long, deep sigh.

"Did I hurt you very badly?" he asked.

She shook her head, snuggling against his chest. "I didn't think it would be so . . ."

Whatever she had been about to say was lost as she caught his hand and pressed it against her belly. In a voice of wonderment she asked, "Do you think we made a baby?"

Morgan swallowed his disappointment at the stark reminder that she had come to him to get with child, rather than out of any sense of longing or sexual desire. "We won't know for at least a few weeks," he replied.

"Is it always like that?"

"You mean the wait to see if one has conceived?"

"No, I mean . . . what we did. Our union."

"No."

She turned in his arms to face him, searching his gaze with a small frown. "No?"

"No." He smiled and pulled her back into his embrace. "It gets better."

Lazarus held the *London Review* in his hand, squinting over Flame's column by the light of the moon. This was it. The Cat's Paw, the brothel she had written about.

The smell of sin surrounded him. The fetid stench of debris churned up by the river, the horse droppings, the drunks who relieved themselves in the alleyways, baring their arses to all who passed. Such filth. No wonder Flame had sent him here. To purify. He paused in a shadowed alleyway, eagerly feeling in his pocket for his phosphorous sticks. Such glorious work to be done.

But as he glanced back up at the brothel, a movement near the rear door caught his eye. A man. One of the sinners who frequented the establishment, no doubt. No sooner had he formed that opinion when the first man was joined by two others. The threesome briefly conferred then dispersed, assuming clandestine positions in the dark alleyway that led to the brothel.

Almost as though they were lying in wait for someone.

Panic seized Lazarus. Something was wrong. Something was very, very wrong. He must have made a mistake. A bad mistake. He shouldn't be here. The realization made his throat go dry and his heart pound against his chest.

He took what comfort he could from the darkness, shrinking back against the wall, cowering in fear, trying to make himself invisible. He could hear his father's hoarse voice even now, ringing through the night air. "Idiot! Worthless idiot!"

The sound of footsteps coming from behind him made him reel about in terror. He peered through the darkness, his heart in his throat. His father. He had found him. He walked steadily toward him, his face red with fury, his cane clenched in his fist. Lazarus stood frozen in horrified uncertainty. He could try to hide or run, but that would only make matters worse. Eventually his father would find him. He always did. Next would come the punishment. Quivering in fear, he braced himself for the harsh lash of his cane.

"Evening, m'lord."

Lazarus blinked in foggy confusion. It wasn't his father at all. Merely a night patrolman swinging his truncheon.

"Good evening."

The patrolman peered at him through the darkness, the frown on his face visible even beneath his bushy mustache. "Anything wrong, m'lord?"

Lazarus managed a shrug. "Merely a wife who doesn't appreciate that her husband likes to take a night now and then to share a fine bottle of port with his friends." He smiled, pleased at the ease with which the lie had sprung from his lips. With a vague gesture at a row of men's clubs not far from where they stood, he continued. "She's a fine woman, but the temperance type, you know. I thought I might clear my head a bit before returning home."

The patrolman nodded in commiseration. He leaned against the wall next to him as though they were old friends who had all the time in the world. Apparently glad for someone to relieve his boredom, he discussed his own wife, a woman who Lazarus determined was probably a fat, boring cow, just like her husband. As the minutes ticked slowly by, his frustration built to a near-fever pitch. He wanted to scream at the man, to rail, to pummel him with his fists. Instead he leaned casually against the rough brick wall, his face fixed in an idiotic expression of placid joviality.

"I don't suppose you'd have a wee nip of something on you?" the patrolman asked, glancing hopefully at Lazarus's pockets. "Something to take the ache out of my feet?"

"That'd be lovely, wouldn't it? But I'm afraid I drank my last pint."

"Ah, well. I'm sorry to hear that."

At last the patrolman sighed and straightened, sending him a reluctant nod of farewell. "Watch yourself for thieves, m'lord. Never can be too sure who you might run into. All sorts of riffraff hereabouts." That said, he went on his way, whistling and swinging his truncheon as he disappeared around a corner.

Lazarus watched him go, then moved automatically in the opposite direction. He had no idea where his feet were taking him. He simply walked and walked, his head spinning. He found no relief from the muggy warmth that filled the night air. His hands shook, his stomach churned, and sweat drenched his clothing. Twice he was certain he heard his father's footsteps behind him, but when he turned, the man wasn't there. But he was watching. Lazarus could feel him watching.

He stopped and pulled his copy of the *London Review* from his pocket. Yes. He hadn't read it incorrectly. The Cat's Paw. A brothel located on Garner Row. Yet they had been there waiting for him. It had been a trap. He was certain of it. He had come to cleanse, to purify. To burn the sinful house to the ground, just as Flame had directed.

Just as Flame had directed.

She had tried to destroy him. As his mind stumbled toward that inescapable conclusion, a sensation of crushing loss swept over him. For a moment he was broken, filled with such inconsolable grief that the weight of it nearly bent him in two. He had trusted her, and she had returned his trust with betrayal. He had seen something different in her, something rare and pure and bright. A glorious flame. He had thought she could be saved. But there was no hope.

His panic and despair turned to rage and self-loathing. His father's words echoed in his ears. *Fool! Idiot!* Did she think he wouldn't see? Did she think he wouldn't know? *Whore.* She was no different from any other of her kind. He didn't want to do it, but he had no choice. Just as his father had had no choice. She had to be punished. She had to be shown the way.

He became suddenly aware of a hoarse, gasping sound and realized it was coming from him. Laughter. He had been running, but he wasn't aware where his feet had taken him. He looked up and smiled in recognition. Of course. The Lord had brought him to this place to do His work, and so it should be done.

He cautiously approached the building and peered in through a window. He saw a man and a woman writhing together. Fornicating. Their eyes glazed with lust, oblivious to everything around them. He could hear every sordid and despicable noise they made. Their moans, their purred whispers, even the sound of their flesh slapping together as they moved. He watched in horrified fascination, choking back the bile that rose in his throat.

Such evil. Such ugly sin.

He waited until their lust had been sated and the couple drifted off into a sound sleep. With sweaty, shaking hands, Lazarus dug the phosphorous matches from his pocket. The window was already ajar, making his task that much simpler. All he had to do was lean forward and touch the burning flame to the drapery. In a matter of seconds the fire leaped to the rug. The flame swept around the room, licking and devouring everything it touched with a brilliant, righteous purity. He stepped back from the window as a thick stream of smoke poured from the room.

That was when the couple awakened and realized what was happening. He watched the man and woman as their lustful writhing turned to agonized pain and shrieks of terror. The sights and sounds sickened him. He wanted to stop it but he was powerless, incapable of moving. He could almost feel his father's heavy grip on his shoulder, firmly fixing him in place, commanding him to watch.

Eventually their screams faded away, leaving nothing but the sounds of cracking timber and billowing flame. Lazarus stared at the fire in gut-wrenching horror as tears streamed down his face.

She had left him no choice. He had to do it. She had to be taught a lesson.

All for you, my love. All for you.

Chapter 15

A thick film of greasy ash coated everything. Scores of smoldering timbers lay strewn about. They glowed eerily red, sending shimmering waves of heat pulsing toward the sky. Scattered bits of debris, most of it charred beyond recognition, lay juxtaposed next to items that had barely been scarred, reflecting the brutal leapfrog pattern of the flame.

The grim spectacle of the aftermath of the blaze should have been awful enough on its own. But there was also the matter of the stench to contend with. Buckets of water taken from the Thames had been used to quench the blaze. As a result, the docks reeked of raw sewage. But that wasn't the worst of it. The odor of badly burned human flesh drifted through the muggy air. Four bodies, burned nearly beyond recognition, lay stacked in a nearby dray. One blackened appendage protruded from beneath the rough wool blanket that had been used to cover them.

The men from Home Secretary Chivers's office

worked side by side with the men from London's newly
established Fire Brigade, combing through the smoldering
ash with handkerchiefs tied over their noses. A horde of
spectators hovered nearby, shaking their heads and making the sign of the cross, filling the air with the sound of
their dire whispers and gloomy murmurings.

Julia stood among that crowd, frozen in a stupor of
horror and disbelief as she gazed at the devastation before
her. The Tern's Rest . . . or what was left of it. The occasion of her last visit, a mere week ago, had been to sell her
interest in her father's warehouse to Henry and Annie.
They had toasted the bright promise the future held for
them all. Now the tavern was rendered to smoking ash.

And Henry and Annie? Julia's anguished gaze drifted
back to the burned appendage that hung from the dray.

She felt Morgan place his hand on her arm. Although
he stood beside her, his words sounded as though they
were coming to her through thick layers of cotton and
gauze. "You look as though you're going to faint."

His words served to shake her free from her stupor.
"Of course I'm not," she snapped. "I wouldn't dream of
doing anything so ridiculous."

Although she knew her reaction was nothing but misdirected anger on her part, she nevertheless took immediate offense at his words, as though they were some
reflection on her mental stability or moral fiber. She was
not a frail female who was subject to fits of vapors. No
one had used her or forced her into doing anything
against her will. She had deliberately baited Lazarus,
knowing there would be consequences. This was her fault.

There was no escaping the fundamental truth that
Henry and Annie would still be alive if it hadn't been for
her. It should have occurred to her that if their trap failed,
Lazarus might try to extract his revenge by hurting those
around her. She simply hadn't considered it.

Mr. Chivers, spotting her and Morgan amidst the
crowd, approached. He was dressed in his customary im-

maculate fashion, despite the early hour and the heat. "Word travels quickly, doesn't it?" he said by way of greeting. Turning to the scattered debris that covered the docks, he shook his head and let out a dark sigh. "I'm afraid Lazarus didn't come near the brothel all night," he said. "This looks like it might have been his work. From what we can tell, the fire was set deliberately. It could have been him, or maybe just someone trying to line their pockets with a bit of insurance money. We'll know soon enough. I'm sending one of my men down to the property records division to see who owns the place."

"Don't bother," Julia said, amazed that her voice sounded so strong. "The Tern's Rest belonged Henry Maddox. He was my father's bosun mate for years. His wife Annie ran the tavern."

An expression of shocked surprise showed on Chivers's features. He nodded, mulling over the ramifications of that statement. "I see."

"I don't suppose . . ." she began, but she knew even as the words escaped her lips that the question was pointless.

"An older couple?" the Home Secretary asked.

She nodded tightly.

"I'm sorry."

His words fell on her shoulders like a great weight. Breathing suddenly became difficult, the heat was more intense, the buzz of the crowd grew unbearably louder. Amazing. She had felt so prepared for the worst. But then, preparing oneself for something and having it occur were two very different things.

Chivers cast a glance at the dray, then turned toward Morgan. "I wonder if you would be able to help, Lord Barlowe? We haven't found anyone else who could identify—"

"Of course," Morgan replied tightly. He gave Julia's arm a reassuring squeeze, then stepped away, silently accompanying the Home Secretary.

She was only too willing to leave the ghastly chore to Morgan. She said a brief prayer, indulging one last time in a few seconds of irrational denial. Let them be safe and unharmed, she pleaded silently. Perhaps Annie and Henry had left the city for a few days, and it was another older couple who had been found among the ashes. Perhaps—

Chivers lifted the rough wool blanket to allow Morgan a glimpse of their faces. Julia watched in horror, unable to take her eyes away as Morgan's features tightened in grim recognition. She felt bile rise in her throat as her knees went weak and an icy shiver swept down her spine. Despite her earlier protestations of hearty fortitude, she sank onto a wooden crate, grateful for the temporary seat.

Mr. Chivers lifted a second blanket, exposing the remaining two bodies. Morgan gave them a quick glance and shook his head. The grisly task accomplished, the men returned to her side.

"Any chance one of those two might be Lazarus?" she heard Morgan ask.

Mr. Chivers shook his head. "Highly doubtful. I thought if you recognized one of them, that might lead to something. . . ." He let his words fade out, giving a somber shrug. "They're both older men, and neither one is in any condition to run from a pursuer. The pub owner across the way knew them only by their Christian names. They didn't have any trade. Just a couple of old salts who did odd jobs down here by the docks. We found empty pints in both of their pockets. If I were to make a guess, I'd say they had their fill of gin and crawled into that alleyway to sleep it off for the night. Cursed timing on their part."

The three of them watched in uncomfortable silence as Chivers's men sifted through the debris, looking for anything that might lead them to Lazarus.

Morgan let out an impatient sigh and raked his hand through his hair as he surveyed the rubble in disgust. "Christ."

"What happened at the brothel?" Julia asked Chivers. "You and your men saw no sign of him?"

The Home Secretary grimaced. "No sign. If he was there, I don't know how he saw us." He looked at the smoldering ash and shook his head, an expression of bitter disappointment on his face. "We must have given ourselves away. I thought he might not have seen your column, Lady Barlowe. Or perhaps he had seen it but he chose to ignore it. I never expected—"

"None of us expected it," Morgan said.

"But why this?" she asked. "If he wanted to hurt me, why not come directly at me? Henry and Annie had nothing to do with any of this."

Morgan answered before Chivers had a chance. "If Lazarus discovered you had set a trap for him, he may have decided to punish you for your betrayal. That has been his way all along. He uses fire as a means to punish his victims. Not to hurt them directly, necessarily, but to show them the error of their ways."

"I'm afraid I must agree," Chivers said. His sharp, considering gaze moved over Julia. "Who else knows of your connection to this place, Lady Barlowe?"

She thought for a moment. "Any number of people," she said with a sigh. "I came here regularly before my marriage—at least once a week. I made no effort to hide my destination. We have seen in Lazarus's letters that he made a game of following me. Given that, it's highly likely that he might have seen me here."

"Yes, I suppose so," Chivers concurred dismally.

Their conversation turned to the information the Home Secretary had been able to glean from witnesses. Unfortunately, most of it struck Julia as either contradictory or simply unhelpful. One man had seen a suspicious stranger dressed in a cape. A woman had seen a stocky man with a limp. A seaman on leave reported a middle-aged, well-dressed man running through the docks, laughing almost hysterically to himself. And there were more. Tall, short, fair-haired, dark-haired, so bald his scalp shone in the moonlight . . .

After few minutes she simply quit listening. She folded her hands in her lap and stared blindly at the smoldering ash. Beyond her grief and exhaustion, she experienced a profound sense of failure. Her gaze shifted to the dray as the driver climbed aboard. He gave the reins a light shake, setting his mules plodding into motion. The crowd wordlessly parted to let the vehicle pass.

Chivers cleared his throat. "Is there any family to be notified?"

She shook her head. "They had no children. Henry's brother died years before. Annie has—had—two sisters, both of whom reside in Leicester."

"Do you recall their names?"

So dry, so unemotional. It seemed impossible to believe that they were discussing two very dear people whom Julia had known nearly all her life. While she struggled to remember the names of distant relatives, Morgan stepped away, joining Chivers's men as they sifted through the ash and debris. From the corner of her eye, she watched him push the rubble aside with the toe of his boot, intently studying the charred remains. He moved on, then abruptly turned back with a frown, returning to the spot where he had originally stood. Bending down, he sifted through the ash and lifted something from the debris. He studied the object for a long moment with a concentrated frown, then tucked it in his pocket. Curious, Julia made a mental note to ask him what he had found.

"Very well. I'll see to it then," Chivers said, redirecting her attention to their conversation.

Startled that their interview had come to such an abrupt end, she looked up at him and said, "What shall I do now? Should we try to set another trap?"

Chivers shook his head. "Whoever we are dealing with may not be entirely sane, but that does not imply that he is fool. In fact, his actions seem to suggest the opposite, do they not? Continue your column if you wish, but in no case should you attempt to instigate contact on your own."

"That's everything, then?" Morgan asked as he returned to her side.

"For the moment, yes. I would suggest you take whatever precautions you deem necessary to keep yourselves safe. If you receive another letter from the man, I would be most indebted if you would share that with me immediately. Aside from that we simply wait."

She studied him in disbelief. "You're suggesting we do nothing?"

"It has been my experience that time favors the just, Lady Barlowe. Eventually our luck will change for the better."

On that optimistic—and to Julia's mind, supremely unrealistic—note, Chivers bade them good day and returned to join his men.

With nothing more left for them to do there, Morgan placed his hand on the small of her back and guided her toward his coach. He helped her inside and stepped in behind her, pulling the door shut as he did so. As they drove away, the grim reality of the scene came rushing at her. No matter how she tried to push the images away, she couldn't escape them. The shocked crowd. The smoldering debris. The charred limb.

As they moved through the bustling streets, the heat and darkness within the coach grew increasingly oppressive. She felt hollow, hot, and sticky, her nerves shattered to the point of collapse. Perhaps Lazarus was right. She should be punished. While Henry and Annie had been trapped inside the Tern's Rest burning to death, she and Morgan had spent the night wrapped in each other's arms. In fact, they had left so quickly that morning, she hadn't yet had a chance to bathe. The scent of their lovemaking still clung to her skin, marking her guilt as clearly as a hot brand.

She took a deep breath, struggling to control her churning emotions and retain her dignity. They would return to Morgan's estate shortly. There she could retreat to her room and surrender to her feelings in private.

Unfortunately, her husband chose just that moment to fix his attention on her. "Julia?"

Unable to met his eyes, she turned away, staring blindly out the coach window. "Yes?"

"Are you all right?"

"Certainly," she managed in a small, choked voice.

Ignoring her shaky affirmation, Morgan reached out and pulled her into his arms. Embarrassed, she tried to draw back, but her resistance was futile. He cradled her against his chest, ignoring her puny struggles to break free. It was too late to save her dignity in any case. Unlike some women, who turned into gushing faucets of sentimentality at the slightest provocation, Julia was not prone to public displays of emotion. Therefore she was all the more embarrassed at her lack of ability to control her reaction to the morning's events.

She cried for the horrific way Henry and Annie had died, she cried out of guilt for the part she had played in their deaths, she cried out of shame for the comfort she had taken in Morgan's arms while her friends had perished, and finally she cried at her own lack of control— because she felt like a fool for crying but simply couldn't stop herself.

At last she took a deep, shuddering breath and accepted the handkerchief he passed her. She dabbed her eyes dry and blew her nose, then sent him a small, embarrassed smile. "I apologize. I didn't mean to subject you to that."

He brushed back a strand of her hair that was matted to her cheek and kissed the spot where it had lain. "You don't have anything to apologize for."

"Henry and Annie would be alive if I hadn't run that column."

After a long moment of silence, Morgan released a deep sigh. "I couldn't have predicted what he would do. Neither could you. Neither could Chivers."

"It's all my fault."

"No, Julia. It just feels like it is."

Perhaps it was his tone, or the look in his eyes, or just the simplicity of his words. But that statement finally penetrated her own grief and self-absorption. Morgan knew. Moreover, his understanding ran deeper than mere words of consolation. She had seen the scars he bore on his skin, she had heard the rumors of what had transpired in his servants' quarters on that foggy morning over two years ago. For one of the few times in her life, words failed her completely.

Julia had assumed she held a vague notion of the horror he had gone through. But now she wondered. What must it have been like to have fought so valiantly and to have failed nonetheless? To have lost everything he had held dear? The woman to whom he had been betrothed, his standing in society, his notion of his own ability to control his life and protect those around him. All of it gone with a wisp of smoke. Even his reflection in the mirror had changed. The Beast.

A heavy somberness fell over her as the questions drifted through her mind. Too exhausted to examine them at length, she released a sigh and leaned back against his chest, taking what comfort she could from his embrace as their coach lumbered toward Grosvenor Square. To her surprise, another vehicle proceeded them through the tall gates of Morgan's estate. The door was blazoned with the regal family crest of the Earl of Bedford.

"Were you expecting Jonathan Derrick?" she asked.

"No, I wasn't," he replied, studying the coach with a slight frown.

The vehicle came to a halt in the circular drive before Morgan's front door. But to her surprise and dismay, it wasn't the earl who disembarked from the coach, but her

Uncle Cyrus, Aunt Rosalind, and cousins Theresa and Marianne.

Julia reluctantly shifted off Morgan's lap and onto the seat bank opposite him. "Just like bad pennies," she said with a small apologetic smile. "Always appearing at the most inopportune moment." She lifted her shoulders in a resigned shrug. "I suppose I would have had to call on them immediately in any case. At least this saves me the trip."

"You planned a social call?"

"Of course. Clearly I have no choice after the events of this morning. If Lazarus knew about Henry and Annie, he cannot fail to know of the existence of the rest of my family. If he is determined to continue to strike out at the people around me, they are all in grave danger."

A strange, shadowed expression crossed Morgan's face. As a groomsman moved to their door to pull it open, he waved the man off. "See that our guests are shown to the west parlor and offered refreshments. The viscountess and I will be along shortly."

"Very good, m'lord."

Morgan studied her in somber silence, waiting until his servant had stepped away and given them the privacy he obviously required. At last he said, "Has it occurred to you that Cyrus Prentisse may very well be the man we are looking for?"

"You cannot be serious. Uncle Cyrus?"

"You told me yourself that your uncle felt slighted by society for not having been recognized as a peer of greater stature."

"Resentment over his status in society would hardly would indicate a diabolical need to burn all of London to ashes in revenge."

"You must admit he fits the profile of the man we are seeking," Morgan pressed. "Cyrus is directly connected to you and could easily have monitored your movements. It is certainly conceivable that he would have known of your column at the *Review* and of the warehouse you operated with Henry—"

"In which case he would have demanded the entire profits from both ventures."

"Furthermore," he continued doggedly, "it is not inconceivable that he might have harbored a personal grudge against me. The fact remains that he did openly press the suit of both his daughters, neither of whom interested me in the slightest."

"If we are to suspect every father of a daughter you either rejected or seduced in your career as a consummate rake, I imagine the list of suspects would include nearly every household in England."

"It should also be noted that Cyrus Prentisse was not on the guest list for the galas that were being held that year by the Earl of Chilton and Lord Webster. Many in society regarded those parties as the events of the Season. The arson that followed could easily be construed as retaliation for the perceived slight."

"There are many events to which my uncle is not invited," she pointed out.

"Would you at least consider the possibility?"

She ran the premise through her mind. "No," she said firmly. "No. It can't be."

"Julia—"

"Do not for a moment imagine that I am defending my uncle's character," she interrupted with a rueful smile. "In fact, just the opposite is true. But as far as the matter at hand is concerned . . ." She paused, shaking her head. "Lazarus seems to be motivated by sin and redemption. Uncle Cyrus is motivated by money and social status. They are two very different things."

"But if I am right?" Morgan asked.

"If you are wrong?" she countered. "If Lazarus harms them and I do nothing to warn them of the danger? No," she said, a slight shudder running through her frame. "I'm sorry, but I simply cannot abide another death on my conscience."

Before Morgan could further attempt to dissuade her from her course, she opened the coach door and stepped outside. Apparently acquiescing to her wishes, he walked beside her in silence as they made their way to the west parlor.

The informal receiving room was one of Julia's favorite places in all of Morgan's estate. But as she stepped inside, she felt the same tight, uneasy tension she experienced whenever she was near her family. Gazing about the room, she noted that her Uncle Cyrus looked even more smug and superior than usual. Her aunt and cousins regarded her with expressions that could be defined only as gloating satisfaction.

After polite greetings had been exchanged, she asked, "Isn't the earl with you?"

"No, but he was kind enough to lend us the use of his coach for the afternoon," replied her uncle.

"Oh?" Something in his tone told her there was more to come.

"We have glorious news, Julia," gushed her aunt.

"Yes?"

"Jonathan Derrick, the Earl of Bedford," Cyrus Prentisse intoned regally, "has asked for permission to court Marianne. Furthermore, he has made it quite clear that his ultimate intention is to request her hand in marriage."

Fixing a polite smile on her face, Julia turned toward her cousin and said, "What wonderful news. I'm so happy for you both."

Her aunt immediately launched upon a long and painfully elaborate discourse regarding the details of the courtship, the date the betrothal would be formally announced, the wedding plans that had been undertaken to date, the items Marianne had acquired for her trousseau, and a million other details so petty and sundry, Julia forgot them the instant they were mentioned. Glancing across the room at Morgan, she noted that he, too, listened with polite but blank interest. At long last her aunt seemed to run out of breath, and the conversation ground to a merciful close.

A brief, awkward silence followed. Julia hesitated, giving the matter of Lazarus final consideration. Although she knew she was directly proceeding against Morgan's wishes, she could think of no other course but to warn her family of the danger they might be facing. Therefore she took a deep breath and announced, "Actually, it's quite fortunate that you've all come. I had intended to pay a call this afternoon."

"Oh?" said Rosalind.

"I hate to follow Marianne's joyous news with something unpleasant, but I thought you should know . . ." She hesitated for a moment, searching for the right way to frame her words. At last she blurted, "There's been another fire. Another deliberate case of arson."

"Oh dear," sighed Rosalind. "Between those ghastly fires and this dreadful heat, the quality are simply fleeing London. If this keeps up, there'll be no one of any standing left to attend the gala the earl is hosting next week. Then where will we be? Something simply must be done."

"Yes. Well . . . I'm afraid there's something else you should know," Julia continued. "This latest fire occurred down at the docks, at a tavern owned by Henry Maddox, my father's former bosun. It appears as though the fire may have been indirectly connected to me."

"Connected to you?" Cyrus's gaze moved from her to Morgan with a frown. "How can that be?"

In a manner as level and straightforward as she could manage, Julia proceeded to inform them that she was the anonymous author of "The Tattler," that she had been receiving notes from Lazarus, and that she was involved in the failed trap Mr. Chivers had set for the arsonist. So as not to frighten or overwhelm them any more than necessary, she concluded briskly, "I'm certain he will not attempt to retaliate any further, but I thought it only fair you be warned in order that you might take whatever precautions you deem necessary to protect yourselves."

Expressions of appalled shock and stark disapproval greeted her confession.

To Julia's surprise, it was Marianne who spoke first. "You're doing this deliberately, aren't you?" she cried. "You're trying to undermine my courtship. You can't stand the fact that I shall soon outrank you socially."

"I wish you nothing but happiness, Marianne. My only concern is for your safety—"

"How could you involve us in another scandal?" Rosalind wailed, her florid complexion even redder than usual. "After everything we've done for you, Julia. How could you?"

"What will this do to *my* chances?" demanded Theresa. "At least Marianne has a beau. I'll be ruined—all because of her. You cannot allow this, Father."

Cyrus leaped angrily to his feet and turned to Morgan. "Can you not control your wife?"

Until that moment Morgan had been leaning casually against the marble mantel, observing the goings-on without speaking. Now he subtly shifted his posture, standing with his legs spread slightly apart, his full weight resting equally on the balls of his feet. His icy gaze fell directly on Cyrus Prentisse.

"Apparently not," he replied. "It was my recommendation that Julia not issue the warning you just received. Not only did I deem it a complete waste of time, it struck me as foolish in the extreme to expect any sort of gratitude for the risk she was taking in openly exposing her connection to Lazarus."

"Gratitude?" echoed Cyrus incredulously. "What of the risk she has subjected my family to? What of the scandal?"

"There will be no scandal if this discussion does not leave this room."

"You cannot mean that you condone her activities. I warned you from the first that she was too high-spirited, too pampered and indulged. What she needs is a firm hand of discipline. If that task is beyond your capabilities, I would be only too glad to—"

"Before you finish that statement," Morgan interrupted, "I would ask that you remember in whose home you are standing."

Cyrus's expression tightened. "Very well." He nodded to his wife and daughters, who stood and assembled at the threshold of the room. As Cyrus shepherded them out, he turned to Morgan and haughtily intoned, "Let this matter be in your hands, Lord Barlowe. As you reap, so you shall sow."

"Worthy advice for us all."

A resounding silence filled the parlor as they left. Julia watched them go, lost in her uncertainty. Had she done the right thing in warning her family of the danger? Then again, how could she not have done so? It was preposterous to conceive her uncle as the arsonist who was terrorizing all of London, and clearly they had no intention of letting on that she was the anonymous Tattler. Still, a flurry of questions ran unanswered through her mind. What if it was Cyrus? What if it wasn't?

Pushing them aside for the moment, she turned to Morgan and forced a tight smile. "Well, that was pleasant." When he failed to reply to either her words or her tentative smile, she lifted her shoulders in a slight shrug and said, "At least I warned them."

"Yes. So you did."

He moved to the window and watched the Earl of Bedford's coach pull away from his drive, a contemplative frown marring his features. Once the gates had been closed and securely locked behind them, he turned to her and gave a polite nod. "If you'll excuse me."

Morgan retreated to his study and spent the remainder of the day in conference with his secretary. She si-

lently debated whether she should go to him and
apologize for having disregarded his counsel, but that set
a precedent she didn't like. Then again, would it cost her
so much to admit she might have been wrong? She was so
dangerously anxious to please him, she couldn't seem to
think straight any longer.

With nothing to occupy her time, she roamed restlessly about the estate. The day's post brought nothing
but a few invitations and a letter for Morgan. She briefly
adjourned to her room and attempted to focus on her
column but found herself completely uninspired. Failing
that, she moved out to the gardens. The day's heat, barely
tolerable earlier that morning, was now too oppressive to
bear. Defeated, she drifted back indoors, feeling as wilted
as the flowers she had wanted to gather.

At long last the afternoon faded into nightfall. Cook
prepared a light supper of clear soup, poached fish, aspar-
agus, beetroot, and boiled potatoes, followed by biscuits
and an assortment of cheeses for dessert. Morgan proved
as cordial a host as ever, but Julia found herself unable to
feign an appetite. She toyed with her food, sending it back
to the kitchens with an apologetic smile. She did, however, manage to drink the glass of cool, dry wine that was
offered her, as well as the second. As unaccustomed as she
was to spirits, she immediately felt the wine's effect. She
felt fuzzy-headed but relaxed, the restless tension that had
gripped her all day temporarily allayed.

When Morgan adjourned to his own room after supper, she was left with no choice but to do the same. As it
was too early for bed, she sprawled out in a tufted chaise,
attempting to find distraction from her thoughts with a
book. But once again her thoughts kept drifting. Was
Morgan angry at her for openly defying him in warning
her family about Lazarus? Was that why he wasn't coming
to her room? As she could find no other reason for his
absence, she dismally concluded that that must indeed be
the case.

A knock on her door interrupted her thoughts. At her call to enter, Morgan stepped inside. He wore a gray silk dressing robe. Judging by his bare calves and feet, he wore nothing beneath it. In his hands he carried two oversize brandy snifters, each filled with a generous splash of the amber liquor. As he moved toward her, a sensation of giddy pleasure and relief raced through her.

"I'm glad you're here," she said with a soft smile, privately embarrassed by the depth of that understatement. "I was just thinking of you."

"Oh?" He set down the brandy and moved around behind her. Taking the book from her hands, he set it aside and began to gently massage her neck and shoulders. Julia closed her eyes and released a deep sigh. His touch felt heavenly. It was light, yet strong enough to soothe away all the knots and tension she had carried with her that day.

She had never been adept at the politics of relationships, being too forthright in nature. Thus she moved directly to the heart of what had been bothering her. "Were you very angry at me today?"

"Angry?" he repeated, a note of genuine surprise in his voice. "What made you think I was angry?"

"I didn't see you all afternoon."

"My apologies, princess. A score of mundane business matters required my attention. Nothing important, just loose ends that needed settling."

"Then you weren't upset that I openly defied you?"

He made a faint *tsk*ing sound with his tongue. "Did you?" he said. "That sounds rather dire. Why do I not recall it?"

"I'm referring to the fact that I acted against your wishes and warned my family about Lazarus."

"Ah. That. I wasn't aware that was direct defiance. I thought you were simply acting your own mind."

"To most men they are one and the same," she

pointed out. "Particularly if those men happen to be husbands."

"In that case I suppose I have a confession to make. Contrary to public taste, I have never been overly enamored with the concept of a dutiful, obedient wife. I encourage that ethic in my servants but not my wife."

"I see," she said, absurdly delighted by his reply. She was about to tell him so when she suddenly remembered something even more important that she had wanted to discuss with him. Breaking the gentle contact of his massage, she turned around, searching his face. "When we were down at the docks, I saw you pick up something from the ashes. What was it?"

"You saw that, did you?" He reached within the pocket of his dressing robe and passed a charred leather tassel to her. "It jarred a memory," he said with a shrug. "When I dove after Lazarus two years ago, my hand brushed his boot. Later I remembered not only the quality of the leather but the feel of a tassel as it slipped through my fingers."

"Lazarus wears Hessians?" she asked, instantly recognizing the distinctive tassel that hung from the front center of the boot.

He hesitated, then cautiously replied, "Perhaps."

Her excitement at obtaining their first real clue to the man's identity quickly waned. The tassel was far from conclusive. The expensive boot, generally worn by the upper classes, had been all the rage during the reign of the Prince Regent. It was still popular but less so now. It could have been worn by a member of the gentry, a servant who had inherited his master's boots, or simply a patron of the tavern. Like everything else the clue seemed initially significant, but in the end it proved to be as amorphous as Lazarus himself, vanishing like a cloud of smoke.

Nevertheless, one question remained that had to be asked. "Was Uncle Cyrus wearing Hessians?"

"No, he wasn't."

Julia experienced a strange surge of both relief and disappointment. Although it would have been dreadful to discover that her uncle was indeed the man behind the horrific acts of arson, at least they would have found some closure. How she longed to find the man once and for all, to end it completely. Instead tomorrow would bring nothing but another day of anxiety and uncertainty.

"Tired, princess?"

She sent him a small smile and nodded.

Morgan wordlessly helped her undress, then shrugged off his robe and slipped into bed beside her. He must have sensed the depth of her fatigue, for he made no attempt to initiate lovemaking. Instead he cradled her in his arms, running his hands over her body in a touch that was infinitely soothing yet not at all sexual. In time she felt him drift off to sleep, his arm draped heavily across her hip. But despite the comfort his presence brought, Julia was unable to find any rest.

She felt worried and anxious, unable to stop revisiting the emotions that had plagued her earlier that day. A profound sadness over Henry and Annie's brutal deaths washed over her. Tension regarding where Lazarus would strike next swiftly followed. Even petty little annoyances, like her family's reaction to her warning, loomed large and threatening. Try as she might, she couldn't put aside the vague feeling of dark foreboding that hung over her.

Was it nothing but fruitless worry that made it so, or some sort of prescience on her part? The question remained dark and unanswerable. And on that unfortunate note she at last drifted off into a restless and troubled sleep.

Chapter 16

Morgan reined in his mount at the crest of Sheffield Hill. An early morning fog drifted around him. It was not a particularly enjoyable fog, in that it offered no relief from the heat that already filled the air. Instead it felt warm and grimy against his skin. Upon consideration, it was not thick enough to be properly considered a fog at all—just a faint mist that had been tinged yellow from the constant coal smoke and industrial vapors that hung in the air. The sticky warmth and offensive odor was not the weather's only disadvantage. It also obstructed his vision enough to prevent him from seeing who had been following him for the past five miles since he had left his estate.

He did, however, have a suspicion who it might be. Lightly tapping his mount's flanks, he directed the animal into a narrow alley and waited for the rider who had been trailing him. Within moments a sleek chestnut mare appeared at the crest where he had earlier paused.

Leaning slightly forward, he called through the mist, "Over here, Julia."

His wife spun about in her seat, an expression of startled surprise on her face. "Oh. There you are. I didn't realize . . ." Her voice trailed off as she shifted uncomfortably in her saddle.

She was dressed in a pleated skirt of deep forest green that allowed her to ride astride. A pale linen blouse, sturdy brown boots, and matching gloves completed the ensemble. Her hair had been fashioned into a neat braid. A broad-brimmed straw hat festively adorned with silk roses and long streamers of peach and green ribbon added a pretty, feminine touch to her otherwise austere attire. She toyed with her reins as he studied her, looking as guilty as a child who had been caught stealing penny candy.

"Following me?" he asked.

A wry smile curved her lips. "That would be rather difficult for me to deny, wouldn't it?"

"Why?"

"You mean, why was I following you?" At his nod her smile abruptly faltered. In a tone of flat resignation, she replied, "You're going after Lazarus, aren't you? You shouldn't face him alone. I thought if there were two of us, I might be able to offer you some protection."

Morgan wasn't certain what he expected to hear, but that wasn't it. He regarded her in stunned surprise. That Julia might want to offer him protection was completely unheard of . . . and absurdly touching.

"Even if I were intent on hunting Lazarus," he said, "exactly how did you expect me to hunt him down?"

"Well, with the tassel you found yesterday . . ."

"I see." He nodded, impressed at the scope of her thinking, if not the logic. "What would you have me do?" he asked. "Go door to door searching the entire city for a pair of Hessians with one tassel missing? That's a rather ambitious undertaking—and a misguided one as well, I'm afraid."

"I see your point," she agreed after a moment, sending him a small, embarrassed smile. "It was a foolish notion on my part, I suppose."

She gave a wistful sigh and focused her gaze on the horizon. They sat atop their mounts in silence, sharing an unspoken reluctance to leave. As the sun rose higher and shone brighter, the yellow mist burned away, bathing the city in the harsh light of day. There were many places where the sight of London waking up, rousing itself like a sleeping giant to devour a brand-new day, was nothing short of magnificent. Sheffield Hill, however, was not such a place.

It was a working district, and thus despite the early hour signs of life surrounded them. Laborers filled trolleys, carts, and drays, crowding the streets as they headed toward their employ. The hungry wails of infants, the shouts of angry wives, and the grumblings of weary husbands all blended together in a chorus of poverty and discontent. From their vantage point Morgan and Julia had a clear view of the slaughterhouses, tallow works, and tanneries. The by-products of those industries oozed into the river in a thick current of slimy sludge, blood, intestinal waste, and excrement.

Julia gave a light shudder. "And one wonders why the stench of the Thames is so abhorrent."

"This is the most direct route, but certainly not the most scenic. Had I known I had company, I would have taken another path out of the city."

"Where are you—" she started, then broke off abruptly, giving a soft laugh. "Forgive me. I suppose that's your affair, isn't it? I believe I've sufficiently played the part of the shrewish wife, chasing her husband halfway across London in an effort to ascertain his whereabouts. I needn't compound the insult by badgering you with questions. I'll leave you to your pursuits."

She was, Morgan thought, gracious even in her own self-mockery. The prospect of spending the afternoon with her, as opposed to ruminating on his own thoughts, was infinitely preferable. "As it happens, I have a business matter to attend in Kent," he said. "Fortunately it's a rather civil transaction, so I doubt I'll have need of your protection. Might I enjoy the pleasure of your company instead?"

He watched indecision flicker over her face. "I shouldn't intrude—"

"Not at all," he insisted. After a little more coaxing, he at last persuaded her to join him. They rode together through the narrow, crowded streets, increasing their pace to a light, rolling canter as the cobbled ground beneath them gave way to broad dirt roads that would accommodate farmers' wagons. To his considerable satisfaction he found Julia to be a surprisingly good horsewoman. Other than occasionally pointing out a few sights of interest or unusual wildlife, they rode without much conversation. In time the broad open spaces, clear streams, and lush fields announced their arrival in Kent.

As they reined in at the small village of Charlesham, they found the open-air market bustling. "Hungry?" he asked. At her nod they dismounted and made their way through a variety of stalls, purchasing fruit, freshly baked bread, rich cheeses, local wine, and crisp biscuits that had been liberally dusted with cinnamon and sugar. At a tin-smith's stall they selected serviceable plates and mugs. Their marketing complete, Morgan tucked the purchases into a cloth bag and tied the bundle to his saddle.

They mounted and continued their journey. After a few miles' ride, he directed Julia off the main road on which they traveled and onto a narrower path that had fallen into disuse. A thick growth of brambles and weeds nearly hid the route entirely. They rode uphill, moving over a lush rolling meadow dotted with pockets of vibrant wildflowers. Morgan stopped at a shallow stream that meandered through a grove of tall, shady elms. Spread out beneath them was the village of Charlesham, complete with its tall church spire, schoolhouse, modest thatched-roof cottages and regal manors, and bustling market center. Looming a short distance above them was the majestic stone estate known as Snowden Hall.

Morgan reined to a stop and dismounted. Moving to Julia's side, he wrapped his hands around her waist and lifted her from her saddle. As he secured the reins of their mounts to the branch of a nearby elm, she surveyed the lush meadow in which they had stopped. He retrieved a blanket that had been tied to his saddle and spread it out over the lush grass. Prying the cork from the wine, he filled a tin cup and passed it to her.

They sipped wine and nibbled their lunch. Morgan relaxed back against a fallen log, stretching his legs out before him. He felt comfortably full and comfortably wearied from riding, more relaxed than he had been in months. Even the weather suited him. It was warm but not nearly as oppressive as the muggy heat of London. A brilliant blue sky hung overhead, puffy clouds drifted by, bees buzzed in the clover, and a pair of spotted fawns grazed a few yards away. The air smelled clean and fresh, slightly sweetened by the scent of wildflowers. He watched as two young boys held an impromptu race, releasing shouts of joy as they galloped headlong down a dusty road.

After a few minutes Julia let out a contented sigh. "This is lovely," she said, then cast a glance at the nearby estate. "You don't think the owner will mind our stopping here?"

"I don't mind at all."

An expression of astonished delight showed on her face. "This belongs to you?"

He nodded. "In truth, I had almost forgotten about it. Yesterday I received a letter from a local solicitor. Apparently someone is interested in purchasing the place. I came to make certain I wanted to let it go—one of the loose ends that needed my attention."

Her delight faded somewhat at that news. "I see." Schooling her expression to one of polite interest, she asked, "Has the estate been in your family long?"

"No. I purchased it just three years ago as a wedding gift for Isabelle."

A wry smile curved her lips. "You don't believe in giving trinkets, do you?"

He gave a light shrug. "In retrospect, it's just as well I never presented her with this house."

"Oh? Why is that?"

"Isabelle would have been gravely disappointed. She would have far preferred a diamond necklace—the gaudier and more ostentatious the better. Rusticating in the country was never one of her foremost goals. London was her life. The theater, the grand balls, the gossip, the gowns, the crowds—she thrived on it all."

"Then why did you buy it?"

"For myself, I suppose," he admitted. "For the children I had hoped she and I would one day have. Little did I know that the estate was cursed."

"Cursed?"

He nodded and sipped his wine. "Would you care to hear the story?"

"By all means."

Morgan thought for a moment, then began. "Legend has it that once an earl was traveling through Charlesham on his way to London when an axle snapped on his carriage. He was forced to stop for repairs. Having nothing else to occupy his time, he decided to wander through the village shops. In the market square he chanced to see a young peasant woman of phenomenal beauty and fell instantly in love. He had neither youth, nor beauty, nor strength, nor kindness to offer her, but he did have wealth.

"Learning that her family was impoverished, he of-

fered to support her parents and siblings if she would
consent to be his bride. She agreed, but only on the condition that they settle here rather than in London. They
wed, but there was no love between them. In an effort to
make her happy, he built her this house, complete with
fountains, gardens, ballrooms, and glittering halls. He
hired wandering singers and theatrical players to entertain
her, bought her the richest ball gowns, and served her
only the finest food. But in the end she left the old man
for a poor shepherd boy who offered her his heart. The
earl let the manor crumble around him and died shortly
afterward, a broken man."

Julia was quiet for a long moment. "How very sad,"
she finally murmured. "Is that true?"

He shrugged. "Village lore. I never met the man—or
his bride, for that matter. But I thought the story suited
the property's melancholy charm."

"Is that how it strikes you?" she asked, turning away
from him to study Snowden Hall with a pensive frown.
"Melancholy?"

He gave the manor a cursory glance. "Yes. Empty
and dilapidated. A bit of foolish whimsy on my part that
resulted in nothing but a drain on my coffers."

"I see a house of great promise," she declared, as
though defending a long-lost friend.

Morgan smiled and pulled her to him. "Ever the opti-
mist, aren't you?" He removed her riding hat and set it
aside, then eased her onto her back, her head resting in
his lap. He released her hair from the tight braid into
which she had secured it and ran his fingers through the
thick, fiery masses, massaging her temples and scalp until
her eyes drifted shut and small sighs of pleasure escaped
her lips.

"Do you ever think about the future?" she asked after
a long moment.

"What do you mean?"

She hesitated, then opened her eyes. Her sherry gaze

locked on his. "Our future. What will happen between us."

Morgan's hands stilled in midstroke. Clearly she had raised the issue for a reason. What could he possibly do if she, like the young bride of legend, secretly planned to escape? If she longed for a different lover, a better lover, one who was young and beautiful? Force her to remain with him out of a sense of pity and duty? The thought was even more unbearable than losing her completely.

A score of emotions poured through him, the strongest of which was primitive possession. Julia was his—as essential to his very being as the air he breathed or the food he ate. He could no longer imagine his life without her in it. They were legally wed, bound together in the eyes of God and man.

Temporarily overwhelmed by the depth of his emotions, he retreated into the comfortable shelter of dry humor. "Barring any dramatic separation, I imagine we will be stuck side by side, growing old and gray somewhere together. You will watch my hair fall out, and I'll watch wrinkles form around your beautiful eyes. We'll sip tea, rock our chairs, and discuss the glorious, bygone days of our youth."

She wrinkled her nose. "That doesn't sound very romantic."

"Is that what you want, princess? Romance?"

A bittersweet smile curved her lips. "That's what every woman wants."

Unable to stop himself, he drew his fingertips across the satiny perfection of her cheek. "In that case I shall have to oblige you and fall tragically, deeply, hopelessly in love, won't I?"

She rose from the position in which she had lain and turned to face him. "I expect nothing less."

Their eyes locked and held. The air between them felt heavy with unspoken words and missed opportunities. For a moment Julia thought he might kiss her. She would welcome it. In fact, she would welcome more than that. She would welcome being taken right there, right then, on a coarse wool blanket beneath a blue sky in the middle of a field of wild spring grass.

Apparently he was of a like mind. He leaned toward her as though to pull her into his embrace. But the laughing shouts of the young boys who had been racing on the road below them suddenly filled the air. Their intimacy shattered, the moment abruptly ended.

Morgan recovered first. "Would you like to see the house?" he asked.

Battling her disappointment, Julia managed what she hoped would pass for an enthusiastic smile. "Yes. Very much."

He helped her to her feet. Together they packed the remains of their lunch and tied the blanket and cloth sack to Morgan's saddle. Gathering the reins of their mounts, they walked the short distance that led to Snowden Hall. The closer one drew to the estate, the more magnificent it became. The manor house had been constructed of local quarry stone. Although the stones had glistened like the purest of alabaster in the morning sunlight, the duskier beams of the afternoon sun caused them to glow like softly mellowed gold.

Despite its stunning construction, it was evident that the estate had fallen into disrepair. Random pockets of stone crumbled like powder, giving the facade a somewhat pockmarked appearance. The fountains had long since gone dry. Overgrown strands of withered ivy filled the flower beds. The boards that had been hung over the windows to protect the glass had been torn aside, perhaps knocked down by a storm or collected by local villagers for use as kindling.

Its numerous flaws notwithstanding, to Julia's mind the estate had a magic all its own. She could easily picture a flood of guests arriving on a snowy winter's eve, the hearths blazing, and the warm amber glow of candlelight spilling from the windows to welcome them.

Morgan withdrew a key and unlocked the front door, ushering her inside. To her considerable delight, the interior proved just as promising. Morgan's home in London was graced with an undeniable richness but with an undeniable masculinity as well. Snowden Hall had been built to suit a woman. The rooms were large and spacious, grand without being too formal. Plaster ceilings, great mullioned windows, rich wainscoting, and oak parquetry flooring added a wealth of luscious detail that reminded Julia of a great multitiered cake from a fancy confectioner's shop. There were, of course, a few minor flaws. The house was empty, the floors were stained, the walls were patched, and an occasional windowpane was splintered and cracked. But as their footsteps echoed through the bare rooms, her imagination went to work, mentally correcting the defects and filling the spaces with an abundance of comfortable furnishings.

They left the main level and ascended a broad, curved stairway that led to the upper floors. Again, Julia labeled the rooms in her mind as they passed. A guest suite. A private library. A nursery. Morgan opened a set of broad doors that led to what was clearly the master bedchamber. She stepped inside to find a large room with a tall bank of windows that faced south, bathing the chamber with rich, golden afternoon sunlight. She moved toward the windows, her back to Morgan as she gazed out at the weed-choked gardens and sun-scorched hills.

He moved up behind her, staring out over the barren grounds. "I had forgotten how much work the place needed."

"It's beautiful," she corrected. "Perfect."

"You think so?" He sounded surprised.

She nodded. It was everything she had always dreamed a home could be. Yet she couldn't help but acknowledge that the house wasn't hers. Standing there, she experienced the same flood of emotions she had felt in that moonlit garden years ago, when she had watched Morgan gather another woman into his embrace. Longing and blind desire poured through her, accompanied by a shameful sense of reaching for something that wasn't meant to be hers.

She should just let it go, content herself with what they did have. But that had never been her way and never would be. Gripping her medallion, she rubbed the shiny gold between her fingertips, searching for guidance. Was it really too much to ask? Was it really so impossible that her husband might come to care for her—even a fraction as much as she cared for him? Perhaps if she just tried a little harder, perhaps if she just gave a little more. . . .

"Julia?"

Unable to confine her feelings to mere words, she spun around and locked her arms about his neck, pressing her body against his in a kiss of stark urgency and need. Thus far Morgan had always taken the lead in their love-making. But Julia couldn't wait. She had to tell him what she felt, and this was the language in which they communicated best.

There was no softness in her embrace, no slow, budding desire. Her need was too overwhelming to allow for grace or modesty. She poured all her hunger and longing into that single kiss. She kissed him with all her heart and soul, kissed him as though they were about to be swept away from each other forever unless they could find some common ground to cling to.

She felt Morgan's initial shock at her embrace quickly fade, escalating into the same primitive urgency that had seized her. He locked his arms around the small of her back and pulled her even more tightly to him, returning her embrace with a possessive fervor that sent fiery tremors racing down her spine. Their passion ignited, blazing out of control. Julia burned with longing and lust. She wanted to touch him everywhere at once, and to feel his hands caressing her naked flesh in kind.

He dropped down to one knee, pulling her to the floor with him. "We have no bed," he murmured against her hair.

"It doesn't matter."

"I can get the blanket from my horse."

"Don't leave me."

The command was primal, necessary. She pulled mindlessly at the buttons of his shirt, shaky and clumsy with desire. He followed her lead, fumbling impatiently with the row of tiny hooks and eyes that lined the back of her blouse. Somehow they managed to rid themselves of their clothing. Boots, socks, drawers, riding skirt, pants, blouse, shirt, all of it lay crumpled and abandoned in a disorderly pile.

Having no bed to retreat to, Morgan stretched out beside her on the wooden floor. As they renewed their kiss, his hands moved voraciously over her skin, caressing and exploring, heating her flesh with his touch. Julia mimicked his motions, almost desperate to return the pleasure he was giving her.

After a moment he tore his mouth away from hers. He nuzzled the sensitive skin at the nape of her neck, nipped at her collarbone, and teased her nipples with his tongue. He kissed her belly, her thighs, and the back of her knees. Every place his lips brushed her skin felt inflamed, singed by his touch.

Needing more than to passively accept the mere touch and feel of Morgan's kisses, she pressed her mouth against his neck. His skin felt like coarse satin beneath her lips, the taste was slightly salty on her tongue. As she moved lower to kiss his chest, she felt his muscles leap to life, subtly tensing wherever she pressed her lips. Emboldened by his reaction, she brazenly explored his body with her mouth, licking and tasting and sucking, reveling in that newfound source of pleasure.

She moved farther down, across his ribs and belly, then abruptly halted at his stiffened manhood. She cupped him gently in her palm, experimentally running her fingers over the silky skin of his penis. His member throbbed in reaction to her touch. But did she dare kiss him there? She cast a questioning glance at her husband, only to find his eyes closed, his breathing shallow, and his jaw tightly clenched, as though he were exerting every ounce of his will to hold himself back.

Overwhelmed by carnal curiosity, she reached a bold decision. As he had not objected to the touch of her fingers, surely he would not object to her kiss. She bent down low, lightly pressing her lips against the tip of his throbbing member.

She heard Morgan's sharp, quivering intake of breath, a sound that was more reflective of pain than pleasure. But the low moan that followed assured her otherwise, as did the way he dug his fingers through her hair, as though urging her on.

She drew him into her mouth, lightly swirling her tongue around his hardened staff. He felt silky smooth and yet rock solid, pulsing with life. She would have drawn the experience out longer, but all too soon she heard him give a hoarse groan and subtly shift away from her.

"Julia—" he managed, but even that single word seemed to be an effort, torn from deep within him.

He reached for her and pulled her upward. Bracing himself on his elbows above her, he kissed her with deep, savage possession. His hands moved over her body in an almost frenzied pattern, tracing her every curve and hollow. A tide of hot, quivering desire churned within her, mounting and building with each passing second.

Julia's sexual experience, outside of what she had learned with Morgan, was barely enough to fill a thimble. But she was intuitive enough to recognize that there was a rare glory in their lovemaking, that they had been given a unique and precious gift. But despite the dizzying heights to which they soared, she was overcome with a sadness she couldn't quite dispel, a sense that something elemental was missing between them. She wanted more—she needed a release for the emotions that swelled within her.

But the words she longed to say stuck in her throat, hopelessly blocked by fear and uncertainty. Unable to utter a single word, she cowardly decided to pour her heart out through her touch and let her actions speak for her. With every soft kiss she pressed against Morgan's flesh, her heart cried out, *I love you.* With every loving stroke of her hands against his skin, she silently whispered, *I love you.* With every brush of her lips against his, her thoughts screamed, *I love you.* Over and over, with every impassioned embrace, with every lingering touch and soft caress, with every smoldering glance, with every fiber of her being. *I love you.*

She would have made the moment last forever if she could, but the physical ache building within her would wait no longer for release. Nor, it seemed, could Morgan wait any longer to attain his satisfaction. He rolled so that the hard wooden floor rested beneath his back. Then he caught her about the waist and lifted her up, lowering her slowly down upon his thickened member. Julia's eyes widened at the foreignness of the position, but her body seemed to respond of its own accord. Her innermost lips parted to allow him admittance to the warm, silky chamber between her thighs.

Slowly realizing that it was up to her to establish the rhythm of their lovemaking, she leaned forward and grasped his shoulders. She lifted her hips, then brought them back down, proceeding with cautious uncertainty. But even that slight movement was rewarded with an audible sigh of pleasure from Morgan. Her courage bolstered, she lifted and lowered her hips, playing with the tempo and the depth of the motion. She moved slowly at first, then with increasing speed and intensity as her belly began to churn, sending quivering pulses of desire through her limbs.

Her breath came in short, gasping pants as tension seized her. Yet she sustained the motion of her hips, impaling her body over and over against the steel rigidity of Morgan's staff. She felt as though she were flying and falling at the same time, racing headlong toward a cliff from which she she would surely plummet and never be seen again.

Suddenly a shuddering explosion of wonder and desire filled her body. Her limbs tingled and stiffened. Wet, liquid release poured through her as she arched her back and cried out, unable to silently contain her pleasure. In the next instant her strength vanished completely, and she collapsed against Morgan's chest, shattering like a pane of glass.

He shifted slightly, driving into her with long, hard, pounding strokes that filled her completely. Like her, he was unable to find his release in silence. As his body stiffened and his seed poured into her, he let out a low moan of hoarse, shuddering satisfaction.

Their lovemaking ended, he pulled her tightly against him. They lay spent and exhausted, tangled within each other's arms. Sweat slickened their bodies, coating their skin with a warm, silky glow. Slowly their passion receded, fading like the tide drifting back out to sea.

The sudden, sharp sound of tolling bells broke the contented silence that had enveloped them.

Julia started, as did Morgan. They jerked upright to a half-sitting position, listening intently. Fortunately it quickly became apparent that what they were hearing was not the shrill and chaotic tolling of London's recently established Fire Brigade. Instead it was a different, soothing kind of bell. Resonant, deep and steady. Church bells, alerting the local parishioners of the commencement of late afternoon mass.

Having apparently reached the same conclusion,

Morgan sent her a sheepish grin at their alarmed reactions. But there was no recapturing the selfish bliss in which they had lost themselves. Reality came slowly back. They had found a temporary shelter here, but it was time to return to London.

He silently helped her to her feet, and they began to dress. Julia glanced around the room as she did so, feeling a sudden and compelling need to take stock of her own situation. The wooden floor was beautiful, she decided, but it had felt cold and hard beneath them. A feather mattress would have been infinitely nicer, but there was no bed here for them share. Furthermore, the windows poured in too much light, and the plaster walls were split and cracked.

Next she applied the same harsh scrutiny to her own marriage, forcing herself to see it for what it truly was, rather than what she hoped it might be. In a moment of bitter irony and understanding, she could well appreciate her husband's dilemma. The house was simply too small a gift for a true lady and too grand a gift for a simple sea captain's daughter. No wonder he had forgotten about its very existence. It was part of a dream Morgan had held in the past, a dream that had vanished with the fire that had nearly taken his life.

Besides, they had already exchanged wedding gifts. He had rescued her from the odious suitors that her Uncle Cyrus had presented her. She had brought him a promise of capturing Lazarus. Expecting any further depth of emotion from him was simply unrealistic.

As she fastened her riding skirt, she contemplated their future once again. Her waistline was still slim, but there was the distinct possibility that in their union they had conceived a child. If that were the case, would Morgan cease coming to her altogether?

He had made it abundantly clear that he wanted an heir. A male heir, presumably. Like most men, he would probably continue to try until he had reached the ultimate goal of creating male progeny to carry on the family name. And once they had done so? She took a deep breath, wondering how she would bear it if he stopped coming to her altogether. Even if their lovemaking meant nothing to him, she didn't want to lose his touch.

He moved to her side and helped her fasten her blouse. That accomplished, he lightly brushed aside her hair and placed a gentle kiss against the nape of her neck. "You have the oddest look on your face," he remarked. "What are you thinking?"

She gave him a soft smile, swallowing hard past the tight lump that filled her throat. "I was thinking," she said, "that if we do have a child right away, I hope it's a girl."

Chapter 17

Flame surrounded him. It burned the linen sheets and seared the finely knit lace canopy. Licked and swirled up the tall mahogany posts. Scorched the plump downy pillows. Everywhere, nothing but flame. Wild, greedy, hateful flame, devouring everything it touched. So hot, so agonizing, so terrifying. So inescapable.

Lazarus awoke with a startled cry, drenched in his own sweat. He had unleashed the fire, and now it was too strong to contain. Now the flame was after him. He had been doused with kerosene, and his own bed was on fire. His heart thumped madly in his chest as he released a cry of sheer, anguished horror. Panting in terror, he instinctively beat back the flames. Over and over he blindly swatted at the blaze, desperate to put it out.

Not again. It couldn't be happening again.

Please, God, not again.

Then, just as quickly as the flames had erupted, the fire vanished. Lazarus blinked, gazing about the room in

muddled confusion. The chamber was dark and still, illuminated by nothing but faint beams of silvery moonlight.
Everything was in its place. It was all familiar, all meticulously orderly. He was alone. There was no fire.

Or was there?

Seized by panic, he threw back his bedclothes and
scurried across the room. He curled up in a corner and
rolled into a tight ball, clutching his knees against his
chest as he rocked back and forth. A high, frantic whimpering rose from his throat as his gaze locked on the bed.
He was too late to stop it now. He had excited the memories. He tried to beat them back, but the flames engulfed
his mind.

Just as the blaze had consumed them both. The man
and the woman who had writhed in agony on the bed.
The slut and the man she was with. *Slut.* He repeated the
word again, using it to give himself strength. To see things
properly, as they truly were. To put everything in perspec-
tive. It didn't work.

He was a child again, watching and listening. But it
wasn't a dream or a vision. It was a memory—one he
couldn't banish, no matter how hard he tried. The sharp
odor of kerosene filled the room. Flame ravaged the bed.
He covered his ears, desperate to block out the sounds.
He heard them anyway. The man and the woman's tor-
tured screams. His own piercing wails. His father's deep,
booming voice, ringing out above him like the voice of
God.

*"Whore. Harlot. Evil temptress. You brought this upon
yourself. The flame of your desire shall perish at last. Your
sin shall be cleansed."*

Lazarus struggled to break free and save her. The
attempt was useless. He was a small, weak boy, defeated
by his own childish impotence. His father's hand clamped
down on his shoulder in a viselike grip, holding him in
place. He had to see. He had to see what sin wrought. He
had to learn what happened to those who defied the law

of God, who turned away from the path of righteousness and glory.

"*Fire rained down from heaven as the Lord blasted the sinners with the heat of his anger,*" his father continued. "*The world was purified at last. Go forth and sin no more, or you shall feel the stinging lash of His mighty wrath against your flesh.*"

Lazarus watched, unable to look away as agony knifed through him. His whimpering drew louder. He was crying, sobbing now, his throat choked with tears. In his fear and horror, he had released his bladder. A warm trickle of urine streamed between his legs. The shame of it made him sob harder.

His father was right. She had to be purified. There had been no choice.

But the words meant nothing to him.

He cradled his body into a tight ball and watched the woman writhing in the flames, screaming in agony as the fire devoured her flesh. His small, fragile world abruptly shattered. He didn't care what she had done. He didn't care about sin. He was seven years old, and he loved her.

Mama.

"You have a most unusual look on your face, Lady Barlowe," Thomas Fike remarked as he dipped his brush into one of the thick globs of paint that were smeared across his palette. "What are you thinking of?"

Julia shrugged. "Nothing in particular. Last night's ball at Lord Calderfield's."

"Yes," he said, nodding. "It was rather a bore, wasn't it?"

She made a noncommittal reply and smothered a yawn. Indeed. As far as the Season's harried round of galas was concerned, it had been a rather dull affair. The evening did, however, have two good points. The first was that her Uncle Cyrus, Aunt Rosalind, and cousins Marianne and Theresa had all been in attendance. After an initial period of awkwardness, they had behaved in a manner that was remarkably civil. Apparently they were so delighted at the breakneck pace at which the Earl of Bedford's courtship of Marianne was proceeding that they chose to forgive Julia for her inadvertent entanglement with London's notorious arsonist.

The second bright spot of the evening was that she had spent most of it at Morgan's side. Despite the severe trepidations she held as to the future of their relationship, at the moment the days were passing in a glorious blur of romantic intimacy and exploration. Were it not for the looming threat of Lazarus that hung over them both, she might have been completely happy.

"If you would be so kind as to drop your right shoulder ever so slightly, Lady Barlowe," the young artist instructed, interrupting her thoughts.

She did as requested, then sent him a small smile. "'Lady Barlowe' sounds so formal, does it not?" she said. "I'd prefer 'Julia,' Mr. Fike."

"I'm honored, Julia," he replied absently, his focus on the soft beams of light that streamed in the room through the bank of windows behind her. Releasing a sigh of impatience, he stood abruptly and shifted his easel to a position more to his liking. That accomplished, he reseated himself and sent her a quicksilver smile. "Then you shall call me Thomas."

"Very well, Thomas."

She stood alone on an elaborately staged podium, feeling absurdly self-conscious. She wore her gown of brilliant red silk, the very gown she had worn on the night that she and Morgan had become lovers. Thomas Fike, upon seeing her in the shimmering creation at Viscount Trycore's had declared that that was exactly what she should wear in the portrait he had been commissioned to create. She wore her hair elaborately swept up and her medallion about her throat. A large oval mirror was angled behind her. Although she maintained a motionless pose, her thoughts were anything but still.

Of all the rooms in Morgan's estate, Fike had selected the vast, empty ballroom as the ideal site for the portrait he had been commissioned to paint. He had declared that the light and staging were best here, and that the open doors and windows would allow the fumes from his paints to dissipate somewhat. To Julia the ballroom had been an odd choice, but she had bowed to his artistic caprice and acquiesced. Morgan had not voiced an opinion on the subject at all, short of remaining steadfast in his decision not to take part in the portrait—a fact that seemed to bother her far more than it did Mr. Fike.

She glanced about the room. Notwithstanding the fact that she and Morgan had shared their first true kiss here, to her mind the chamber remained slightly melancholy, redolent of romantic defeat. Perhaps that was why the room appealed to him. Mr. Fike had spent a considerable amount of time studying the portraits of Morgan's ancestors. No doubt he was determined to have his own work as reflective of the true state of their relationship as were the paintings that filled the front hall.

To that end she had felt the young artist's gaze on her and Morgan whenever their paths chanced to cross at various balls and late night suppers. He had watched them with a stare that was intent and judging, as though taking measure of their relationship. He seemed to have formed some conclusion, for he moved his paints and easel into their home with a bossy imperiousness, as though he knew exactly what sort of mood he wanted to achieve and would settle for nothing less.

"Now that," said Fike, "is exactly the sort of expression I am hoping *not* to see on your face when I paint your portrait. You look decidedly vexed."

"What sort of expression would you like to see?"

He absently waved one thickly laden paintbrush in her direction. "The usual. Something dreamy, subtly mystifying, sensual. As though you're a goddess and the honor of your touch will bestow life upon mortal man. Think of Cleopatra. Helen of Troy. Aphrodite."

Julia smiled and arched her brows skyward. "That's quite a look."

"I have every confidence in your ability to deliver such a look. In fact, I suspect you shall put your sister seductresses to shame." He regarded her with a smile that was blatantly suggestive, his deep brown eyes smoldering with dramatic intensity, as though she were the only woman in the world. Then, as quickly as one might extinguish a candle flame, his gaze sobered and he returned his attention to his canvas. "But don't bother now, because I'm still working on the background."

She regarded him with amusement. The more time she spent with Thomas Fike, the more she understood why London's foremost hostesses coveted him as a guest. With his soulful chocolate eyes, thick blond hair, and seductive manner, he was the unparalleled rake of the Season. Furthermore, he had a stature and self-assurance that few men possessed. In many ways he reminded her of her husband. Yet unlike Morgan's sleek elegance, there was a blunt edge to Fike's beauty, a coarseness that seemed to lurk just beneath his smoothly polished surface.

"Now that," he commented absently, furiously spreading paint across the canvas, "is a far more interesting expression."

"Is it? Hmmm. I was thinking of your reputation."

He shrugged, his gaze fixed on the canvas before him. "Most of the rumors you hear are gross exaggerations." He paused, sending her his most provocative smile. "I would hardly have time to paint at all if everything that was said about me were true."

Julia sent him a look of cool reproof. "I meant as an artist in demand."

"Ah." He smiled. "In that case the rumors are quite

authentic. In fact, I find that my talents in that area are actually underestimated."

"I see," she replied, smiling at the unabashed vanity on his part.

A movement near the doors caught her eye. Morgan strode into the room, moving directly to where Thomas Fike had set up his paints and easel. In a show of deferential grace, the artist stepped aside to allow his patron to examine his work.

A frown darkened Morgan's expression as he gave the canvas a cursory glance. "If you've finished for the moment, Mr. Fike," he said brusquely, "my wife and I have an engagement this afternoon."

"Very good, my lord." Fike gave a low bow, then wiped his hands on a nearby cloth and deposited his brushes in a solution of turpentine. He made his way toward the broad doors, turned, and nodded. "Until tomorrow, Julia."

Aware of her husband's sharp—and unquestionably disapproving—look at the use of her Christian name, she nodded and sent Fike a faltering smile. "Yes, until tomorrow."

She waited until he had left the hall, then stepped down from the podium on which she had been posed and moved to Morgan's side to study the canvas. As Thomas had mentioned earlier, at this early stage the work consisted of nothing but broad brushstrokes that suggested the background of the piece. There was nothing there to cause the intense frown she had seen on his face. Surprised at the harsh tone Morgan had taken with the man, she said, "Your dismissal was rather abrupt, was it not?"

"It was my understanding that there was a depth to Fike's work, that he was possessed of a singular ability to capture the essence of his subjects. That is why I hired the man. I am not paying him to seduce my wife."

Morgan, jealous? While the idea seemed ludicrous, there was no mistaking the edge to his voice. Even more ridiculous was the distinctly feminine surge of pleasure she felt at learning that she was capable of arousing such an emotion within him. "Actually," she rejoined lightly, "he reminds me of you. Or rather, the man you used to be. The irrepressible rake, out to conquer any female who had the misfortune to cross your path."

" 'You shall put your sister seductresses to shame,' " he mimicked in disgust. "What utter rubbish."

"I seem to recall your saying something in the vein of . . ." She paused for a moment, thinking. "Now what did I overhear you say in the garden that night? How the glory of the moonlight paled in comparison to the radiant luster of the young lady's alabaster skin?"

He winced and pulled her into his arms. "No need to be cruel, princess."

She tilted her head back to study his eyes. "Then give me credit for having a bit more sense than to take his words to heart. I suspect his only intent was to provoke an expression of smoldering desire on my face."

"Did it work?"

"Yes."

His dark frown instantly returned. "It did?"

"Absolutely," she averred with a smile. "I was thinking of you."

"Ah." He let out a satisfied sigh and tightened his embrace. "Very nice. Very nice, indeed." He captured her lips with his own, bestowing a kiss of heated passion and infinite longing, a kiss that warmed her to the very soles of her red satin slippers. At last, with a display of obvious reluctance, he pulled back.

Julia studied him through a haze of unfulfilled lust, struggling to reclaim her wits and say something intelligent. At last recalling what he had said when he had interrupted the painting session, she remarked, "I wasn't aware we had an engagement this afternoon."

"No?" Morgan regarded her with a puzzled frown. "I'm certain we did. In fact, I had my secretary make a note on my calendar, lest I forget. It's a new addition to my schedule, but one of which I hope you'll approve."

"You're already so busy as it is," she said. "What with fencing lessons, daily business affairs, morning rides, the House of Lords . . ."

"True. But I'm confident I can make room for this latest task."

"Oh?"

"Every Thursday afternoon: make love to Julia."

She arched one delicate auburn brow. "Just Thursday afternoons?"

"As it happens, I find that marriage has made me remarkably more flexible in regards to my time. I also have Thursday nights available, as well as Friday mornings, Friday afternoons, Saturdays. . . ."

"My, my. You certainly are accommodating, aren't you?"

With a rakish smile he reached for her hand and placed it on the straining bulge between his legs. "Unfortunately, princess, the same can't be said for my trousers." He bent down and lifted her into his arms in one smooth, effortless motion. "Shall we?"

Morgan carried her through the main floor and to the upper level, blithely ignoring the shocked gasps and knowing smiles of the servants they passed. Although a deep blush heated her cheeks at the brazen, blatant manner with which he proceeded through the house, Julia didn't object. Nor did she object as he kicked the door to his bedchamber shut behind them and gently deposited her in the center of his bed.

All things considered, it was a rather pleasant way to pass a Thursday afternoon.

*H*e was here. Lazarus was here.

Morgan could feel his watchful, hovering presence so close at hand, he could reach out and touch him if he so desired. In fact, he probably already had. The more he thought on it, the more convinced he grew that he knew the man. With that in mind, he gazed about the room at the guests who had assembled in Jonathan Derrick, the Earl of Bedford's, home, determined to identify him once and for all.

It was a relatively minor event, having drawn only one hundred or so attendees. That paltry sum could be directly attributed to two factors. The first was Derrick's bumbling social incompetence. Although his rank and title served to make up for a great many of his shortcomings, the man seemed to drift about in a perpetual fog. The second factor was the dreadful heat and constant threat of arson, the combination of which had driven a good portion of better society out of the city well in advance of the end of the Season.

Nevertheless, a good number of hearty souls remained, and of those most had chosen to attend Derrick's small gala. Morgan mentally composed a suspect list in his mind, weighing the threat that each man posed. There was Cyrus Prentisse, of course. Roger Bigelow. And all three of Julia's original suitors, each of whom had offered for her hand: Lord Edward Needam, whose current mistress exhibited a subtle but distinct bruise at the nape of her neck. Sir William Bell, already drunk and stumbling, despite the early hour. The Honorable Peter Trevlin, who was in the midst of flirting with a pretty young servant boy who looked no older than fifteen. A wretched group, to be sure, but was there a killer among them? Doubtful, Morgan conceded. So who was he overlooking?

The light touch of Julia's hand on his arm drew his thoughts back to her. "Have you seen Aunt Rosalind and Uncle Cyrus?" she whispered, nodding her head at a spot across the room. "They look positively beside themselves with glee."

He followed the direction of her nod across the room. Sir Cyrus Prentisse and his wife sat on a low, carpeted podium in a pair of grossly ornate, thronelike mahogany chairs that would have looked ostentatious had they been occupied by Albert and Victoria. Given that it was Cyrus and Rosalind seated within, they looked patently ridiculous. A slim trickle of guests filed by, dutifully offering best wishes and good fortune on the occasion of their daughter's betrothal to the Earl of Bedford, an event that had been formally announced just moments earlier.

"It appears as though society is finally paying Cyrus Prentisse his rightful homage," he remarked.

"For the moment," Julia returned, releasing a soft sigh. "But I suspect that by this time tomorrow he will be simmering in a stew of resentment once again, mentally compiling a list of all the imagined slights he suffered tonight." She shook her head and said, "But I am happy for Marianne."

Morgan's gaze shifted to Marianne Prentisse and Jonathan Derrick, watching as they strolled arm in arm through the sparse crowd. Not a bad match, despite the gap in their ages. They were both blond and pale, but they complemented each other in unexpected ways. Marianne's sharp features and piercing gaze countered the air of shaggy dim-wittedness that constantly hung over the Earl of Bedford. In return, the earl's simpleminded state of befuddlement served to make his young fiancée look somewhat less haughty and less concerned with rank and prestige.

"Not exactly a love for the ages, but they do appear remarkably content," he said. The rueful smile that curved Julia's lips told him that she understood at once to what he was referring.

Apparently deciding to enlarge upon the announcement of his betrothal as a theme for the party, Derrick had leased a score of richly detailed wax figures from the House of Madame Tussaud. Placed conspicuously throughout the hall were life-size replicas of famous lovers. Romeo and Juliet embraced near the buffet. The legendary King Arthur and Queen Guinevere reigned over the champagne fountain. Samson and Delilah stood at one end of the dance floor, Antony and Cleopatra waved from another.

Unfortunately the earl had not taken the weather into consideration when making arrangements for the display of the carved figurines. Or perhaps he had simply under-estimated the heat that would be generated by a hundred or so bodies milling about. In any case thin rivulets of wax had begun to drip down the faces of the fabled lovers, giving one the unhappy impression that they were dissolv-ing in tears.

Julia shook her head. "The poor man. Imagine going to all this trouble, only to have everything go to ruin like this."

Morgan shrugged. "Perhaps the weather will change."

"I do hope so."

A storm had been brewing all day, but it had yet to break. Instead the heavy clouds that loomed overhead served only to intensify the heat, as though compressing it into an even denser, muggier mass. Even the gusty breeze that stirred through the trees did nothing but pitch the hot air about, causing men to chase after their hats and ladies to clamp down their skirts.

The storm seemed to bring with it a mood of simmer-ing tension as well. Tempers were short everywhere. Hackney drivers hurled insults at each other as they jos-tled for position in the streets, shopkeepers argued with their clerks, servants were berated by their masters, and packs of dogs snarled over bones. Perhaps it was this at-mosphere that had inspired Morgan's conviction that the city could not stand much more of the constant heat—nor the constant threat of arson. He had the distinct impres-sion that things were coming to a decisive head. Lazarus was here, and he was preparing to strike again.

"For such a happy occasion, you look decidedly grim," remarked Julia.

"My apologies." He forced a smile and turned toward her. "I was just thinking of—"

"I know," she said, somber understanding filling her eyes. "But let us put him behind us for one evening, shall we? Let's be selfish just this once and claim the night for ourselves. We'll worry about him tomorrow."

Unable to resist her gentle entreaty, he nodded and gazed about the room, searching for a suitable diversion for them both. "Where would you like to begin?" he asked. "A glass of champagne? A plate of smoked oysters? A tour of the gardens?"

She smiled softly and shook her head. "A dance, if you please."

He gave a low, formal bow. "It would be my honor," he replied, offering his arm as he escorted her onto the dance floor. As the opening strains of a waltz filled the room, he pulled her into his embrace, holding her far more closely than what was dictated by the convention of the dance. Yet to Morgan his grip on her still wasn't tight enough.

He could not banish the fear that they had somehow come full circle. As though the events of late were entirely surreal, merely the beginning and ending to a dream. He would wake up tomorrow, and it would all be over. Even the gown Julia wore served to reinforce that worry. She had selected the shimmering, peppermint pink satin she had worn on the night they had met at the Devonshire House. While it seemed impossible to believe that she might leave his life as abruptly and as dramatically as she had entered it, fate had taught him how very fragile even the sturdiest foundations to one's life could sometimes be.

"What are you thinking?" she asked.

His eyes moved slowly over her face, as though memorizing every delicate feature. "Have I told you yet how beautiful you look tonight?"

She smiled and brushed her hand over the fabric of her gown. "You remember this?"

Unwilling to ruin what was obviously a happy reminiscence for her with his own gloomy trepidations, he smiled and replied, "Very well." Defying the rules of convention and decorum, he boldly followed the path her hand had taken, tracing his palm over the smooth curve of her hip. "I remember thinking when I first saw you that you looked like a cross between a luscious, sugary confection and a stunningly wrapped gift."

She arched one slim auburn brow. "That was your first impression of the gown?"

"No. As flattering as the gown is to your beautiful body, my first impression of the garment was that I would have far preferred to see it pooled at your feet."

Although his reply obviously pleased her, she clucked her tongue in mild reproof. "I thought you were supposed to be a reformed rake."

"A reformed rake?" he echoed, keeping his tone deliberately light. "What a ghastly notion. Isn't that rather like praising a stallion for behaving like a gelding?"

A slight, preoccupied smile touched her lips. "What was your initial impression of me?"

"Aside from the fact that you were the most stunning creature I'd ever seen in my life?"

"Aside from that," she returned, as a faint coral blush colored her cheeks.

Morgan thought for a moment, swaying in time to the music as he led her across the dance floor. "I had a variety of impressions of you," he finally replied. "But to my great relief, not one of them proved to be true. I suspect they were more a product of my own experiences and cynical expectations than anything you projected."

"That sounds rather dire."

"To begin with, I thought that Mr. Randolph was your husband."

"Mr. Randolph?" she echoed, giving a choked, horrified laugh. "He's old enough to be my grandfather."

"That's not so uncommon. A young, beautiful woman marrying a wealthy man with one foot in the grave and the other resting on a banana peel. From what I'm told, those marriages can be remarkably contented—so long as the husband allows his wife enough freedoms and liberties. Particularly those meant to compensate for certain inadequacies that might occur in an elderly man's bed." He paused, giving an indifferent shrug. "That was my initial impression of you. That you were a married woman searching for a mildly amusing diversion. And on that particular evening, it appeared as though a rousing game of Beauty and the Beast suited your fancy."

Julia looked appalled. "Yet you agreed to leave your companions and follow me?"

His eyes locked on hers. "The truth is, princess, I would have followed you anywhere."

She shook her head. "Had you known what I intended to lead you into, I suspect you would have run screaming into the night."

"Had I know then what I know now," he replied firmly, "I would have run directly into your arms."

Julia searched his gaze for a long moment, her brows drawn together in a troubled frown. "I lied to you."

"Did you?"

"You asked me once if I harbored any anger or resentment toward my father for his actions, specifically the fact that his drinking and consequent bad judgment led to my future being placed in the hands of my Uncle Cyrus. At the time I denied it, but of course that wasn't true. I was furious at my predicament—particularly because my choices were so limited that I had no option but to approach you with the outlandish and rather humiliating proposition that we wed." She smiled and shook her head. "Strange, isn't it? Were my father here today, I would thank him profusely."

He pulled her even more tightly into his embrace. "So would I."

"You say the oddest things," she remarked, studying him with an expression he couldn't define.

A pang of regret spiked through Morgan. He captured a fiery curl that had escaped from the elaborate, upswept arrangement in which she had styled her hair. Closing his fist about that stray lock, he gently rubbed his knuckles against the silky softness of her cheek. "Perhaps they wouldn't sound so odd if I said them more often."

The steps of the dance led them to cross the path of Roger Bigelow and Isabelle Cartwright. The other couple sent them a cool nod as they swayed past, looking supremely beautiful and staggeringly self-aware, their gazes moving around the room as though searching for the most prestigious guests to which they could attach themselves.

As Morgan returned his attention to Julia, he found that she had also been watching the other couple as they swayed past. But rather than share his amusement, an expression of profound sadness was etched on her face. "What is it?" he asked.

"Lord Bigelow and Miss Cartwright."

"What about them?"

She took a deep, shuddering breath, as though struggling to find the words she needed. At last she managed, "When I think of the circumstances that brought us together, I imagine you must be consumed with regret at what might have been. I don't blame you a bit. I'd be angry, too, if I had to settle for—"

"Settle? You cannot mean to apply that word to yourself."

"Then you mean you don't wish that Miss Cartwright—"

"I don't wish anything." He ran his hand lightly down her spine, his gaze locked on hers. "What I am consumed with, princess, is a profound sense of awe and undeservingness at the wealth of gifts I have already been given."

Tilting her face toward his, she searched his eyes. He could almost pinpoint the exact moment her disbelief was transformed—first to wary hesitancy, then to joyous acceptance of his words.

Before he could speak again, a sharp bolt of lightning illuminated the horizon. A rolling boom of thunder immediately followed, silencing the orchestra. As the music came to an abrupt and awkward halt, so did the waltzers. A sharp gust of wind rattled the windows as it swept through the room, extinguishing the vast majority of candles that illuminated the hall. Startled, nervous laughter sounded among the guests, followed by a scattering of applause that built to a hearty crescendo as fat drops of rain began to fall. The storm had broken at last.

A second bolt of lightning split the sky. Whether it was by fate or by chance Morgan would never know, but in that instant, as lightning lit up the room, his attention was turned away from Julia and toward a back wall. To his surprise he found his gaze locked on Thomas Fike. The young artist stood by himself near a narrow flight of stairs that led toward the upper floors. His darkly brooding expression was immediately transformed to one of startled dismay at having been caught staring at them. He quickly turned his back on Morgan without so much as a nod of acknowledgment.

The lightning faded, and the ballroom darkened once again. As Jonathan Derrick's servants busied themselves rushing about the room relighting the candles, Morgan's gaze remained fixed on Fike. No longer alone, he was leaning toward a woman Morgan couldn't identify, whispering something in her ear. The woman tilted back her head and emitted a shrill peal of laughter, flirtatiously rapping Fike on the arm with her silk fan. Fike propped one booted foot upon the staircase and leaned closer to the woman he was evidently intent on seducing. Even from the distance at which Morgan stood, his choice of foot-wear was clear. Fike was wearing Hessians.

"Morgan? What is it?"

He slowly returned his attention to Julia. "Thomas Fike," he replied. "It appears as though he's been watching us most intently."

"Yes, I've noticed that," she returned offhandedly, absently smoothing down the folds of her gown. "It's rather disconcerting, isn't it?"

"Why didn't you mention it earlier?"

She studied him with a small frown. "I didn't think it significant," she replied. "According to Lady Whitcomb and Lady Ausprey, he makes a habit of surreptitiously studying his clients whenever they are not formally posed. He claims that enables him to capture the true essence of one's personality, rather than the stiff expression one fixes on one's face when sitting for a portrait. From what I've heard, his work bears that claim out."

Perhaps, Morgan thought, *perhaps.* A reasonable explanation. And yet . . . something about Thomas Fike wasn't right. Whether it was his instinct that caused him to form that impression, or his irritation at the man for having flirted so blatantly with Julia, Morgan couldn't say. He knew only that he wasn't quite ready to dismiss him from his mind.

As the orchestra lifted their instruments to begin another waltz, he took Julia's arm and escorted her from the dance floor. Morgan's longtime friend Edward Southesby joined them as they resumed their previous place in the crowd. After greetings were exchanged, Southesby remarked, "Do you realize, Morgan, that the evening is half over, and I have yet to enjoy a waltz with your beautiful bride? I wonder if she might favor me with that exquisite honor?"

Receiving Julia's assent to a waltz, the two moved away to join the other guests who filled the dance floor. Morgan watched them for a moment, unable to shake the brooding sensation of unease that gripped him. Satisfied that Julia was in good hands with Southesby, he returned his attention to Fike. The artist was once again standing alone, sipping from a drink.

Morgan scanned the crowd, looking for the woman with whom Fike had been speaking. While she seemed to have disappeared entirely, he was surprised to note that Home Secretary Chivers was in attendance. As the waltzers continued their graceful promenade around the dance floor, Morgan moved across the room to speak with Chivers. "I didn't expect to see you here," he remarked.

"Actually, I arrived only a moment ago," Chivers replied. He gave a light shrug. "I don't normally mingle in society, but I thought it prudent that the Yard make its presence known until this Lazarus person is apprehended. One never knows what one might learn. As I've said before, luck favors the prepared mind."

"I imagine carrying a loaded pistol doesn't hurt much, either."

"You noticed that, did you?" Chivers pulled his jacket closer to his body. "And here I thought I was so discreet."

"Expecting problems?"

The Home Secretary hesitated for a moment, as though choosing his words carefully. At last he replied, "Given the number of years I have spent in this line of work, I've acquired what my mates at the Yard have come to refer to as a nose for trouble. That intuition led me here tonight. Of course, I'm wrong as often as I'm right, but still—"

"What do you know of Thomas Fike?" Morgan asked directly.

"The artist?"

"Yes."

"Not a great deal, but I am privy to the latest gossip. He's rumored to be quite the ladies' man, is he not?"

"So I've heard. I've also noted that he seems to have

developed a particular interest in my wife—one that strikes me as rather excessive, given our present circumstances."

Chivers frowned. "I see. He's here tonight?"

"Yes. Over by the—" Morgan nodded at the rear stair, then stopped abruptly as he discovered it deserted. Fike was nowhere in sight.

"Viscountess Barlowe?" Chivers asked immediately.

Morgan looked toward the center of the room. But the previous waltz had ended, and a new group of dancers had assumed the floor. Southesby and Julia were gone as well. His heart in his throat, he scanned the room. It wasn't possible. They couldn't have disappeared. Not that quickly. *Damn it.* Where the hell was Southesby? Where was Julia? Why hadn't he been watching her?

As his gaze returned to the rear stairway, a feeling of ominous dread spread through his veins. Morgan moved instinctively toward the stairs, taking them two at a time as he rushed toward the upper floors. Chivers followed without a word. On the second level they found a long, dimly lit hallway filled with a series of closed doors. They stopped for a moment, studying the doors as they gained their bearings.

Then Morgan heard it. The shrill, piercing sound of a woman's scream filled the darkened hall.

Chapter 18

For a long while he had conquered the fire. He had controlled the blaze that raged within him. But now it was getting out of control. Conquering sin alone wasn't enough. He had made no sacrifice. There had to be a sacrifice, or the flames would bellow out of control, eating away at him until they destroyed him completely.

It was already happening. The world was spinning around him, events moving too quickly for him to grasp. The dream kept coming back, terrorizing him night after night. He couldn't sleep, couldn't function. He was inadequate, fumbling, and confused. It was getting noticeable; people were beginning to remark upon it. Something had to be done. He turned and gazed across the room. There was only one sacrifice that would be worthy.

Flame. His beloved Flame.

She had started the fire that consumed him.

Her death was the only thing that would end it.

* * *

Julia stepped from the ladies' retiring room, the small tear in the hem of her gown adequately repaired. Edward Southesby was a lovely man and a charming conversationalist, but perhaps the most awkward partner with whom she had ever shared a waltz. Spying him standing outside, enjoying a pipe with another gentleman, she sent him a smile that she hoped would convey the inconsequential nature of the damage. The poor man had been horrified at his clumsy misstep.

Receiving his polite bow in return, she considered the matter closed and moved discreetly through the ballroom, searching for Morgan. Unfortunately her husband was nowhere to be found. Thus she drifted somewhat aimlessly about, feeling ridiculously alone and conspicuous. Soon, however, she was rescued from her abandoned state by the host of that evening's gala.

She greeted Jonathan Derrick with a warm smile. "My sincerest congratulations."

He looked momentarily puzzled by her words, as though he had been occupied with some deep inner contemplation. Then understanding broke across his features. "Oh. I see. You mean this marriage business. Yes, yes. It's about time I took care of the matter. I suspect Miss Prentisse will do very nicely, don't you?"

"I'm certain you'll be very happy together."

"Yes. I'm certain we shall." He hesitated, a look of pained consternation on his face as he lumbered along beside her. "There's been some talk of the unseemly speed of our courtship. Perhaps I should have waited a month or two before offering for her hand." He gave his head a helpless shake. "It was not my intent to cause your family embarrassment by pressing my suit with undue haste."

Julia sent him a reassuring smile. "Perhaps people will assume you were so swept away by the depth of your emotions for Marianne that you could not contain yourself another day."

His puzzled expression returned, then he gave a startled bark of laughter. "Ah, an impetuous love match. That's very amusing. Very amusing indeed, Lady Barlowe."

Julia's smile slowly faded. "You sound so flippant."

"Flippant?" He echoed, looking stunned by the suggestion. "At four and forty years of age, I can hardly be expected to play the part of the lovestruck swain, now can I?" He shook his head. "No, I am merely being realistic, my dear. Your uncle is a pious man, and he has raised two lovely and virtuous daughters. I believe that Miss Prentisse and I will suit each other. All I can hope is that we share a few years of comfort and companionship."

"I see."

A small smile appeared beneath his bushy mustache. "You sound as though you disapprove."

"It's not my place to either approve or disapprove."

Despite her words he gave a small shrug and continued. "The lower one's expectations, the less chance that one will be disappointed. I far prefer a ship with stable moorings to one that has been swept away upon a passionate sea. Not all marriages can be love matches like yours. Not everyone has the temperament for it."

A love match, Julia thought. Was that how she and Morgan were perceived? That notion—no matter how misdirected—sent a quiet thrill racing down her spine. *A love match,* she repeated silently to herself, savoring the phrase. Perhaps she wasn't so ridiculous to believe that something in Morgan's touch, something in his gaze, reflected a new depth of feeling between them. If others saw it as well, perhaps it truly existed.

Catching sight of her cousin across the room, holding court and preening before a flock of well-wishers, Julia reluctantly redirected her thoughts to the conversation at hand. "You've certainly made Marianne very happy."

"I'm glad. She's been generous enough to forgive me this fiasco."

"What do you mean? The party is lovely."

"You're too kind," Jonathan Derrick replied absently. He took her arm as they walked, leading her across the room. "Do you remember last Season? A visit to Madame Tussaud's was all the rage. I thought it would be dreadfully clever to engage her services for this event. But this atrocious weather is conspiring against me." He cast a despairing glance at a pair of melting wax lovers and gave a deep sigh. "I can only hope that the unfortunate condition of the figurines is not as apparent to everyone else."

"I'm certain it's not," she returned politely.

As they moved past a pair of doors that led to the dining salon, the earl's expression of troubled anxiety returned. He stopped for a moment, watching his servants bustle about the great hall as they made the final preparations for the evening meal.

"We'll be serving a lamb stew," he muttered. "Dreadful. No one serves lamb stew. I should have remained firm in my decision to serve some sort of fowl. People enjoy fowl, do they not?"

"I'm certain the lamb will be—"

"I'm not any good at this sort of thing," he interrupted, almost as though speaking to himself. "But it is obligatory. Always taking, never giving back. Not the thing at all. One must host in return. Particularly when one has an engagement to announce. My mother was a lovely hostess. Lovely. Do you see the alcove about the stair? The one with the Roman statue?"

"Yes."

"When I was a small child, I used to hide there and watch the galas my parents would host. That was forty years or so ago, of course. Everything was different then. This hall would be filled, always a veritable crush. But I could pick my mother out instantly. She would float across the room dressed in a gown of vivid silk, like some sort of beautiful butterfly. Her hair was almost your color, did you know that?"

"No, I didn't."

"Perhaps in the future Miss Prentisse will take care of these matters for me. But then, of course she will. She'll be the new Lady Bedford, won't she?" he said, as if the thought had just occurred to him. He shook his head, an expression of grave befuddlement on his face. "How very strange."

Julia experienced a sudden urge to comfort the man. Morgan had labeled the earl as merely socially inept, but to her his ramblings struck a deeper chord. Although he seemed to mean well, Jonathan Derrick exuded a perpetual air of lost innocence and confusion. He reminded her of one of those unfortunate souls who went through life with an expression of bewildered pain in his eyes, like a shaggy puppy who didn't understand why he was repeatedly kicked.

The earl looked at Julia and gave a sudden start, as though surprised to find her still standing beside him. "Well," he said, forcing a choppy laugh, "well, now. That's enough of that."

He had taken her arm a few minutes earlier. At the time she had assumed that it was nothing more than an absentminded gesture of politeness on his part. But as they stepped away from the main ballroom and moved toward an outside terrace, it became evident that he was steering her in a particular direction. Julia came to a firm stop, regarding him with a puzzled smile. "Where are we going?"

He blinked in startled surprise. "Forgive me, Lady Barlowe. I thought I had mentioned it." He gestured across the vast lawns toward a building that was barely visible through the thick summer foliage. "I have an engagement gift waiting to be presented to Miss Prentisse after supper—a rather large painting of a mother and child that I thought she might enjoy." He paused, an embarrassed blush staining his cheeks as he admitted, "The truth is, I transformed the boathouse into a private studio and painted it myself. But now I'm not at all certain whether it's worthy of Miss Prentisse. The last thing I wish to do is to embarrass her further. I wonder if I could trouble you to view the piece and render your honest judgment of it. I shall not be offended in the slightest should you suggest that I wait for a more private moment to present it."

"I see." She hesitated, instinctively disinclined to leave the ballroom. Then again, it would be rather rude of her to refuse her host's earnest request. That decided, she cast an anxious glance at the sky. The fat droplets of rain that had fallen earlier had temporarily ceased, but it looked as though the dark clouds brewing above them might open up again at any moment. "I suppose we shall have to hurry if we don't want to find ourselves soaked by this storm," she said.

Jonathan Derrick rewarded her with a beaming smile. "Wonderful. I am forever in your debt."

He led her away from the terrace and along a crude stone path that meandered through the trees. Random gusts of wind shook the branches overhead, causing murky shadows to leap and sway over the ground beneath them. Residual droplets of rain spilled from the leaves and fell upon the slick stones. Twice Julia stumbled and would have fallen were it not for the firm grip he had on her arm.

"I suspect that you are saving me from the embarrassing fate of being memorialized in print," the earl said as they walked. "An award for the most grievous error in judgment is hereby given to the Earl of B, who made a folly of the celebration of his engagement by showing the poor taste to present his fiancée with the dismal gift of a painting he himself executed. The 'Trotter'? Is that it?"

"I beg your pardon?"

"You know. That dreadful social column that everyone buzzes about."

She sent him a wan smile. " 'The Tattler,' I believe."

"Ah, yes. That's it. Stuff and nonsense, but I suppose it is better to be noticed than to be passed by completely."

His words were nearly an exact echo of Morgan's sentiments. Nevertheless, her column was a subject Julia preferred not to discuss. Fortunately their arrival at the boathouse spared her the necessity of a reply.

He released a satisfied sigh. "Here we are at last."

Until that moment she had been concentrating on the rough ground beneath her feet. Now she looked up to see a small wooden structure that overlooked a large pond. Although the storm clouds blocked most of the moonlight, she could still make out the basic details of the building. With its thatched roof and profuse blossoms filling the window boxes, it reminded her of a quaint storybook cottage. The shutters had been firmly latched shut, but brilliant rays of light shone from within, escaping between the shutter slats and beneath the doorjamb. The earl gave a small, polite bow, opened the door, and ushered her inside.

Julia took two steps into the cottage and abruptly froze.

Dominating the center of the simple, one-room structure was a large bed that had been dressed in crimson satin sheets. Hundreds of brilliant white candles blazed from every surface that surrounded it. They cluttered the mantel and the shelves and tables. Flickering candles filled the windowsills. They glowed from atop the headboard and the wall sconces. The burning tapers were even arranged in thick clusters on the floor. Everywhere she looked, she saw tiny, writhing buds of flame.

Her gaze swung back to the bed. Above it hung a giltframed portrait that had been draped in black gauze. The painting depicted a redheaded woman holding a small blond boy in her lap. But it was apparent even at a glance that the hand that had executed the portrait was unstable at best. The woman's features were grotesquely distorted, as though she were wracked with pain. An expression of pure terror filled the child's face. Completing the background were scores of ominous, swirling, blistering flames.

A series of disjointed thoughts flashed through her mind. First and foremost was that she had found Lazarus at last. He had been so close all along. Jonathan Derrick, the Earl of Bedford. Now she knew. Now she finally had a face to attach to the mysterious arsonist who had terrified all of London. But what she could do with that information at the moment was frighteningly little. For what she was viewing, she realized in horror, was a funeral pyre. Her own.

She turned to find him intently watching her. He tilted his head toward the painting. "Do you like it?" he asked. "I did it for you, my love. All for you."

She managed a tight nod and took a step away from him. "It's very well done."

"Do you think so? Truly?"

"Yes."

"I can't tell you how it pleases me to hear that."

"It's . . . very well done," she repeated, at a loss for any other words.

"Splendid." His gaze moved past her to the painting. "Splendid. I wasn't at all certain that you would like it. Not at all."

Julia took a deep breath, willing herself to remain calm. *Later,* she silently swore. She would allow herself to fall apart later. Panic and hysteria were rarely productive emotions, and at the moment she needed all her faculties. Pushing back the terror that threatened to engulf her, she forced herself to rationally examine her situation. But her options, she realized with a feeling of sinking dread, were limited.

Escape was the first thought that came to mind. She was all too willing to obey that primal instinct. Unfortunately the windows were shuttered and latched closed; the swarms of candles that blazed in the sills served as an additional barrier. Furthermore, Jonathan Derrick stood between her and the room's only door. Nor would she be heard if she cried out for help. She was simply too far from the ballroom.

If she couldn't flee and she couldn't expect help, she had no option but to fight. She cast a discreet glance around the room for some sort of weapon. Nothing. Not a mounted sword or a set of dueling pistols. Not a glass vase or a letter opener. Not a broom, or a pot or a pan. The room was nearly bare save for the painting, the crimson-sheeted bed, and dozens upon dozens of flickering candles. Just as she was about to give in to despair, she caught sight of a long, dark shape near the side of the mantel.

A firebox poker.

A tiny spark of hope was lit within her. If she could just get to it. If she could just stall him long enough to reach it . . . She took a small, backward step in the direction of the mantel.

Jonathan Derrick's gaze immediately snapped toward her. He studied her with an intense frown, as though puzzled and displeased with her motion, but not entirely certain why.

Julia glanced again at the painting. Her initial impression was that it had been of her. Then she remembered the earl's earlier words. *Her hair was almost your color, did you know that?* With that in mind, she forced a tight, wavering smile and guessed, "Your mother?"

For a long moment she thought he wouldn't reply at all. Then he slowly nodded. "I painted it from memory."

"You must have loved her very much."

"Yes. Very much."

"She died in a fire?"

Another long pause, as an expression of intense pain contorted his features. "Fire was the only way to cure her of her sin. The only way. My father had no choice."

She shook her head, watching him closely. "I don't understand."

"It was her sin that drove him to it," he said. "I saw it all. My mother and the man she lay with, the way their naked flesh slapped together in the dark. So evil. So foul, so dirty. My father had to purify, to cleanse. He had no choice but to do it." He fixed his gaze on the painting as he intoned, " 'The heat of his wrath shall cleanse the body of sin. Through fire one shall purify one's soul.' "

A glimmer of ghastly understanding spread through Julia. She retreated another step, conscious of the candles that lined the floor. The slightest misstep might cause her skirts to brush against a burning flame and ignite.

"I want it to be beautiful," the earl continued, his gaze returning to her. "If we have to do it, it must be done right. It has to be beautiful."

"What has to be beautiful?"

"Your death, of course," he replied. A note of almost desperate pleading entered his voice as he nervously wrung his hands. "There will be pain. I don't know how to do it without pain. I wish I did. I don't enjoy it; I don't enjoy it at all. I hope you can believe that."

She swallowed hard. "Yes, of course." *Just a little more time,* she thought. Just a little more time until she could either talk him out of his insane plan or reach the poker. "I thought you and I were working together," she said. "Look at how much we've done to rid London of its sin. Do you remember the foundling home in Westchester? They now have a new board of trustees, and the children are receiving twice their previous allotment of food, as well as warm coats and shoes without holes. And that gin house on Turner Street? The one that sold opiates to—"

She broke off abruptly as the earl began muttering to himself. Rhythmically shaking his head back and forth, he retrieved a length of thick crimson ribbon from his coat pocket and wound it between his hands. Combating a sensation of mounting dread, Julia watched him tighten his fists about the satiny strands. "What is that for?"

"To tie you to the bedposts."

Her heart slammed against her chest. So much for talking him out of it. "I see you've given this a great deal of thought," she managed.

A relieved smile curved his lips. His face was even more florid than usual; tiny beads of sweat glistened on his skin. His pale blue eyes burned with equal parts zealotry and confusion. Yet at the same time there remained a childlike earnestness about him, as though he were struggling to find the right answers. "Yes," he gushed. "You do understand. I was so hoping you would. We don't want this to be unpleasant."

She took another small step toward the mantel. "No, we don't."

"Flame. My dearest Flame. It has to be you. There has to be a worthy sacrifice, or the dreams will keep coming back. My father won't leave me alone. He won't ever leave me alone."

"Where is your father now?"

"Here. Right here," he answered, his voice rising several octaves. "He's with us now, watching. That's why I have no choice."

"I see."

As he dragged his fingers through his shaggy mop of blond hair, his excited expression plummeted to one of utter despair. "Sin. So much sin. It won't ever end, will it? He'll never let me rest."

Until that very moment Julia had been consumed, perhaps quite properly, with her own safety. In her fear she had questioned her ability to fight off a man as large as Jonathan Derrick. But with his words that suddenly changed. She was filled with a new sense of strength and purpose. There was no time for doubt or hesitancy. After what he had done to Morgan, to Henry and Annie Maddox, to Sarah Montgomery, and to countless others, he had to be stopped.

She took another step and felt the mantel bump up against her back. Slipping one hand behind her, she fumbled blindly until her trembling fingers wrapped around the thick iron poker.

"What was that?" he suddenly demanded, his head cocked and alert.

She froze, her heart in her throat. Had she given herself away? No sooner had that thought filled her mind than a low rumble of thunder shook the room. A strong gust of wind immediately followed, then the sound of driving rain.

The sudden fury of the breaking storm was apparently lost on Jonathan Derrick. As though listening to a voice only he could hear, he gave a vague nod and said with an eerie, boyish giggle, "Yes. Yes, I will. I understand." Tightening the ribbon about his fists once again, he moved toward Julia. "Flame," he said. "My beautiful, precious Flame."

She took a deep breath and clenched the poker in her hand, bringing the weapon up and ready to strike. She would have one good swing, perhaps two if she was lucky.

Another sharp gust of wind rattled the windows. The door flew open behind them. Her first thought was that the force of the wind had caused it to open. Then she blinked in disbelief as the figure of her Uncle Cyrus filled the doorway. He stepped into the cottage, soaking wet and looking thoroughly annoyed. Behind him loomed both Morgan and Home Secretary Chivers.

Cyrus, as usual, was the first to speak. He gazed about the room and said, "Really, Julia, this is most improp—"

Then everything seemed to explode at once. Jonathan Derrick spun around with a sharp, startled cry, an expression of naked horror on his face.

Julia's gaze flew to Morgan. "Laz—" she began, but she didn't need to finish the word. Evidently the macabre setting was enough to impress upon Morgan exactly with whom he was dealing. Shoving Cyrus aside, he leaped across the room in a flying tackle, hurling his full weight against the Earl of Bedford. Dozens of candles scattered across the floor as the two men rolled toward the bed, locked in a fierce struggle.

But it quickly became apparent that Morgan was the only one who was fighting. Jonathan Derrick lay curled up in a tight ball beneath him. Covering his face, he emitted an eerie wail that was almost inhuman—a sound like the agonized, frantic bleating of a sheep that was being slaughtered. Over and over again he pleaded with his father to stop beating him. His cries filled the room, echoing off the cottage walls in a pitch of shrill, fevered hysteria.

Morgan, at last hearing what Derrick was saying, drew back, his fist frozen in midair. Swallowing a surge of pity and horror, Julia allowed the poker to slip through her fingers. Home Secretary Chivers, who had held his pistol fixed on the two combatants, slowly lowered the weapon, an expression of grim sobriety on his features. Even Cyrus Prentisse was temporarily silenced.

Breathing hard, Morgan rose to his feet, his gaze locked on Julia. She wasn't aware of moving, or even of deciding to move. But somehow she made it across the room. In the space of less than a second Morgan's arms locked around her, holding her as though he would never again let her go.

Julia hesitated outside the door to Morgan's library, unaccountably nervous. It was foolish on her part, but she couldn't help it. In the aftermath of the abrupt ending to the Earl of Bedford's gala and his subsequent arrest, she had not had a chance to speak privately with her husband. Nor had they spoken on the long, stormy carriage ride home. At the time she had been perfectly content to wallow in the comfort and security of Morgan's arms. But she couldn't help but feel that the events of the evening had occasioned a profound shift in their relationship, one that they had no choice but to discuss. There were too many unspoken words between them already.

Refusing to allow herself to put it off any longer, she tightened the belt to her dressing gown and stepped inside. Like her, Morgan had removed his formal attire in favor of something more comfortable. His gray silk dressing robe fell open to reveal the sleek, bronzed lines of his chest. Beneath it he wore only the tailored, black wool slacks she had seen him in earlier.

He sat with one slim hip propped against his desk, his attention absorbed by the thick leather volume he held in his hands. As she entered the room, however, he immediately looked up and sent her a soft smile. "Good," he said. "I've been waiting."

"Not too long, I hope."

"No, not too long." His gaze moved over her body in a manner that was neither overtly sexual nor blatantly possessive, but instead fell somewhere in between. He gestured toward a crystal decanter. "Brandy?"

"No, thank you."

She seated herself across from his desk in a plushly cushioned chair that allowed her to draw her feet up beneath her. Deciding to deal with the issue of Jonathan Derrick before delving into the larger concern of the future of their relationship, she asked, "What will happen to him?"

Morgan shrugged. "Chivers ordered him taken to Bedlam. There will be hearings on the matter, of course, but I imagine he'll remain there the rest of his life."

"You sound almost disappointed."

A small frown touched his lips, but he didn't deny it. Glancing at the book he held, he rose and slid it back into its place on the shelves. "I suppose in some ways I am," he admitted, turning back to her. "After all these years I created a monster in my mind, some sort of evil Goliath I would have to slay with my own hands. Instead, all I felt for Jonathan Derrick was pity. It's somewhat humbling to have one's life nearly destroyed by so small and weak a man."

Although Julia could find no adequate response, she was nonetheless intensely pleased that he had shared his feelings with her. Shifting the topic slightly, she asked, "How did you find me?"

"Fortunately your Uncle Cyrus was keeping a closer eye on you than I was. He watched you leave with the earl and was most displeased when you failed to return to the salon. Apparently he was of the opinion that your prolonged absence with a man who was not yet a member of the family was most unseemly, particularly given that your destination was so isolated a spot. Thus when he saw me, he insisted that I do my husbandly duty and return you to the ballroom forthwith."

She smiled and shook her head. "And to think I always resented him for his ridiculous preoccupation with proper society."

"It appears we both owe him a world of gratitude for that ridiculous preoccupation."

She nodded, but as she recalled the events of the evening, her smile faded. "I still don't understand how our paths could have crossed. When I returned from the ladies' retiring room, you were nowhere to be found."

"Ah. So that's where you disappeared to."

"Where did you think I was?"

Morgan leaned against the bookshelves, a rueful smile curving his lips as he reluctantly explained, "Home Secretary Chivers and I jointly applied our vast powers of reason and intellect and deduced that Thomas Fike was the mastermind behind the arson. That unfortunate conclusion was further reinforced when Fike displayed the profoundly poor timing to disappear from the ballroom at the same instant you retired to mend your gown. Naturally we feared the worst and were determined to rescue you from the clutches of that dastardly fiend."

She tried and failed to imagine the scene that must have followed. "What happened?"

"Not a great deal," he replied, lifting his shoulders in a bored shrug. "We followed him upstairs to an upper-floor bedroom."

"And?"

"There's really not much to tell. You may be interested to learn, however, that Lady Beecher's shrill cries of ecstasy sound remarkably like cries of pain—particularly when one hears them from behind a closed door while running down a hall."

As the implication of what he was saying sank in, she studied him in wide-eyed disbelief. "You didn't."

"Like the proverbial bull charging through a china factory." He folded his arms across his broad chest and continued. "Imagine our surprise after we forced our way into that locked bedchamber."

Julia bit back a giggle. "Imagine Lady Beecher's surprise."

"Indeed. Evidently Thomas Fike took it upon himself to entertain the lady while her husband was downstairs numbing his companions with a dreary recital of the far-reaching implications of the tax rates that have been levied on the West Indies."

"I see."

Morgan shook his head, grinning broadly. "It was most embarrassing for us all. And I suspect the worst of it is yet to come."

"What do you mean?"

"Needless to say, I imagine the extortionate rate the young scoundrel is charging me to paint your portrait is about to be quadrupled."

"That's the very least you deserve," she returned with a soft laugh. As she regarded him, however, her mood slowly changed to one of quiet contemplation.

"What is it?" he asked.

She shook her head. "Nothing. I just noticed where you're standing, that's all."

"Where I'm standing?"

"The lamp," she clarified after a moment's hesitation. "You're standing directly beneath the lamplight. You never did that in the past. It seemed that whenever we spoke, you were always in the shadows."

"And what did you see? The Beast lurking in dark corners, or your phantom lover in the gardens?"

"You were never either man, were you?" she returned softly.

"No, I never was." Their gazes met and held for a long moment. Morgan crossed the room and held out his hand. She placed her palm in his, allowing him to assist her to her feet. "But until I met you, I thought I might be. I thought a great many ridiculous things."

"Such as?"

"The usual rubbish. That what was important in life was having the right tailor and the fastest horses. Spending a ridiculous amount of money. Drinking the best cognac and socializing with people of the proper class and rank. But now I know that none of that matters."

"It doesn't?"

"Not one damned bit."

"Then what does matter?"

He smiled and gently placed his hands about her hips, pulling her closer to him. "Loving you," he said, his breath falling against her temple like a warm caress. He paused, shaking his head as he ran his hands lightly down her back. "Amazing, isn't it? I suspect I've known all along, but it took nearly losing you to a madman to finally bring that point home."

Her heart in her throat, she snapped her head back and searched his smoky gaze. "Say that again."

A slow, teasing smile curved his lips. "Nearly losing you to a madman?"

"Morgan—"

"I love you, Julia."

Although those four little words were everything she had hoped to hear, she couldn't quite convince herself that the emotion that had engendered them was real, and not a product of the ordeal they had just been through. She studied him in trembling disbelief, asking, "Just when did you finally reach that remarkable conclusion?"

"Finally? I think I've known it from the moment we met."

"You mean the Devonshire House?"

He thought for a moment. "No, not there."

"Then when?"

"Very well. If you wish to be precise, I knew I lusted after you at the Devonshire House. I don't think I loved you until we reached your father's warehouse. Perhaps it was the scent of overripe cheese and rotten cabbage that brought out the suitor in me."

Her smile broadened as she remembered the events of that night. In retrospect, it had been a preposterous plan. Yet the outcome had far surpassed her wildest dreams. She studied her husband, her throat thick and heavy, clogged with unspoken words. In an attempt to gain control of her emotions, she tore her eyes away from his, gazing blindly about the room.

He lifted one hand and gently stroked her cheek. "Nervous, princess?"

Her gaze snapped back. Apparently his thoughts had turned reminiscent as well, for that was exactly what he had asked her on that fateful night at her father's warehouse. "Hardly," she replied, echoing her original response. Their conversation was as fresh in her mind as if they had shared it just hours ago, rather than months.

"I'm glad to hear it." He gestured vaguely around the library. "Interesting choice."

"It's certainly private," she gamely replied. "And spacious."

He arched one dark brow. "How much space do you think we'll need?"

Biting back an embarrassed grin, she answered, "The bigger the better."

"Any other preferences I should know about?"

"Just one."

"Oh?"

"I think you ought to know that I'm madly in love with my husband."

"Lucky man." A slow, seductive smile curved his lips. Bending down, he lifted her into his arms and carried her across the room toward the burgundy velvet settee upon which they had first become lovers. "How fortunate for you that his only wish in life is to accommodate your every whim and desire."

She wrapped her arms about his neck, nuzzling her cheek against his chest. "I'll try to do the same for him."

Morgan gently set her down on the settee. His smoky gaze searched her face with a look of shattering, loving reverence. Lowering his head, he placed a light kiss atop her left breast, directly over her heart.

"You already have, princess. You already have."

Epilogue

Kent, 1860

Morgan paused in the foyer of Snowden Hall. Suspended on the walls above him were the ancestral portraits that had once filled the grand entrance hall of his London town home. His gaze moved automatically to the newest addition in the line of paintings, the nearly life-size portrait of Julia that he had commissioned Thomas Fike to create shortly after their marriage.

Despite the embarrassing fiasco over misidentifying the man as Lazarus, the cocky young artist had indeed proved himself to be worthy of both his exorbitant fee and his reputation as a portraitist. Morgan had flatly insisted at the time that all he wanted was a simple portrait of his wife, but Fike had given him much more than that.

Apparently having determined on his own exactly how the portrait should be accomplished, Fike had positioned Julia in a gown of shimmering crimson, standing alone in the center of a vast, empty ballroom. In the tall oval mirror behind her was a shadowy reflection of Morgan himself, gazing at his bride with an expression of brooding longing.

If Fike's intent had been to tell the story of their relationship—as the ancestral paintings preceding it had—the man had admirably accomplished his goal. Other than the brilliant red of Julia's gown, there was no hint of fire. Fike had focused instead on the longing and secrecy that had been so central to their relationship, managing to capture both the darkness and the promise of light. Moreover, no outcome was suggested by the portrait, and that pleased him as well. It simply captured the essence of a particular moment in time between a man and a woman, leaving future generations to finish the story as they chose. Very satisfactory, indeed.

Turning away from the portrait, Morgan left the hall and stepped outside. Although it was just mid-August, a fresh crispness filled the breeze, promising an early fall. Following the high, gleeful sound of childish laughter, Morgan made his way to the lush, informal gardens that encompassed the rear of his estate.

His two tiny daughters raced back and forth armed with butterfly nets, swooping the gauzy fabric over an occasional stray insect, then over each other's heads.

He stopped to watch, filled with a sense of satisfaction greater than any he had ever known. Both girls had inherited their mother's remarkable sherry eyes. The eldest had his dark hair, the younger her mother's rich, shimmering russet. They were both—in his own biased estimation—stunningly beautiful. His gaze moved next to his wife. She was seated on a blanket, the remains of a picnic lunch spread around her.

Catching sight of him, she held out her hand and greeted him with a soft smile. "I was hoping you would join us."

He moved across the lawn. Brushing his lips against hers, he said, "There's nowhere else I'd rather be."

He sat beside her and crossed his legs, then eased her

back until her head rested in his lap. He removed the simple clip that held her hair in place, gently massaging her scalp as he ran his fingers through the long, fiery strands. The afternoon sunlight reflected off the small gold medallion she wore about her throat.

Saint Rita, patron saint of the impossible.

Indeed. Years ago he would have sworn it was impossible that he could ever be so contented. But just as Julia had breathed life into the desolate shambles of Snowden Hall, so she had given him a new sense of purpose and direction. The gulf between the hardened, bitter man he had once been and the man he was now seemed so disparate, it was sometimes difficult for him to believe they were one and the same.

"It's so beautiful here," Julia said, her voice coming out like a long, silky sigh.

Morgan brushed his hands through her hair. " 'I asked for all things in order that I might enjoy life. I was given life in order that I might enjoy all things.' "

"That's lovely," she said, smiling up at him.

"But not original, I'm afraid. A passage in a book I once read."

"Lovely, nonetheless."

"How are you feeling?"

Her hands moved automatically to her full, ripe belly. On occasion Morgan was secretly convinced she was carrying a son and was filled with a sense of pride beyond measure. Other times he was ridiculously thrilled at the prospect of a third daughter, who would bring even more laughter and beauty into his life.

"It depends on the moment you ask," she replied with a small, contented smile. "Tired, wonderful, huge, excited, clumsy, and overjoyed."

"You look stunning."

He ran his knuckles over her cheek as their gazes met and held. So much. He had been given so much.

The sound of their daughters' high-pitched laughter

drew their gazes away from each other and toward their children. The girls came running toward them, breathless and excited. Their hair was messed in tousled disarray, their gowns were smeared with dirt, their skin was flushed and rosy. They leaped onto the blanket, tumbling over each other like exuberant puppies as they wrapped their chubby arms about his neck. "Papa, Papa, we want a new game!"

Morgan thought for a moment, overcome with a profound sense of gratitude.

Of all he had been given, perhaps the most significant gift was a deep reverence for life, with all its pain and all its glory. Every loss had meaning. And every day was a new reason for celebration.

"A new game?" he echoed. He could not change the past, but he could embrace the present. He lifted his scarred, reddened hands.

Mimicking his motions, his daughters lifted their own tiny, dimpled hands, watching him with expressions of rapt adoration.

Clapping his palms together, he began to recite, "Patty-cake, patty-cake . . ."